"The course of true love never did run smooth."
WILLIAM SHAKESPEARE
A Midsummer Night's Dream, Act 1, Scene 1 (1600)

LOST

LOVE'S

RETURN

A NOVEL

Alfred Nicols

ISBN: 978-1-953865-16-8 (Paperback)
ISBN: 978-1-953865-17-5 (eBook)
ISBN: 978-1-953865-28-1 (Hardback)

Library of Congress Control Number: L2021903575

Any references to historical events, real people, or real places are used fictitiously. Names, characters, and places are products of the author's imagination.

Books Fluent
3014 Dauphine Street
New Orleans, LA
70117

For Landy Teller, who inspired me to write,

And for Mary, who lived with the time spent writing.

CONTENTS

PART ONE

World War I

– 1 –

PART TWO

The Great Depression

– 105 –

PART THREE

World War II

– 179 –

ABOUT THE AUTHOR

273

ACKNOWLEDGMENTS

274

READER'S GUIDE

277

World War I

CHAPTER 1

HE MAY BE A SISSY

JULY 1918
FRANCE

The last fifteen miles of Peter's journey from America to the Western Front was a foot march, along a muddy trail, laced with bomb craters. His pack cut into his shoulders, the mud sucked at his boots, his rifle got heavier by the mile. In the distance, the sounds of exploding artillery got ever louder and more menacing. But he was thinking about Hannah.

In the two years since he had last seen her in the spring of 1916, Hannah had seldom been off Peter's mind for long. In the first days and weeks after she left, he'd thought about her almost constantly. He had imaginary conversations with her, pictured them together: in the classroom, at her parents' house, making love whenever and wherever they could. After several months, he would occasionally go a day or more without thinking about her, but in two years it had never been a week. Initially, thoughts of Hannah always gave him a sad, lonely, lost feeling, yet a warm one.

Then, a year ago, the letter came from Michigan. Suddenly his thoughts became not thoughts of him with Hannah, but thoughts of Hannah with this other man. Jealous, bitter thoughts. He tried hard not to, but he would picture Hannah making love to this other man, in the same way she had made love to him: kissing him, hugging him, stroking him, teasing him with her beautiful naked body, making her familiar sounds of pleasure when her time came.

Marching along, he wondered what Hannah would think if she knew he had joined the Army, gone off to "do his duty," as Grandpa Montgomery called it; wondered if she would care if he was killed. He began to wonder if Hannah had loved him at all, or was just using him, like she might have used others, wherever her father's timber cuts took them. He wondered if he would ever feel about another woman the way he felt about Hannah.

~

When he reached the trench on the front line, Peter climbed down a ladder, put his pack and gun down, and sat on a ledge dug into the side of the trench. At not quite twenty, he had thought little about death when he arrived in these muddy trenches in the Marne Valley. He knew that he would ultimately die, but he had always pictured it as an event in his distant future. Now his death became a constant reality, always at the forefront of his consciousness. On his first day, it was the threat of German heavy artillery: big rounds thundering out of the sky, with loud, eerie, whizzing shrieks, followed by deafening blasts, blowing clouds of mud, dirt, and smoke high into the air, which then rained down upon them.

A round landed down the trench from him, caving in a huge section of the parapet, the force of the explosion causing his left ear to seep blood.

"Help! Help!" a platoon member screamed from around a curve. "Byron . . . he's been buried! We've got to find him before he suffocates!"

Peter grabbed his shovel and rushed down the trench. He and Arthur Weems began to dig into a big mound of dirt, along with two more men digging from the other side.

When Peter's shovel struck something, he dropped it and pawed furiously with both hands. He uncovered three fingers, then a whole hand. When he got to the wrist, Peter grabbed it and started to pull. Out came a whole arm, bloody and mangled, severed at the shoulder, trailing ragged pieces of muddy cloth.

"No reason to be in a hurry now," the platoon sergeant said from behind Peter, barely audible above the artillery bombardment. The soldiers methodically dug out the dead man. It was Byron Drake, one of the eight who had shared Peter's tent in his early months of service.

But it was on his second day in the trench that the great likelihood of imminent death came home to him even more dramatically. He and Arthur had climbed up on the fire step, their eyes barely above the edge of the parapet, surveying the scene. The French farmland in the Marne valley had topography reminiscent of his Grandpa Montgomery's South Mississippi farmland: gently rolling fields for the planting, a few trees along the drains, patches of forest on the hillsides. But these fields were now pitted with bomb craters filled with water from recent rains and strands of barbed wire. Its trees were ghostly skeletons left charred and leafless by artillery blasts.

Suddenly, a sniper's bullet grazed Peter's helmet, knocking him backward into the bottom of the trench. "You knobhead! You young fools can't listen . . . can't wait to die!" came the voice of Sergeant Mulholland, shrill and emphatic, in a heavy British accent. "Trust me! Won't miss you again . . . you bloody knobhead!"

Peter looked up, muddy and dazed. Crawling to his feet, he sat on the fire step, his dented helmet in his hands. Mulholland was a British sergeant assigned to advise the American reinforcements. He was lean and tall, a man with poor posture and a long neck poking out from his drooping shoulders. His face and head were shaved, giving him a look reminiscent of a condor. With rains having left deep mud in the trenches, mud covered Mulholland to his knees.

"Put your helmet back on, Montgomery, and you might as well shave off your pretty blond hair, before it breeds more lice than you want to carry around on yer scrawny arse."

Shock merged with anger. Peter was relatively short, but lean, muscular, and athletic. He had never before been called scrawny. He immediately found himself hating this Mulholland. As Peter sat trying to imagine being shaved bald like Mulholland, the German heavy artillery, well off in the distance to the south, again let off a series of mortars, screeching their way down behind them.

"What's this rotten smell, Sergeant?" asked Peter. "Keeps making me nauseated, and all."

Mulholland smirked. "Whole lot of stuff, Montgomery. With this rain, no way all the loos aren't overflowing everywhere. We put in that lime and creosol. Only makes it worse. But mainly it's the smell of the dead . . . the smell of rotting flesh."

"You mean we don't bury the dead?"

"When we can. Out there in no-man's-land . . . hard to get them without a truce, and a truce ain't often. Can't go out there in daylight and not get shot. Night, you got all that barbed wire in the dark . . . use any light, machine guns'll cut you down."

Peter realized three fellow soldiers had gathered around, listening to Mulholland expounding on the subject, all overpowered by the stench. Mulholland lit a cigarette and blew out a puff of gray smoke that drifted down along the trench in the warm, humid air, mingling with the stench of death.

"You mates want a smoke?" he asked, handing out cigarettes. Mulholland continued: "At times, them bloody bombs just blow the chap into small pieces . . . arm here, leg there, head over there, parts of the middle scattered everywhere . . . not much left to bury, especially after them rats work on it. Even when a chap's buried whole, them rats'll dig him up. Enough dead around, them rats'll only eat the livers and eyeballs."

"Rats!" Jake Brewer, a chubby, freckled-faced private from Texas, interjected. "So many rats! One ran across my face last night . . . jumped up on me . . . tried to chew through my pocket, get to my tobacco. Why don't we kill 'em?"

"Waste to try. I hear pair'll breed a thousand in a year. Got miles of holes and tunnels to hide in. Kill them? That's just something else to stink. Bury them . . . other rats'll dig them up and eat on them, then leave those rat carcasses out rotting." The sergeant took another long draw on his cigarette, holding it between two fingers. With confidence and a macabre smile, he added, "But rats do prefer human eyeballs and livers."

Peter noticed Jake Brewer's chubby face, usually ruddy in the oppressive summer heat, had paled.

Sergeant Mulholland's now stubby cigarette burned his fingers and he flipped it down the trench, where it quickly went out on a wet duckboard. "Got a proposition for ya Yanks. There's one rat . . . bigger and meaner and smarter than the others . . . and I've been in these bloody trenches for three years. A few months ago, while I was sitting dozing, he jumped on me and tried to take my bully beef right out of my hand. Slapped at him and he bit my arm. Named him Bruno, big brown bastard. Kill Bruno and you'll get an extra bottle of rum."

"How we gonna know it's Bruno?" Peter asked after a pause.

"Big as a house cat, face like a bear, and missing his tail."

"Missing his whole tail?"

"Almost. Tried to shoot him . . . all I got was his tail . . . right up against his furry brown arse. Now, whenever I spot him, he's back in a hole before I can get off a shot."

There was a silence as the group tried to visualize the big brown rat, the size of a house cat, face like a brown bear . . . with no tail.

"Gotta get out of these wet boots before I get the trench foot." Mulholland started down the muddy trench, the duckboards squirting up streams of water where he stepped. As he neared the corner in the zigzag, he looked back.

"Don't you mates stick your head up for that sniper . . . even for an instant! He's the best the Huns got . . . And shave your heads before the nits make a good crop. The lice'll eat you anyway, but it'll help."

"Everybody in my family gets bald by thirty-five," Arthur Weems said, as Mulholland passed from view. "Every hair I've got until then is precious. I ain't shaving off nare a damn one."

Peter had always been proud of his thick blond hair, and he wasn't worried about becoming bald. But his scalp itched. He sat on the fire step, took off his helmet and scratched. When he looked up, Arthur was sitting across from him on the edge of a hole dug out in the side of the trench, grinning. Arthur said nothing; his grin said it for him. Peter had the gorgeous locks the lice would most want.

~

Arthur, two years older, was Peter's best friend in the unit. They had both joined the Army in the summer of 1917, then been assigned to the same eight-man tent in newly opened Camp Shelby in South Mississippi, not far from Peter's home in Glasper. Peter and Arthur had much in common, both small-town Southern boys from a Scots-Irish Protestant tradition, with Arthur from the small town of Dempsey in north-central Louisiana. But more than anything else, what they had in common was their love of baseball. Both had played for their school teams and both loved the game.

Arthur had one of the new crystal radios, and at every opportunity they tuned in to the fortunes of their favorite team: the Chicago White Sox. The White Sox were having a great season, and every time they won Peter and Arthur would celebrate the victory.

"Why dontcha come home with me to Glasper. It's only an hour away," Peter had said the first time they had a weekend off. "We've got a team in town, semi-pro we call it, you know, and we play teams from other towns on weekends. Anyone shows up we can usually work in . . . get to see you in action and all."

Arthur had smiled. "Think they'll let me play?"

"Sure will. We'll play any who shows up, and all . . . usually play some fifteen-year-olds and some forty-year-olds."

When they'd arrived in Glasper, Peter learned the locals had lined up a home game against a rival team from the nearby town of Summit. As it turned out, some of the regulars did not show and Arthur was needed. Big and presumably slow, Arthur was made the first baseman.

Peter's decision to bring Arthur had been validated and a friendship further cemented at the end of the ninth. Summit was leading seven to six. Peter got a leadoff single. Drew Irby, a local farmhand, struck out. Wink Strange, the high school baseball coach, struck out. Up stepped Arthur, with two outs, one out away from a loss. Arthur looked at Peter on first, then hit the next pitch over the center fielder's head into a cow pasture for a homer, winning the game. Peter's teammates had made it clear that he should bring Arthur home with him any time he could.

Peter's family had also taken a liking to Arthur. He was warm and friendly and had been taught proper manners, always important to Peter's mother. In time, it became apparent that Peter's older sister, Evie, exactly Arthur's age, was enamored with Arthur. Peter realized they were slipping out and meeting late at night, and once he saw them kissing out on the lawn in the moonlight. Peter began to wonder if Arthur might become his future brother-in-law.

On October 15, 1917, back at Camp Shelby, before they left for Europe, Peter and Arthur had listened to the last game of the World Series on Arthur's crystal radio. The Chicago White Sox had beaten the New York Giants to win the Series. Their team had won it all!

~

"Quit scratching and put your helmet back on. You never know when you're gonna need it," Arthur said, still grinning.

Peter complied. They sat for an hour, both dozing. Then the heavy artillery started up again, this time quite close.

A round roared in from above and hit in front of them, not fifty feet away, violently shaking the ground, raining dirt and debris down upon them. The force of the explosion sucked the air from the soldiers' chests, the pressure of the blast seeming to make their heads explode. Not a man was left standing, all face down in the muddy trench, covering their heads with their hands, cowering in terror, waiting for the next round to find its mark. Acrid smoke began to fill the trench. Another round came in, again close enough to rain down dirt and debris. The shelling continued, on and on, in ten-second intervals.

Ears ringing, Peter's head throbbed. His ear was bleeding again. At times, the German shells hit in front of the trench, other times, just beyond. Always there was the terrifying sense that the next round would find its mark. Finally, the point of impact began to move away to the west and after another two hours, the shelling ceased.

Mud-covered men gradually began to get up and stand in the trench, most breathing heavily. Peter got up and sat back on the fire step, adjusting his helmet. It was then that he noticed Arthur on the other side of the trench, his back to him, kneeling on the muddy duckboards, elbows on a hole dug into the trench wall for rest and sleep, a bolt hole or funk hole Peter had learned it was called.

Arthur prayed aloud, some intelligible, some incoherent muttering. "Lord, please don't let me die. Please spare me. Please don't let me die." Peter could make out a shaky, earnest tone. He also heard something about rats and eyeballs and livers. Finally, it appeared Arthur was reciting the Lord's Prayer. "Our Father who art in heaven . . . Thy kingdom come, Thy will be done." Arthur's voice trailed once more into incoherence until Peter finally heard "forever and ever, Amen."

Arthur got up and sat on the edge of the bolt hole. Having removed his helmet to pray, he put it back on. Then looking up, he realized that Peter had been watching him, probably had heard his prayers.

"You praying not to die, Peter?"

"Hadn't been. Reckon I'm gonna start."

"Then pray for me too. I don't want to die so young." Arthur added a slight smile. "Not before I can marry your sister."

They sat across the trench, facing each other, knees almost touching. The artillery was silent. Three large brown rats ambled single file across the mounds above Arthur's head. He did not see them and Peter gave them no comment.

"Don't know why in hell I volunteered for this," Arthur said. "Fool! . . . Bored. And thought I was volunteering for some big patriotic adventure. How about you?"

Peter wiped away mud that was smeared on his face. He spat on the duckboards. "Fella came in the store one morning . . . my parents' general store, you know . . . and put a big poster in the front window. It was a gray-haired man in a blue coat, red bow tie, white top hat with a wide blue band pointing his finger and all. 'I want you for the U. S. Army,' it said."

"Same picture I saw in Dempsey, before I joined . . . was at the post office."

"Grandpa Montgomery . . . he had fought in the Civil War . . . wounded at Shiloh," Peter said. "His older brother had been killed in battle at Nashville. Grandpa got the poster out of the window and brought it to the back where I was sitting at a table with Pa and Evie. 'Them Germans been sinking our ships and killing our people,' he said. 'Now that Zimmerman . . . that Zimmerman . . . he's done been caught trying to get them Mexicans to invade us. There's a time you gotta go fight and stand up for yourself.' Then he looked at the poster and looked at me, serious-like, you know, before he put it back in the window. Went to the recruiting station the very next day and signed up."

~

That night Peter slumped back in a bolt hole, sandbag under his head, his feet out on the duckboard, trying to sleep. The weather had improved; the stars were out; the guns were silent. Down the trench a small light flickered as another soldier lit a cigarette. Someone was coughing. Peter began thinking about a time when he was eight years old, and he'd learned that he had an aversion to blood, to killing, to seeing any death at his hands.

"Wake up, Little Peter! Get up, Little Peter!"

Startled, he'd awoken to find Grandpa Montgomery standing over him. The lamp was on in his room, but it was dark outside the window.

"Huh?"

"Get up. I'm taking you with me squirrel hunting."

"Squirrel hunting? It's dark outside."

"We gotta get out there before daybreak. That's when hungry squirrels come out looking for something to eat. Gonna be a hunter, gotta learn to be in the woods at daybreak," Grandpa had said.

They walked along a ridge as the first light crept among the towering hickories and white oaks. Leaves crunched under their feet. He could hear his grandpa breathing heavily.

"Let's sit here." Grandpa had settled against a massive oak and pulled him close into his lap. He cradled the new shotgun, his small hands on the smooth stock and the cold barrel.

"Bought you this little four-ten. Won't kick much. Think about how we been practicing on cans with the twenty-two. Just sight on the squirrel like you do a can and pull the trigger . . . I'll tell you when to shoot."

He had felt a surge of exhilaration, a euphoric sense of pride. He was going to be a hunter, a big man in the Montgomery tradition.

"There's one," he'd said to his grandpa, spotting a squirrel as it leapt from limb to limb. He'd put the bead on it and pulled the trigger. The squirrel clung for a moment to a branch, lost its hold and fell heavily to the ground. He'd run excitedly to the spot where the squirrel fell.

Then his world had suddenly changed. Beneath him was a helpless creature still suffering. One shot had hit the center of its chest and a stream of blood trickled down from the wound, a crimson line across the thin white fur. The squirrel looked at him with big, sad eyes that seemed to say, "Why did you do this to me?" Then the squirrel twitched and died.

Peter began crying, then sobbing uncontrollably, running back to his grandfather, leaving the squirrel where it had fallen.

"Where's the squirrel?"

He gave no answer as he continued to cry. His grandfather got up and retrieved the squirrel by the tail. "Let's go, Little Peter. I killed my first squirrel at six but you may be too young right now, or maybe you're not meant to be a hunter."

On the way home, he and his grandpa said nothing. His mother was up and fixed him breakfast, but he wasn't hungry. Sitting in the kitchen, staring at his eggs and ham, he could hear his father and grandpa talking in the living room.

"I'm a little worried about our Little Peter," Grandpa told his father. "We may have us a bit of a sissy to deal with. Hope he grows out of it."

His grandpa never quit calling him Little Peter, and he never took him hunting again.

~

Peter wondered how he would feel killing a German soldier. Surely it would be different. The German soldier would be trying to kill him first.

He fell into a restless, shallow sleep, his mind drifting between dream and reality, past and present, until he was roused before dawn for the morning stand-to. He stood watch for an hour on the fire step, bayonet fixed, ready for an enemy attack, which most often came in the hazy light of dawn and dusk.

By late morning, Peter was assigned to repair the duckboards in his section of the trench, which took less than five minutes. Arthur was assigned to pump water from the trench, a much more challenging task.

Peter sat in the dugout where he had slept, with his feet in the trench, holding a narrow wooden slat not needed for the repair. In his mind he was at the plate on the dusty clay ballfield in Glasper. On the mound was Cleve Dallas, the big left-hander from Summit.

Reality intruded as up the trench Peter saw a big brown rat running toward him, heedless of his presence. It was Cleve Dallas's change-up.

In one motion Peter stood and swung the slat, catching Bruno flush in the face. The rat fell at the feet of Jake Brewer, blood gushing from his mouth, clearly dead. Peter stepped over and poked the rat with the slat. The monstrous creature had no tail.

"I'll go tell Mulholland, if you'll share the rum," Jake said with a grin. "You can have it all."

Soon after, Jake arrived with Sergeant Mulholland, who had a bottle of rum in hand. "Little Peter, I hear you killed Bruno. Bloody hell, that's great. Oh, there he is. That's him."

Peter flushed in anger. "Don't call me Little Peter! If you call me that again, you'll be sorry!"

Mulholland bristled. "Little Peter, you're under my command, ya knobhead. I'll tolerate no insubordination. You'll have loo duty every day. I'll call you what I bloody please! What you threatening me with, shooting me when we attack and making it look like a Hun?"

"No, but I'll be praying you're the first one the Huns hit."

Mulholland stammered, struggling for an appropriate response. Then he smiled. "Little . . . uh . . . Private Montgomery . . . uh . . . you got spunk. When we go over the top tomorrow, I like knowing I'm fighting with a soldier with your kind of spunk. You'll be on my right."

With that, the sergeant handed Peter the bottle of rum and walked away. Peter pitched it to Jake, who had a look of panic. "What's he mean 'when we go over the top tomorrow?'"

No one offered a response, but they all realized what was coming. Attack plans were always the subject of rumor, but for security reasons were kept from the rank and file until shortly beforehand.

～

In midafternoon Peter's platoon of thirty-eight assembled in their longest section of trench, packed shoulder to shoulder, some sitting on the fire step, others on the edge of the dugouts, many standing.

Addressing them was their platoon leader, Lieutenant Tom Crawley, a twenty-four-year-old West Point graduate. Crawley was a six-footer of medium build with a strong voice and a Midwestern accent. His recently-shaved head had an alabaster cast in sharp contrast to his thick, dark eyebrows.

"Tomorrow morning at five-forty we go over the top. Let's all synchronize. It's three-twenty-five."

Peter looked at his watch. It was three minutes slow. Along with numerous others, he made a necessary adjustment.

"Our objective is to take the enemy positions to our front, clear and secure them, then push on to the Marne and beyond to Chateau Thierry. Intelligence shows two machine gun nests in front of our platoon. The enemy is on the ridgeline, about three hundred yards to our front."

Arthur was on Peter's left and he began to cough loudly. Lieutenant Crawley stopped talking and looked his way. Arthur suppressed his coughing. "Let's have no smoking until I finish," Crawley admonished, but Arthur wasn't smoking.

"The sergeants and I will check equipment: guns, ammo, grenades, wire cutters. Mulholland has gone over the top at the Somme. He will tell you what to expect, how to stay alive."

Mulholland stood beside Crawley, lanky frame slouched as usual, his long neck protruding from his bowed shoulders, his voice as strident as ever.

"Mates, the Somme was in July of sixteen. My company was almost wiped out. Don't want to walk in a line abreast . . . do that and bloody machine guns'll mow you down. When we start taking fire, get down, look for cover. Return fire from cover. Crawl forward for more cover . . . run forward to more cover. If our artillery is hitting close to the Huns, that's the time to run forward."

Lieutenant Crawley interrupted. "Our artillery will lay down a creeping barrage ahead of us. Stay behind that."

"Don't go right into them machine guns," Mulholland warned. "Get around behind them, get under them. They're big and heavy . . . can't be sighted quick like a rifle, most sighted for a field of fire, not a single chap. Get close. Use your grenades . . . use your handgun."

Lieutenant Crawley stepped forward again. "Be at your position with the climbing ladder in place at four-forty. Tonight, we will send out a party to cut gaps in our wire."

After Crawley and Mulholland had finished and the group dispersed, Arthur looked at Peter. "You been praying? For me and you?"

"Heck yeah, you know I have," Peter lied.

"You better."

About midnight, before Peter finally dozed off into a restless sleep, he remembered his promise. "Lord, protect Arthur and don't let him get killed," he prayed silently. "And me too." He remembered such a prayer should include the phrase, "If it be Thy will," so he added that. He had been taught that every prayer should end with, "In Christ's holy name, Amen," and Peter followed the formula. Remembering Arthur's prayers, Peter added, "And, Lord, if we die, please don't let them rats eat our eyeballs." Livers didn't seem that special.

CHAPTER 2

BIG GUNS KILL PEOPLE

I t was still dark, but a faint light appeared on the horizon. Suddenly, as far as Peter could see in each direction, the sky was ablaze with exploding artillery. Incendiary rounds lit up the landscape. The ground shook. He gripped his rifle with one hand and the step-up ladder with the other. Arthur and Jake were on his right, and Mulholland on his left. The sergeant had a light machine gun, a Lewis, with a strange circular magazine on top the size of a small, thick pie plate.

Mulholland handed Peter a small but heavy canvas bag. "Extra grenades. Weems says you can throw well. You get close enough . . . nothing better."

"One minute!" Lieutenant Crawley shouted from down the trench to Peter's left. "Fix bayonets!" Bayonets clicked into place up and down the trench. Peter could hear his heartbeat and feel it in his throat. His mouth had a metallic taste. He sensed a chill in the center of his back. It was the longest minute of his life. Finally, the lieutenant blew a shrill whistle and they scrambled up the attack ladders and over the top.

"Get behind me," Mulholland shouted. "I know where the wire's cut." As instructed, they moved forward, not in an exposed wave, but in fours and fives following single file. Mulholland was in front of Peter; Jake and Arthur followed him. The sky in front was ablaze. Overhead it screamed and shrieked. They were sandwiched between cannons firing behind them and shells exploding in front. The noise was deafening. Ahead, machine guns clattered. Bullets whizzed by, making a dull-sounding splat as they hit the mud.

"Get down!" ordered Mulholland. "Crawl! They can't see us . . . they're firing blind!"

Crawling was difficult, as Peter's knees and elbows slipped in the mud. He dug them in hard and managed to squirm forward. German artillery shells exploded around them, one hitting a water-filled crater to Peter's right. Water and mud showered down. He was engulfed in rancid smoke. The Germans began exploding flares as a foggy dawn crept across the battlefield. Peter saw the shadowy figures of scores of men crawling and running every direction. Men fell as machine guns swept their ranks. Others were blown into the air by the shell blasts. Men moaned and shrieked in agony.

When their group came to a small depression, Mulholland set up his Lewis. "Run for the next cover," he yelled. "I'll try and keep them ducking." Peter heard Mulholland's gun clatter in short bursts of three and four rounds.

While two others stayed behind with Mulholland, Peter, Arthur, and Jake Brewer ran forward, skidding down the slope of a huge crater and sinking up to their knees in mud. It had a reek of rotten flesh. Peter felt something furry. It was the head of a rotting horse, wearing a ghoulish expression, with its teeth and eye sockets staring at him from the bleached skull.

Early light revealed their progress. They had made half the distance to the German positions on the ridge. Most survivors had taken cover. The German artillery intensified, and a round exploded directly behind them. Mulholland's gun went silent.

"Think they got Mulholland . . . maybe Davis and Beasley," Arthur cried. "There's a ditch over there, going up toward them . . . maybe we can get to it."

Peter struggled out of the deep mud, feeling the horse's tail under his hand. Peeping over, he saw the ditch where Arthur wanted to take cover. Bullets struck the mud inches from Peter's face. They had been spotted!

"What we gonna do?" Jake cried out, knee-deep in mud at the bottom of the trench.

"I ain't doing nothing right now," Arthur replied. "They must be looking right at us."

Minutes passed. The machine gun fire moved to their left.

"We need to do something," Peter shouted. "I'm going for the ditch!"

"We'll all go! They won't get us all," Arthur yelled back.

Peter scrambled from the crater and dashed for the ditch, twenty yards away, Arthur and Jake following. Almost immediately, the machine gun opened up on them. A bullet struck the butt of Peter's rifle, a splinter striking him in the right cheek. As he approached the edge of the ditch, a shell exploded to his left, the force of the explosion sending a rush of air past his face. His left leg numbed and collapsed under him. Peter tumbled into the ditch and Jake fell in behind him.

"Think I've been hit," Peter said.

"God yeah! There's a hole in your legging . . . and you're bleeding bad."

Peter looked down at his left leg. Midway between Peter's ankle and his knee was an inch-square hole with blood pouring from it, soaking the muddy garment and staining the water in the ditch.

Jake scowled. "Get our bandages!" Each of them had been issued a small pocket kit with two sealed bandages. Jake got Peter's out first, then his own. He unwrapped Peter's legging to above the wound. Out spurted blood. Both sets of bandages were placed around the wound, and Jake tightly rewrapped the legging.

"Still bleeding . . . but not that bad anymore," Jake announced.

Intense, radiating pain replaced numbness. Peter lay on his back, dizzy, about to vomit. The relentless, deafening sounds of artillery shells and machine gun fire continued. Jake lay on his back beside him as minutes passed.

Peter suddenly remembered Arthur had been behind him when they left the shell crater and that Jake was behind Arthur.

"Where's Arthur?"

"He got hit."

"Let's go back for him."

"He's dead . . . half his face blown off."

Rage replaced Peter's nausea. He rolled back onto his hands and knees and started dragging himself up the ditch toward higher ground. He heard Jake panting behind him. The ditch got deeper, its steep sides affording brief protection, then became little more than a depression scraped into the earth. Winded, Peter rolled over on his back and Jake joined him.

The clattering of the machine gun to his left seemed near now. Peter wormed his body to the top of the ditch and peered over. The machine gun was close, not more than twenty yards away, firing off to the left down the ridge.

He rolled onto his side and pulled two grenades from the bag that Mulholland had given him, gently placing them near the top of the bank. Back on his stomach, he squirmed around for the best possible position from which to throw a grenade. He grasped the pin and pulled it, tightly holding the safety lever.

He was in center field on a dusty ballpark in Glasper. He caught the line drive on one hop and threw home, trying to cut down the runner at the plate. The grenade took one bounce at the top of the bunker, skipped by the machine gun, fell below and exploded. The machine gun fell silent. Peter took aim with the second grenade and let it fly. He had found the range and this one went straight in on the fly before it detonated. Crawling out of the ditch, Peter started pulling himself across the open ground toward the machine gun nest.

"Where the hell you going?" Jake called out under his breath. Peter kept crawling forward. Jake remained in the ditch, paralyzed by fear.

Reaching the parapet of the machine gun nest, Peter cautiously peered over the edge. In the bottom were three lifeless, bloody bodies.

A deep trench led away from the machine gun nest toward the main German positions. Peter heard guttural voices, and two German soldiers appeared. They did not notice Peter as they looked at their dead comrades. Peter aimed his rifle at the closest one and fired. The German paused, wobbled, then fell forward into the mud. His comrade fired at Peter, hitting the parapet inches from his face. Both struggled to reload. Peter fumbled weakly with the bolt action rifle. As the German took aim, Peter heard a rifle crack immediately to his right. The German pitched backward. Peter looked up at Jake, who was maneuvering his bolt to chamber another round.

Peter and Jake lay on their backs staring at billowing clouds of smoke and dust. Peter touched Jake on his arm in silent gratitude. Down the ridge, another German machine gun clattered furiously.

"Let's go for that one," Peter said, weakly. "Probably the other one Mulholland talked about."

"We ain't got no cover. You're hurt bad."

Weak and dizzy, Peter crawled toward the machine gun, skirting the German line, hidden by the high parapet. Jake realized that without standing up on the parapet, the Germans couldn't see them, and he followed.

It took fifteen exhausting minutes, and twice they were almost hit by their own artillery, but they worked their way to a spot less than twenty feet below the second German machine gun nest.

Jake crawled up beside Peter. "Let me take this one."

"Together," Peter whispered weakly.

They edged closer. Peter took two grenades from the bag, handing one to Jake. They pulled the pins and held the safety levers. Jake awaited Peter's lead.

"Now!"

The German machine gun was still clattering loudly when the grenades bounced over the parapet and fell below. They detonated seconds apart and the gun fell silent.

Jake crawled to the edge of the parapet and peered over. Two appeared dead, but another sat, holding his rifle, staring blankly ahead. As Jake's movement drew his attention, the German struggled weakly to lift his rifle, then fell sideways, his helmet burrowing into the brown mud. Jake lowered his rifle. The man was dead.

Jake and Peter positioned themselves on the edge of the parapet, bracing for another onslaught that might come down the trenches. Five minutes passed and Peter slipped into unconsciousness.

The artillery retreated behind the German trenches. Down the hill, soldiers from their regiment advanced across open ground. Their machine guns silenced, the Germans had retreated from their positions on the ridge.

Four soldiers approached and Jake spotted Lieutenant Crawley among them. The lieutenant recognized Jake, but not the unconscious Peter.

"Brewer . . . this man dead?"

"No, sir, but he's bled a lot . . . we've got to get him help."

The lieutenant turned to the soldiers behind him.

"Usury! Blake! Go find a stretcher bearer for this man. Get a stretcher yourself if necessary and come back for him. You get this gun, Brewer?"

"Yessir . . . me and Peter did."

"Good work. Somebody in another platoon got that other gun down there about thirty minutes ago. When you got this one the enemy retreated."

Jake pointed at Peter. "He got that other one."

The lieutenant had a look of astonishment.

"You fellas got both of them?"

"Yessir."

"My God!"

Lieutenant Crawley acted as if he wanted to say something else, but then walked on. Jake sat with the unconscious Peter as scores of soldiers passed them in pursuit of the fleeing Germans.

∼

Peter lapsed in and out of consciousness as he was jostled on a stretcher to the Dressing Station behind the front lines. He was barely aware as a medic swabbed on iodine and bandaged the wound. Consciousness seeped back in during a blood transfusion in the Casualty Clearing Station several more miles to the rear. He became aware of men moaning inside the tent. One called out to his mother in an eerie, mournful voice. Distant artillery fire punctuated strained voices mingled with the sound of engines and horses' hooves.

"Let's go on and amputate, right below the knee," he heard a voice say, in an accent that reminded him of Lieutenant Crawley. "He's had morphine, but we'll need ether."

"Maybe ought to wait, mate. He might not have to lose it." This voice was British. Peter tried to look at the source of the voices without raising his head. The American appeared young—maybe thirty—tall, close-cropped hair, beard just days of neglect; the British voice came from an older man, short and stocky—likely fifties—bald, with a prominent handlebar mustache.

"Sure to get infected, if we don't, and he'll die . . . or they'll have to amputate later, further up . . . probably even at the hip."

"Back at Edmonton we've been using the Carrel-Dinkins irrigation. It's saving many, like this. Got some in here yesterday."

"Where's Edmonton?"

"North Middlesex. Bit north of London. Specializing in orthopedic."

"Can we get him there before it gets infected?"

"Think we should try, mate. Always somebody on the train, boat . . . along the way . . . who can cut it off, if need be. Let's clean it up. Hold it open, I'll probe around."

Peter felt a bolt of pain, so bad it made him nauseated.

"Tibia looks good. Fibula is completely shattered. Let's get out that little piece of bone. Good it's fibula shattered; big ole tibia will hold it all together, bear the weight, serve like a splint."

"Let's clamp off this vein; it's where most of the blood's coming from," the American said.

The pain intensified. Peter gritted his teeth to hold back an urge to cry out.

"We'll need to get the Carrel mixed and irrigate, 'tis what we need to do now . . . comes in two containers . . . ye don't mix it until you're about to use it."

They methodically cleaned, irrigated, bandaged Peter's wound. The older surgeon patted Peter on the shoulder. "Think we've done all we can for ye here, ole chap, try to move you out soon. Good luck to you and Godspeed."

As they walked away, Peter heard, "Hope we're not making a mistake . . . that they have to cut it off at the hip or it gets so infected he dies."

"It's not infected yet, mate . . . it's not infected yet."

CHAPTER 3

A WOMAN'S TOUCH

Peter endured the painful journey by ambulance from the Casualty Clearing Station behind the front to the coast, across the channel by boat, by train to London Station, then by ambulance to Edmonton Military Hospital in North Middlesex. Tall windows and chimneys loomed through a morphine-induced haze as he looked up from the stretcher at the sprawling three-story brown brick structure.

His ward consisted of a dozen beds on each side of a narrow aisle, a scene of white and grays: patients in white gowns on white sheets, iron beds, a floor of dark gray terrazzo, and light gray walls. Anemic daylight filtered through the window overhead. Nine panes topped by a hinged transom dissected the weak illumination, casting geometric shadows. From his bed, the first on the left as one entered the ward, he could see into a part of the nurses' station, separated from the ward by a wall, the top of which was glass.

Just hours into his first day at Edmonton, Peter awoke to find someone's hands on his leg. A young woman was attending to his bandaged injury. Only the sleeves of her blue denim dress showed beneath a full-length white apron that was snugly bound at her waist with a white cloth belt. The apron was topped by a white starched collar, and she wore a white veiled cap, fitted tightly across her forehead. A tuft of auburn hair peeked out from the cap. Thin and petite, she had a delicate figure, almost child-like. Peter found her beautiful, with a rosy complexion, high cheekbones and wide-set hazel eyes.

She glanced up at him and smiled warmly. Pulling aside the dressing, she adjusted the tubing running into his wound, casting her practiced eye over it while changing the dressing and replacing the nearly empty bag of liquid suspended above his foot.

She leaned over him, putting her hand briefly on his forehead, smiling again. Pressing her fingers into the underside of his wrist, she studied a watch on her other wrist.

In a pronounced English accent, she said in a soft voice, "Shall I get you something for pain, Private Montgomery?"

"No ma'am, I'm fine."

"You sure? I shall certainly get you something if you ask. Shattered bones are painful, mind you, very painful. You shan't heal as well if you're in pain."

"I'm fine," Peter said again. In truth, the pain was excruciating; at times a hard ache, at other times—particularly if he moved—a sharp throbbing sensation.

"Then you rest. I shall be back to check on you again soon."

With that Peter gave her a somber look.

"Ma'am," he beckoned her, then paused and looked away.

"Are they gonna cut off my leg, and all?"

She struggled for a response.

"Now don't you think about anything like that, mind you," she said. "We don't need to think about anything like that."

Then she added, with a resolute look, "We shall work together not to let that happen, Private Montgomery, we surely shall . . ."

She took his hand and patted him softly on the forearm, smiling. "Now you rest. You just try and rest."

As she walked away, Peter felt comforted.

～

Two hours later the routine was repeated. As she was pressing her fingers into Peter's wrist, checking his pulse, he heard a loud voice, two beds over: "Miss Baker, I'm thirsty. I need a drink. I need a drink now. Please!"

"He's not thirsty," she said to Peter, under her breath. "He only wants attention. He'll ask me to marry him . . . like he always does. I try not to be annoyed."

After finishing with Peter, Nurse Baker went to the nurses' station, returning with a large container of water and a glass.

"Oh, thank you!" Peter heard the other soldier say. Glancing sideways, Peter saw the patient take one gulp and put aside his glass. "Have you thought about it? Are you gonna marry me? I'll take you to Texas to a big ranch. I'll dress you in fine clothes. We'll go to the beach at Galveston for the summers."

"She's not going to marry you, she's gonna marry me," said another voice from a bed across the aisle, not far from Peter's. "I'll take her to Colorado. We'll spend summers in the mountains. I'll find gold and we'll be rich."

Looking at one, then across the aisle at the other, Nurse Baker said, in a voice loud enough to carry through much of the ward, "With this war, and all we're going through, marriage is the last thing on my mind." With that she gave them a weak respectful smile and retreated.

When she entered the nurses' station, her supervisor, Janet Humphreys, looked up from a patient chart. Elizabeth Baker was twenty; Janet Humphreys was thirty-one, childless, widowed in the first year of marriage when her husband was killed in battle on the Somme. Janet was a robust woman, of medium height, with a freckled face and bright red hair.

"I wish these patients wouldn't hassle me like they do," said Elizabeth. "They always embarrass me so . . . make me feel so self-conscious."

"Hassle?"

"Oh, they're always flirting with me . . . asking me to marry them and stuff like that. It embarrasses me."

"Elizabeth, you are a lovely young woman . . . but even beyond that these boys are bored and lonely and far from home, and you're around, love. They don't mean to be that cheeky. They're just having a little fun. Lord knows, I even get a proposal from time to time." Janet smiled at Elizabeth. "But maybe only once or twice a year." With that she looked back down at her work.

"Do they treat Hilda and Rachel like that? I never hear them complain . . ." Hilda and Rachel were the other two nurses who had regularly attended to the patients on this ward during the six months Elizabeth had been at Edmonton. The nurses all worked two at a time, on twelve-hour shifts. Hilda was fifty-four and unmarried . . . skinny, skin wrinkled and loose. Rachel was a war widow in her mid-forties, a portly frump. The strain of constant twelve-hour shifts took a toll on any tendency either of them might have to smile.

"I don't know, love. You'll have to ask them." Janet's look had a tint of sarcasm.

~

Elizabeth Baker quickly became the center of Peter's universe. He had a constant longing to see her, to hear her voice, to have her smile at him, to feel her touch. Often, he could see her in the part of the nurses' station visible from his bed. He couldn't take his eyes off her. She would catch him staring at her and would smile his way before looking away. Fearing he might make her uncomfortable, he tried not to watch her at every possible moment, but he had little success. When her shifts were over and she left, he felt intensely lonely.

~

Something about Elizabeth reminded Peter of Hannah Nixon, his only prior love interest. Hannah had come to Glasper the summer Peter turned sixteen. Her father had been transferred from Williamsburg, Pennsylvania, by the Susquehanna Timber Company. Susquehanna had purchased a large tract of South Mississippi virgin pine and Hannah's father was to oversee the timber harvest.

At sixteen, the raven-haired Hannah had had a much more womanly figure than Elizabeth. But Elizabeth had the same rosy complexion, high cheekbones, and wide-set hazel eyes, and Elizabeth's English accent reminded him of Hannah's Yankee brogue, both foreign-sounding and so different from any of the girls in Peter's small south-Mississippi school. The students had been seated alphabetically, placing Hannah next to him in the classroom. Being new and a Yankee, Hannah hadn't found early acceptance, and she'd kept to herself.

"There's not much point in me trying to make many friends,"

Hannah had said to him one day, as they were leaving the last class of the day. "As soon as I make some friends, my father will move us to a new timber cut. I've never lived anywhere more than about two years—Pennsylvania, Ohio, New York, Indiana. Even thought we were going to Michigan once, when I was twelve. Then we didn't . . . this is the first time we've been in the South."

Hannah was smart and sharing, always being more prepared than he was, which was not difficult, and he'd come to like her.

Not long into the school year, he'd been struggling with math. As school was adjourning one day, she'd said to him, "Come out after school this afternoon, if you'd like, and we'll study some together."

He'd reflected on her offer. "I'm gonna take you up on it . . . I mean, you know, if you're serious, and all."

The Nixons had rented a large, two-story house on the outskirts of Glasper. Hannah had a big, loud family with an older sister and two younger brothers. It seemed their house was always chaos, with her mother always shouting at her younger brothers, trying to call them down or breaking up a fight.

Hannah was neat and studious, clearly her mother's favorite. Hannah's father, Horace Nixon, worked long hours and was seldom home. It had not been difficult for Hannah to persuade her mother that the only reasonably quiet place in the house for them to study was her bedroom upstairs.

"She wants us to keep the door open," Hannah had told him firmly.

They kept the door open. But the third time they'd studied together, when they were alone upstairs, Hannah had moved over close to him and said in a soft voice, "I want you to kiss me. I'm so lonely . . . and I think I need to be kissed today." Caring little about her motives, and with no prior experience, he'd done his best to accommodate.

His improved grades had come to the attention of his parents, and Hannah's parents had noticed that she was adjusting to this Mississippi move unusually well. The two dating and spending a great deal of time together received tacit encouragement from both sets of parents, subject to a ten o'clock curfew imposed by Hannah's father. Much of that time had been spent parked in the Montgomery Ford on a forest lane two miles outside town, making love.

Hannah had constantly worried that she would become pregnant. Repeatedly they'd resolved not to "go all the way" *again*, until they were acceptably old enough to marry, knowing that a pregnant girl would not be allowed to continue in school. Then, once more, passion would overcome them. When they had "gone all the way," they'd managed to reason that more than one time in a day was no more likely to get her pregnant.

In August, right before he was to start his senior year of high school, Peter had arrived one afternoon to pick Hannah up and she'd come running out to meet him. She had been crying. "Peter, we're moving again," she'd said, choking back tears. "We are going to Michigan."

He'd reached out and hugged her to him, as she'd sobbed against his chest. "Maybe we need to get married and I could stay here in Glasper with you. But Father says I'm his child with the most potential for college, and he wants me to go to college, study to become a schoolteacher . . . and I do want to."

Peter had told her he would marry her if that's what she wanted.

They resolved to write often, and Peter had tried, in spite of the fact that he was not much of a letter writer. Over the months her responses had gotten shorter, slower to come, somehow less warm and personal. Her early closing of "I love you, Hannah" was replaced with "Love, Hannah." Finally, a year after she left Glasper, subsequent to two letters from him to which she hadn't responded, Hannah had written that she had married, but that she would always love him.

From the time Hannah left for Michigan, until he'd left for the Army, he had cared about little except playing baseball and "running the roads"—as his worried mother called it—drinking and smoking with his friend Dennis Langley, hanging out wherever they found it convenient, being what the locals called "young fools going down Fools' Hill."

Lying in his bed in North Middlesex, thinking about how much Elizabeth reminded him of Hannah, Peter realized that Hannah had contributed to his decision to join the Army.

CHAPTER 4

MUTUAL ATTRACTION

When Elizabeth came to his bed, Peter sought ways to keep her there. Trying to ask sensible questions became his strategy.

"What's the stuff in the bag you keep changing, Miss Baker?" he asked in late morning on his eighth day at Edmonton.

"It's called Carrel-Dinkins solution; comes in two parts that must be mixed up right before use."

"What's in it . . . uh . . . what's it supposed to do?"

"I don't know exactly what's in it, Private Montgomery. Definitely supposed to help with infection. I shall find out for you."

"What's in this Carrel-Dinkins solution?" Elizabeth asked Janet, when she returned to the nurses' station.

"Don't remember the exact chemical names, love, but it's basically chlorine mixed with some type of soda in a weak solution. It helps with infection but is not strong enough to irritate . . . mixed together, it's not good for long, that's why we have to mix it up every day, from the two packets."

Elizabeth went back to Peter. "Some type of chlorine, mixed with some type of soda," she told him. "We must constantly flush the wound with it; helps keep it from getting infected. We *are* working together to keep that from happening, aren't we, Private Montgomery?"

She gave Peter a warm smile. He smiled back. "Thank you . . . ma'am

29

for finding out for me. I been wondering about what it was."

~

Previously, Elizabeth had approached Peter's bedside from his left side, adjacent to the next patient. She began to approach from his right side, next to the wall, standing close to his head. Her voice softened, as if she wanted their conversation to be private. After she'd learned that he was refusing morphine, she'd rarely taken his pulse when she came to inspect his wound and replenish the solution. She began to check his pulse again, every time. Short-staffed, the nurses usually felt the patient's forehead for a gross observation of temperature, only using a thermometer when fever was suspected. She began to feel his forehead, and then always take his temperature with a thermometer, standing patiently waiting for the thermometer to have time to make its reading. Studying Peter pleasantly, Elizabeth leaned against the wall, arms folded in front of her.

Early in the afternoon of his tenth day at Edmonton, as Elizabeth pulled the thermometer from his mouth, while still looking down at the thermometer, she asked him, in her soft voice, with the accent that he had come to love, "Where are you from, Private Montgomery?"

"Glasper."

She looked up from the thermometer, with a bit of a smirk. "Where, pray tell, is Glasper, Private Montgomery?"

"It's . . . uh . . . it's in Miss'sippi and all."

"Now I *have* heard of that . . . that's a state of the United States, is it not?"

"Yessum—"

"'Tis a pity you're here with me, Private Montgomery . . . so far from home . . . so far away from your loved ones." She gave him a quizzical look, as if seeking information.

But she did not pause long, and with a jaunty motion, she turned her head and walked back to the nurses' station. Peter embraced happiness. This small show of interest seemed most positive.

From this point, he was not continually challenged to come up with sensible-sounding questions or feign interest in some technical aspect of his hospitalization. Now, often Elizabeth took the lead in their dialog. After several days this was noticed by her other ardent admirers. With pronounced aloofness, Elizabeth ignored their snide remarks.

"Where in your America is Mississippi?" she asked him, two days later, when she came to check and treat his wound.

"It's in the South . . . uh, some say the Deep South."

"Would I know about anything close by?"

"Well, uh . . . well . . . there's Louisiana, you know, on one side. That's the closest other state to us in Glasper, and all. I been there several times, to Baton Rouge several times . . . and once to N'Olens. Then there's Alabama on the other side, you know. I never been there, except going through on the train to come over here. Tennessee is way up to the north . . . never been there. Down below is the Gulf of Mexico. My grandpa took me down there once, when he was going on a vacation, to see his cousin."

"Isn't there a big river Mississippi?"

"Yessum . . . it's real big, mile wide they say, and runs down the side. We have to cross it and all, to get to Baton Rouge and N'Olens."

The next day, she asked, "How big is your Glasper?"

"Oh, it's not very big, Miss Baker. Only about three streets running down to the railroad, and to a road running up alongside the tracks and all . . . and with Main Street going right down to the train depot. Of course, there is a few cross streets too, you know. The train and the train station is kind of the center of everything."

"How many people live there?"

"Oh, gosh . . . I don't know . . . there's a sign at the railroad station, people see . . . you know, coming into town on the railroad. It says: 'Welcome to Glasper, home to a thousand friendly people, and a few ole sore heads.'"

Elizabeth chuckled. "It's my bet that the chap—the one who made the sign—is indeed an ole sore head." She looked pensive. "I've never been outside London, not once in my whole life."

"Didn't your family take you anywhere else?" he asked. "On a vacation or something . . . to see some relatives who lived somewhere else, or something like that?"

She took on a strange, dispirited look. "No," she said, walking away.

Peter wished he had not asked the question.

~

One day in Peter's third week at Edmonton, when Elizabeth entered the nurses' station, Janet turned in her chair to face her, with a concerned look.

"Elizabeth, I must talk to you," she said, "as a friend . . . like I would if you were my sister, my daughter. We've been working here, twelve on, twelve off, for six months together; I've come to feel very close to you. Take this chair and sit beside me."

Elizabeth sat.

"I fear that you, my dear Elizabeth, are making a mistake. You are letting yourself become romantically attracted to this Private Montgomery. And, Lord only knows, I truly understand why . . . that blond hair, those beautiful blue eyes." She looked away from Elizabeth, down at her desk. "When he first came here, an Indian orderly . . . the one that wears the purple turban . . . was bathing Private Montgomery, cleaning him up a bit, had him naked. I couldn't help but observe him. He certainly has a lovely body . . . a body that would excite any woman. Oh, I know, my dear Elizabeth, you haven't noticed his body."

Janet gave Elizabeth a sly smile. Elizabeth felt herself blush. "Janet, he's such a gentleman."

"Oh, yes, love," Janet responded, with another sly smile. "I'm sure that's what attracts you to him." After a pause, Janet said, "Elizabeth, in time, Private Montgomery is going to leave here to go back to America, probably back to his American love, and you, my dear Elizabeth, are going to be left a prissy little thing that's sad and empty indeed."

Elizabeth felt herself flush. "I'm not prissy!"

"You weren't until Private Montgomery came along." With that Janet turned back to the work on her desk. Elizabeth returned to the patients on the ward.

~

Midmorning two days later, Elizabeth and Janet were engaged in an exchange far less benign, both with angry raised voices.

"You can't go, and that's that!" Janet virtually shouted at Elizabeth.

"I must go! I must!"

Elizabeth dropped in a chair, face in her hands, and she began to cry softly.

"I must go. I must! She has been my closest person. We're like sisters . . . she's like my only relative. I never remember a time without her."

"If you go, then don't come back here. I don't want you back here. We mustn't risk it. Who is this Agnes Dixon you think you must go to . . . makes her someone you want to risk catching this awful flu for, risk bringing it back to all these sick men, maybe killing half of them? Soon half England—half the world—will be dead from this. It gets worse every day." Janet's voice was lower now, and it had a defeated tone.

Elizabeth wiped her eyes on the back of her hands and looked up.

"I don't know where to start."

An orderly walked by, pushing a clattering cart. Janet looked at him, annoyed, then back at Elizabeth.

"In my earliest memories Agnes and I were only four. We would lie in bed together, holding each other . . . alone, shivering . . . afraid."

"Why? Where were you?"

"In a wooden East End tenement, two rooms, an awful, shared outhouse in the back alley. Her mother and my mother lived with us. At night, they would put on bright clothes and perfume and go out and leave us . . . usually they left together, but never came back together. Sometimes they came back in the night, sometimes the next day. We were always scared they wouldn't come back at all, that some bad person would break in and get us. It was just Agnes and me. We were so little . . . and we were always so frightened."

Tears flowed again down Elizabeth's cheeks.

"One day—I remember it was, like the middle of the day—well up in the morning . . . they had us put on clean clothes they had washed the day before. They made us sit down at a little table and my mother said, 'We're taking you to Barnwell to live. That's what we've decided is best for you.'"

The orderly came back by with the clattering cart. This time Janet and Elizabeth paid him no attention. Elizabeth stopped talking, sitting with her chin slumped against her chest.

"Barnwell?" Janet said in time. "I may have heard of that."

"It is a blessed place, an orphanage for the likes of Agnes and me."

"Did you like Barnwell?"

"Going there was the best thing that ever happened to us. All our time there we were inseparable best friends."

"How long did you stay in this orphanage?"

"Until I was twelve."

"How did you get from there to here? Get to be a nurse?"

"It was because of Dr. Prince . . . the other special person in my life."

"Dr. Prince?"

Elizabeth had stopped crying. "Janet, it's a long story. Maybe some-day—if our lives allow—I can tell you all about it. But not today. I must go to Agnes. Nothing else matters to me right now."

"Elizabeth, please don't. Please . . . we so need you here."

"I must," Elizabeth said, in a dejected but firm voice.

Elizabeth started down the hall to the stairwell, but then turned around. Walking past Janet, never looking at her, Elizabeth approached Peter's bed. She stood and looked at him as he slept.

"Goodbye, Private Montgomery," Elizabeth said in a soft voice. "I shall be praying for you and for your leg." She turned and walked away.

CHAPTER 5

DYING A VIRGIN

An hour earlier, Elizabeth had received a message from Dr. Prince that Agnes was critically ill in Queen Mary's Annex fifteen miles away, which was devoted to the quarantine of Spanish Flu patients. Still wearing her uniform, Elizabeth boarded the tramcar, which had less than a dozen other passengers, and took a seat against a window on the left, midway back. The tram clattered along the track, swaying gently from side to side. At intersections, the sun sent bright beams between the shadows of the dark brick buildings. The streets were busy and she passed stoic horses pulling utilitarian carts, spoke-wheeled vehicles with bug-eyed headlights, hat-clad pedestrians, people on bicycles, shops and store fronts, and an occasional bobbie with his black pointed helmet, baton in hand. Other trams and double-decker buses passed in the opposite direction, each time making an abrupt loud clatter.

At twelve, Barnwell sought to integrate orphans into society, and a favored choice for girls was domestic work for prominent families. Agnes had been placed with J. B. Clifford, a wealthy banker, and Elizabeth with John Prince, a renowned surgeon. Suddenly Elizabeth and Agnes were separated by five city miles and the expectations of their employment. At times, months passed with no contact.

The last time they had been together, Agnes had wanted to meet for lunch at The Fairy Cake, a sweets shop with pleasant outdoor seating and daily specials, long a favorite place not far from Barnwell.

Elizabeth had been working twelve-hour shifts at the hospital with few days off and was exhausted. Coming from North Middlesex, it was nearly an hour, by tram or bus, but she wanted to be agreeable, knowing Agnes was still having difficulty dealing with Wilber's death. Elizabeth expected Wilber and his death to be a primary topic of conversation. She always offered what comfort she could, but Elizabeth was not looking forward to it.

For two years, whenever they were together, Elizabeth had heard much about Wilber. Agnes had fallen deeply in love with him, shortly after he came to work for the Cliffords as a groomsman. Agnes had even talked him into coming to one of their lunch meetings so Elizabeth could meet him. Stocky and broad-faced with shaggy light hair, a prominent belly, and droopy dark eyes, Wilber reminded Elizabeth of Doctor Prince's Clumber Spaniel.

Wilber made Agnes happier than she had ever been in her otherwise rather sad life. Her voice had a sparkle about it, and she started taking great pains with her appearance. Then Wilber went off to join the war and was killed on the Western Front, where he was also buried.

The Fairy Cake was on a corner, across the intersection from the tram stop. Elizabeth had left the tram and walked by a harnessed white horse hitched to a parked floral cart, side blinders framing his eyes. She'd spotted Agnes under the familiar green awning, in a back corner to the right, seated at a round table topped by a white cloth.

Agnes had risen, pushed back her black metal chair, and greeted her, with a phlegmatic expression.

"Hi, Elizabeth. I *love* that blouse."

That day she'd worn a plain calf-length black skirt, topped by a long-sleeved white blouse with a high ruffled collar, practically her only casual clothing, since she spent almost all her time in nurse's uniform. She'd worn garnet earrings and a matching pendant, given to her on her sixteenth birthday by Mrs. Prince. Her hair had been pulled back by a broad black band. Mrs. Prince had also given her red lipstick in a metal tube, only on the market for a few years, and Elizabeth had worn it for the occasion.

"You look beautiful, Agnes," she'd said, trying to reply in kind. Agnes was a large woman, big-boned at twenty, portending signs of becoming portly in time. Her dress was plain; brown skirt topped by a long-sleeved beige blouse with an open collar showing cleavage. Her left cheek had been scarred by acne. Agnes had worn no makeup, lipstick, nor jewelry. Her flaxen hair was thick, cut short, and parted in the middle. She had lost weight since they last met, and her face looked drawn and tired.

"Already, I ordered tea," Agnes had said as Elizabeth took a seat opposite her. "Would have ordered you some, but didn't know how long you'd be, and I feared it would get cold."

"I know, love, it's a long ride these days, and the trams are not always on time, especially now with the war." Elizabeth wished she hadn't said that.

"We'll order lunch now," Elizabeth had said to the approaching waiter, a small, thin, gray-bearded man, wearing khaki trousers and a dark blue shirt.

"Daily specials . . . not much these days," he'd cautioned, "with the war and rationing. Cupcakes aren't like before . . . with potato meal and not much sugar. But you're in luck today, dearies. We have potato soup with a bit of cabbage, or rice with a bit of fish."

Neither of them had been confident the fish would be fresh. They both ordered the potato soup. The waiter hurried off and was back in record time with their soup.

Agnes' face had worn a mantle of grief. They had met only once since Wilber died four months before.

"How are things with your work with the Clifford family?" Elizabeth had asked, holding a spoonful of potato soup in front of her, blowing out a breath to cool it.

"Oh, fine. Well, much better in fact. The Cliffords took another girl from Barnwell—Josephine—she's thirteen. Took my place as scullery maid, and I'm now assistant cook." Agnes stirred her soup, putting a spoonful into her mouth.

They had discussed Josephine, her respective good and bad qualities, the difference in Agnes's duties as an assistant cook, compared to those as a scullery maid. Turning over to Josephine some of the dishwashing, cleaning, rabbit and poultry dressing duties of a scullery maid had been most positive. She had become very fond of Josephine and enjoyed helping her start a life outside the orphanage.

"How are things with your nursing?" Agnes had asked.

"There's good and bad," she remembered saying. "The good is that I feel so needed, like I'm doing something worthwhile. The bad . . . we are so short-staffed. I'm working twelve-hour shifts with almost no days off, and I'm so exhausted all the time . . . and there is such a dreadful sadness in it. Most of the patients are young like us. We have deaths every week, and so many are losing their arms and legs."

Agnes had sighed. "Do you ever get close to any of them?"

"I guess I get to know most of them who stay for any time, but in a detached sort of way. I'm warned to guard against getting close. They will leave and the war will only bring more. But it is hard not to sense what they are feeling when they lose an arm or a leg. Death is never far away, even for the young these days."

She'd realized too late that she had turned the conversation down the dark path of Agnes's grief. Wilber had been just twenty-one.

They had finished the soup, and they sipped the last of their tea. The cupcakes sat untouched. Agnes wiped her eyes with the back of her hand, and they sat in silence.

"Are you still a virgin?" Agnes had asked, looking up at Elizabeth intently.

Elizabeth had been stunned for a moment.

"Well, yes," she'd finally answered, truthfully. "Why would you ask me that? I've never asked you anything like that . . . that private."

"I wish I wasn't," Agnes had said, in a low sad voice, looking down. "Wilber wanted to do it. Not right at first, he wasn't that kind, but after a time. I told him I wanted to, but I wanted to wait until we married. You know that's what they always taught us at Barnwell, the Christian thing. He would suggest it again, from time to time, but he never pushed it that much, never acted mad . . . always said he understood, respected me, but he couldn't help but want me . . . that way. I came close several times, but always held back."

Agnes had picked up a cupcake, broken it in half, then put it back down. She'd given Elizabeth a forlorn look.

"I wish I'd let him . . . wish we'd done it. I wish I had his child. At least I'd have something left of him and he'd have left something of himself, when he died." Agnes had looked down, deep in thought, and stroked the acne scars on her left cheek. "I won't find another man that'll want me. I'll never have another Wilber. You and I both know I'm not very pretty, not pretty like you are. I'd be a fool not to know that. . . . I'll die a virgin. I know I will."

"You won't die a virgin!" Elizabeth remembered saying. "There are plenty of men who will want you in time. Another Wilber will come along. I know he was special, but in time you will have another chance at love."

"No. I'm sure now; I'll die a virgin."

There had been another period of silence, both of them looking down.

"You've never had sex? You're so pretty, and I know all the men are after you all the time," Agnes had said.

"No."

"Have you ever come close, wanted to, but all that Barnwell stuff held you back?"

"No."

"Really . . . never come close? Never wanted to do it, have sex with a man?

"No, Agnes," she'd said. "I get flirted with a good bit, but never by a man I trust, never by a man I am that attracted to, and never one I want to do that with. Besides, who would want a skinny little thing like me?"

She'd attempted to console Agnes, with little success. In time they'd parted, going back to their separate worlds, sprits dampened, but fortified by friendship. They had shared too much to ever be otherwise.

~

The tram stop at Queen Mary's Annex was in the middle of the block, right in the center of the large three-story structure. Annexed to Queen

Mary's Hospital in administrative terms only, the aging gray building had been a sanatorium for patients with tuberculosis. Only recently had it been converted to a facility for the treatment of those acutely ill from the ever-growing and deadly influenza epidemic.

Elizabeth's dread grew as she ascended the stone steps, as broad as the tramcar was long. At the far side of the large lobby, three women sat behind a waist-high counter. As Elizabeth approached, a pudgy, middle-aged woman looked up, with an impassive expression.

"I'm looking for Agnes Dixon. What floor and ward is she on?"

"Gertrude . . . Agnes Dixon . . . look for her." She pointed to her left with her thumb. "Go over there."

Elizabeth moved to the center woman, frail and gray. Her arthritic fingers sifted through cards in a metal container. She pulled a card, looking down at it, then up at Elizabeth.

"Not here anymore. She died yesterday."

"Dead! You sure? Agnes Dixon?" Elizabeth said, in a hysterical voice.

"Yes."

"Oh no! Please . . . please look again."

"I'm so sorry," the woman said, in a sympathetic voice. "Your sister?"

Elizabeth began to cry. "No, but my most special person in all the world. Where is she? I mean where is her body?"

"She was probably in the group they took out yesterday . . . late afternoon. Many deaths yesterday. Mostly young. Not that many older people dying from it."

"Will there be a funeral?"

"No time for that. Funerals put people together and spread it. If nobody's made a request in advance, I think they are taking them to a cemetery up in Waterlink . . . about twenty miles away, putting them several to the hole."

Elizabeth felt weak and dizzy. Turning away, she started to cry harder. She could not imagine a world without Agnes.

CHAPTER 6

I MISSED YOU

Elizabeth grasped the heavy brass handle, pushed the door open, and went back outside. She took a seat on the bottom step and sat weeping, overwhelmed by memories of Agnes, all they had been through together, and all that Agnes meant to her. When she had finally cried herself out, Elizabeth wiped her eyes and headed back to the tram stop, and back to her flat.

Sparse, dreary, and eclectically furnished, the flat was one that the hospital had obtained for her, just three blocks from work. Converted from a storeroom, it was a large rectangular room on the second floor of an old tenement. The walls were stained from roof leaks. Lighting was a naked bulb hung from the high ceiling, augmented by a brass bedside table lamp, a black floor lamp with a discolored cream shade, and the ambient light of a tall window with two cracked panes at the top. Dingy white curtains across the bottom half provided a measure of privacy, hanging almost too close to the rust-stained cast-iron radiator that stood underneath. A faded brown couch with the armrests worn through to padding sat on a frayed dark green rug. A blond table with two chairs was behind the couch.

Left of the entrance in a corner was a counter with a square sink and a two-burner hot plate. Mismatched dishes, cups, and cheap glasses were stored on the bottom shelf over the sink. A meager assortment

41

of canned goods sat alongside. The top shelf was empty. Tan curtains that could be pulled back from both sides separated a sleeping area at the back. A smaller, faded green rug next to the bed gave slight comfort from the scarred and splintered wood floor. Another set of tan curtains lent modesty, if not privacy, to the minimal bath that consisted of a wall sink, a toilet, and a tiny shower. A chest and an open hang-up rack stored Elizabeth's limited wardrobe.

By the standards of most nurses assigned to Edmonton Military Hospital, it was premium accommodations. Most lived at the nurses' annex on the grounds, where they had one modest room, often with a roommate. Janet Humphreys had lined up the flat for Elizabeth when she was assigned to Janet's ward. Janet also lived in the building, as did four senior nurses.

Janet let Elizabeth know right off that she was most fortunate to not be in the crowded nurses' annex. "You're a jammy little lady," she had said, when showing her the place. "It's a three-block walk; and it can be cold, wet, and dreary, mind you; but having a bit of quiet and privacy is great when you do have that rare time off from work." Then Janet added, with a hint of drama, "And who knows, love, some day you may need a place with some privacy."

By the time Elizabeth had returned to her flat from Queen Mary's Annex, it was late afternoon. She had trouble getting the key in the keyhole but it finally seated and she unlocked the heavy old door, entered, and closed it gently. The slightest force in closing made a startling loud clunk that reverberated up and down the narrow concrete hall. She did not relock it. She seldom did except when she wanted to sleep, as visits from other nurse tenants were not uncommon. The unwritten rule: try the door, but don't knock, lest you disturb someone in need of sleep. Taking off only her nurse's veil, she lay down. Tears welled up again. Exhaustion finally overcame grief, and she slept.

"Elizabeth." She awoke to Janet touching her arm. The last light of the day cast shadows through the high window. Janet had turned on the floor lamp. "If you are going to sleep, you might want to take off your uniform and put on your nightie."

Elizabeth made no response.

"Did you see Agnes? How is she?"

"She's dead."

"Oh, no, I'm so sorry. Did you get to talk to her before she passed away?"

"No. She died yesterday. They had already taken her to be buried. I never got past the lobby."

"The funeral?"

"No funeral. They are dying so fast there is no way, unless someone has lined it up in advance. And funerals are discouraged . . . risks spread of this awful flu." She rolled over and hid her face, crying softly.

"Elizabeth. Get some sleep and come back in the morning." Janet gently patted her on the shoulder. "You will come back, I hope? I need you." Then she added, in a contrite tone. "I'm sorry that I overreacted. Even if you had gone in and seen Agnes, we would have worked something out; waited a few days to see if you got sick . . . or something."

"I will be back in the morning," Elizabeth said, rolling back over to face Janet with a weak smile. "I don't know what else I'd do right now . . . and I do feel needed."

Janet nodded and eased her way out the door.

～

The next morning, Elizabeth arrived at the hospital fifteen minutes early. When she went into the nurses' station, Hilda, always the indolent one, was sitting at the metal desk, looking bored. Rachel was on the ward, attending patients.

"You're back . . . and you're early. Good," Hilda said, jumping up. "I'm tired and I'm leaving." She squirmed into her black coat, tight for her frame, picked up her purse, and scurried out.

Elizabeth looked through the glass at Private Montgomery. He was asleep. She had an urge to go to him; wake him with a medical procedure; hear his voice; hope he would smile at her. There was something about him; he was different than the other soldiers. She resisted and walked down the ward to Rachel, who was changing the dressing of a new soldier who had arrived in her absence. His leg had been amputated at the knee, and a dressing covered half his face.

"When you finish the leg, I'll do the one on his face," Elizabeth said to Rachel. "You look tired. You can leave if you like. Janet will be here soon."

"I am . . . and I will. Glad you're back."

After Rachel left, Elizabeth looked at the new soldier's chart. A Brit, Sergeant Blackstone was a stocky man with dusty blond hair, beginning to bald at the temples, his right eye covered by the bandage. He gave Elizabeth a feeble look with his exposed left eye, groaned in pain, but did not try to speak. Part of his right cheekbone had been lost. If he survived, he would be crippled and disfigured. She felt a visceral sense of sadness and despair. She finished the dressing on the head wound and walked toward the nurses' station, glancing over at the still-sleeping Private Montgomery as she passed.

From the nurses' station, Elizabeth watched Private Montgomery through the glass partition. She could no longer resist her impulses. She would check his leg wound.

The Carrel-Dinkins constant irrigation had been suspended and the wound was being allowed to dry and heal. She pulled back the bandages. He was healing well. It would not be so very many weeks before he could be ready to be discharged.

"You're back," he said. "You weren't gone long, but . . . uh . . . I missed you. And . . . uh . . . I was afraid you might not return."

Elizabeth eyes met his. "I missed you too," she said, her voice low, sincere, ripe with emotion. Given their circumstances, her comment was inappropriate. She felt herself flush and turned and walked away. For his part, Peter Montgomery felt an intense mixture of joy and bafflement.

That afternoon the relationship that had developed between Peter and Elizabeth took a new turn, a turn that brought it around to Peter's love of baseball.

She had been at the far end of the ward, attending to several patients, and was returning to the nurses' station. "Miss Baker!" Peter called out to her as she was passing, something he had never before done. When awake, he watched her every move, not unusual for the patients who were conscious and alert. She had gotten used to him watching her, and she usually smiled at him. Unlike many of the other patients, Peter had never called out to her. Elizabeth responded and approached Peter, as was her custom, from his right, next to the wall.

"Look here at this, Miss Baker!" he said, directing her attention to the letter he had received that day. "It's from my papa, I guess they . . . my family and all . . . finally found me here in North Middlesex. Looks like it took a while. This letter was written over a month ago. Guess I should've tried to write 'em from here and all. But most of the time not feeling like it, and, you know, didn't have anything to write with and all."

"Well, we shall have to change that right away. I will find you writing materials and help you get something right out to the post. Is everyone there in Glasper doing well . . . all your family?" Elizabeth paused, before adding, in a lower tone, slowing and trailing off at the end, "All your special people . . . those you love and care about, who love you and care about you?"

"Well," Peter responded, "Papa says the war has made it hard to get some of the stuff they needed . . . at our store, you know . . . to make good profit and all, but they're getting by. And Cousin Odell in Picayune died. Didn't much know him. Heart attack, they think. And a big thing, Papa says it looks like my White Sox won't win the pennant in the American, them Red Sox will—and them Cubs will win the pennant in the National."

Elizabeth struggled for something to say. "What's your White Socks?" she finally responded.

"It's my favorite team, you know, baseball."

"Baseball team?"

"Yes ma'am. Baseball is mighty big for us in the United States."

"I don't believe we play baseball here in England," Elizabeth said, with an air of confidence.

"Your school didn't have a baseball team?"

"No."

"Well surely this big London has a baseball team, big place like this. Lots of big places in the United States, places like New York and Chicago and Boston, they have two teams."

"I've never heard of baseball here in London. Not in all of England." Elizabeth glanced back at the nurses' station, where Janet gave her a look, a look she had come to know all too well.

"Janet needs me. Maybe in time you can teach me about baseball."

"I'd like to. It's about my favorite thing." Then he looked down at his wounded leg. "But I figure my baseball playing days is about over; sure won't be playing shortstop or center field."

She came back in an hour and approached the right side of his bed, leaning against the wall, close to his turned face, arms folded daintily in front of her.

"Is this baseball anything like rugby?" Elizabeth asked Peter. "I went to a rugby game once, with Dr. Prince, when I was about fifteen."

"Can't say, Miss Baker. Don't know nothing about rugby. What's it like?"

"I know little about rugby, either. Only went to that one game. They played it on a big field with two big 'H'-shaped posts on each end and men run around all over this big field with a ball about the size of a melon. They knock each other down and kick the ball on the ground and at this big 'H'-shaped thing."

"I've never seen nothing like that. They don't do that rugby in the States. At least not that I've heard of."

She smiled. "One funny thing I liked. At times they all got in a pile, all lying on top of each other. Then the ball comes squirting out of the pile and they all run off after it. Maybe I can go see rugby again someday." What Elizabeth really wanted to say was, "Or watch a baseball game with you." But she resisted the urge.

"I wish you could see a baseball game someday, Miss Baker," Peter said. "You'd like it, I'd expect."

"I wager I would."

Elizabeth walked back to the nurses' station. Janet was at the desk.

"You know anything about baseball? Ever seen it?"

"Well, I did go to a game not long ago with my cousin William . . . out at Chelsea. It was a big deal . . . almost twenty thousand people came."

Elizabeth's voice took on a tone of excitement. "They have a baseball team at Chelsea?"

"No. It's a Yank game and was a game between Yank teams, one from their Army and one from their Navy. Navy won, as I recall. Two points to one point. Looked right to the end like their Navy was going to win two points to love, but their Army scored a point right at the end."

"You think they will have another baseball game out at Chelsea?"

"I doubt it. This was a special event, a part of some kind of national observance the Yanks had."

"And was baseball fun to watch?"

"Rugby has more action. Much more exciting to watch if you ask me."

"Even so, I'd like to see a baseball game."

"No doubt Private Montgomery likes baseball."

"I'm going to see if Sergeant Blackstone needs more morphine."

Elizabeth made a point of staying away from Peter for two hours. The first hour he was sleeping anyway. The second hour she glanced at him out of the corner of her eye, when she passed up and down the narrow aisle. Two hours was all Elizabeth could manage.

She approached Peter with a self-satisfied smile. "Amazingly, I have learned that Nurse Humphreys went to a baseball game not long ago, Private Montgomery."

"I knew you folks would have baseball teams here in England, here in this big London."

"Oh, it wasn't a game between English teams. It was two Yank teams, one Army and one Navy. Big event, Janet said, out at Chelsea . . . huge crowd."

"Bet my Army won."

"No, I'm sorry to tell you, Private Montgomery, Janet said the Navy won, two points to one point."

"Did Janet like baseball?"

"She did. I hope to hear of another game being played some time soon. I'd love to see a baseball game."

"I'd sure like to go with you, Miss Baker. Teach you all about it."

"I think that would be fun," Elizabeth said. She felt herself blush and fled.

CHAPTER 7

BASEBALL STRATEGY

Shortly after daybreak the next morning, Elizabeth and Janet were walking together the three blocks from their flats to the hospital. With September had come a drop in temperature and a chilly fog, smelling of burning coal. Both were starting the day fatigued from the constant twelve hours on, twelve hours off. Elizabeth was cold. She had not dressed for the chill. As they turned the corner for the last frigid block, the wind picked up and pressed their skirts against their thighs.

"Elizabeth," Janet said, "you have got to stop spending so much time talking to Private Montgomery. Some of the other patients are resenting it, complaining they are not getting their share of attention."

"Who?" Elizabeth's voice was suddenly defensive and laced with an atypical anger. "Who? Which patients? I want to know specifically . . . which patients are you talking about?"

"Well, just some of them."

"No! I want to know which ones. Specifically! *Which ones*?"

"Well, I don't know . . . love . . . just some of them."

"Well, you tell me which ones and I shall see to it that they have all the morphine they can stand. I shall see that their bandages are changed before there is even a hint of blood! You tell me which ones are complaining. Which ones! I shall see that they have more water than they can possibly drink."

"Don't get so upset, love, but it's obvious to anyone paying attention that you have something special going with Private Montgomery, that you spend any time you can with him."

"Maybe so, but I don't neglect the patients. Not ever! You and I both know we are far too busy at times. At times we could use much help, but you also know that other times we have little to do. What's the difference in me talking to Private Montgomery and you sitting on your royal working a puzzle or reading the daily?"

Janet attempted no response. They reached the hospital, walked up the steps to their ward, relieved Hilda and Rachel, and went to work.

Suddenly realizing that Janet meant well, and was likely right, Elizabeth made a point of starting her shift at the far end of the ward, making Peter her last stop. She walked around to her usual position next to the wall. Before she could say anything, he was holding up letters, quite excited.

"Look here at this! Another letter from Papa, and another one from my sister Evie."

"Are all still doing well, all your special people at home? Did you hear about any *more* of your special people back home this time?"

"Well Evie . . . she's my sister, two years older 'n me . . . she's working hard to finish her nurse training . . . in Baton Rouge. She wants to come over here—here to this Europe—treat wounded soldiers and all."

"Is Evie married?"

"Oh, no. Don't think she's ever even had a boyfriend or anything. Do reckon she was kinda sweet on my buddy Arthur, you know. Took him home with me once. Arthur was sweet on Evie too . . . but he's dead now. Got killed when I got wounded."

"Was Arthur from Glasper?"

"No . . . from Dempsey, Louisiana. Met him at Camp Shelby—that's in Mississippi—where I got my training and all. He was my best friend . . . you know, in the military. I can't believe he's dead now. And it seems so wrong . . . him dead and me alive. He was a much better fella than me . . . and he prayed to the Lord to spare him. Whole lot more'n I did."

Elizabeth struggled for something to say.

"I'm so sorry. I can tell Arthur's death was such a loss for you . . . so many are losing their special people in this awful war."

Elizabeth again wanted to come out and ask Peter if he had any-one special back home but felt self-conscious after Janet's comments that morning. And she was afraid if she asked, she might get an answer she didn't want to hear.

"Papa's letter was mostly about baseball . . . who does for sure gonna win the pennant, go to the World Series and all. He knew that's some-thing I'd want to know about."

"And what's the pennant?"

"Well, that's when you win your division. Then, you know, you get to go represent your division in the World Series."

Elizabeth loved to hear him talk, with his strong, warm voice and his accent, so different from hers, especially when he was so clearly excited. His crystal-blue eyes grew even wider and had even more allure. And to her, his grammar was simply a part of his accent, part of his uniqueness.

"Did your favorite team win the pennant?"

"Oh, no. Papa says this war got most of our good White Sox play-ers, and them Red Sox, they got that Babe Ruth. He's a great pitcher, you know, and can hit too."

"Have you ever seen this Babe Ruth play, Private Montgomery?"

"Oh, no. Never been to no Major League game. They're all played in them big cities way up north . . . mighty far away from Miss'sippi."

He held the letters out to her. "You want to take a look?"

She reached out and took them.

"For a man, your papa has a very nice handwriting, that he does, Private Montgomery. I'd wager he is a special man, indeed a good man, your papa."

He was slow to respond, reflecting. Then he answered her, in a seri-ous tone, "Don't think I ever thought about it, and all, but he really is. He works hard at the store, almost all the time, except Sunday. Every Sunday he always takes us to church, both in the morning, and again at night. Our church has two preachings on Sunday, you know. He even prays in church sometimes; he's an elder and all. And he always prays to bless the food before we start eating. And he don't cuss—well, maybe a little bit, when he's real mad—and he don't smoke or chew. But he does drink . . . some whiskey in his chair at night after supper."

She handed the letters back to him. "Do you think you shall pray in church someday, Private Montgomery? Do you think you shall bless the food for your family?"

"Yessum. I guess I will, if I ever have a family and all. That's the way it is with us Montgomerys, you know. Did your papa pray and bless the food and all?"

"No, Private Montgomery, my father never blessed my food. I must go now and see if Janet needs help with anything."

He folded his letters together, and held them against his chest, as he watched her return to the nurses' station.

~

"What is it you like so much about this baseball, Private Montgomery?" she asked him the next day.

Never considering it before, he had to think about it. "Oh, I don't know . . . don't know to tell it. I reckon it's just something that's fun, something everybody does around home. I guess all over the States and all. I like the feeling I get when I play good . . . get a good hit or make a good catch or something."

"I would wager you obtain many good hits and produce many good catches; I bet you do, Private Montgomery."

"I'm not one to brag and all, but yes ma'am, some said I was the best player around Glasper. Then, a few did say Johnny Long was . . . but I think it's because he got more home runs. I didn't hit many home runs, but I'm faster and always got good wood on the ball . . . got on base a whole lot more than he did and scored more runs and all. And I definitely was a better glove man."

"I hope you will teach me more." With that she left him, sensing that she had already let this conversation go too long.

~

A day later, she checked his wound, and then went to his side, leaning against the wall; as usual, her arms folded in front of her.

"What does it take to get on base, like you do so well, Private Montgomery?"

"Well, uh, you have to hit the ball where nobody catches it and throws you out. Uh, gets the ball to first base before you get there and all. Of course, that's a grounder—like when it bounces along the ground. If they catch it in the air, before it hits the ground and all, you're out anyway—don't have to throw it to first base—can even be a foul ball, if they catch it in the air you're out. 'Course you can try for extra bases, try for a double or triple or something, if you want to. If you go for extra bases, they can throw you out there too, but then they have to tag you out."

"Tag you?

"Yessum, that's when they touch you with the ball . . . it can be in your glove and all, glove counts, if the ball's in there. Most of the time to get a hit, on a grounder, you have to hit it in the gap . . . uh, that's between the infielders."

Elizabeth smiled, as if she comprehended it.

Later, back at the nurses' station, Janet confronted her, with a concerned countenance, talking in a low, serious tone.

"Elizabeth, as much as I've warned you, it's obvious you've let yourself fall in love with Private Montgomery. He will be going back to America soon, and you will be left here, sad and lonely, an empty young woman indeed."

Elizabeth said nothing, walked to the side past Janet, took a seat at the metal desk, rested her forearms on the surface. Then she turned around in the chair and faced Janet.

"You ever fallen in love?" she asked in a strained, earnest tone.

Janet looked down and did not immediately answer. Her expression was sad.

"You know I have. And you know I lost him to this God-awful bloody war."

"When you fell in love, did you know he was going off to fight in France? That he might be killed. That you might well be left sad and lonely?"

"I suppose. I certainly suppose I should have."

"Then why did you let it happen? Why did you let yourself fall in love?"

"It just happened. It may not have been love at first sight, as it is called, but it was close."

Elizabeth turned away. Janet picket up a water pitcher and started down the ward.

~

The next day, when Elizabeth approached to refill his water pitcher, Peter was brimming with more information about baseball.

"Forgot to tell you that you can also get on base with a walk," he said.

"A walk?"

"Yessum. That's when the pitcher throws four balls before you get three strikes. Three strikes is all you get, you know . . . three strikes and you're out."

"I take it a strike is when you strike at the ball and miss it?"

"Well, yessum, that's one way to get a strike. 'Course you can hit the ball and it goes foul where nobody can catch it. That's a strike too. And if the ball is over the plate and you don't swing at it, that's a strike too . . . of course it's gotta be in the strike zone. And even if a foul is a strike, it can't be the last strike, you know. You can't be out on a foul unless somebody catches it in the air."

"Sounds like a strike is a bit more complicated than swinging the bat, trying to hit the ball, that it does."

"Yessum. But not that much, not when you get to knowing about it good."

~

Two mornings later, Elizabeth arrived for her shift, approaching Private Montgomery to check his wound. She went around to her usual position against the wall and greeted him.

"Good morning, Private Montgomery. Did you sleep well?"

"Good morning," he said, in a somber tone.

"Did you not sleep well? Are you having pain?"

He was slow to answer, looking away.

Still looking away, he said, "I ain't having no pain . . . no more than usual. But I ain't sleeping very well."

"Is there something wrong . . . something I could help you with?"

"No ma'am. I just been thinking too much about all them I was with when they got killed, and believing I was going to be next . . . And I been wondering why it was them and not me."

"I know it must be hard, Private Montgomery, to have to think about those things. Can I get you anything?"

"No ma'am?"

"I'll check on you again soon."

She smiled at him and went on to the next patient.

An hour later she returned. "Is there anything you need I can get for you, Private Montgomery?"

"And I been thinking about them I killed," he said, looking up toward the ceiling, as though they were in a continuation of the earlier conversation. "I never wanted to kill nobody . . . nobody."

"They wanted to kill you. It was them or you."

He made no response, never looked at her.

Feeling uncomfortable, she returned to the nurses' station.

Throughout the day, his mood remained unchanged. Elizabeth had come to realize that Peter could be down and moody at times, but she had never seen him like this.

~

The very next day, after making their rounds on the ward, surgeons Emery Drake and Gregory Clark met with Janet and Elizabeth in the nurses' station. Both were familiar and had been with the Edmonton staff since Elizabeth first arrived. Emery Drake was sixty, drawn and wrinkled, clean-shaven, with silver-gray hair. He spoke in a pronounced West Country accent.

"Ye need to make arrangements for the Yanks to come and retrieve Corporal Mayfield and Private Montgomery. They've both healed so well no special orthopedic care is necessary. We have another delivery of severely wounded due tomorrow. We need the beds."

Elizabeth felt her heart sink. "Where will they take them?" she asked Janet, when they had left.

"The Yanks have a big base, out west, toward Southampton. There's several thousand there . . . mainly a place to billet for various purposes. I think they do some special training there."

"Do they have medical care? We know they are not *completely* healed."

"Basic. Not the care we can give."

"How long will they be there?"

"Don't know, love. Could be a long time. Getting people back to America would not be a priority right now, I suspect."

"Can I be the one to tell him?"

"Yes, love," Janet said, with a tender look. "I told you this day was coming for you."

When Elizabeth made no response, Janet said, with a sad look, "Elizabeth, to be fair, I'll admit, we have little control over when we fall in love."

Elizabeth braced herself, then stood and went to tell him.

Peter was asleep. She stood for a full minute, looking at him, his chest rising and falling as he breathed. When she sensed that she would cry, she returned to the nurses' station.

An hour later, looking through the glass, she saw he had awakened. When she approached him, he smiled.

"Private Montgomery, this is a day you will never forget."

Saying nothing, he raised his eyebrows inquisitively.

"The staff surgeons met with us this morning. They have determined we have done all we can do for you. You will be discharged from the hospital today."

"Today?"

"That's right. Someone will be coming this afternoon to pick you up."

"That's good news. This ole bed's gotten mighty old."

She knew what she was feeling, but she struggled with what she could say. "I've so enjoyed learning about your game of baseball." She bit her lip and started to walk away. His voice stopped her.

"Miss Baker, you're so wonderful . . . and so beautiful. I'm so lucky you were here for me. Every day I lay here, I was just wanting you to come, wanting to see you . . . wanting to hear your voice. I'm ready to get out of this bed . . . but I'm going to miss seeing you, so bad."

She reached over and touched him on the hand, a warm, lingering caress, like none she had ever dared with a patient. She wondered if the look in her eyes had said even more. Then, she leaned over and kissed him on the forehead. "Take care, Private Montgomery, I'll miss you too." And she walked away.

CHAPTER 8

REUNION AND REVENGE

The following Saturday it rained for most of the afternoon, but looking out the window, Elizabeth saw that it appeared to have stopped. Good. She had the walk to her flat and she hadn't dressed for rainy weather. She would have this weekend off, her first in many weeks, but she was not excited. She was emotionally down, and it wasn't the weather.

Leaving work and emerging into the hospital lobby, she saw him, leaning against a wall, garrison cap pushed into his thick blond hair. He leaned on one crutch, supporting his injured leg. He had propped the other crutch against the wall. When Peter recognized her, he broke into a broad smile. He was in full military uniform: an olive drab high-collar jacket with button-down flap shoulder straps, five big buttons down the front, and two sets of buttoned-down pockets, on the chest and at the thigh. He had a khaki-colored calf-length boot on his good leg, a heavy beige sock covering his bandage on the other.

"Whatever are you doing here, Private Montgomery?" she said, unable to hide her surprise.

"I wanted to see you."

"Are you all right?"

"I'm fine."

There was awkward silence.

"Whatever brings you to see me?"

He paused, striving for his best answer. "I'm no good at this kind of thing, but I reckon I wanna see if we could have a date . . . sometime. If I could take you out to eat or something."

At first, she struggled for any response. Then, as inexplicable to her as the kiss on the forehead, she found herself saying, "I have not had a day off from work in more than a fortnight, and I do not know when I will be off again. I would be happy to dine with you tonight."

This response brought another smile to his lips, and Elizabeth did so love Private Montgomery's smile.

~

Earlier that day, Peter had approached Sergeant Burney Whatley, who was over the local motor pool at the base where he was quartered. Whatley was also from south Mississippi, having joined the Army in 1908 to escape the poverty of a hardscrabble farm in the area's sandy clay hills. A swarthy, unkempt little man, wrinkled by a life of sun, alcohol, and tobacco, Whatley looked ten years older than his actual age of thirty-two. He had been an instructor in Peter's prior training. During training, when Whatley learned Peter was from "home," he had occasionally struck up a conversation. Whatley had heard accounts of the battle in which Peter was wounded, and Peter's bravery. He had a reputation of being one who could bend the rules on the use of military vehicles, for the proper people, with proper incentive.

"What do you need a vehicle for, Montgomery?" asked Whatley.

"I wanna go to London."

"Why do you need to go to London?"

"I wanna go see a woman."

"A woman. What kind of woman?"

"Nurse . . . while I was in the hospital."

"Ever been to see her before?"

"Just in the hospital."

"What makes you think she wants to see you?"

"I don't, but I wanna see her."

"Does she already have a man?"

"Don't know."

"Don't know! Never asked? Jesus! You young fools are all alike. You'll get in a mess. She probably ain't sleeping alone."

Peter'd had enough.

"Sergeant, if you'll let me have something, I'll be appreciating it. If you ain't, it may cost a lot, but I'll get there somehow."

"I'll be breaking regulations," Whatley said, "but them that can bust me is always wanting it for themselves. They'd croak if I ever got tight on the regulations, right now in the middle of this war. I'll help you out if I can. I don't have much to let you have . . . well, there's that ole Packard dump truck . . . we use it to pick up garbage at the mess hall, every Tuesday and Friday. Won't need it again until Tuesday."

"I'll take anything that'll get me there."

"Hate to send you off driving a smelly dump truck to see a woman you're interested in." The sergeant hesitated for a few moments, then smiled. "I've got a better idea. Ever ridden a cycle?"

"Few times. My friend Dennis had one for a while, until he wrecked it, and his pa took it away from him. Not that much to it."

Whatley pondered. "You couldn't handle it—if your right was the bad leg—but the left doesn't do much, and with the sidecar, won't have to put the left down. Montgomery, let's go with this Harley with the sidecar. I wouldn't do this for everybody, Montgomery, and you damn well better let this be between us . . . us Miss'sippi fellas."

"Sarge, you can count on it," Peter said, with a grin.

⁓

Peter and Elizabeth made their way to the Harley, and he opened the door to the sidecar for her. It had a big bucket seat with an impressive rolled leather back. Before she got in, wishing for a scarf, Elizabeth took off her nurse's veil and pushed it into the pocket of her apron, letting her hair hang loose behind her. Once in the sidecar, she got over as close to Peter as she could and they put his crutches against the door. She put her left hand over his forearm as he gripped the handlebar. She felt a thrill at the wind in her hair, the roar of the Harley drowning other sounds on the street.

He sensed his garrison cap was about to blow off, and tucked it under his right thigh, also letting his thick blond hair blow in the wind. After driving a short distance, he pulled off to the side. "Where you wanna go,

Miss Baker?"

"Please call me Elizabeth, and no more Miss. I looked at your charts. You will soon be twenty, and I will not be twenty-one until March. And we are not patient and nurse. Now we are, uh . . . friends."

"Tell me which way to go . . . Elizabeth?" He liked calling her that; it gave him a positive feeling, bordering on euphoria. "Don't know much about London."

"Peter, I'd like to get out of London, take a ride out into the country but it *is* getting late, and this weather is most unpredictable. First I'd like to go home and change . . . then we can decide."

Elizabeth directed him to her flat. Instructing Peter to park in an alleyway behind the building, she handed him his crutches. "You need to stay completely off that leg. I did not think you were well enough to be discharged, but they needed the beds . . . so many more coming in with fresh wounds."

They went through a back door and up the stairs to her flat. She tried to help, gripping his hard, muscular arm. She unlocked the door; they went inside, and she shut the door, more gently than usual. It hardly made a sound.

"You sit here on this couch for a moment. I shan't be long." She went into her bedroom space and pulled the curtain.

Peter couldn't bear the silence.

"I sure wanna take you to a nice, fancy place, and all, somewhere you'll be excited about. Where you think you might wanna go . . . Elizabeth?"

"Oh, I shan't want you to spend much," she said through the curtains. He heard her pulling out a drawer and closing it.

"I *wanna* spend some money . . . ain't had nothing to spend any on since I got in the Army. Can't spend none in a trench gettin' shot at, or in an ole hospital bed."

"Well, there's Captain Jack's. It's quite far away, down by the river. I've been once with my friend Janet. It was loud and I didn't like getting bothered by men I did not know, one in particular. I told Janet I was leaving and she left with me. It has a nice river view and I could probably enjoy it with you, when I would not get any unwanted attention."

The curtains parted and Elizabeth came back out. She had on a white knitted sweater with a tight collar and a knee-length black skirt, topped by a khaki jacket with flap pockets that came to the mid-thigh, over which was a wide black leather belt. On her head was a black knitted cap, having a slight dome, at the top of which was a thumb-sized bun. It covered her ears, her long auburn hair coming out from under and flowing down on both sides. Black leather boots came almost to her knees.

"Do I look like a motorcycle girl?" she said, standing in front of him.

"The prettiest I ever seen." Peter had the excitement in his voice and the sparkle in his eyes that he had when he talked of baseball.

~

When they got to Captain Jack's, the night was early by the standards of the clientele and London nightlife. Not being regulars, and expressing no preference, they were given a small booth for two in a corner near the front entrance. It lacked the intimacy they would have liked, but they did not object. Peter put his crutches in the corner of the booth beside him.

The waiter came, a stocky man of middle age with bushy hair and a heavy beard. He wore a black bow tie and a colorful red and yellow vest over a white shirt, sleeves rolled halfway to his elbows.

"What'll ye have?" he said in a pleasant voice, with a pronounced Cockney accent.

"Fish and chips with beer or ale," Elizabeth said.

"What pig's ear would you like?" the waiter said, writing on a pad.

"I should like a recommendation."

"I do not see you a Guinness . . . think a Bass will be more to ye liking."

"Then I shall please have a glass of Bass."

"What will you have, my Yank?" he said, turning to Peter, and noticing his uniform.

"I'll have what she's getting."

"I have not had much beer or ale," Elizabeth said, in a frank admission, after the waiter brought their drinks.

"Me neither. Me and Dennis . . . we was bad to drink whiskey, when we could get it, and I drank some rum in the Army, but I ain't drunk much beer."

"I'm so glad to be here with you," Elizabeth said, reaching over and touching him on the back of his hand. "This was my first night off in a long time, and I had nothing to do. Some of the nurses do, but I don't go out at night to the pubs alone. Janet was off too, but she was going to see her aunt in West London."

Elizabeth sat looking at Peter contentedly. He began to feel self-conscious.

"What about them other fellas there with me? How's they doing?"

"Corporal Dunn, two beds over from you, he has been discharged. A Sergeant Gladstone, he's British, from Cambridge, he took your bed. Other than that, little has changed. How are you doing? Do you like where you are now?"

"I still have some pain . . . but it ain't that bad. And I'm just in a regular barrack. Not like the hospital; it's temporary, made out of lots of wood and that wrinkled tin, all painted white. Crowded too. Four rows in one big room, twice as many as in your ward. Junky, too. Everybody has some personal stuff, mostly in a trunk at the foot of the bed and in a duffel under their bed. 'Course I ain't been there long enough to get much personal stuff."

She took a sip of her Bass that the waiter had brought and continued to look at him attentively with her wide-set hazel eyes.

He continued, "Nothing to do but lie around. Don't know when I will be going home and all, they say it may be a while. Ships is short and lots of people to take back."

There were about twenty people in the place at that point and two couples were dancing to a piano player's tunes. They finished their food and the first ale and ordered another. Elizabeth felt warm and secure. Something about Peter made her feel that way. She was confident that he would be considerate, never pushy, always a gentleman. It had been a long month, a long week, a long day; and she needed this.

Two men came in, not noticing Peter and Elizabeth as they passed by. They went to the back of the establishment, taking one of the few tables still available. Without a doubt, they had been drinking elsewhere. Both were large men, but one impressively so. He was at least six-five, two hundred fifty pounds, slightly bald, with broad muscular shoulders, thick arms, and a massive neck. Soon they had large steins of dark ale in front of them and were eyeing the crowd, assessing the prospects.

"I hope they don't see us," said Elizabeth. "I don't like them."

"Why not?"

"I so *really* don't like them. They're from the Billingsgate fish market, and they talk and smell like it. That big one . . . he's the one who kept bothering me the night I was here with Janet. He kept forcing me to dance when I didn't want to . . . and kept groping my bottom and pulling me up against him."

Peter began to watch them. Elizabeth avoided looking their way. Two single women were in the place, sitting together smoking, both well in their forties, both with abundant gaudy make up. Peter did not know much about that side of life, but it occurred to him that these women were prostitutes.

The big muscular man got up from his companion and took one of these women out to the dance floor. Peter saw him move his right hand well down on her buttocks, saw him spread his legs unnecessarily far apart, and saw him pull her up against his crotch as tightly as possible. Midway through this dance the man noticed Peter watching. Then he seemed to be looking at Elizabeth. When this dance ended, he abandoned the woman and headed straight to the table where Peter and Elizabeth sat. Paying no attention to Peter, he focused on Elizabeth.

"I know you, little sweetie. I danced with you here before. Let's dance, little sweetie," he said, in a rough, loud voice, grabbing her by the arm.

"I don't want to dance," she said, pulling away.

"Come on. Just one, little sweetie. Your little cripple Yank here won't care. He can't dance much on them crutches."

"I'm with him and I don't care to dance with you," she said angrily, pulling away again. Peter tried to stand up and get between them. The big man pushed Peter roughly back into his seat.

"Watch it, little one," he said. "You don't wanna get hurt. This cunt here wouldn't be sleeping with you if you weren't a Yank, with all your Yank dough."

It happened so fast that to Elizabeth it seemed a blur. Peter's hand went to the bottom of a crutch and he stood, swinging it with all his strength, the top part catching the fishmonger in the face with a loud thud heard over the piano music. The big man dropped to the floor unconscious, a gash over his left eye, blood pouring out upon the dark wood. People gathered around him, trying to turn him to better assess his wounds. Peter stepped back and stood, as if in a daze, watching, still holding the crutch by the small end.

"Peter! Let's go! Let's go quickly!" Elizabeth pushed Peter's other crutch into his hand. He positioned both crutches under his arms and they went out the door, far faster than he had ever tried to move on crutches.

CHAPTER 9

WE MONTGOMERYS

Once out the door, they hurried toward the Harley. It was parked against a piling well down the dock, beyond more than a dozen cars. Elizabeth wanted to run as fast as she could, but could not leave behind Peter, rhythmically hurrying along, one crutch span at a time. When they reached the motorcycle, Peter handed the crutches to Elizabeth, braced himself on the handlebar and, standing on his bandaged foot, oblivious to the pain, tried to kick the starter with his good leg. The engine failed to respond. He did it again, trying harder. Again nothing! Elizabeth heard loud voices coming out of the pub, shouting down the dock at them. She began to feel panic as Peter kicked a third time. On the fourth kick, the Harley sputtered, but died. On the fifth, it started, stumbled and finally began to run. They jumped onto the Harley and sped away, just as a crowd of a half-dozen men were about to reach them.

"Stop! You better bloody stop!"

Peter didn't. He accelerated, as fast as he dared. In their haste, they had placed the crutches in the sidecar between them. As she leaned over to get closer to him, she noticed blood on one of his crutches and on her left sleeve.

To the throaty roar of the Harley, they rushed past occasional trams, pedestrians, people on bicycles, and vehicles with bug-eyed headlights beaming at them, their spoke wheels flickering in the streetlights. Each time the sidecar hit a bump, they wobbled, side to side, before the Harley regained stability. Peter was speeding far beyond his skills. They rounded a corner and the sidecar struck a tram track. Suddenly Elizabeth felt herself soaring three feet above the ground. Her stomach flipped. She couldn't breathe. Peter struggled to avoid rolling over. Finally, the sidecar came back to the ground and he regained control. He pulled to the side and stopped, visibly shaken, but not nearly as much as she was.

"You all right?" he said.

All she could do was nod.

"I think we've shook 'em." He pulled her over to him, hugged her, and kissed her on her forehead. "Where you wanna go now?"

"Home . . ."

While he maneuvered the bike at a much slower speed, she directed them back the long trip north, across London to her flat in North Middlesex. There she told him to park the Harley in the narrow alley in the back, tucked behind steps.

Inside the flat, he sank onto the couch, still feeling the effects of an adrenaline rush. She sat beside him, leaned against him, putting her face on his chest, her hand on the side of his waist. There they sat quietly, both trying to recover their composure.

"I'm scared," she said.

He made no immediate response.

"Aren't you scared?"

"Well . . . uh . . . guess I'm still kinda shook up, and all, you know. But now that we're safe, and I'm here with you, I've got nothing that much to be scared about."

"Are you not worried that big man will come after you? Or try and have you arrested?"

"I ain't thought about something like that. I guess when you go over the top, and see fellas dying all around you . . . and figure you gonna die too, any moment, it ain't easy to get too scared about something like that."

She put her arm around him, hugging herself even closer to his muscular body, smelling the scent of his sweat, feeling the rise and fall of his chest as he breathed. She began to calm down, and she felt an intense rush of desire, a level of desire for a man that she had never felt before. They lay there, his head back, his eyes closed, his heavy breathing slow.

She thought about the events of the night, the events of her week, the war, the epidemic, her last conversation with Agnes before she died, all the dead and dying, so many so young. Suddenly she realized that this night, with this man, she wanted to lose her virginity. If she died young, it would not be like Agnes, not as a regretful virgin.

She got up and knelt in front of him. "Let's take off this boot," she said, unlacing his single boot and working it off. She placed it neatly beside the couch.

"I saw you putting all your weight on your wounded leg, when you stood up to strike with the crutch, when you tried to crank the cycle. Is it hurting?"

"Little bit . . . not that bad."

She gave his bandaged leg a close inspection. "There doesn't seem to be any blood coming through anywhere. I shall keep checking on it."

Elizabeth got up and sat back beside him. "I'm off tomorrow and Sunday," she said, pushing far enough away to focus on his crystal-blue eyes. "I'd like for you to stay with me, if you'd like. Maybe we could ride out in the country and have a picnic . . . a romantic picnic, like I've read about in novels. Would you like that?"

"You know I would."

He remembered his only picnic, with Hannah right before she announced she was leaving for Michigan. They had made love, their last time, under a big beech tree beside a creek on his grandpa's farm, with only his denim jacket and leaves beneath her. He could still recall the feel of the dry leaves beneath his palms as he held himself above her, the sounds she made as she found her pleasure.

Elizabeth became conscious of the spot of blood on her left sleeve.

"I think I will go take off this jacket, try and wash out this blood, change into something more comfortable."

Giving him a warm smile, she went into the bedroom area, pulling the privacy curtain. She took off her sweater and her jacket, putting the sweater in the bottom drawer of her chest. She scrubbed at the blood in cold water, and then hung the jacket on a peg usually reserved for bath towels.

In front of her mirror, Elizabeth picked up her hairbrush and stroked it through her auburn hair half a dozen times. Taking off her bra, she stood in front of the mirror and surveyed her small breasts. With her hands she pulled her breasts together, yearning for cleavage she didn't have. She longed to be well-endowed, like Agnes and Janet.

She sat on her bed for a few moments, trying to decide what to do next, what to put on. He had committed to spending the night with her. What point was there in dressing again like she was going back out?

She usually slept in a plain, straight flannel nightshirt. She had two, warm and comfortable, but large for her petite body. But there was another option; for her eighteenth birthday, Mrs. Prince had given her an expensive flannel nightgown that she had never worn. Going to her chest, she pulled it out of the back corner of the third drawer and laid it out on the bed. It was snow-white and full-length, with a lace collar interwoven with a bright pink ribbon, lace-trimmed cuffs and hem. When she had presented it, Mrs. Prince had commented, "This could be for your wedding night." Perhaps she would not live to get married in these awful times. Agnes had not.

Elizabeth pulled the nightgown over her head, put her arms in the sleeves and pulled it down full-length, reveling in its seductive softness. She went back to the mirror, picked up the brush ,and stroked her hair again. She pulled the nightgown up over her waist and slowly stepped out of her underwear, which she pitched into a wicker basket in the corner.

Unlike her entrance dressed as best she could to be a "motorcycle girl," this time Elizabeth made a shy return to Peter, quickly sitting beside him on the couch, snuggling up close and putting her face against his shoulder. He looked down at her, raising his eyebrows in surprise.

"My. You did change clothes. You sure did."

She turned her face up to him. "Well?" she said. "We agreed you will stay the night with me. I've had all the going out I need for one night." She made no mention of her nightgown. If he thought this fancy garment was her nightly attire, it could do her no harm.

He was momentarily at a loss for words. "I don't keep this ole heavy, tight uniform on at night, that's for sure. But I don't have no pajamas or nothing like that . . . nothing like you gone and put on."

She felt herself wanting to say: "The less the better." She didn't.

"Fact is, I don't even own no pajamas, or nothing. Always slept in my underwear . . . all my life, and all."

"Well, you will not want to stay in this heavy jacket with all these buttons." She unbuttoned his military jacket, starting with the top button. "My! These big buttons are hard to undo."

"Let me do them. I'm kinda used to them and all, you know."

"No. Let me do them. I want to." She continued to fumble with the first button until she managed it, not because it was difficult, but because her hands were trembling with emotion.

She went button by button to the last, then she pulled open his jacket, slowly, almost ceremonially, one side at a time. "Now!" she said, in a strong voice of accomplishment.

He needed no encouragement to stand up and finish the job, shucking off his jacket and pitching it on the end of the couch. Sitting back beside her in his sleeveless undershirt, he reached out and pulled her to him. She laid her head on his chest, her fingertips stroking his neck down to his collarbone, lingering on the texture of his chest hair coming out the top of his shirt. He put his cheek against her hair, taking in her alluring feminine scent.

Peter wondered if she had noticed the bulge in the front of his heavy trousers. Elizabeth sensed a warm wetness of her own. At once they both feared they would somehow go too far too fast, that they would somehow spoil this divine moment. They did not want to in any way ruin something yearned for ever so long.

"Tell me what it was like growing up in your Mississippi," she finally said, pulling away and looking up at him, wanting to overcome the sudden awkwardness.

"Well . . . uh . . . ain't much to tell about. Glasper ain't nothing like this big London. Most everybody there knows most everybody else. Glasper is the county seat of Duncan County, you see. That's where the courthouse is, and all, and the sheriff's office, and the post office, and most all of the business places, where you can go to buy things . . . like our store. And there's three churches and the biggest school in the county, they're in Glasper. That's where the railroad stops, there in the center of Glasper, you know. The railroad is the key to about everything, most everybody and everything comes and goes on the railroad."

"Peter, I think you must have a close, loving family." This comment brought her a deep, visceral emptiness; but she did want to know about his family . . . and what he would be going home to.

"Well, there's just four of us. Me and Papa and Mama, and my sister Evie. She's two years older 'n me . . . think I told you a little about Evie once. We're not a big family like so many. There's them in Duncan County with a dozen kids, but not us. There's just us four.

"Papa and Mama, they own Montgomery Mercantile. It's the biggest store in Glasper . . . well really the whole county. Papa bought it with money my grandpa loaned him from the family of Burnell Ledbetter, when he died, and all . . . I was about two. Papa had worked for Mr. Ledbetter for a while before he died, don't know how long. Papa said he was a good fella, that he taught him the business. Said it weren't an easy business to get the hang of, know what would sell, what to stock, said that's the hardest part. But it does seem to me we sell almost everything."

"How about your mother? Does she work in this Montgomery Mercantile?"

"Most every day, if she's needed; house is close by, you see. It's a funny business, our store and all. Some days, not much business, especially when it's raining or mighty hot or mighty cold, or when folks is planting or getting in the crops . . . then they ain't got time for nothing much else. And usually really slow on Wednesdays and Thursdays . . . fact we close at noon on Thursdays. Sometimes we'd go hours without a single customer. But Saturday! Oh, my, Saturday can sometimes be something, especially right before school starts up and before Christmas. Sometimes Papa and Mama and Evie and me, all the four of us, we can go so hard we don't ever get to sit down all day long. Always glad that didn't come in baseball season."

"Your mother? Does she cook? Is she a good cook?"

"Oh, yeah, Elizabeth." He did so love calling her by her first name now. "Most everybody says she's one of the best cooks in the whole county. 'Course she has a good place to show herself off with our store and all, you know. She cooks cakes and pies, stuff like that, and sells it at the store, where there's people coming in all the time. Some say her egg custard pie is to kill for."

Elizabeth looked up at him affectionately, enthralled, loving to hear him talk, loving the enthusiasm with which he talked about his home. She squirmed even closer. When she did, he hugged her gently.

"What did you do at home in Glasper that you remember most? What are you looking forward to going back to?"

"Well, there's baseball. You know all about that. And I'm so afraid I ain't gonna be able to play much ball anymore, with this leg, and all. And there's lots of huntin' and fishin' and all . . . lots of that goes on. I love to fish, but ain't no hunter, which was an embarrassment to my grandpa. He couldn't accept nobody that wasn't no hunter, not no Montgomery. But I just don't like it."

"But you do like to fish?"

"Sure do. And we got good fishing round Glasper, especially lots of big cats, you know. Now, so much of what we did, that I remember so much about, was churching and all. We churched twice ever' Sunday, then again on Wednesday night. Prayer meeting, it's called. Then there's a big revival, you know, whole week of preaching out at the campground ever' summer. We is Baptist, got the biggest church house in the county. Then there's the Methodist. They got the next biggest. Then there's the Presbyterian. Theirs ain't that big. Ain't nothing else. Ain't no Catholic churches, ain't no Jew churches, nor nothing . . . not in Glasper. Now there is some of those in some of the bigger places, like Hattiesburg, and all. Biloxi. I hear there's lots of them Catholics, and even a Greek church. But nothing in Glasper but Baptist, and Methodist, and Presbyterian."

Elizabeth began to play with the small patch of chest hair she had come to love, coming out above his undershirt near her face. She felt a tension, a tension unique for her; a tension that needed something other than talk.

"You know, Elizabeth, I wouldn't say this to many people, sure not to my Mama and Papa, but I hated all the churching and all. Them preachers, they go on and on talking about sin, this sin, that sin, the next sin.

Ain't supposed to lie, and steal, and kill, and take the Lord's name in vain . . . that's cussing and all, you know. And that adultery—that's the worst—they're always preaching on that. And if anybody thinks there's any of that adultery going on, that's all they talk about around the store, and all. I doubt there's anywhere more gossiping goes on than our store."

He paused, took a deep breath, began to stroke her hair softly, then went on: "And they're always talking about gettin' saved, asking if you know for sure you been saved, 'cause if you ain't and you die, you're going to hell and all."

Neither of them spoke for a full twenty seconds. His breathing became discernibly more labored.

"Elizabeth, I ain't stole, and I ain't much of a liar and I don't do no cussing, and I couldn't commit no adultery, not being married and all. But I sure have done some killing." His voice had a tremor in it, a tone of anguish. "I don't even know how many I've done killed . . . least five or six . . . maybe more'n that . . . and I never wanted to kill nobody. Nobody."

"Peter, you couldn't help it. You did what you had to do, because you are a soldier, and this is a war, an awful, senseless, bloody war. When soldiers fight a war, they kill people. Because that is war."

"I try to think I done it because it was my duty . . . they call it. And my family, they expected me to go do my duty and all. And I killed 'em because they was trying to kill me first. But I'll always wonder if they was just like me; they didn't want to kill nobody neither. Somebody made them think killing me was their duty, and all . . . that them German fellas I killed was just fellas like me, not knowing what they was doing . . . just doing what they thought they was expected to do. Like I was."

"Peter, the Germans started this awful war. They deserved what they got. You have nothing to feel bad about."

"You think them German fellas I killed knew who started it?"

Elizabeth wasn't sure how to take the question. Was it an expression of cynical doubt . . . or sincere hope? They lay together, close and tender.

"You need to tell me about *you*, Elizabeth," he said. "You've learned all about me . . . in the hospital and all, and now here. And I don't know nothing about you. Tell me about your family, your growing up, your school, your churching, and all."

A minute passed. Then another. Peter found himself in the grip of an apprehension. Maybe she had been married before; maybe he had been killed early in the war, now in its fourth year. Maybe tonight he was standing in for a memory.

"You don't have to tell me nothing if you don't wanna. I know there's times when people don't wanna talk about the past. Sometimes there's been bad things they don't wanna talk about . . . it brings back bad memories and all."

"It is not that bad, I suppose," she said, moving away enough to look into his face. "My life has just been so different from yours, that I don't know where to start. There is no family, like yours, to talk about. I have only the vaguest memories of my mother. I know nothing at all about my father. If I have brothers or sisters, I know nothing of them. I have no place like Glasper. No regular church. No baseball. No fishing."

She put her head back on his chest, no longer looking at him. Other than small segments with Dr. and Mrs. Prince, never before had she shared much with anyone other than Agnes about the events of her life, her feelings, her pain, her loneliness, her hopes, the person she really was.

She told him about her early childhood in the East End slum, where her mother shared a wooden shanty with another woman, and with Agnes, another child about her age, and how the two women stayed inside for most of the day, sleeping a large part of the time, then dressing and putting on strong perfume and going out at night. She told him about how cold and dirty it was, and how scared she always was as a child. She told him how she and Agnes were taken to the orphanage.

Peter began to wish he had not made her revisit these painful memories.

"You don't have to tell me about all this, and all, if you don't want to. I can understand if you don't want to. I can only know what I know about you now. That's all I need to know."

"No. I want you to know who I am, where I have come from as a person, like I now know where you have come from as a person. Then I hope you want to accept me and want to be with me, knowing all there is about me."

"I'm definitely gonna do that. I'm sure gonna do that."

"Looking back, I know that being taken to Barnwell was the most fortunate event of my life. It is very structured there, with everyone wearing the same clothes and having the same haircut. The boys and girls are largely kept separated. They want to give children like me and Agnes all the basic protection and necessities that a young child needs, and a basic elementary education."

"I bet you was good in school . . . made the best grades of anybody, and all."

Elizabeth strived for the most modest tone she could manage. "I did quite well."

"I didn't make the best grades, probably not good as I should have," he said, "got by, and all, but probably spent too much time fishing and playing baseball. How long did you stay at this orphanage, this Barnwell?"

"When I was twelve, I was sent to do domestic work for Dr. Prince. So much of my life, Peter, so much of who I am today, comes from going to work for Dr. Prince. His name was John Prince. He was a prominent surgeon, with a big house and an office in a very fine neighborhood called Mayfair. Going to work for the Princes was a blessing for me indeed."

"Is Dr. Prince still alive?"

"Yes. But he is quite old and it is beginning to show. He uses a cane now. Mrs. Prince is showing her age too, but she is still able to get around quite well. She never forgets my birthday, and always buys me something for Christmas. I love them so and visit them whenever I can."

"I'd sure like to meet them, Dr. Prince and Mrs. Prince. Do you think I could ever go with you to meet them?"

"Peter, I shall certainly try for us to do that, if you would truly like. I know they would enjoy meeting you." In that, Elizabeth was most sincere. Mrs. Prince had long insinuated that she thought Elizabeth was a trifle slow in finding her a man, always quizzing her, "Are you seeing anyone special these days, my dear Elizabeth?"

With her right hand, Elizabeth again began to unconsciously stroke his chest, above the top of his undershirt, stretched and baggy from age. He noticed her doing it. He liked it.

"When I was about fourteen," Elizabeth went on, "Dr. Prince decided I should help him in his clinic. I was expected to clean the clinic, which was not very large, and I was also allowed to help with his patients, eventually even help with some of his surgeries. Then, one day, when I was seventeen—as we were finishing up for the day—Dr. Prince told me he thought I should train as a nurse, and he wanted to enroll me in a training program at St. Thomas Hospital. Then the war came, and so many trained nurses were needed in the military hospitals."

Elizabeth raised her head, looked him in the eye and dramatically announced, "And that . . . Peter Montgomery, is how I came into your life!"

She put her head back on his chest. He gently stroked her hair, her shoulder, the side of her back. They lay in silence, basking in the moment, in the warmth of each other's bodies.

Peter broke the silence. "Did you ever see your mother again? Do you know what happened to her?"

"No. But about two years ago I went back to the East End looking for her. One person remembered her and told me to go look for Beatrice Denny at the fish market, that she was the woman we lived with when I was little. Took a lot of searching, it is such a big market, but I finally found her, a gray, wrinkled woman, at a table dressing fish. She said my mother had died of a fever in 1913."

"What about your pa?" Peter asked. "Did you ever find out anything about him?"

She fell silent. Finally, she answered the question, in a voice that let him know she was about to cry, "I asked Beatrice Denny if she knew anything about my father . . . if she knew who he was. 'Ain't no knowing little lassie,' she said. 'Your mamma didn't know. Weren't no way for her to know.'"

Elizabeth began to weep. Peter said nothing, continued to stroke her as she cried. In time she stopped and looked up at him, tears still flowing down her face. "Peter, my mother was a whore. Whoever he was, my father is unknown, because he paid to be unknown." This was something she had never before said aloud to anyone else.

She pushed her face tighter against his chest. There was neither sob nor sound, but tears continued to seep from her eyes.

Suddenly Peter could hear his grandfather's voice, words he had heard all his life: "We Montgomerys . . . we Montgomerys . . . we Montgomerys."

"We Montgomerys are hunters."

"We Montgomerys believe the Bible is the word of God."

"We Montgomerys do our duty in time of war."

These words had brought Peter heartache, pain, and resentment so many times in his life. They were now words he realized he had been blessed to hear. He hugged Elizabeth harder than ever.

They lay there together on her couch, in this embrace, her against him, his arm around her. In time he stopped stroking her. All was quiet and still. Peter was not about to break the silence. There was nothing he could think of to say.

Then she said to him in a voice so soft it was barely audible, "Peter, do you have anyone special back home in America, someone special who you know is waiting for you?" She could be haunted by the question no longer.

"Nah," he said, in a firm, sincere tone. "I ain't got nobody back home."

It was a moment of mutual gratitude. Her question and the tone of her voice had answered a question for him too, one that he had harbored for at least as long.

There was another period of silence. Her breathing became more pronounced.

"Peter, have you ever made love, had sex?"

He struggled to answer. Should he lie? He remembered his father's voice, something he'd heard more than once. *Don't ever lie, boy. Do and you'll just have to tell another lie to cover that one up. And before long you gonna need more lies than you're smart enough to think up.*

"Yes," he answered, with all the modesty he could muster.

"Many times?"

"Well, I dunno. Guess not that many."

"I'm a virgin."

"Certainly ain't nothing wrong with that," he said. "But it'd be alright if you weren't."

"Will you make love to me tonight?"

"You know I will," he said, trying not to sound too excited. "Right now?"

"Not quite. I have never taken off my clothes in front of a man. I know I'm skinny and my body is not that attractive. I would like to go take off my clothes and get in the bed under the covers and then have you come to me."

With that she got up and pushed through the curtains, headed toward her bed. Peter got up and took off his clothes, throwing them randomly on the couch. Then he sat down and waited, naked and eager.

"I'm ready . . ." she said. Not long had passed, but to Peter it had seemed an eternity.

CHAPTER 10

PASSION, PAIN, AND PLEASURE

P eter got up, hobbling on his bad leg, ignoring the pain, and went to Elizabeth's bed. He had never felt more excitement, but it was tempered by huge anxiety. With Hannah there had always been the nagging fear that she would become pregnant, but there was never any anxiety over his ability to give her pleasure. She had always been the aggressor, always let him know what pleased her, always showed him the way.

Lying in his trench in France, thinking back on Hannah, thinking back on her letter announcing that she was married, it had occurred to him that she might have married because she had finally gotten pregnant. Maybe she had wasted little time in Michigan finding another lover. Maybe pleasing Hannah might have been so easy because she was experienced in what pleased her. He was not her first.

He was anxious. Peter had never wanted anything more in his life than to please Elizabeth, make her first experience a wonderful one, and make her love him.

When he got to the bed she said, "Peter ,will you just come under the covers with me, hug me at first, hold me, and help me get comfortable with all this? It's so new to me and I am afraid I will not know what to do."

She pulled back the covers for him. In the ambient light, he glimpsed her naked body, almost full-length, her dark pubic hair against pale white skin. She may not have been as voluptuous as she desired, but she was so very feminine; she could not have been more desirable nor aroused him more.

He lay on his back, pillow under his head, and drew her close. She put her face on his chest, her right leg over him, stroking the center of his hairy chest with the tips of her fingers. Feeling her pubic hair pressing against his thigh gave him almost instant arousal. With his hand, he turned her face toward him and kissed her cheek, then her eyelids, then her neck, gently nipping on her earlobe.

She giggled softly. "That tickles." Her heavy breathing let him know she enjoyed it.

"I want us to kiss, like lovers do in the books," she said. "In romance stories, lovers kiss and kiss. You shall have to teach me."

He moved to kiss her, his left hand behind her head, his right along the side of her left cheek. Peter had done a lot of kissing. When he and Hannah were in their most acute fear of pregnancy, they had sat in the car, parked in the woods, and did everything they could for sexual pleasure other than that which could get her pregnant. Their bodies would be chapped and raw from the experience.

He brought his lips to hers. Her lips were stiff and taut.

"Relax your lips," he said. "Try to make them do what mine do."

He tried again. "That's better . . . but relax. Open your mouth more."

He brought their lips together again and let his tongue stroke the inside of her lips, moving along them in a soft, slow caress. Her lips tightened. That had startled her. But then she relaxed and began to enjoy it. He moved his tongue inside and touched it to her tongue. Again startled, her tongue abruptly retracted. He pulled away from her and looked down at her.

"Lovers use tongues when they kiss," he said.

They came back together, and they kissed more, and more, and the kisses were joined by caresses, and the caresses became more and more focused, more and more intimate.

"It is so big, Peter," she said, taking him in her hand.

"I think everybody gets a whole lot bigger when they're ready to do it . . . and you will too."

"I'm afraid you shall surely hurt me. You do know I'm a small woman."

"Elizabeth, I'd never want to hurt you."

"Peter, if I ask you to, will you stop?"

"You know I will."

His promise gave her comfort. It gave him anxiety.

"Then I think we shall try now. I so want you. I so want you to be my first lover." She quickly followed that with "Oooo," in a low descending tone. It was apparent to him that it was pain, not pleasure.

"Is it hurting?"

"Yes, but not that bad."

"You want me to stop?"

"No. Not yet. Just be still for a moment."

He did his best.

"You may try a trifle more."

He did, ever so little, ever so slowly.

"Am I hurting you now?"

"Not much at all now . . . you may do more."

Suddenly, stimulation overcame apprehension and her body was ready to receive him. It began to feel good to her; she was ready for more. But there was not to be much more. Peter had lasted as long as he could this time. Elizabeth sensed that it was about to be over, and it was. Yet, as brief as it was, this first act of intercourse, it still gave her a warm feeling of pleasure, a vague sense of completeness, a sense of satisfaction all its own. For, whatever it meant, if she died now, died young, she would not die as Agnes had, a regretful virgin.

They resumed the position that had now become familiar: him on his back, pillow under his head, arm around her, hugging her to him, stroking her, her face on his chest, her hand stroking him.

"I know it weren't very good to you . . . me hurting you and all . . . but I hope we can try again, and it'll be better."

"We will definitely try again, Peter. I know it will be better for both of us when I am not so anxious."

Peter hugged her tighter and kissed her at her temple.

They lay together without speaking for half an hour.

Then he said in a flat tone, with no emphasis: "I'd like to try to do it again, if you'd let me."

"Peter, if you want to, I'm willing to."

This time it was different. Their kisses were more spontaneous. Their touches and caresses were less awkward, her arousal less dampened by apprehension. On and on he went, higher and higher she soared, until there seemed a cessation of sensate awareness, her body suspended in infinite nothingness. Then out of the place where they were joined together came waves of electric tingling, a suffusion of warmth that spread over her, then hard, throbbing pelvic contractions.

She let out a low, soft moan of pleasure, and it was over, save for a lasting warmth and a strange, euphoric high. Suddenly she realized that the pulsing, throbbing sensations she felt were not all hers, that they were accompanied by his own. A simultaneous act of mutual completion.

Afterward she pulled up the bedcovers over them, the light of the single lamp continuing to spread over the bunched curtain and across the ceiling. She assumed a fetal position with her back to him, and he turned upon his side to mirror her position. She pushed her body back, trying to touch him, trying to press against him, full-length. She took her instep and stroked along the top of his foot. He put his arm around her, embraced her warmly, then softly kissed her hair. She went to sleep.

Opening her eyes again, Elizabeth realized the morning sun had found its way across the Channel, across London, and now a bright beam of sun was streaming into the room through a high east window. Her eyes focused for a moment on a cracked windowpane in the upper left corner of the window, a sight that had greeted her every morning that she had lived in the flat. Dust particles floated and danced happily in this sunbeam.

She turned to face him and was startled to find him propped on his elbow, looking at her adoringly.

"Elizabeth, you're so beautiful. I can't believe I'm here with you like this. I must be dreaming."

She leaned up and kissed him on the cheek. She had never felt beautiful but loved hearing it from him.

Naked and unashamed, she got up and went to the toilet, then out to the kitchen corner, looking for something she could find for them to eat. She heard the toilet flush and returned to find him back in the bed. On a tray she had two cups of hot tea and a saucer with two hard, dry rolls, a bit of blackberry jam spread upon them.

"All I could find," she said, apologetically.

They sat propped in bed, legs crossed, tea in their laps, enjoying this breakfast together. When they had finished, she put the empty cups on the tray and carried them through the opening in the curtains to the sink. Coming back and standing by the bed, she reached out and touched his thigh through the bedding. He looked at her nakedness, felt a hard surge of desire. She sat on the bed and rolled over on him, her face close, looking into his eyes.

They made love again, and though it seemed impossible, this time it was even better for Elizabeth.

She had not only lost her virginity, she had learned that she could enjoy sex with a man, this man. Maybe, she thought, the most satisfying sexual pleasure would always come in the company of love.

For on this day of her life, in the fall of 1918, she was definitely in love—deeply, passionately in love—with a young American soldier from a faraway place called Mississippi. She should have known it the day he left the hospital, a day she went home to a strange and wretched emptiness.

By midmorning of this beautiful, sunny autumn Sunday, Elizabeth knew she had to take this man and go outside. She wanted to experience Peter, love, fresh air and sunshine, all together, all at once. It seemed the best life had to offer, and she wanted it.

"Can we take the cycle and go for a ride?" she said. "Out to the north, out of town, out in the country?"

"I wanna do whatever you wanna do."

"I wish we had some bread and wine and cheese, and we could have a picnic in the country, like they do in the romantic books I've read."

"Why don't we?" Peter responded, excited at the idea.

"I don't know where we could find any cheese or wine and bread on a Sunday morning."

"Know anybody around here?"

"Sure, half the nurses I work with live quite close."

Peter pulled out some money. Far more than should be needed.

"See what this'll do for us."

Elizabeth looked down, felt herself blush for some unexplained reason, then she smiled. "I'll be back."

He heard her start to knock on doors, talking to those who responded, in muted tones. Minutes later, she returned with a loaf of bread, fresh bread for a change, a thick slice of cheese, two bottles of wine, even a picnic basket. She handed him most of his money back.

"Must've found some bargains," Peter mused.

"The wine and the picnic basket came from my friend Janet. She would not take any money. Said she would trade it for a love story, if I had one to tell."

"You gonna tell her about us?"

An obvious warm flush colored her face and neck. "Maybe . . . maybe not. She is my best friend and it is the most exciting thing that has ever happened to me. But it is rather private, isn't it?"

~

She sat in the sidecar, as close to him as she could, locking her hand across his forearm; and they drove north from London into the countryside of Essex, a patchwork of farms and fields, thatched stone farmhouses with colorful cottage gardens, quaint villages with names like Netteswell and Spellbrooke and Thornwood. The sun shone brilliantly, with huge billowing clouds rising up in the sky. The road was bordered by hedges at times, by stone walls at others. The throaty roar of the Harley set a tone of adventure and excitement as they crossed small streams on stone bridges.

They continued northward past Bishop's Stortford, and then crossed the River Stort, turning west into Hertfordshire. It was there they found, near a village cemetery, a spot in a grassy meadow under a huge spreading oak. She got a blanket out of the Harley's saddle, spread it out, and they sat.

Elizabeth started to open the picnic basket, but hesitated, getting as close to him as she could and pushing him over on his back. She leaned over and kissed him, not a kiss of passion but a happy kiss of warmth and affection. Pulling away, she sat back up, and he followed. Opening the basket, she pulled out the bread and cheese. She handed him a bottle of wine and a small corkscrew with a wooden handle.

He looked at the contraption.

"How do I do it?"

"You have never opened a bottle of wine before?"

"Had a little whiskey and beer, and all, but no wine. Have you?"

"No," she admitted. "I guess we shall have to learn together."

They successfully uncorked the bottle, and they had the romantic picnic of her fantasy. The wine was a dry Cabernet Sauvignon.

"Want any more?" Peter asked.

"No. I think I prefer ale."

"Me too."

He poured what was left in the glasses on the ground and pushed the cork back in the bottle. They rolled over on the ground and began to kiss, this time with passion. Hungering for more, they did not want to stop, but they were close to the road and far too obvious to enjoy sex, there in open view.

That night when they got back to London, they finished the bread and cheese. Having no ale, the beverage was hot tea. Peter wanted to pick up where they had left off on the blanket beneath the oak, as did she. She quickly realized that she had become sore, and it was more pain than pleasure. She never let him know it, for she loved him and wanted to make him happy. She did find pleasure in that.

～

When Peter awoke at daybreak, Elizabeth was fully dressed in her nurse uniform, touching him on the shoulder. "I must go back to work. Stay as long as you like. Don't worry about locking the door; leave it open. There is little here for anyone to pinch anyway, and we've never had a problem."

"I'll drive you to work with the Harley."

Elizabeth wanted to avoid hospital gossip. "No, Peter, I don't think that would be wise. I don't think we should call attention to ourselves."

She smiled at him.

Peter stood up, pulled her to him, looked into her face.

"I sure do wanna see you again, Elizabeth . . . soon as I can."

"I'm on days—twelve hours—but will be here every night. If you get here first, just come in and wait. If I have arrived, and the door is locked, call out softly."

She quickly kissed him on the lips and walked out, gently closing the door behind her.

Peter got up and dressed. He figured he best get the Harley back to Sergeant Whatley as early as possible. Grabbing his crutches, he put them under his arms and headed out the door. But, as he got to the stairs, he turned and went back into Elizabeth's flat. He picked up their unopened second bottle of wine. With that, he headed back toward his barracks.

～

Peter entered the motor pool on the Harley and drove up in front of the tin shack that was Sergeant Whatley's office. Whatley had heard the un-mistakable sound of the Harley and came out, even more unkempt than usual, his uniform wrinkled and grease-stained, his boots only partially laced. It was clear that he had enjoyed a weekend of his own, romancing bottles. He squinted in the sudden bright light.

"Got a little something for you, Sergeant Whatley." Peter pulled the bottle of wine from the saddlebag on the Harley. "Worth a whole lot more, but this's all I could manage. Maybe next time, I can do better. Have a little better jump on it then."

Whatley smiled when he saw the wine. "You're a good 'un, Montgomery. Most of them officers don't bring me nothing. I ain't no wino, but it won't go to waste. How about it Montgomery, did you find her? Did she give you a little?"

Peter was offended by the crass comment, but he was not about to get crossed up with Sergeant Whatley.

"I did find her. She's a lovely little lady; she hasn't got another man, and I had a good time." That was all Peter was going to offer.

Whatley gave him a smirking grin, but questioned Peter no further. He sensed that it would do him no good.

～

Sergeant Whatley accommodated Peter when he could, and Peter quick-ly mastered public transportation from his barracks to North Middlesex.

For the next two months Peter Montgomery and Elizabeth Baker epitomized young love at its zenith. They talked, they laughed, they walked together, hand-in-hand in the sunshine, huddled together in the chilly fog. Occasionally they visited a park or a palace, a cafe or a pub, but most of the time they stayed at her flat . . . in bed. They kissed, caressed, joined together, over and over, in passion and pleasure. In eagerness, he came to her whenever he could; with joy, she received him.

As a wounded soldier, awaiting his return home, Peter had no duties, little to do at his barracks. Sometimes he would come into town knowing she was working and wander around London looking for something special to buy her, some special food to share. Then he used the key she had given him, waiting long hours in her flat for her to get off work.

Peter bought a briar pipe and smoked it while walking through the city streets, or just sitting alone at her place. It calmed the tension he felt, waiting for her, wanting her. Elizabeth worked long, tiring hours, yet came home to him eager and excited, knowing he would be there to take her in his arms and love away her stresses.

CHAPTER 11

A PIPE AND A PEARL

Elizabeth's work schedule at the hospital became brutal; days off were hard to come by. More wounded soldiers were brought in daily, and there were insufficient nurses to attend to their needs. After the night she and Peter first slept together, it was a full month before she would have another weekend off. She wanted the next one to be as memorable as that first time. Early one Wednesday morning, as she was dressing for work, he still lay in bed, fidgeting with his empty pipe, watching her dress.

"Saturday night I want us to celebrate our anniversary," she said to him, pulling her blouse over her bra and buttoning it.

Distracted by her actions, he tried to concentrate on what she had said.

"Our anniversary?"

"Yes. Saturday night will be our one-month anniversary."

"Sounds good to me. What do you wanna do to celebrate?"

"You will have to wait until Saturday night," she said, a hint of mystery in her smile.

"You know I'll take you out anywhere you wanna go, to celebrate and all."

"Wait until Saturday night," she said, this time with a look of stern resolve to keep him guessing.

In midmorning, Elizabeth approached a young man in his hospital bed, leg bandaged and suspended on cables. In her hand was a nurse's file folder, on top a blank sheet. "Good morning, Private Jones," she said. "Aren't you from Georgia?"

"Yes ma'am . . . south of Macon."

"Isn't that close to Mississippi?"

"Yes ma'am . . . there's Alabama between."

"People in Georgia eat what they eat in Mississippi?"

"Yes ma'am . . . I guess pretty much so."

"What would be a good dinner for a special occasion where you grew up?"

"You mean like Christmas . . . or something?"

"Well, not Christmas . . . more like what your mother would have, if she wanted to celebrate your homecoming . . . perhaps cooking some of your favorite dishes for dinner."

"Well . . . that'd probably be fried chicken . . . and butter beans . . . and cream corn. Probably some cornbread or biscuits . . . maybe peach cobbler or apple pie."

"What would you drink with this meal?"

"Be some sweet tea."

She wrote it all down carefully.

A few minutes later, Elizabeth was in the nurses' station, eying Janet at her desk. Janet had grown up in a stable middle-class family in Bristol; she liked to cook. When they were off duty together, Janet often invited Elizabeth to share a meal in her nearby flat. Elizabeth was not much of a cook.

"Can you teach me to fry chicken?" she now asked Janet.

"*What*?" Janet first said, then seemed to comprehend.

"Don't know where you could get a chicken to fry the way things are right now . . . but I could fry it, if I had a good enough stove. You and I don't have much stove these days." Janet was well aware by this time that Peter was frequently sleeping over. He had even taken them both out to eat a week earlier. Janet had become very fond of Peter and realized he was as enamored with Elizabeth as she was with him. "You must want to show your Peter that you are good wife material."

Elizabeth avoided a direct answer. "I want to cook him a special meal, and I'm told that fried chicken would be something he would like."

"How about a rabbit? Janet said. "Rabbit might be easier to get right now."

"I don't want rabbit."

"Lord. I'll start asking around about a chicken. My Uncle Cleve has chickens on his farm, but that's thirty miles . . . What else do you intend as a part of this meal for your Peter?"

Elizabeth looked at her list. "Something called *budder* beans and *cream* corn. Maybe peach cobbler or apple pie . . . cornbread or biscuits."

"We'll have to go with apple pie . . . shan't likely find peaches," Janet said. It seemed Janet had gotten into this special meal and intended to help make it happen. "What for heaven's sake is a *budder* bean?"

In time, through diligent inquiry, they were able to learn that a *budder* bean was a *butter* bean, a lima bean, and *cream* corn was simply creamed corn.

Over the next three days, as Janet focused on the culinary fare, Elizabeth began to focus on ambience for the occasion, making her little flat as romantic as possible for her anniversary dinner, also with Janet's help. Janet's background gave her superiority on both fronts. They bought a new white tablecloth for the tiny table. Janet lent dishes and glasses. They even bought a glass candlestick and red candle. Janet donated another bottle of wine, this time a Chardonnay that she thought appropriate for chicken. Elizabeth would also be sure they had beer and ale. Making this all happen, both women slipped off from their nursing duties from time to time, taking care to keep it brief so no patient's needs would suffer.

Two days before the special day, it occurred to Elizabeth that she wanted to give him a present, an anniversary present. Janet suggested an item of apparel, maybe a sweater.

Elizabeth was not sure. Peter never seemed to want to wear anything except his military attire; and she did not know anything about size or what might please him. Then it occurred to her that with his pipe smoking he used the paper containers tobacco came in, packing it with a little stick he had whittled. She'd seen those who smoked pipes carry their tobacco in special leather pouches. She'd get him one of those, and maybe a fancy pipe tool.

Patients' needs slowed in midafternoon, and so she went off to the pipe shop near her flat. They would have a good selection.

Once there, she looked at several leather tobacco pouches, trying to decide. Her eyes fell on a beautiful white pipe, and she had to inquire about it. "One of our finest," the shopkeeper informed her. "It's a classic meerschaum, made from a special clay from Turkey. Meerschaum pipes can be a bit fragile, and they are expensive, but many think they give the finest smoke, and I'm one of them . . . Look at this one." He showed Elizabeth an intricately carved pipe, depicting a bearded man.

"I like this plain white one. Is it expensive?"

He gave her the price, and it was more than she had. It would not have been, had she not bought new bedding, a lamp and lamp stand, and two fancy pillows, wanting to make her little flat a bit more elegant. Confused, she left, buying nothing.

"What did you buy for him?" Janet later asked.

"Nothing. I had decided to buy him a tobacco pouch for his tobacco . . . and I found several that I liked. But they had this beautiful white pipe. I wanted to buy it, but I didn't have enough money. . . . I tried to think of something to sell and get some money, but I don't have anything. I'm going back tomorrow and get the tobacco pouch."

Janet went out and came back with her plaid purse, pulling out a cache of pound notes, handing them to Elizabeth. "This should be more than you need. What you don't need you can give back to me, and you can pay me back when you can."

～

She and Janet did their best, but the meal was not quite what Elizabeth had wanted. She did find a chicken, thanks to Janet's Uncle Cleve, who met her halfway with it, dressed and ready to cook. But they lacked chicken frying experience and could not get the oil as hot as it needed to be with Janet's puny stove, so the fried chicken turned out greasy and a little more like oil-boiled chicken than true crispy fried chicken. The lima beans wound up navy beans and the creamed corn wound up potatoes, since those were the closest things they could find. No cornmeal was available, so they opted for biscuits.

Janet took pride in her apple pies, and she made one for dessert. Elizabeth did her best to do sweet tea, which Janet thought too strong and not sweet enough, but Peter had developed a taste for a strong ale anyway, which she would have available. Even though their initial experience with Cabernet Sauvignon had not been positive, they had both learned to like Chardonnay, and Elizabeth bought a second bottle to add to the one Janet had provided for the occasion, along with ice to chill it.

When he came in, Peter immediately noticed much effort had been expended to make this a special occasion.

"Look at these nice new dishes," he said. "You just buy them?"

"They're Janet's . . . she loaned them to me."

"And look at this fancy candlestick, candle, and all."

"I bought that, Peter, so we could dine by candlelight. You sit there on the couch and enjoy your pipe while I finish up."

Peter sat, occasionally glancing back over his shoulder at her moving dishes to the table.

"Anniversary dinner served," Elizabeth presently announced. "Let's see how I did."

She sat down across from Peter, the meal served, the wine poured, the candle brightly flickering. She reached across and took his hand in hers.

"Think we should bless it," he said.

She bowed her head, closed her eyes, squeezing his hand.

"Lord, thank you for these and all our blessings. Christ's name. Amen." That had been the Montgomery family prayer at every meal of Peter's life growing up.

"You're quite a cook," Peter said, about halfway through the meal.

"I couldn't have done it without Janet's help." She felt compelled to be honest, and not wanting him to expect that skilled of a domestic partner quite so soon.

"Bet you did most of it." She started to respond with the real truth but decided she had been truthful enough. So she just smiled warmly at that comment.

"Go sit on the couch while I clean off the table . . . let me get you some more ale," Elizabeth said, after they had finished eating.

"Think I'll take the rest of that wine," he said, to her surprise. He sat on the couch and put his wine on the table, took out his briar pipe, and started packing it with a whittled stick.

"Wait," she said, taking his pipe.

She went into her bedroom and came back, standing before him.

"I got this for you, to celebrate our first month's anniversary."

Elizabeth brought the gleaming white meerschaum out from behind her back. He took it in his hand, looking at it admiringly, stunned and speechless.

"You like it?"

"It's the prettiest pipe I've ever seen. You shouldn't of bought me something so fancy."

"And I got you this." She handed him a metal pipe tool.

He stood up and hugged her, holding the pipe and pipe tool in one hand behind her. "You're so wonderful," he said. He looked like he wanted to say something else, something profound, but he only hugged her again.

"You try your new pipe," she said. "I will finish cleaning up."

He gave his new meerschaum another long, loving look, and laid it on the table next to his wine. After a few moments, he went over and put his hands on both of her shoulders as she stood at her sink stacking the last of the dishes. "Come with me," he said. Peter had his own surprise.

He led her to the mirror near her bed and positioned her in front of it. "Close your eyes." She felt him put something around her neck.

"Take you a look now."

When she opened her eyes, he was holding a little gold necklace behind her neck, with a small pearl dangling beneath her chin. "You can do the catch thing. I've never done one of them like this." She reached back and closed the clasp.

"Oh, Peter, it's beautiful. I love it." She turned and faced him, putting her arms around his neck, and kissing him. They kissed with all the passion that now consumed them. Finally she reached her hand down and found that he was as ready as she was; his fly was cooperative and easy to open. It was that kind of special night.

The next morning, Elizabeth finished washing the dishes wearing only the gold necklace with the white pearl. Peter sat on the couch smoking his new white meerschaum, watching her, a man accustomed to the lust he always felt at the sight of her naked body. Any thought she might have had that she needed to be more voluptuous was a vain worry indeed.

~

November 7, 1918, four days before Armistice Day, Elizabeth had worked twelve straight days and she had been given a Thursday off. They spent Wednesday night and started Thursday in her flat, most of it in bed together making love. They opened a bottle of Chardonnay, and had a pretend picnic in bed, with wine, bread, and cheese. By afternoon they were ready to do something together outside the flat.

The weather was gray and overcast, looking like rain, and they took an umbrella. Although in moderate pain and limping, Peter had on both boots and was determined to walk without the crutches he had come to despise. They walked to Edmonton Green Station and took the train to Silver Street. The clouds broke and the sun came out. In Pymmes Park, they strolled around and sat for a time on a bench, huddled together, where they kissed. Not kisses of passion, just warm, tender kisses of love and affection. Peter got out his new meerschaum, which had already taken on a soft gold patina, packed, and lit it.

The day before, Elizabeth had realized that she was two weeks late with her period, and she wanted to talk to him about it, wanted to ask him if he thought they would get married, but she would not mar such a beautiful day together with the weighty issues of reality. After all, she had never been that regular. The issue of a pregnancy had never been discussed. If she carried his child, she thought it might make for assurance that he would come back for her; if she got pregnant, he reasoned, she would be anxious for his return.

So they talked about the war, how Allied victory seemed in sight, what the patients she was treating were saying about the battlefield. Elizabeth asked when he would be returning to America. He did not know but thought it might be soon. For the most part they simply sat, him holding her cuddled against his chest.

As the day waned and the sun started to set, the temperature began to rapidly drop. They left the park and walked back to Silver Street, where they found a small pub. Being early, most of the tables were vacant. They took one in the back, against a dimly lit wall, and ordered ale. She reached out and took his hand. "You're so wonderful," she said.

"Not as wonderful as you."

Both wanted to say "I love you." Neither managed to be the first to say it, as true as it was. But he did say, looking at her: "I don't know much about getting married . . . and I don't have no house or no job or nothing. But soon as I get home, I want to look for a job . . . and then I want to come back for you."

She waited for, and so wanted, a formal proposal, the traditional one; "Elizabeth, will you marry me?" It did not come. Maybe he thought it was already implied by what he had said.

Disappointed, she didn't respond immediately. She wanted to be in a position to say "Yes. I'll marry you." Finally she said, "I hope you will come back, Peter." She gave him a coy smile, not one he was accustomed to seeing. *You might be coming back for our baby too*, she thought.

They ate, then made their way back to her flat. Twice before that day they had engaged in passionate sex, once before the indoor picnic, and once right before they went out. Well-sated with food and wine, they slept the night, warm and close and tender.

She almost overslept, so she dressed hastily, and kissed him on the cheek before rushing out, leaving him naked in her bed. She would be going back on night duty, and Peter would be going back to his barracks for a few days.

CHAPTER 12

A HORROR AND A WHORE

Back at his barracks, Peter was under the command of Sergeant Oscar Duck. At thirty-two, Duck was an old timer, having been in the service since he was nineteen. In a young and rapidly expanding wartime army, Duck should have been a first sergeant, even a sergeant major, but he was a staff sergeant. Twice he had gone up the ranks and twice he had been busted back down, once for allegedly assaulting a female civilian working for his unit, the second time for cowardice.

Weighing almost three hundred pounds, Duck had narrow shoulders and a large posterior, which stuck up high behind him, cantilevered there by his big belly that protruded a good four inches over his lowslung belt. He walked with short steps, swaying from side to side, and his voice had a gurgling sound as it passed through his baggy throat.

"GET UP MONTGOMERY . . . GET YOUR ASS UP! YOU'RE MOVING OUT."

Peter opened his eyes. Sergeant Duck stood over him, poking him in the chest with clenched knuckles. Stunned, Peter could manage no words. Duck poked him again, this time hard enough to be painful.

"Get your ass up!" Duck said again, this time not as loud.

"What?" Peter said, blinking. "What for? It's still dark outside."

"Get to packing. I've got to get you to Liverpool by dark . . . Here's another duffel. Show me your stuff. I'll help you."

"Where's Liverpool?" Peter said. Duck was already stuffing Peter's belongings into an extra duffel he had brought.

"Two hundred miles north of here," Duck said over his shoulder, still packing Peter's apparent belongings into the duffel. "Get in your uniform, Montgomery. We've gotta hurry . . . got the others already outside waiting."

"I can't go today," Peter said. "I've got somebody I've gotta tell I'm leaving . . . where I'm going. I need to wait until tomorrow. Why can't I wait until tomorrow?"

"Montgomery, if we average twenty miles an hour, don't get stuck, and have no flats I'll be lucky to get you to Liverpool by the time this ship leaves. SHUT UP AND GET YOUR ASS DRESSED."

"Give somebody else my spot. I'll wait for another ship," Peter pleaded.

"Shut your ass up and get dressed. You're getting some kind of award in New York, and this ship is waiting for you and them others outside."

Dressed as best he could, in a sleepy fog of shock and horror, Peter stumbled out the door, carrying one duffel and Sergeant Duck carrying another.

"You'll have to consolidate your stuff in one bag on the way, Montgomery, one'll probably be all you can take on the ship . . . but we don't have time for that now," Duck said.

Outside, Peter found four other soldiers in a Hudson open-sided ambulance, with huge spoked tires, a convertible seat up front, a bed in the back with benches on each side that could be folded down or up, depending on the needs of the occasion. Canvas tops and sides on a metal framework were available, but they were rolled back. The front seat, next to Sergeant Duck, was a Lieutenant Thomas, and Peter, two young staff sergeants, and another private were on wooden fold-downs in the back. There was room for another on the padded front seat with Sergeant Duck, even as big as he was, but Duck failed to see it that way.

Most travel between London and Liverpool was by train, but this was obviously a rushed trip that allowed no time for train schedules. From its inception, Peter realized the ride on the hard slat benches was going to be punishing. The roads were rough and springs on the Hudson ambulance minimal.

At Northampton it began to rain, a cold, heavy drizzle, so they all got out and put up the canvas on the ambulance sides and top. Even with the canvas, the Hudson was far from dry. The others had donned heavy outerwear before they embarked, but Sergeant Duck had not given Peter the opportunity.

Peter's outerwear was in one of his duffels. He tried to tough it out, but in time relented and rummaged around until he found his heavy jacket. Duck, not being one to go long without food, had brought water and conventional troop rations: hard bread, sardines, corned beef, and a large bag of chocolate bars. As they started up with the canvas in place, Duck enjoyed his first snack of the trip, his first of many chocolate bars.

"I can't believe they're doing this to us!" Peter said in a loud, anxious voice. He was frantic about contacting Elizabeth, letting her know what was happening to him.

"I was told they think the war is about to end and we're wanted for some big awards ceremony in New York," said Sergeant Garner, who was sitting across from him.

The rain abated north of Birmingham, but they left the canvas in place. In the back, with the canvas up and no windows, two sergeants and two privates sat entombed and silent, leaning forward, elbows on their knees, trying to brace for the next bone-jarring bump. Peter was wet and cold. But the main reason he was miserable was worry over Elizbeth, being forced to leave England with no opportunity to contact her. He was worried about what Elizabeth would think about him leaving her without a word, and he realized all she knew about him was that he was from a small town in Mississippi named Glasper. He knew it was unlikely she could contact him.

Somewhere north of Wolverhampton, Peter started making plans to do the only thing he could think of; see if Sergeant Duck would get in touch with Elizabeth, when he returned to London, explain why he had left without a word. He remembered a shirt that might have a pencil in its pocket, one he used to write Elizabeth occasional notes that he left in her flat. Rummaging through one of his duffels, he was able to find his pencil.

No one had spoken for almost an hour. "Does anybody have any paper I could write a note on?" Peter asked, in a jarred broken tone.

"I think I've got a letter from my mother," Private Boone said. "Nothing that private in it." He found his duffel and dug around until he found his mother's letter, handing Peter the first page.

Peter made crossed lines across the written side, slid down the bench to have some room, started to write. He soon realized he would have to wait until they had to stop for something, which happened from time to time. He had never paid any attention to the names of streets on his trips to see Elizabeth, simply went by landmarks. When he could, he started carefully writing the landmarks, as he remembered them. *Go out the camp and turn left . . . go about five miles until you come to a church on the right, then take a left at the church. Go awhile until you come to a long bunch of three-story brown buildings on the left . . . take a left past the brown buildings and go awhile until you come to a pub on the corner . . . take a right at the pub.*

And on and on he went, until he thought he had done his best to get Sergeant Duck to Elizabeth's flat. After that, his instructions directed Duck up the stairs and told him Elizabeth's flat was the door to the left of the stairs.

A sick empty feeling came upon Peter. He saw Elizabeth alone in her flat and Sergeant Duck there with her, an obnoxious drunk, grabbing Elizabeth by the arm, trying to force her to do things she didn't want to do. He remembered rumors he had heard about how Sergeant Duck had gotten busted the first time, probably something that would have sent him to a court martial and a military prison had the victim been of another ethnicity. He folded his note around his pencil and held it for the next ten miles, then slowly unwrapped it, crumpled it into a wad, stood and stuffed it in his right pants pocket.

"Can I have another piece of that letter?"

Boone shuffled around in his duffel and found his letter. This time he gave Peter the last page, containing only a few lines and his mother's signature. Peter folded the paper in half, tore it in two, keeping the bottom half, blank on both sides, handing Boone back the top half with the writing on it.

They stopped again, this time for a herd of sheep in the road, and he quickly scrawled:

Elizabeth Baker—nurse
Edmeter Hospital
Go to second floor—go right
Tell her what happened to me
That I'll contact her soon as I can—

Peter folded this note and put it in his left front pocket of his jacket. Then he pulled out his wallet and all the money that was in it. Six fives and thirteen ones. Private Boone, sitting beside him, looked at the money and then at Peter.

"How much money's in that big wad?" he asked, impressed with Peter's show of cash.

"Forty-three dollars . . . I think," Peter said. After all, Boone had been nice enough to share his mother's letter with him, maybe he deserved a response. Then he folded all nineteen bills and put them in his pocket with the note.

"Montgomery, you can stay in a whorehouse for a week on that," Sergeant Garner piped up, seated across from Peter. "But don't think you're going to get a chance for even one visit, unless it's back across the pond," he continued, in a louder tone intended for the group. He was attempting to bait Peter into giving an explanation of the note and money.

Peter had given all the explanation he intended to give. He thought about writing a note to Elizabeth, telling her how much he loved her, explaining his abrupt exit. But such a letter would be private, Peter had no envelope to seal it in, and he didn't know what he could say, since he was confused about what was happening to him.

As he was contemplating what he would say, considering asking Boone for more paper, they started up again, almost immediately being jolted by the bumpy road. Somewhere out beyond the canvas, Peter heard loud, startled sheep. If he could get Duck to find Elizabeth and tell her what had happened when he found her, that seemed his best bet, maybe his only hope.

~

After nightfall they crossed the Mersey River on a ferry. They had left London over thirteen hours earlier. With herds of sheep in the road, rivers to ford and other impediments, they had averaged almost eighteen miles per hour. While still on the ferry, they began to hear the sounds of Liverpool Harbor at night. Strange, almost eerie sounds invaded the windowless rear of the ambulance, still completely enveloped in canvas.

"Where's them American ships?" they heard Duck ask when they pulled off the ferry.

"Probably be at Pier's Head or King George's Pier," someone answered him. "What's the name of the ship you're looking for, old chap?"

"*Saint Louis*," Duck said.

"Go up and take a left and head toward Pier's Head. Ask up that way."

In almost total darkness, they continued to bounce along. Sounds of the city began to intensify. No one spoke. The ambulance stopped again.

"Looking for an American ship . . . *Saint Louis*," Duck shouted.

"What kind of a ship is it?"

"A big ship that's taking troops back to America."

"Go down this road and take your fourth main left . . . that'll put you at Pier's Head. Several big Yank ships there."

When they stopped again, Duck shouted, "Which one's the *Saint Louis*?"

"Last one up at the far end," someone answered.

They stopped again. "You got those we're expecting from London?" an American voice asked.

"Got five," Duck said.

"I hope you got them all . . . they've had us holding up all afternoon for you."

Duck opened the canvas. "Get out! Hurry! You're holding up the ship."

"Everybody get out and I'll pass out the gear," Sergeant Garner commanded. After they jumped out, he started pitching their duffels out the back of the ambulance. Lieutenant Thomas had been waiting outside when Duck opened the canvas, and he retrieved his bag and started toward the ship.

"Lieutenant Thomas?" the midshipman queried, looking at his manifest.

"Right."

Each identified their respective bags and started toward the ship, being duly checked off the manifest. Only Peter remained.

"I've still got my stuff in two bags," Peter said to Duck.

"Hell. Don't matter to me, if it don't matter to the Navy. Pick 'em up and get your ass on the ship, Montgomery."

"I need to talk to you, Sergeant Duck," Peter said in his most humble tone.

"Damn, Montgomery! Don't you see there's no time for talking . . . that *big ship* is waiting JUST FOR YOU!"

Peter pulled the note about Elizabeth, together with his wad of nineteen bills from his front pocket, offering them to Duck, whose eyes widened at the cash.

"What's this money about, Montgomery?" Peter had gotten his attention. "Where'd you get all that money? . . . how much is it?"

"Forty-three dollars."

Duck knew this was his whole monthly pay.

"I'll give it to you . . . if you'll do something for me."

"Hurry up!" the midshipman shouted. "The ship is waiting for this last one, Montgomery."

"Dammit! Give us a minute!" Duck shouted back. "We'll be right there!"

"Montgomery, I hope what you want is not criminal," Duck said, with a smirk and in a tone of self-righteousness.

"I want you to find a woman for me, when you get back to London . . . and tell her I didn't want to leave without seeing her. Tell her about all this, and all . . . tell her how this happened to me so quick. Tell her I didn't have no chance to tell her about it. Tell her I will find a way to come back for her."

"That's all I gotta do for forty-three dollars?"

"That's all. But I *really, really* need for you to do it."

"Give me the money," Duck said, and Peter handed it over.

"Who is this woman?"

"Here's her name and where you can find her," Peter said, pointing out his note about Elizabeth. Duck tried to read it, but the light was too poor for him to make out the writing. "This tell me what I need . . . to find her?"

"Yes." Peter was confident that Duck would know where Elizabeth's hospital was, since so many wounded American soldiers had been treated there. Duck stuffed the money and note in his left pants pocket.

"I'm counting on you, Sergeant Duck," Peter said, in an almost pleading tone. "And be sure to tell her I'm coming back for her."

"Come on!" the midshipman shouted. "We can't hold this ship up any longer for this high-level conference!"

Duck got back in the ambulance and started out from the dock. Peter, with his two bags, limped up the gangplank onto the USS *Saint Louis*, a 9,700-ton cruiser destined to return him to America. None on board for the return voyage would be unhappy . . . except him. He did think, for all that money, he could count on Duck. Either way, he had little choice. Peter and Elizabeth had shared much about their respective lives, but no addresses. They had never seen any reason to be specific about anything like that. Although actually in North Middlesex, Peter considered her flat somewhere in London. He could follow familiar landmarks and get there easily. She knew he was from a small town by the name of Glasper in a part of America called Mississippi. That's all they knew.

～

Flush with Peter's money, Duck decided he would forget looking for military quarters for the night and find himself a hotel room, swanky if possible. In time he wound up at the Parrot Hotel on Scotland Street, procured himself a room on the second floor, threw his bag on a chair and lay back on the bed, exhausted. When he had so abruptly awakened Peter at four that morning, he had already rounded up all the others, and then he had driven more than fourteen hours.

Though tired, sleep eluded him, and he got up and went down to the hotel's first floor pub, which was busy and noisy. Duck approached the ornate bar and ordered a pint of ale, an advertised special, the white-painted sign displayed on the wall behind the bar. Two patrons left and he spotted a vacant table next to a wall. A waiter came up, middle-aged, thin and hairy, dressed in a long-sleeved white shirt with matching vest and bow tie.

"That's good stuff, old chap, that Knotty Oak," the waiter commented dryly, as he cleaned off the table.

Duck thought about using some of Peter's money to procure himself a woman. He figured with one of the dollars a basic old whore might be arranged; one of the fives should give him a shot at a sweet young beauty. He decided against it, doubting he had the stamina for sex at this point.

He drank the pint of Knotty Oak, rather rapidly, and went back to the bar for another. There were two waiters behind the bar, in identical dress. The one who had cleaned off his table turned to wait on him.

"That Knotty Oak . . . mighty good," Duck said.

"Best we've ever found, old chap. Good buy, this special."

When Duck finished his third pint, he began to feel an urgent need to urinate. He had noticed a number of patrons coming and going through a door back in a corner, and he suspected that was where the toilet was located. Walking through this door and down a short hall, his suspicions proved well founded.

Standing in front of the toilet, he held the top of his pants with his left hand and used his right to open his fly, and he stood enjoying blessed relief. For the first two or three seconds, until he got on target, his stream missed the toilet to the left. The floor was already wet anyway; he was not the first drunk with poor aim. With his left hand in his pocket and his right attending to the business at hand, there he stood for about twenty seconds; he had drunk quite a lot of ale. When finished, he pulled his left hand back out of his pocket to assist refastening his pants. The money had long ago been transferred to his wallet, but the note with information about Elizabeth was left in his left front pocket. It came out with his hand and landed on the floor in the wet urine. Duck started to reach down and pick it up, but it was already soaked, the writing bleeding into illegibility.

"CRAP!" Duck stared at it for another moment, after which he stomped the urine-soaked paper with his boot and walked back out into the pub.

Something about relieving himself, and getting up and walking around, had made him feel more invigorated, more virile. The bartender looked up as he approached.

"More Knotty Oak, mate?"

Duck nodded in affirmance, and the bartender turned his back and poured him another pint. Duck stood, forearms across the bar, displaying his money.

"Come into a little windfall. Think I want to use a little on a woman," he said, when the bartender returned. "Anything you can do about that?"

The bartender looked at the money, then at Duck, studying his drunken state.

"Likely could be arranged, but it's late and would be expensive. What can you afford?"

"What about five U.S. dollars?"

"Little late and little notice, old chap."

Duck counted through his remaining money. "Would ten do?" he said in a drunken slur.

The bartender raised his eyebrows in a look of mild shock. "That's quite a bit. Think I can make it happen. But you and the ole Knotty Oak may not be up to much. You'll pay in advance, and if I get her, and you don't want her, or can't do it, there'll be no refund. You understand that, don't you, mate?"

"No worry," Duck replied. "Never asked for a refund."

"I'll see what I can do, mate. Go sit and enjoy your Knotty Oak."

The bartender conferred with his assistant, then went to the coat rack, starting to put on his coat and hat. Duck got up from his Knotty Oak and approached him.

"What's your name, fella?"

"Max."

"Mack?"

"No, *Max*."

"Max. I like 'em young. For that money, you need to get me a young one."

"How young you talking about?"

"Young as you can get. Younger the better."

"Too young, can be jail, big man."

"I've always taken my chances."

The bartender found the right woman. Cassie Drinkwater. He and Cassie had worked together for more than three years. Cassie wasn't young, but she was petite. The main thing: at twenty-eight she had more than a decade of experience . . . the experience he needed. She could be counted on to separate this obnoxious drunk from his whole windfall.

The next afternoon, he met Cassie behind the pub. The bartender took the watch, Cassie got her promised fee, they split the windfall, then Duck's wallet went into the pub garbage.

~

Two days later, an agreement was signed between Germany and the Allies to end all hostilities on the Western Front. Celebrations broke out all over Britain; people danced in the streets; shouts of joy rang out everywhere. Peter and Elizabeth should have been there, celebrating together the end of this war that had affected their lives so profoundly. They were not. Instead they were separated by hundreds of miles of vast ocean.

PART TWO

The Great Depression

CHAPTER 13

DISEASE AND DISTANCE

The second day of the voyage was Peter's twentieth birthday. Mercifully, no one wished him a happy birthday, for it couldn't have been more unhappy. He couldn't believe he had been forced to leave England with no opportunity to contact Elizabeth, tell her he was leaving, no opportunity to tell her how much he loved her, no chance for them to make plans to get her home to Mississippi as his wife. Surely Sergeant Duck would let her know what had happened! He had given the man a month's pay!

Peter started thinking about how he could reconnect with Elizabeth, as soon as possible. He would immediately write to her. Maybe the telegraph would be available. He knew he soon would be discharged. Perhaps he could find a way to immediately return to England. But what would be the point of that? They would want to live in America, where he had contacts and could provide for them.

Peter had never been more anxious. Surely, if Sergeant Duck explained why he left without a word, Elizabeth would understand, and she would wait for him to reestablish contact.

On board, Peter learned that the rushed departure was because he was among a group of thirty-nine who were to receive the Distinguished Service Cross for valor, the ceremony at the military facilities on Governors Island.

The crossing was to take six days. On the third day, the weather took a turn for the worse, and the ship began to violently lurch in the stormy North Atlantic. Many of the soldiers aboard became seasick, including Peter. A day out from New York, he began to choke and cough. His head ached. He ached all over, alternating between chills and fever. By the time the ship docked, Peter's fever was 105° F. He had contracted the Spanish flu.

Among those in the Hudson ambulance with Sergeant Duck, three were infected: Peter, Lieutenant Thomas, and Private Boone. None would make the awards ceremony for which they were being rushed home. Private Boone would die four days after their arrival in New York.

Peter was placed in a large warehouse on Governors Island that had been converted into a hospital facility. For almost two weeks he lay delirious and near death, on the verge of drowning in bloody fluids accumulating in his lungs, coughing up blood. At the end of the second week, his fever began to subside and he appeared better, but then bacterial bronchitis and pneumonia set in, with a chronic fever, a deep cough, and recurring chills.

Finally, in the second week of January 1919, he was deemed well enough to be discharged, from the hospital and from the Army.

Peter was summoned to the Governors Island post headquarters. "Please sit down, Private Montgomery," the officer said, in a deep, authoritative voice. Sitting behind a gray metal desk, the speaker was a trim man, about fifty, with wiry gray hair, in an immaculately pressed uniform. His dark eyes focused upon Peter with piercing intensity. The placard on the desk read: *Colonel Pierce Oswalt.*

Peter sat.

"You have much to be happy and proud about at this time, Private Montgomery," Colonel Oswalt announced. "You have survived what has killed so many of our best, both on the battlefield and in the hospital. I have your discharge papers, and I am to present you with the Distinguished Service Cross. Do you know about the Distinguished Service Cross, Private Montgomery?"

"Not much, sir."

"It's our nation's second highest military honor, second only to the Congressional Medal of Honor. It is recognizing your extraordinary bravery in combat in France. Your country is very proud of you, Private Montgomery, and grateful for your extraordinary courage. And I am here to express your country's appreciation and present this to you."

With that, Colonel Oswalt summoned a photographer, who photographed him pinning the Distinguished Service Cross on Peter's chest in front of the American flag.

"Lieutenant Glick, would you see that this brave young man is given highest priority in being returned home to Mississippi?" he asked his adjutant, a lanky first lieutenant, equally clean shaven in an equally immaculate uniform.

"Private Montgomery, good luck and Godspeed."

Peter was considered decorated, discharged, and given his leave. And he left, still coughing, numb, weak, and bewildered. He had survived near death in combat, near death in the great Spanish flu pandemic, and was now on his way home to Glasper, Mississippi.

~

The trip home by train took almost as long as the voyage across the Atlantic, with layovers and changes of railcars. His family had been notified that Peter was being discharged and was on the way home, but there was no way for him to provide a definite day and time of arrival. It didn't matter to his sister Evie. The minute she heard he was coming home, she left Baton Rouge with the intention of being in Glasper to greet him.

Montgomery General Mercantile sat on a corner of Main Street, in the second block from the train station. It had big bay windows facing out onto two streets, stocked with items most likely to tempt the locals: mule collars; garden plows; bolts of bright cotton cloth; shoes and boots; pots and pans; butter churns . . . even a black pot-bellied stove.

In mid-afternoon on Friday, January 17, 1919, a cold winter day by Glasper standards, a shout rang out across the store, "It's Peter! It's Peter! He's home!"

Evie was racing to meet him, scattering a scoop of dried beans in her haste. As she got to her brother, she threw the metal scoop high in the air and it landed with a loud crash. Peter dropped his large duffel bag on the floor and Evie, gawky and plain as ever, a full two inches taller, hugged him as hard as she could. His papa came to greet him, overjoyed. His mother was not there; she was struggling to recover from a mild case of the flu and had left a short time earlier to go home and rest.

Peter was then greeted with another hug. Following his papa was a young woman Peter had never seen before. She had short, medium brown hair, closely set dark eyes, and was full-figured, with ample cleavage showing above the cut of her blue-and-white print blouse.

"I want to hug him, too!" she said in a loud, excited voice. "I've heard so much about you." With that, she hugged Peter, pressing her ample bosom tight against his chest. She stepped back. "You're as handsome as Evie said."

"This is Emma Bateman," Peter's papa interjected, at first being at a loss for words. "She has been working for us since Evie left us and went off to Baton Rouge." He gave Evie a look of playful disdain.

"Nice to meet you," Peter said, feeling self-conscious. "Sounds like they held back on you with some of the bad stuff."

∼

Getting reconnected with Elizabeth had been constantly on Peter's mind from the moment he was awakened before dawn in London by Sergeant Duck. He loved her so and intended to marry her and bring her home to Glasper as soon as he could. He felt such an aching emptiness, such a miserable anxiety.

The afternoon he got back to Glasper, Peter inquired at the telegraph office in the railroad depot about communicating with Elizabeth by telegraph. The telegraph agent, Carl Allen, dashed that hope. Transatlantic cables were very limited. With the world in the grip of a pandemic of unprecedented proportions, while winding down from the greatest military conflict in history, personal communication such as Peter wanted would not be approved.

His only immediate option was to write to Elizabeth, and that posed a problem. He had paid no attention to the address of Elizabeth's flat.

He decided that he would write to her at the hospital, although in London there were more than forty hospitals treating wounded soldiers, and this did not even include hospitals in outlying suburbs. Edmonton Military Hospital was actually in North Middlesex, for most of its history known as North Middlesex Hospital . . . only called Edmonton during the war. Even worse, he misremembered the name of the hospital as "Edmeter" Hospital.

CHAPTER 14

I LOVE YOU

The Montgomery residence was two blocks down a side street from the store. The house was set well back from the road, with a circular front drive, bordered by large, straggly azaleas. Little grass could grow under giant oaks in the yard. Their two-story white house, large by Glasper standards, had started out as an impressive Victorian, then fell short when the expense of the ornate woodwork ran afoul of Peter's father's Scotch frugality.

After eleven o'clock, on the night of his arrival back in Glasper, Peter was lying on his bed, thinking about Elizabeth. Evie knocked and peeped in the open door. A light on in the hall at the top of the steps illuminated her standing in the doorway.

"Can I come in?"

"Sure."

Evie sat in a simple walnut wooden chair across from Peter's bed.

"I have missed you so. Tell me about where you've been, what you've seen."

"Not much to talk about . . . I'll tell you what I can."

Intuitively, she sensed that she should not go right to the battle where he was wounded.

"What's the ocean like? I've seen it once, from the beach at Biloxi . . . water going out as far as I could see. But I know that's not like being way out on the ocean."

"You sure can't feel all them *waves*, standing on the land . . . some days they is mighty big and throw you around. They made me so sick. I never vomited so much before. And looking around at all that sky and water, nothing but water as far as you can see, in every direction, makes you feel mighty small . . . like you're nothing but a little speck, or something."

"What was England like?"

"That London is so big you just can't believe it. You can go on and on and on, like you are going all the way from here to Hattiesburg, and there's nothing but big buildings, all stuffed together, almost all of them more'n one story, with funny things sticking out these big chimneys where the smoke comes out. They say each one of 'em is where a different fireplace comes out the same chimney."

"You didn't ever get out of London?"

"Well, I got taken to Liverpool, but it was raining for most of it, and they had me shut up in the back of this ole ambulance where I couldn't see out."

Then he remembered taking Elizabeth out of London for their picnic. "One time I did get out in the country on a sunny day, and out there was pretty farms, kind of like here, but not near as many trees—and little places like Glasper, where lots of the houses have funny-looking roofs made out of straw." With those images, he came very close to telling his sister about Elizabeth, but he didn't.

Evie could no longer contain her curiosity about the source of his injury.

"You feel like telling me about when you got shot? If you don't want to talk about it, I'll understand."

"Don't think I'll ever want to talk about it. Like to forget it . . . much as I can. But if I'd talk to anybody about it, it'd be you. What do you want to know?"

"I don't know. Were you scared . . . knowing you were going to be shot at . . . knowing you might be *killed*?"

"Yes, I was real scared . . . When they gave the orders to get out of the trench and go out across that field it got kinda like being in a dream.

There's bullets hitting all around, and some shot and hollering . . . you pretty much don't know what you're doing or why you're doing it."

"You ever think about not getting out of the trench . . . not going out and getting shot and killed?"

"No."

He did not try to explain why, but there was a definite reason he would not disobey orders and stay in the trench. It wasn't about patriotism or honor; it wasn't an issue of courage or cowardice. He had bonded with a group of other men, trained with them, found companionship in them. Together they had suffered in the wretched trenches of this wretched war, and he would be loyal to them, even to death.

"Did it hurt bad when you got shot?"

"Not at first . . . I just kept on fighting . . . trying not to get killed." He saw visions of his bloody wound, but he was not about to describe that to her. "But it got to hurting real bad when they got me in an ambulance and I started calming down some."

With her nurse's training, Evie was most interested in how his injuries were dealt with, how he got to the hospital in England, his stay at the military hospital, what it was like. As best he could, he explained, and she listened intently, occasionally asking specific questions about his treatment. Again, he came close to telling her about Elizabeth, but held back.

Evie came over and sat on the edge of his bed, taking his hand. "I'm so glad the Lord took care of you and didn't let you get killed."

After a pause, he said, "You think it was the Lord's will that I wasn't killed?"

"Must have been. We know the Lord is over everything."

"I'm not so sure about all that." The war had made Peter confront theological issues that his sister had not yet seen. "Some of them fellas I was with was mighty good fellas . . . probably some lot better 'n me . . . don't know why the Lord would want them to die and not me."

"That's the way the Lord's will is. We don't know everything about His will."

He said in a soft, contemplative voice: "Evie, I'm not so sure the Lord wants to be in on everything. I think He may be willing to let us kill ourselves and kill each other if we are of a mind to." They sat silently, both trying to make some sense out of God's will.

Shortly after one o'clock, she squeezed his hand, and leaned over and kissed him on his forehead. "I've kept you up too late . . . I'm sorry. I didn't realize how late it is. I know you are exhausted. You go to sleep now."

At the door, Evie turned back and looked at him. She had a strange sense of dread but could wait no longer.

"Peter, what about Arthur? Did he come home with you?"

Peter hesitated.

"No Evie . . . Arthur's dead. He was killed when I was wounded."

She put her forehead against the door facing for a moment; then she looked up at him.

"Did he suffer?"

"No. He died quick-like."

Evie said nothing, and she was gone. Peter heard faint sounds from her room. He thought she might be weeping. No. He was certain of it.

Half an hour later, Evie lay awake still. She felt him touch her on the arm. "Can we talk a little more?" he asked.

"You know we can." She moved over, and he sat on the edge of her bed.

"I'm wondering how you know if you're in love. Have you ever been in love?"

Shocked, she hesitated, searching for an answer. This was not a question she had ever expected from Peter.

"Maybe," she finally said.

"I think I'm in love," Peter said, in an almost apologetic voice. His sister was the only person in the entire world he felt comfortable talking with about this. And for the next two hours Peter told Evie all about Elizabeth, leaving out the sex. A little after three, Peter gave Evie his summation.

"Whenever I was with her, I had this happy feeling, happier than I've ever felt any time before. It's like she's all I can think about . . . I always had this funny, tingly feeling whenever I heard her voice, and whenever she would smile at me or touch me . . . and whenever we kissed."

The emotion in Peter's voice as he talked about Elizabeth, the look on his face, gave Evie a warm, tingly feeling of her own.

"Evie," he said, "she's all I can think about. I want to get back with her so bad."

"We'll have to make it happen. I'll do anything I can to help . . . and I know Mama and Papa will too."

"I don't want to tell them anything about it, at least not right now," Peter said, going back to his room.

~

"Evie! Peter!" their mother shouted up the stairs. "Come to breakfast . . . your breakfast is ready; eggs are no good cold."

Both Peter and Evie fought for an unwilling consciousness after too little sleep.

"We're coming," Evie finally shouted down the stairs.

Evie led the way, Peter in her wake. Halfway down the stairs, when they turned onto the landing, Peter caught the aroma of the bacon frying, a smell that throughout his life had meant his mother was cooking breakfast. He could never smell bacon and not think of this place, of her, feeling a sense of well-being.

Peter's father, P.W. Montgomery, was already seated, leaning back contentedly in his customary wooden captain's chair, at the far side of the large round breakfast table, his back to the big bay window. In the center of the table was a round lazy Susan, already beginning to accumulate food in dishes of various sizes.

Peter's grandfather, the first Peter Wilson Montgomery, was referred to as "Pete," often "Big Pete." His father always went by "P.W.," and he was "Peter" . . . at least that was his decided preference. It was from P.W. that Peter had inherited his classic chiseled features, his broad shoulders and narrow hips. At forty-five, P.W. was still an impressive six-one, a hundred eighty pounds, lean from hours of lifting merchandise and stocking shelves. His hair was a thick salt-and-pepper gray, and his voice a deep monotone.

By contrast, Peter's mother, Lila Montgomery, was a petite woman, barely over five feet and a hundred pounds. She had a decidedly nasal voice that could get in two words to P.W.'s one. Her hair had now turned silver-gray, and her thin face had begun to wrinkle. It was Lila's genes that had predisposed Peter to be only five-foot-seven.

"Lord have mercy, boy, your mama done tried to fix you everything possible for any breakfast, all at once," Peter's father said, looking at Peter.

"Well, not quite," Lila said. "We're not having waffles and pancakes at the same time, but we are having ham and bacon. I've got to fatten him back up some. He's come home skinny as a scarecrow and with that awful cough."

"Wow!" was all Peter could say.

Peter and Evie did their best to do justice to their mother's efforts. Simply eating a small portion of everything she had prepared proved a challenge. Profuse comment was made about how much Peter had been missed, and how good it was to have him back home. No effort was made to question him about his experiences.

"I've got to get on back to the store," P.W. finally announced. "Emma's there, but Saturday is our busy day, you know. We'll take all the help you kids feel like giving us."

"I'll be up to help right away," Evie said. "Peter is still kinda sick and he didn't get much sleep last night. We should let him sleep some more, unless we can't do without him."

Upstairs, minutes later, Peter came into her room and asked his sister, "You got any stationery I could write to Elizabeth on?"

"I think so, but it might not be exactly what you're looking for . . . maybe a little bit girly." She went over to an ornate white desk in her bedroom and retrieved a box of stationery, handing it to him: extra-heavy paper, a soft mauve, lightly scalloped on the edges, not full business-size, but almost. "All I got," she said.

"You think it'll be okay?"

"Don't know why not. It's not *that* girly."

Shortly after eight o'clock on Saturday morning, January 18, 1919, a fatigued Peter Montgomery sat down at a feminine little desk in his sister's bedroom to compose a letter to Elizabeth. This letter he had desperately wanted to write for more than two months, during which it seemed every power in the universe had conspired against him. He found no pen; but a graphite pencil would do.

Dear Elizabeth,

I know Sergeant Duck told you why I had to leave without letting you know—now you is wondering why it's been so long and me not writing and all. What happened—I got real sick. Caught that bad killing flu. Really—really sick. In the hospital for two months. Heard them saying several times I was going to die that day. 'Course I didn't—wouldn't be here writing you this.

Got back home to Glasper yesterday. Don't know what I'm going to do yet. Can work for Papa, but don't want that always. Evie wants me to get you to come here and get a job nursing with her in Baton Rouge and me maybe go get more school or some special training. Says we can live with her. I like that. What about you?

I want to get you with me more than anything ever in my life. I'll try and write often now—now that I can.

I love you and want you with me so bad—so bad.

Peter

What Peter had not said aloud to her, he put in his first letter to her: "I love you."

When he went to the post office to buy appropriate postage and send it off to Elizabeth, Postmaster Bryan Scruggs looked at it and then at Peter, inquiringly. "This isn't much address, just this Edmeter Hospital, London, England. That London is a big place, more people than three or four states around here combined."

"That's all I got, Mr. Bryan," Peter replied. "It's a big hospital and everybody probably knows where it is."

"They'd better."

"Best I've got." Peter felt confident the address was good enough to get it to Elizabeth. Surely everyone in London was familiar with Edmeter Hospital.

Peter yearned to write to her every single day, but he wasn't much of a writer and didn't have much to say. He did write her again on the day after his first letter:

Dear Elizabeth,

Mama cooked another good supper last night. They are really trying to feed me since I got home. Think I'm too skinny—still cough a bit but maybe it's getting better.

Going to hang around and work for Papa at the store I guess but I want to be looking for something else. Evie likes Baton Rouge and wants me to come stay with her and look for something there. Papa's not much for it, but he has this girl Emma and says he can maybe get by with her help if I want to go and be with Evie.

He says he knows not much exciting in Glasper for a young man who been off in the world and all. Not much else to say now.

I want to be back with you so bad. I love you.

Peter

On Wednesday, January 29, 1919, midway into the second week since his return to Glasper, Peter was again at the post office, sending his sixth letter to Elizabeth. They had all been as short as this second one and closed with: "I love you, Peter." Mr. Scruggs had stopped making inquiries into the adequacy of the address, simply taking Peter's money and applying the postage.

"How long do you think it'll take for a letter to get to London, England?" Peter asked Mr. Scruggs.

"Probably three or four weeks," he responded. "Probably go up to New York, and then on over there on a ship. I bet it could make it in a little over two, if it caught a ship about to go out, and if some censors didn't hold it up now that the war is over."

"And if I was getting something back it might be as little as two more weeks after that?" Peter asked, in a somber monotone.

"Well, *if she got it* and wrote back right away. Like I've said, I question if this is enough address to get it to her."

As he left, Scruggs called after him, "We'll send it on and both hope for the best."

CHAPTER 15

A BUXOM CHAUFFEUR

O n Monday morning, after his arrival in Glasper the previous Friday, Peter began to work for his parents at Montgomery General Mercantile. Emma Bateman and his father were there when he arrived.

Emma had grown up on her Uncle Marcel McCoy's farm near Kershey, a hamlet eighteen miles out from Glasper by way of a dirt and gravel road. For most of the war, she had worked in a factory in Hattiesburg sewing uniforms for the military. Near war's end, demand had slowed and she was laid off. Uncle Marcel, who had raised her, was a patron of Montgomery Mercantile, generally coming in with his hired hand, Luke Cox. With little prospect for a paying job for her in Kershey, Marcel came into Glasper one day looking for work for Emma. The timing was right, as Evie had left for Baton Rouge and someone was needed to fill her place.

It soon became obvious to Peter's mother that Emma had set her sights on Peter, and she was not happy about it.

Toward the end of his first week home, Peter's father had left for work and Peter was still finishing his breakfast. Lila said to her son, standing at the kitchen sink with her back to him, "Peter, I can tell Emma is interested in you. You don't want to get involved with her. She's six years older than you are . . . been off there living in Hattiesburg for the war, and she has not likely been saving herself for her wedding night." Lila said nothing further, never looking back at him. Peter, without replying, got up and left for work.

Emma constantly flirted with Peter, smiling at him, touching him at any opportunity, subtly leaning over in front of him to expose her ample bosom. He couldn't avoid noticing what Emma was flouting, but his mind was on Elizabeth.

In the back of Montgomery Mercantile, tucked away in a corner, was a table that was the social and relaxation center of the store. P.W. and Lila drank their coffee here, often in the company of friends and regular customers. Here P.W. sat to read the newspaper and or work on orders for merchandise, while Lila sat and knitted. At times hours would pass with no customer, nothing to do but kill time and hope for business.

Three weeks after Peter's arrival back in Glasper, business had been brisk for most of the day, but it had subsided. Around one o'clock, P.W. had gone up the street to get a haircut. Lila was in the front, measuring off four yards of cotton print for Bettie Dee Agnew, the only customer in the store at that time. Peter picked up a tin of sardines and some soda crackers, sat down at the table, put his first sardine on a cracker, and started eating it.

Not missing any chance to be with him, one-on-one, Emma took a seat across from him. She had a large biscuit and a bottled root beer. A small container of molasses was kept on the table, along with sugar, salt, and pepper, as well as a container of paper napkins. She punched a depression in the biscuit with two fingers and poured it full of molasses.

"Want a biscuit?" she said to Peter, touching him on the shoulder.

"No. I'll go with my sardines and crackers."

Peter looked up and saw Dennis Langley Jr. coming through the door with a broad smile on his face. He and Peter both wanted to hug the other but hugging among men was not a part of their culture. They vigorously shook hands.

Dennis was Peter's lifelong best friend. Considerably larger than Peter in both height and chubbiness, he had a broad forehead, a pudgy nose, and thin white-blond hair. He wore neatly pressed khaki pants, a dark blue wool jacket, and an eight-paneled newsboy cap of black and gray tweed. The time Peter had spent in the Army, Dennis had spent at

Vanderbilt, an experience that had refined his grammar and tempered his Southern accent.

Dennis's father was president of the only bank in town. The two families were mainstays in the local Baptist Church and they were close. Peter and Dennis even had nicknames for each other, born of youthful experiences. Dennis was "Money Clip" and Peter was "Flask."

Dennis put his left hand on Peter's right shoulder, still pumping his hand. "Flask! Flask, my man!" he said excitedly. Noticing Emma looking bewildered, he shifted gears. "Peter, it's so great to have you home! I've missed you, buddy. Nobody around to have fun with since you left."

Peter responded with a big, warm smile of his own. "It's great to be home. Missed everything we always did together."

Dennis sat down at the table with them. Peter lost interest in his sardines and crackers. Emma took a bite out of her biscuit and molasses, swallowed and said, "I'm Emma." Apparently, she needed to call attention to herself to get any.

"Oh, sorry. I'm Dennis Langley. Sorry to butt right in on your lunch, and not even introducing myself."

Peter said nothing. He was never one to take much initiative in making appropriate introductions, and he wished Emma would leave the scene.

"Flask, tell me about it all. All you've done since you left. Mama sent me a clipping from the news . . . about you getting a big bravery award and all. Can't wait to hear more about that."

"Not much to tell. How's that school up there in Nashville . . . that Vanderbutt, or whatever . . . can't exactly remember the name."

Dennis chuckled. "*Vanderbilt.* It's fine . . . Nashville's okay. But I don't care much about school. Can't wait to get through and get home."

"What're you doing home now?" Emma said in a cold tone.

"Oh, it's Uncle Randolph. He died Tuesday over in Marley and I had to come home for the funeral. Going back to Nashville on the train tomorrow afternoon."

Emma took a bite of her biscuit, looking bored.

"Come out front, Flask . . . got something to show you."

Peter got up, and he and Dennis went out the front door of the store, leaving Emma behind.

"Up there." Dennis pointed up the street about twenty yards. "Red one."

Peter followed Dennis up to a shiny new red Buick. "WOW! Where'd this come from?"

"Key Buick in Hattiesburg, first fancy one they've gotten since the war. Dad says Key owed him . . . got him out of a tight one when his credit dried up a while back."

Peter approached the gorgeous vehicle and rubbed his hand over the shiny hood, stepping back to admire the fancy chrome spoke wheels. "Some car!" Peter was never one for superlatives, but this was the most impressive automobile he had ever seen.

"How about us taking a ride in it to Joe Don's Place in Hattiesburg tonight?" Dennis said. "See what we can find . . . if you know what I mean? Hear there's lots of stuff shows up there on Saturday nights."

Peter looked up from the chrome wheel, vague comprehension beginning to register.

"Stuff?"

"Girls . . . women . . . looking for love . . . looking for excitement, *looking for you and me.* If we can't pick us up some stuff in this thing there's no hope for us, Flask, my man."

"I don't know . . . never been much for any ole woman." He wasn't going to try and explain it, but the only woman for him was Elizabeth. He would go, but only to be with Dennis.

"Now, come on, Flask, you know there's other pleasures . . . more than drinking and getting drunk, ole buddy. And just because you find you some stuff, and get a little of it, doesn't mean you have to go back . . . marry her or anything."

Peter made no response, but he definitely knew about other pleasure. He reached into the open window and stroked the leather seat.

"I want to go, y'all," Emma said. They had not noticed her, but she had quietly slipped up. "I love that Joe Don's Place."

Peter and Dennis both looked up, stunned, having no idea their conversation had not been private, not knowing exactly what part of it she had heard. They made no immediate response. "Dennis and I will have to talk about it," Peter finally said. "We might not even be coming back until tomorrow."

Emma stood there for a moment, looking at them, and then she said, in an indignant voice, a mad, hurt look on her face, "Well, if y'all don't want to me to go, then go on and go without me . . . See if I care." She turned around and stomped back toward the store.

"Who is she?" Dennis finally said.

"She's a girl they hired to work at the store when Evie went off to Baton Rouge."

"Hardly a girl. How old is she?"

"I don't know, maybe about twenty-five or twenty-six . . . older than us."

"You like her?"

"Guess she's okay."

"Anything you don't like about her?"

"Don't know much about her."

"Can she drive?"

"She drives the deliveries all the time, usually in our ole truck."

The two pondered the Emma issue. Then Dennis opened the door to the Buick and reached under the passenger seat.

"Check this out," he said, pulling out a fifth-sized bottle from a brown paper sack. "Bacardi Gold . . . hundred proof."

Peter looked at it briefly and quickly stuffed it back in the paper sack.

"Never cared much for rum," he said.

"Tonight you will, some of the best," Dennis replied, with an air of confidence that the war had not changed Flask that much. "What time you want me to pick you up?"

"We close at five in winter. Is that too late?"

"Pick you up after five-thirty . . . that'll be plenty early."

Peter started walking back to the store. About halfway, Dennis called to him. "Come back, Flask . . . let's talk a minute more."

After Peter came back, Dennis said, "About this Emma. Maybe we ought to take her. You know we've been known to get drunk and wreck . . . This hundred proof is stout . . . *and we've got something big to celebrate*, you comin' back home, and all. Don't think I'd ever come up with a lie that would fly if I wrecked the Ole Man's new toy, that quick after he bought it. At some point we might could use Emma to drive. We'll probably have more fun if we don't have to try and stay sober."

"I don't know. I'll have to think about it. I'm still kinda weak and tired from the flu an all," Peter replied.

"She does have a body," Dennis said, grinning, making a descriptive gesture with cupped hands. "We're not gonna find any stuff in Hattiesburg tonight with anything to beat that."

CHAPTER 16

YOUNG DRUNKS

I t rained on them, off and on, the hour-long trip to Hattiesburg.

Joe Don's, a vintage honky-tonk of renown, was located a mile out from town on a pothole-laced gravel road, a rambling, unpainted shack of many rooms, every surface of gray wood. The main room was a dance floor of wooden planks, with two dozen roughhewn tables scattered along the outer walls, most seating more than four. Two kerosene lanterns at each end of the smoky room cast a soft orange light. Against one long wall was a cast-iron stove, vented through the wall, providing poorly distributed heat.

In the corner was a crude bandstand, where on Saturday nights musicians entertained with fiddle, flattop guitar, banjo, the occasional harmonica, and a worn upright piano, not tuned in years. Alcohol flowed, legal and illegal. Patrons could bring their own or buy from Joe Don, who prided himself in not having much markup.

Responding to public demand, over time Joe Don had added a card room, pool room, and a few crude bedrooms out back for the drunks who needed detoxification, occasionally for those bent on getting some "stuff" and others inspired to let them have it. But Joe Don proudly maintained that his was a clean establishment, known by the locals to mean several things: only a certain level of intoxication was acceptable, generally measured by the demeanor of the drunk; cheats at gambling were unwelcome; and whores were not to be tolerated. The definition of what constituted a whore was vague and undefined. As everything else, it was subject to the present mood of Joe Don Benton.

It was eight o'clock, nearly two hours after dark, when the new Langley red Buick, now well spattered with mud, pulled up in front of Joe Don's Place, stopping in the muddy gravel parking lot. Their arrival would set the tone for the night. Dennis and Peter were in the back seat, already into the legacy of Facundo Barcardi Massó, in the form of rum and coke. Cuba Libre, sans lime. In the front seat was their chauffeur, Emma Bateman.

The trio got out and headed in, heedless of the cold rain. Already mellow, Flask and Money Clip could care less that their shoes were muddy, clothes and hair wet. Emma was not happy about any aspect of this situation.

Joe Don's was definitely a seat-yourself, serve-yourself establishment, with a cover charge for men only, which Dennis paid as they entered. Only two tables were empty, one in the back near the door, another opposite the corner bandstand, which they took. Dennis pulled the rum from its paper sack and placed it proudly on the table, as if he expected it to be the only such bottle in the house, definitely liquor that should impress any stuff he could lure their way.

"I'll get us some more Coke," he announced and headed toward the bar on the back wall.

"I don't drink no alcohol," Emma announced, "but I like Coca-Cola." She reached over and affectionately took Peter's hand. A skinny young blond was singing *Wildwood Flower* at the top of her raspy voice in front of a band . . . guitars, banjo, and fiddle. There was no amplification, and she was no Maybelle Carter. The out-of-tune piano stood mercifully silent.

The patrons at Joe Don's were a mixture of laborers, loggers, railroad workers, farmers, sawmill hands . . . together with their women, or women seeking their company. Men outnumbered women two to one, and the women were all Emma's age or older, most much older. Whatever Dennis had heard about Joe Don's being a prime place for two naive twenty-year-olds to go, hoping to hook up with some prime stuff, it did not appear especially promising at this point. In fact, they may have brought with them their only potential stuff. Emma had no interest in Dennis Langley, but of course, from the day she first met Peter, Emma Bateman was attracted to the returning young war hero, wounded and with a limp, but also with captivating crystal-blue eyes. Peter was definitely the strong silent type. It did not hurt his stature that he came from a local family of obvious prosperity, a young man with potential to give her the security she coveted.

Dennis returned with Emma's Coke. She nodded a word of thanks but did not drink from it. Dennis surveyed the scene, failing to spot a single unaccompanied female. Emma surveyed Peter, who surveyed the scene in general, mainly the band and his rum and Coke. The strong smell of tobacco smoke made him want his pipe, but he had forgotten to bring it.

A big raw-boned man, about forty, with dark hair beginning to recede at the temples, dressed in a red plaid shirt and blue denim pants, approached their table. He had weathered skin and was missing the last three fingers of his left hand. From the look on his face, he recognized Emma.

"Emma," he said in a deep, cheerful voice, "Where you been? . . . Haven't seen you here in a while."

"Not been in here in a while. Got me a job in Glasper . . . been staying around there."

"Well, come on out here and dance with ole Jesse Jack and tell me about Glasper," he said, giving Emma a gentle tug on the arm.

"He's telling a good story and I want to hear the rest of it." Emma gestured toward Peter, indicating she had no interest in dancing with Jesse Jack. The only story that was being told at this point was the lie that Emma had just uttered.

"I dance with him who brung me," Emma announced to Peter and Dennis as he walked away. Once more, later in the night, Jesse Jack made another try, with a similar result. Peter was quite the storyteller. If that was a hint to her younger companions to dance with her, one in particular, the hint was slow to register. For another hour, they sat and drank. Dennis and Peter were down to a third of their bottle of Bacardi and Emma on her second Coke when Dennis finally felt compelled to ask Emma to dance.

"You kinda like my man Flask, don't you?" Dennis asked, when they were out on the dance floor, rum and Coke having long ago relaxed his circumspect choice of words.

"What's this *Flask*, you keep calling him?"

"Just something that goes back to high school . . . when we were running together all the time."

"I don't like it. Wish you'd call him Peter." They danced on for a moment. "I do like him a lot," she admitted, "but he don't pay me no attention. He got him a girl somewhere?"

"Not that I know of . . . you know he just got back from Europe and the war and all."

The band finished its number and they sat back down with Peter. "It's your turn to dance with her now," Dennis said to Peter.

"I'm no dancer," Peter replied, looking at Emma apologetically.

Emma announced that she needed to visit *the ladies place* and went back toward the entrance, obviously knowing where it was.

"Flask, go on and dance with her, at least once . . . you're going to hurt her feelings."

"Never tried to dance . . . don't know how."

"Pick one of the slow ones . . . then hold her up next to you and move your feet around some. There's nothing to it."

Emma's exit made them both realize a need of their own. Realizing what was likely in store for Emma if they left her alone, they alternated trips to the *latrine,* as Peter's military experience inspired him to call it. On his way back, Dennis picked up more Coke and ice, but neither needed it quite yet. Emma still had half her second Coke.

A short time later the band went to "Some of These Days," made popular by Sophie Tucker in 1911. The little skinny blond singer was no more a Sophie Tucker than Maybelle Carter, but Dennis realized this was about as slow a dance as the night might offer.

"Come on Flask, get out there with Emma and show her how you can dance."

Peter found himself out on the dance floor with Emma, having taken dancing lessons from the Bacardi school of dance. He tried his best to do as instructed: move his feet around some and hold her up next to him.

"You're a great dancer, Peter," she repeatedly whispered to him. "I love dancing with you . . . and you sure are a hard muscle man."

Sensing her opening, Emma would drag Peter out on the dance floor, even when the tune was not remotely slow.

Close to midnight, as they were returning from the dance floor to the table, a drunken Peter's bad leg collapsed under him and he fell, knocking over his chair with a crash, drawing looks from all over the room. Emma tried to get him to his feet, and she found herself being assisted not only by Dennis, but by Joe Don Benton.

"You young folks done got too drunk to stay in here," Joe Don said sternly.

"We'll leave," Dennis said, with a bit of a slur.

"You going to have to go out back and sleep it off," Benton said, with authority. "I don't let drunks leave here and get hurt."

"I've had no alcohol, and I'm not drunk," Emma asserted, in a strong positive voice. "I drove 'em here and I'll get 'em home."

Looking at Emma, Benton relented. "Let me help you get 'em in the car and be sure you're the one driving." Benton escorted the trio to the new Langley Buick. A slight drizzle was still falling.

"Hurry up, dammit, I don't wanna get wet!" Benton said, as he pushed Dennis into the back seat.

"Put him in here," Emma instructed, gesturing to Peter and the front passenger seat. As instructed, Benton helped Peter into the front seat with Emma. Peter was the drunker, probably contributed to by his recent injuries and illness. Within two miles, he had passed out, slumped in the corner of the passenger seat against the door. Almost equally drunk but conscious, Dennis babbled incoherently in the back seat, something about being told a lie about the stuff at Joe Don's. Emma paid them little attention, concentrating on her commitment to Joe Don Benton.

Occasionally she reached over and touched Peter on his thigh, and once she said in an admiring tone, "Peter Montgomery, you hard muscle man, you're my favorite dancer ever."

CHAPTER 17

A SUCCUBUS

O nce Emma Bateman began working at Montgomery General Mercantile, traveling back and forth each day from Kershey on eighteen miles of poor road, impassable at times, was definitely not practical. A room in the back of Eva Nell Winstead's dress shop became available and was rented, a block and a half down Main Street. The large single room had a double bed, frayed green couch, table with two chairs, a minimal bath, and a kitchenette. Entry was from an alley that ran along the back of all the establishments on Main Street.

Arriving back in Glasper at almost one o'clock, with her two drunken companions, Emma carefully maneuvered the Langley Buick down the alley and parked near her door. Dennis was asleep on the back seat and Peter had become semi-conscious, incoherently mumbling, at one point trying to sing. Emma thought she could make out "one of these days" from his lyrics. Maybe in his drunken stupor he was thinking about their first dance together, to that Sophie Tucker classic. Then, somewhere in his singing, she heard what sounded like, "One of these days, leeezzz-beeeth." Emma couldn't remember anything like "leeezz-zz-beeeth" in any of the lyrics they had danced to.

She got out and walked to the car door behind her, opened it, and rather roughly shook Dennis. "Wake up!" she said. "I need help."

"*Help*? Where are we?" Dennis said, still slurring his words.

131

"Help me get Peter inside . . . don't think he can stand up."

With Dennis's help, Emma got Peter inside and put him on her bed, taking off his shoes. She found a blanket at the foot of the bed and spread it over him. "You stay here," she commanded Peter, who was too drunk to do much else.

Dennis had plopped down on the couch. "Get back in the car," she said to Dennis in a forceful voice.

"Why? Where are we going?"

"I'm taking you home."

"I'll drive myself."

"You ain't driving nowhere. I told Joe Don I'd get you home and I am."

The Langley residence, a columned mansion, was about a mile away on the edge of town. As she was about to enter the drive, Emma turned off the headlights, and slowly drove around to the side of the house. Dennis was in the front passenger seat.

"You can sleep here in the car for a while or go on in," she said, in a low, firm voice. "Don't matter to me. Did what I promised . . . got you home."

"How are you going to get back?" Dennis asked.

"Walk," Emma said.

She walked as fast as she could without running, anxious to get back to Peter . . . worried about him getting up drunk and falling, worried about him trying to find his way home. Emma didn't want him to leave, not tonight. The rain had faded into a soft chilly mist. She pulled her jacket as tight as she could around her neck and covered the distance in fifteen minutes.

When she came in the door, she was winded, breathing hard. In the dim light of the lamp she could see Peter, lying on her bed, the blanket pulled tightly under his chin. Emma sat on the couch, looking over at Peter, watching the rhythmic rise and fall of his chest. When she had caught her breath, she went over to him, standing by the bed, and touched him on his shoulder through the blanket.

"How are you doing, my darling?" she said in a soft voice.

He looked up at her with weak, glassy eyes, still most intoxicated.

"I don't feel so good. I'm dizzy and headachy."

"You just let Emma take care of you," she said, and pulled the blanket up even closer to his chin.

"I feel worse when my eyes is open . . . and can't hold my head up good," he said.

"Then you just keep 'em closed."

"And I'm cold," he said, in a weak, mournful tone.

"It's probably them damp clothes you got on," she said. "We need to get them off you and get you good and dry."

With that, she gently rolled Peter to each side until she had pulled off his shirt and undershirt. She reached down, unbuckled his belt, then opened his fly.

"Pick yourself up for me a little. Let's get these ole pants off too."

She pulled off his pants and underpants simultaneously, followed by his socks. She had not envisioned it like this, but she had him where she had been imagining him; completely naked and in her bed. She gently pulled a sheet and blanket over him, then found yet another blanket to use.

He lay still and quiet, apparently drifting off to sleep, the heavy smell of alcohol on his breath. For a while she sat on the couch across from the bed, watching him sleep, then she got up and methodically took off all her clothes, folding and placing them neatly on her dresser. Turning off the lamp, she left the room in total darkness.

Emma got into bed with him, pressing her naked body against his, gently stroking the tips of her fingers across his hairy chest. She put her head down on the pillow beside his, knowing what she wanted as soon as he was capable, in the mode of a succubus biding her time.

An hour later, he began to stir, to stammer, to talk incoherently, something about ships and picnics. Emma slipped her hand down across his stomach, and on below, until she found what she wanted, got it how she wanted it, and then put it where she wanted it. When, in his drunkenness, Peter realized what was happening, who he was with, his desire to be faithful to Elizabeth, his conscience, cried out for him to stop. It was too late! When he pulled away and lay back on the bed, Emma moved to be beside him, her cheek on the pillow, her arm across his body. "I love you, you big ole good sex man," she murmured. He made no response. Emma said nothing more. She did not repeat it. At that point she did not want to know if he had heard her.

For ten minutes they lay there together, the covers pulled up over them, naked, silent. Then he got up and sat on the side of the bed, elbows on his knees, face in his hands, still quite intoxicated, but his head beginning to clear enough for him to have some balance. He got up, found a light, turned it on, started locating his clothes and putting them on.

"What are you doing, Peter Montgomery," Emma said, in a voice of disapproval.

"Going home."

"But you can't go home. You're still drunk, and ain't no way you can explain yourself."

"I'm going home." He walked out of her place and down the alley toward Montgomery Mercantile.

Dawn was breaking. The rain had abated, but a chilly mist still hung in the air. When Peter got to Montgomery Mercantile, he pulled out his key, opened the back door, and went in. In a back storeroom he took two horse blankets off a stack for sale, placed a sack of flour on the floor for a pillow, covered himself with the horse blankets, and went to sleep.

He slept until mid-morning, when church bells rang out across the town. He waited until he knew his family would be seated in their accustomed pew on the third row of the Baptist Church, then slinked home. Up in his room, he climbed back in bed.

In mid-afternoon, he awakened. His hangover had subsided and he was hungry. Downstairs, he found the remains of the Sunday dinner. All he found he really wanted was some leftover fried chicken and cornbread, and sweet tea. His mother heard him and came into the kitchen.

"What happened to you last night? Why didn't you come home?"

"We had car trouble in Hattiesburg . . . had to spend the night over there."

"Well, we worried about you. You could have somehow let us know." She gave him a disapproving look and walked out. Peter finished his chicken, put the bones in the garbage and his dirty dishes in the sink. He hurried back up the stairs. At Evie's desk he took out the now familiar stationery, and he wrote:

Dear Elizabeth,
I'm not doing so good here without you—
I sure hope you're doing better than me—us not being together
and all—
I love you—so much—
Peter

He could not believe he had not been faithful to Elizabeth the way he intended to be, the way he hoped she was being faithful to him. Now he had even more reason to be unhappy. Guilt.

He dreaded going to work the next morning, seeing Emma, dealing with her. He knew that Mondays were usually busy and they needed him. In good conscience he could only wait so long to show up. When he arrived an hour late, it was indeed a busy Monday morning.

His father was closing the sale on a potbellied woodstove, a major sale. His mother was showing Nannette Rigby a set of fancy dishes, a potentially big sale. Emma was about the mundane business of measuring ten pounds of cornmeal for Emery Blackstone. The minute Peter walked in Homer Lee Howard came in, wanting biscuit flour. Peter savored the opportunity to find Homer Lee biscuit flour. Homer Lee decided he wanted a gallon of black strap molasses, and Peter got it for him.

Throughout this hectic morning, all four of them were occupied servicing customers. At times Emma passed him, giving an oppressively intense look. He avoided her gaze.

In late morning, the store traffic slowed. Then the store cleared of customers. Lila decided to go home and wash some clothes, and P.W. went to the bank. Peter was left alone with Emma.

He hoped what was coming was not a confrontation, just a mutually embarrassing recognition of what had happened. The minute he sat down at the table in the back, he saw Emma approaching him, with an ardent look. She took a chair, reaching over and grabbing his hand.

"You was mighty good to me, Peter Montgomery," she said. "You're the best big ole long-last man ever there's been. I can't wait for you to give me more good loving."

He looked away.

"Emma, I'm sorry that happened. Please forgive me for doing that to you, and all."

Her face reddened. Her voice became high and angry.

"You mean that's all there is to it? Didn't mean nothing to you? You just wanted that one time. You got what you wanted like all you men wanna do, and now I'm nothing. I'm trash. Trash you're gonna just throw away like I'm nothing . . . nothing at all. Trash for you to use and throw away."

"Emma, I didn't mean for that to happen. You're not trash and I'm not treating you like trash. It just happened. I don't even know how. I'm so sorry."

Emma got up, storming down a store aisle and out the front door. The little bell tinkled, and Peter was glad she was gone; he didn't know what else he could say. He hoped a customer would come in before Emma came back. To his relief, several did.

～

The ensuing weeks brought a period of uncomfortable respect between Peter and Emma. She appeared to respect the fact that he had no romantic interest in her and did not intend to engage in more sex with her. He respected her apparent appreciation of this.

Five weeks after her seduction of the drunken Peter, in midmorning, Emma was leaving Montgomery Mercantile to make a delivery in the trusty delivery truck when P.W. Montgomery shouted to her, "Emma! On the way back, stop by the post office and get the mail out of our box. I'm expecting a rebate check from American Hardware, anxious to see how much it is."

Emma did as instructed and picked up the mail. As she started out the door of the post office, Bryan Scruggs called out to her: "Come back. I've got something else, for Peter." Emma went back to the counter.

"Here's a stack of letters returned from London. I told Peter his Elizabeth Baker wouldn't likely get those letters with no better address than he was giving . . . tell him I'm mighty sorry. I was really pulling for him . . . could tell he was anxious for her to get them." Emma had a strange look on her face. Scruggs couldn't tell what to make of it.

On the way back to Montgomery Mercantile, Emma made a quick stop by her room, where she dropped the letters in the drawer with her underwear. She'd read them later.

CHAPTER 18

AN ISSUE OF ABORTION

losing time approached at Montgomery Mercantile the following Friday and the store cleared. Lila left first heading for the front door.

"Going up to Eva Nell's and get some things she has hemmed for me," she said before leaving P.W. to lock the door behind her. Peter was restocking the seed bins. Emma stood by idly, looking out the window near the side door.

"I'm leaving too," P.W. announced. "You young folks lock up for us." He walked out the side door.

Emma locked the door behind him and walked up to Peter, giving him a steely look with her beady dark eyes. In a stern voice, she said, "I need to talk to you about something serious. Come up to my place."

"Let's talk here, if you need to talk . . . nobody here but us."

"Then you go lock that back door and meet me at the table."

Peter did as instructed and returned to the table, feeling a sense of dread. Emma was already seated.

"You sit down," she ordered.

Peter sat.

"You and me got something serious to talk about. You done got me pregnant."

Peter felt a cold chill sweep over him.

"I ain't had no period in a long time. Yesterday after we closed at noon, I went to Hattiesburg and saw Dr. Perry, somebody I went to when I lived there. He done some test and says I'm pregnant."

Peter's cold chill was now augmented by queasiness. He was speechless.

"You gonna have to decide what you gonna do about this, Mr. Peter Montgomery. I didn't get in this all by myself and I ought not to have to deal with it all by myself. I ain't having no illegitimate young'un. You can marry me and give your young'un a name or you can help me get one of them abortions . . . and you oughta have to take care of lining it up and you oughta be the one paying for it. But if you ain't responsible enough a man to take care of what you done, I'll take care of it and pay for it myself."

Peter said nothing, looking down.

"Well, what you gonna do about this baby you done gone and given me?"

With that, he looked directly at her and said in a firm, strong voice, tainted with anger, "I don't know, Emma. I'm going to have to think about it. When I make a decision, I'll let you know." He left by the back door, leaving Emma sitting there.

～

Thursday of the following week, P.W. Montgomery was sitting in his easy chair, enjoying his favorite nightly toddy, George Dickel Tennessee sour mash whiskey, with a touch of water, over ice. As was customary, the store had closed at noon, and he had gone fishing, his first time this year. The bream were biting and he had caught two dozen.

Peter had eaten the evening meal with his mother and father and had gone upstairs to his room. Lila sat down on the ornate Queen Anne couch across from her husband. "P.W., I think we've got us a problem with Peter," she said, a concerned look on her face.

"What kind of a problem? He's gone off to that war and gotten shot, and nearly died with that flu and all . . . and he seems a little down. But he's trying to help us with the store . . . and he needs a little time to find himself . . . We need to understand he's been through a lot."

"But for the last week he's hardly eaten anything at all, and he's gotten all hollow-eyed again, like he was when he first got home." They sat without speaking for a few moments. Lila looked directly at P.W. and frowned. "Try and talk to him. Find out what's wrong; see if he needs help. You know I hear some of these soldiers, when they come home, all that war and killing has messed up their heads, and they need special medical treatment for all that."

~

Two days later at the store, P.W. put his hand firmly on Peter's shoulder, standing at the cash register. "Son, when we close today, I need to talk to you."

The store cleared of customers and Lila left to prepare the evening meal. Emma walked by Peter, and muttered under her breath, in a harsh tone, "You need to come up and talk to me tonight! I've waited as long as I'm gonna wait on you making up your mind." Then she went out the door, leaving Peter and P.W. alone.

"Son, let's sit at the table and talk a bit," P.W. said.

Peter sat down across from his father, who now wore a somber, concerned look.

"Son, your mother thinks something is wrong with you. She thinks we might need to get you help . . . you know, some professional doctoring or something."

When Peter said nothing, P.W. began to feel self-conscious. Reaching out and fidgeting with the saltshaker on the table, he said, "We about need to fill this up."

More silence. Then P.W. said, "Well, guess that's all I got to say. I promised your mother I'd talk to you. If you think you'd like to talk to some professional . . . you know, somebody who knows about this war kind of stuff and how to help a fellow deal with it, we'll find you somebody."

P.W. stood up and started toward the door. As he was about to reach it, Peter said, loud enough to carry across to him, "Papa, come back. I do think I want to talk to you."

His father came back and stood across from Peter.

"Papa, Emma says she's gonna have a baby, and it's on account of me."

P.W. sat back down, resumed fidgeting with the saltshaker, then the pepper shaker, which was near full.

"You been having sex with that Emma?" he said.

140

"Just once, the night me and Dennis went to Hattiesburg before he went back to Nashville. Dennis wanted to take her with us to be our driver. We got real drunk . . . and somehow I wound up in bed with her at her place. I was too drunk to know what I was doing . . . but I did it to her. Well, I kinda did it to her."

"What do you mean *kinda*? Did you do it to her . . . or not?"

"Well, yessir, I guess so."

"How sure is it that she's expecting?"

"Says she went to a doctor in Hattiesburg last week and he was certain."

"You sure it's yours?"

"I don't know, Papa. She's been after me ever since I got home. And I don't think she's been fooling around with anybody else. You think she may have been?"

"Nothing I've noticed, but I don't get around at night or anything."

They both sat pondering the situation. Then P.W. added, "I guess no man knows positive a child is his . . . sometimes married women even sneak around and have them by somebody other than their old man."

He lined the salt and pepper shakers up against each other and placed them precisely back in the center of the table.

"What do you plan to do about it?" he asked his son.

"Emma says she's ain't having no illegitimate young'un. That I'm gonna marry her or she wants to get one of them abortions . . . and she'll expect me to line it up and pay for it, but if I ain't, she will."

"Guess you can't stop her if she's a mind to, but I'm not for an abortion," P.W. said. "We don't want that. Even if we're not positive about it's your young'un, if you done it to her—even once—we can't be sure it ain't yours. If it is yours, it's my first grandchild. I'm not wanting to lose my first grandchild to no abortion."

Peter looked toward the front of the store. P.W. looked at his now well-aligned salt and pepper shakers.

"Guess I'll marry her," Peter said. "I don't want to, but it seems like my only choice."

"Probably what your mother and I would think . . . for the sake of the child." Then P.W. said, in a soft, sad voice, "I'll go tell your mother."

"Don't tell Mamma yet. I don't want to deal with that right now."

Father and son looked down, and Peter said, "I told Emma today I was going to come up and tell her what I was going to do after we closed."

"All right." P.W. walked out the side door of Montgomery Mercantile and Peter sat at the little table alone, taking up his own fidget with the salt and pepper shakers. He got up, located the large container of salt, re-filled the saltshaker and put it back on the table. Then he left by the back door, heading down the alley to see Emma.

~

A farm truck was parked adjacent to Emma's door. Peter paid it little at-tention, since the back of Clyde Tanner's seed and feed store was directly across the alley and vehicles were frequently parked there.

When Peter walked in, he was face to face with Emma's uncle, Marcel McCoy, who was sitting on the couch across from the bed. He was a massive man, with a full beard, dressed in denim overalls cov-ering a dark brown shirt. He had on heavy boots and was cradling a single-barrel ten-gauge shotgun—the kind used by market hunters to slaughter ducks on the water—the bore an inch across. He stood up, towering nearly six inches over Peter.

"Sit down on that bed over there, boy!" he shouted. Peter did noth-ing, just stood looking at Marcel McCoy and the barrel of the shotgun pointed at him.

"You hear me boy! Sit down on that bed! We're gonna talk!"

Realizing that Peter was not intending to sit, McCoy proceeded to light into Peter where he stood. "Now you listen to me, boy . . . you lis-ten to me good! Emma tells me you done gone and knocked her up . . . "

Peter still said nothing, but he moved his gaze from the barrel of the shotgun to look directly at Marcel McCoy, who was red-faced and shak-ing. For a moment Marcel was taken aback by Peter's look. He obviously was not feeling terrified as was expected. McCoy gathered himself and continued, "You're gonna marry my Emma, boy . . . you're gonna marry that girl! You understand me . . .?"

Hyperventilating, McCoy caught a deep breath, and he thrust the barrel of the ten-gauge menacingly toward Peter's face. "You know what that baby will be boy, what my Emma's baby will be if you don't marry that girl? A bastard! And you know what you'll be, boy? You'll be a sorry, no good, worthless son-of-a-bitch!"

When Peter still failed to react, Marcell McCoy said, in a low, raspy, sinister tone, "And you know what us McCoy men do with sorry sons-of-bitches who do our women wrong? You know what we do with them, boy?" McCoy pulled the hammer back on the shotgun, cocking it with a loud click, and pointing it directly at Peter's face.

Peter took a quick step forward, snatching the gun from the hands of the startled, wide-eyed Marcel McCoy. He stepped back, uncocked it, then popped open the breach. It wasn't even loaded. He handed it back to McCoy.

"Mr. Marcel," he said, in a modest, respectful tone, "I ain't scared of you and I ain't scared of your gun. I've been shot at, and I've been hit. I've killed half a dozen men . . . didn't even know why I was killing 'em . . . except maybe they was trying to kill me, and today I'm wishing they had." Then he took a deep breath, and he said in a tone evidencing a degree of anger and contempt, "Mr. Marcel, you ain't never killed no one—and you ain't never gonna—all you're ever gonna kill is a few helpless ducks you ambush on the water, and some hogs every fall . . . and they can't shoot back at you. If I marry Emma, Mr. Marcel, it ain't gonna be on account of you . . . and it ain't gonna be on account of your gun."

Peter turned and walked out the door and back down the alley, headed for the Montgomery residence, to write a final letter to Elizabeth.

At the little desk in Evie's room he took out her stationery and started writing.

Dear Elizabeth,
Don't know how to tell you this—Don't know how I let this happen.
I'm going to marry Emma Bateman.
I don't want to marry anyone but you—for I love you.
But I've gone and gotten her pregnant.
I love you so much—Know I always will. I feel so bad—
so sorry about what I've done. I hope you can find somebody else
who loves you as much as I do—
Peter

He took out an envelope and addressed it to her at Edmeter Hospital. He would mail it Monday, as soon as the post office opened. He left it on Evie's desk, went into his room, and lay on his back on his bed, staring at the ceiling. Presently, he got up and went back into his sister's room, tore open his envelope, took out his letter and wadded it up.

What was the point of it? How can you tell a woman, *in a way that she can understand*, that you love her with all your heart and soul, know you always will, but you are marrying another woman because you've gotten her pregnant? You can't.

$\sim$

On Saturday, April 5, 1919, at eleven-thirty in the morning, Peter Montgomery and Emma Bateman were married before Justice of the Peace Clinton Doolittle in the back of his county store in the crossroads community of Dempey, five miles out from Glasper. Doolittle was chosen by Peter because he did not want the ceremony in town where his parents, especially his mother, might find out about it before it was over and a done deed. He had been specific with the clerk issuing the marriage license. "Don't tell anyone. We're having a surprise announcement gathering."

Emma had wanted her mother and her Uncle Marcel to be present, but Peter wouldn't hear of it. He didn't want Marcel McCoy to have anything to do with it. Peter wanted no family, except his sister Evie, who had come home from Baton Rouge that morning, heading directly to Doolittle's store. Evie would never judge him, would support him no matter what he did, she always had. He wanted her to be with him.

Doolittle made the ceremony as short and simple as possibly legal. At its conclusion, Evie asked Peter, "You got her any kind of ring?"

Peter looked at her, a bit surprised, even embarrassed. "Not yet," he said.

Evie handed him a small gold band. "Bought this for you, thought you might forget." Peter slipped it on Emma's hand. Evie Montgomery was not at all happy about the situation and was not at all positive about Emma Bateman at this point. But that was Evie, she looked out for her little brother when she could.

Peter Montgomery left Doolittle Grocery a man deeply in love with

Elizabeth Baker but married to Emma Bateman, a man committed to accepting what life had in store for him. He resolved that whatever had happened, it had been of his own doing. People around Glasper, Mississippi, came to say that the experiences and wounds of war had somehow made him turn inward.

~

On Sunday, February 9, 1920, more than ten months after their marriage, Emma Bateman Montgomery gave birth to a son she named Casey Bateman Montgomery. Either she wasn't pregnant when she thought she was, or she had lied to him when she told Peter she was pregnant. He neither questioned her about it nor commented upon it. What was the point? He now held his newborn infant in his hands, a wee little six-pound helpless person who needed his support and love.

~

In early March of 1933, Marcel McCoy died. On his death he left a handwritten will. Marcel's large family gathered in the main room of the McCoy farmhouse to read and discuss it. Emma was present, but Peter was not. It was a long, rambling document, and on the sixth page he had written this paragraph:

> *To my niece Emma's husband —that Peter Montgomery*
> *I leave my old ten-gauge duck gun—and I*
> *want him to know that ever since he gave it back to me*
> *them years ago I ain't shot nothing with no gun—*
> *no creature nor critter—the only way we had*
> *any ham and bacon was Luke had to shoot them hogs*
> *without me around.*

CHAPTER 19

BLESSED BY FRIENDSHIP

eter moved in with Emma in her room behind Eva Nell Winstead's dress shop. Although P.W. and Lila were not unkind and made it clear that they were still welcome to work at Montgomery Mercantile, the tension was apparent between Emma and Lila, and Peter felt embarrassment around his mother. Peter found work at a local sawmill and Emma started a seamstress business, capitalizing on her experience in the garment factory in Hattiesburg.

Ever the loving father and realizing the cramped circumstances of the room behind the dress shop, P.W. soon helped them purchase a forty-year-old house in one of the oldest neighborhoods of Glasper. P.W. was not sure it would be big enough for them, if they had a large family. But Emma had let Peter know she'd "had all the young'uns she intended to have."

Throughout the 1920s, Peter and Emma managed to be proudly independent. Sawmill wages were good by the standards of the time, and Emma did well with the seamstress business she ran out of their house.

Then came the Great Depression. Even then Peter and Emma fared better than many families of the time. Ever the hard-driving one, Emma went into high gear with her seamstress business. This was a time for keeping hand-me-downs and almost-rags held together for the wearing, and her sewing skills were in high demand. Peter had earned favor with the sawmill owners, and when production was shut down, they hired him to keep the equipment looking decent in hopes of a sale. Fortunately, years went by without it selling.

~

Late on a chilly morning in 1933, at a low point in the Great Depression, Peter was alone in the maintenance shack of the long-idle sawmill, smoking one of his newer brier pipes, and pondering his future. The owners had finally sold the equipment and he was to be terminated when it was moved out. Unemployment stood at 25 percent and jobs were almost nonexistent.

His best friend Dennis Langley arrived on the scene in his tan Buick. Sitting down in a chair across from Peter, he looked uncharacteristically serious. Peter was confident Dennis knew he was about to be out of work, since there was little that happened in the county that escaped him.

Dennis's father had been the largest stockholder in the Bank of Glasper when it was chartered in 1897. In 1927, upon the death of his father, Dennis and his sister had inherited this stock and Dennis took over as a very conservative president of the only bank in the county.

Dennis had graduated from Vanderbilt and married a prominent Episcopalian classmate from Atlanta. Peter had joined the Army right after high school and married a hard-shell Baptist, who had dropped out of school after the tenth grade, never venturing further from Glasper than the nearby Hattiesburg. There had been little chance that their wives would be close.

Yet neither Flask nor Money Clip had a closer, truer friend. They relished every opportunity to fish together, sometimes merely sharing a few nips and reliving the experiences of their youth. Hopefully, Peter thought, Dennis's bank was not about to join those other failing institutions, with Dennis seeking out a sympathetic old friend.

"Flask, I think I may have a chance to get you a great new job, with a chance to make some good money," Dennis said. "Wouldn't be opposed to that, would you, old buddy?"

"No."

"Here's the deal. Carolina-Pacific is looking for a place to put a new pulpwood operation. Depression or not. It appears that new technologies allow this old resinous yellow pine to make certain grades of paper, and they can get it real cheap. They're buying this place and two hundred acres over there," Dennis said, pointing out the window to the west. "The railroad's here and there's lots of smaller stuff left all around here that hasn't been cut . . . and, also, there's talk of new Roosevelt money coming into this part of the state, for a nursery and reforestation and they want to be in on that."

"Don't know much about pulpwood and paper and all, but I'm flat needing a job. I'll take most any salary they offer."

"Flask, I don't want you to take a salary. A man can't make real money on a salary."

Peter listened. Salary was all he had ever known.

"When these people come to town, I'll put a hard sell on them to hire you on a commission. I'm going to tell them you know the area, know where the wood can be bought, and know how to deal with the local people and get it bought. I'll make them think they need you much worse than you need them." Sounded like craziness to Peter, but he liked it.

Dennis walked to the window. "Let me work it out for you . . . be your agent on this. After all, if you hadn't lied with me that night in high school I got drunk and wrecked Paw's new car, God knows what he'd have done to me." Peter knew the incident had gained him the lifelong nickname, but he didn't realize it was that special to Dennis.

"If they do hire me, I'll do my best to help them buy whatever wood they need," was all Peter could think of to say.

His agent represented him well and Carolina-Pacific hired Peter as the wood purchase agent for the new plant, with a small commission paid on every ton of pulpwood he purchased for them. Southern yellow pine proved well-suited for pulpwood. The economy began to improve, and the plant was a success. Peter did not lose his penchant for quiet reserve, but he did his job well and the plant stayed supplied with all the wood it needed. Carolina-Pacific was happy with their arrangement. After all, they had been told he was the most gifted man around in buying wood, and the plant stayed in production, making them money.

In 1933, the national per capita annual income was $374. Peter made that every three months, and after 1933 it only got better. At the end of every week he would come home with a handsome check, for several years growing larger each week. When he got home on Fridays, the bank was often closed for the weekend. Before the bank opened on Monday, Peter was off and running, often to nearby counties. "Put it in the bank for us," he would say, handing Emma the endorsed check.

Peter sensed the great pleasure his wife got from all the money he was making, the security it seemed to give her. In 1904, Emma's father had run off to Texas with another woman, deserting her, her mother and four siblings, leaving them destitute, and totally dependent upon her Uncle Marcel. Giving Emma his weekly check, seeing her happiness, gave Peter a sense of pride. Pride in his stature as a man, pride in his ability to be a good provider for Emma and his son Casey.

CHAPTER 20

THE HONORABLE THING

The house that Peter and Emma purchased in 1921 was a hip-roofed structure of six-inch horizontal planks, on two-foot-high red brick support columns with matching red brick chimneys on each side. On the roof, a center ridge extended from front to back, and a small dormer in front had a window of six panes. A porch across the front side was supported by four large, square wood columns and was enclosed by a rail with pickets. Wide wooden steps extended to the ground. The center door was framed on each side by tall, shuttered windows, each with twelve panes.

Large oaks dominated the acre lot, making the lawn bare and dusty. The drive and walk were gravel and dirt, packed hard from years of use. In the backyard was a massive oak and beneath this tree was a small bench; Peter's favorite place in all the world to sit and think.

It could be said that this was his place of worship, for Peter would often take his Bible there with him. He would read a few verses, then sit and think about them. Peter grew up a Baptist, a traditional Southern Baptist, not Emma's hard-shell variety. But after the war he never went to any church. Emma offered an excuse for his infuriating infidelity. She told people he was embarrassed to limp into church. That was not it. Emma's church was not his religion. Peter's religion was his own personal mixture of pantheism and ecumenical Christianity—Peterism, it could be called.

He chose to worship alone, on his bench under the big oak in the back-yard, and he did not limit his times of worship to Sundays.

On this bench, Peter also enjoyed his favorite pleasure, smoking his meerschaum pipe. This pipe was reserved for these special times in the backyard. Emma forbade him to smoke any pipe in the house, which had nothing to do with health issues. Smoking was a sin, and he would not sin in her house. That suited him just fine.

Late one afternoon, on a beautiful and unseasonably mild Saturday in November of 1939, Peter sat in the middle of his backyard bench, smoking his meerschaum. From across the yard his son Casey approached him. Peter expected to hear Casey's usual request to borrow the car. He looked up and smiled. His son was quite robust and handsome, the best young athlete in the town, and the source of great pride.

For the last year, Casey had been involved with a girl in his high school class, Carrie Sims, the daughter of the town's Methodist preacher. Her mother taught the eighth grade in the local school. Requests to borrow the car were now coming on a daily basis, and Emma even claimed her son was in love.

Carrie Sims was a skinny, freckled-faced redhead. Initially, Peter thought her not at all the beauty his handsome son deserved. As time went on, Peter realized what attracted Casey to Carrie Sims. She was positive and cheerful, with a captivating smile and infectious energy. When she was present, she seemed to brighten up the scene.

Today, the usual request for the car did not come. Rather, Casey stood in front of Peter and asked, "Could I sit down?" Peter moved to the side, and Casey sat down next to him on the bench. Peter took a draw on his pipe and blew out the smoke in a long, deliberate stream, which drifted away, catching the sunlight as it cleared the shade.

Peter broke the silence. "County paper in the kitchen. Wrote you up good for the game Tuesday night."

CASEY MONTGOMERY LEADS DIAMONDBACKS WITH 17 had been the headline.

"One of your best games, I thought."

"I saw it," Casey responded, almost in a tone of disgust.

Another long draw on the meerschaum, then another long, deliberate stream of smoke. The wind had calmed and it hung like a loose halo above them. Peter was beginning to feel that this would not be about the car keys. Clearly something was troubling his son.

"I'm mighty proud of you son, passing all your classes, helping our team win games like that. Everybody in town who knows who you are says nice things to me about you. Makes me mighty proud."

Casey had almost mustered his courage, was about to get it out, but these prideful comments effectively blunted his initiative.

A mockingbird lit in the old bird bath, splashed around, and shook himself off, a joyful bird by any measure. Yet another long draw from the pipe, another silver-gray stream sent on its way. The lively bird brought no comment. A colorful kestrel landed high in the open canopy of a big pine at the far side of the yard, eyeing the bird bath, mindful of a potential meal. They both noticed the kestrel, but it brought no comment. It usually would have.

"Got something bothering you, son?"

"Yes, sir."

"Want to talk about it?"

"Yes, sir."

"Up to you."

The mockingbird saw the kestrel and dashed for the cover of the privet hedge at the back lot line. The kestrel swooped over the hedge, as if to demonstrate frustrated contempt, then sailed off into a grove of pines beyond. Peter tried another draw on his pipe, which had burned out, so he gently scraped out the ashes.

"I'm in trouble," Casey finally said, in a low, solemn voice.

"What kind of trouble?"

"Carrie's pregnant."

"You sure? Sometimes they think they is when they ain't . . . sometimes they even claim they is when they know they ain't."

"She's sure . . . says she's about to start to show some. Says she's four or five months."

Peter put the now-empty pipe back in his mouth, holding it in his clenched teeth. Casey felt the now-familiar weak nausea and sense of chill coming back. Peter pulled the empty pipe out of his mouth, and he said, "You're not in trouble son, but you are in a bit of a pickle."

Casey didn't find the distinction impressive, but he felt better, maybe just because he'd finally gotten it out. Sensing the threat had abated, the mockingbird returned to the bird bath. Peter got out his tobacco, refilled his pipe, packed it, and lit it.

"What do you intend to do about it?"

"We want to get married."

"That's what most people would think is the honorable thing. I do hope you love her," Peter said in a slow, deliberate voice.

The mockingbird tired of the bird bath and flew back into the privet hedge. A sparrow came and took its place, joined by others. It had been a dry spell and Peter's bird bath was popular. This time Casey broke the silence, in a wordy spurt of fear and anxiety.

"We want to get married; but we don't know how to go about it . . . what's the best way, and all, and we don't know where we can live . . . how we're going to live." Casey was breathing hard and his pulse was up. He started sobbing, "Papa, we're so scared . . . and we're so ashamed."

Peter put his arm gently around the boy. "We'll work it out, son," he said. "It's nothing that ain't happened to lots of other folks."

Peter lit his pipe again and looked at a mockingbird running the sparrows out of the bird bath. "Mockingbirds get lots of praise for their singing, but they can be pretty mean ole birds . . . don't like to share their turf."

Peter turned toward Casey and said, "Look at me, son." They looked directly at each other. "I'm as proud of you now as I was when you came out that door, son . . . in fact prouder." There was a pause, then he went on, "You not hesitating to do the right thing . . . and marrying her's the right thing; that's being a man when you need to be a man. It's lots easier shooting basketball goals than it is to do the right thing in a tough spot, be a man. And it's mighty good that you love her."

Peter put his arm around Casey, hugged him, and said, "I love you, son . . . and if I'm living, I'll be here for you. I'll do my best to help you."

Pride had been verbalized often, love never before now. Casey's lump in his throat was formidable. He wanted to say something in response but didn't know how. Instead, he hugged his father, got up, and went into the house.

As the door closed behind him, the kestrel came in a blur out of the sky, nailed the mockingbird in the bird bath, and stood over his catch, defiantly sticking out his feathery chest; then he flew off over the privet hedge, clutching the mockingbird in his talons. Peter's pipe had gone out again. He scraped out the bowl, half the tobacco still unburned. Then, holding his empty pipe, he sat for a time, pondering.

The pipe took him back to his time with Elizabeth, when she had given it to him in her flat in London in 1918. Now stained rich golds and browns from years of use, it had been new and white then. Twice he had taken it to a pipe shop in New Orleans and had a new stem put on it, and there was considerable wear about the top of the bowl, yet it was still his favorite possession.

Peter sighed deeply, tucked his chin, and closed his eyes. After all these years, he could still smell her, taste her, hear the captivating melody of her lilting English voice, see the whiteness of her naked body in the warm glow of ambient light, the desire in her eyes as she looked up at him, feel the joy in his heart when he realized he had given her pleasure. Wondering what had become of her, he felt tightness in his throat, overwhelmed by his memories.

"Papa?" Peter didn't hear.

"Papa!" Casey said louder, sensing something was wrong.

Peter lifted his head, opened his eyes and looked at his son, who had returned.

His father's strained look alarmed Casey. It made him feel uneasy at all the pain he had caused.

"Papa, I'm so sorry. I know I've shamed you so . . . shamed us all." Casey began to sniffle again.

"It ain't you, son . . . it ain't you. It's just me. And it ain't about shame . . . you tell Carrie we talked and I'll do whatever I can to help you get married."

"I hope that will help her feel better, Papa." Casey wiped his eyes on his fists, turned and again walked across the yard and back toward the house, convinced his father's troubled countenance was all about him.

Sitting on his bench, Peter began to think about what he could do to help Casey and Carrie. They were just seventeen. Simply getting married at their age would probably involve parental help. They would need a place to live. He couldn't imagine them moving in with him and Emma; she would make Carrie miserable. Nor could he see them moving into the Methodist parsonage. They would need money, maybe a car. He had offered to help them, in any way he could, and he would.

Two of the sparrows came back to the bird bath. Peter got up and pushed his pipe into his pocket, his mind beginning to focus on someone who had been there for him in times like these, someone he knew he could count on. He might know someone willing to help shepherd this new life into the world. His sister Evie.

CHAPTER 21

THE GOLDEN RULE

T he trusty Ford stopped at the edge of Duncan County Lake. Two hundred acres of placid water stretched out ahead in the murky darkness. On this cloudy night, the marsh grasses stood silent and still along the lake bank. Even this late in the year, frogs of all species belted out a steady cacophony. The temperature was in the fifties, so Casey and Carrie did not even bother to crack the windows. He slumped down and leaned against the driver's door, pulling her close, stroking her hair and running his hand down the small of her slender back.

"I love you," he said.

"You better."

"You wanted me to talk to him and I did. He said he would help us any way we wanted him to, that he could. We just had to decide what we wanted to do . . . There's no mistake about one thing. He hopes we'll get married. Papa's made some good money in the last few years and will give us any money we need."

A break came in the clouds, with a full moon showing through. Sensing more danger with more light, the frogs quieted down dramatically. Ripples on the water caught the moonlight and sparked brightly.

"I just want to run away and get married and never come back to Glasper," she said, in a voice unusually loud for her. "Would he loan us his car to run off and get married?"

"Probably. Would you tell your parents?"

"No. They'd try and stop us."

Carrie was in no crying mood tonight but was breathing hard.

"They'd be frantic, not knowing what had happened to you."

"I'd try and call them as soon as I could . . . once we're married."

Casey was picturing a frantic, prim and proper schoolteacher hysterically weeping and a devout preacher praying with desperation.

"I want us to talk to your father together," she said. "You shouldn't have to ask him for things by yourself. It would be for both of us. And he can probably tell us the easiest place to get married quick . . . I remember hearing about some people who ran off to some place in Alabama and got married quick . . . think they had to lie about their age."

"Where do you want to try and meet with him?" Casey said.

"Not at your house. Don't want your mother, Miss Emma, in on it."

"How about out here?'

"If it's pretty, there'll be a lot of people out here in the daytime, fishing and all. How about tomorrow at the church in the middle of the afternoon when we're picking up the trash and straightening up the hymnals, like my father has us doing? Nobody ever comes around the church then, never has."

⁓

The Glasper Methodist Church was a traditional, white-framed church on the outside, with a slate roof and a slate-roofed steeple. Inside, it had a high-beamed ceiling with three tall cathedral windows on each side. There was a center aisle and two side aisles, with pews that could seat eighty, light oak with scrolled curved arms at each end. Immediately beyond the front pew were three steps leading up to the altar and pulpit.

Peter and Casey arrived in Peter's Ford and went into the empty church. Carrie was there, having walked from the parsonage. Peter took a seat in the center pew at the front; Casey and Carrie faced him, taking seats on the steps leading to the altar.

"You decided what you want to do?" Peter asked, when Casey and Carrie did not appear anxious to open the dialog.

"Yes sir," Carrie responded quickly. "We want to just run away somewhere and get married . . . quick as we can. We're hoping we can use your car."

"And that you'll loan us a little money for gas and stuff," Casey added.

"When would you tell your parents?" Peter asked Carrie.

After hesitating, Carrie said, "We'd call them as soon as we were married . . . but we wouldn't tell them before . . ." Her voice trailed off sadly.

"They'd worry that something bad had happened to you . . . maybe been kidnapped or something," Peter said.

"Maybe we could leave some note . . . saying we'd gone off to get married," said Carrie, "but not saying where."

"Why wouldn't you want them in on it?" Peter said, influenced by his realization of how hurt his parents had been a generation before, only letting them know about his marriage afterward. "They love you, would want to be in on it."

"I just want to do it simple as possible," Carrie said. "They'd take over: want it in a church; want me to wear white or something—to have bridesmaids and all that stuff."

Peter gave Casey a stern but loving look.

"Son, you know that Golden Rule?"

Casey did, but it was Carrie who articulated it. "Do unto others as you would have them do unto you," she said, slowly and softly, but with confidence. The Golden Rule was the cornerstone of Peterism, something he wanted them to think more about.

"What would you want your son or daughter to do?" Peter said. "Would you want to be at their wedding?"

He fidgeted with his empty pipe. The Glasper Methodist Church sat in silence at mid-afternoon on this autumn Sunday. Peter looked up and gazed at a stained-glass window behind the altar depicting Christ on the Cross with a caption: "God is Love." Another major tenet of Peterism.

Carrie had heard numerous sermons on hypocrisy and blurted out in an agitated voice, "Look! I'd let you and Miss Emma and my mother and father be there if that was all . . . they wouldn't say anything and wouldn't do anything . . . wouldn't make us feel like hypocrites, me about to have a baby and all."

Peter tapped his pipe on his knee softly, then let it rest there, motionless.

"What if you could do it the way you wanted to, and us parents got to be there, but we didn't try to do anything or say anything?"

"That couldn't happen!" said Carrie. "They'd want to pretend I hadn't gone and gotten myself pregnant and I don't want that."

Peter looked directly at Carrie. "I still want to know, what if you could decide exactly how you wanted it to be. You and Casey get married, and I could get everybody to agree it'd be just that way—all parents not try to get involved or change anything—would you let us parents come see you married?"

She looked at the floor. "You know, Mr. Peter, they'd never let it be that way. Never stay out of it."

"I'd tell them . . . real firm. If they didn't let it be EXACTLY what you wanted, then I'd help you run away." With no positive response, Peter announced, "I'm going out and smoke my pipe."

Leaning up against the Ford parked out behind the church, he packed his pipe and lit it.

The bowl of tobacco was nearly gone when he looked up and saw Casey coming out of the church.

"Can you come in . . . talk to us some more?"

The conference resumed where it had been recessed.

"What have you decided, Carrie?" Peter asked.

"I don't know what to do, Mr. Peter. I don't want to hurt anybody . . . but I don't want to be one of those hypocrites Daddy preaches about . . . don't want to feel even worse than I already do. I may be a sinner, but I'm not one of those hypocrites."

"Carrie, I'll tell you what I told my Casey. It's nothing that hasn't happened to lots of other good folks." Carrie looked up at him, tears streaming down her face.

"You know your Bible," Peter continued, confident she did. "It's right there in that Bible . . . mighty plain . . . Everybody's sinned . . . *everybody*. Paul told those Romans that, right there in that Bible."

Carrie's flow of tears began to subside.

"You want to know who the big hypocrites are, Carrie?" Peter continued. "It's not them who commit sex sin, and are sorrowful. It's them that claims to be good but don't know how to love . . . love nobody but themselves . . . can't love nobody they don't start out liking."

Carrie wiped her eyes. "I haven't done much sinning—except my sex sinning—and I sure wish I hadn't."

"I know," Peter said. "And you are a whole lot better person than most folks . . . and don't you ever think otherwise."

Suddenly Carrie felt the great weight upon her heart was not as heavy.

"Can I have a little more time to think about it?" she asked.

"You know you can," Peter said. "No matter what, I'm still going to help you any way you want me to, if I can. You and Casey think about it and let me know what you want to do."

In this small town, both Casey and Carrie were within easy walking distance of their respective homes. He would leave them be in the church to figure it out. Peter got up and started out, but as he got to the church door he turned and said, "Carrie, I love my Casey as much as I ever did . . . before all this, and I told him so. I'm sure your ma and paw are going to be the same with you. They'll always love you and stand behind you and they'd want to be standing right behind you when you get married."

Outside, as Peter started to open his car door, Carrie ran out of the church, once again crying hard. "Mr. Peter, thank you. You're so good. Casey is so lucky to have you for his daddy." She turned and ran back into the church.

~

Three things did not need deliberating; they were issues that had to be faced no matter how this marriage took place: a car; some money; and a place to live. Sunday was not a day for money or a car, so Peter headed for the pulp mill, where he had a small office, only large enough for a desk and three straight chairs. He did not have to look up Evie's number to make the call. She was now a widow living alone in a quaint cottage three hours north in Jackson, where she worked as a nurse.

After she excitedly answered the phone, Peter explained the issue.

"Of course, they can come live with me. I get lonely at times and I'd love some company . . . and I'd *adore* helping care for a baby. When is the wedding?"

"Don't know that yet."

Peter went home happy to have made progress on this issue.

～

The next morning when Dennis Langley arrived at the bank, Peter was there waiting for him, sitting outside his private office on a couch in the bank lobby. Dennis was surprised to see Peter so early on a Monday morning, and there was no way not to suspect something unusual was up. He ushered Peter into his private office and shut the door.

"What's up, Flask? Something wrong?"

"I need your advice."

"You got it."

"Casey has been going with Carrie Sims, Preacher Sims's daughter. They tell me she is pregnant, and they want to get married."

"Where are they now? Lacking less than a year of high school?"

"Right."

"Sims . . . they know about this?"

"No."

"They sure she's pregnant. You know they sometimes think they are when they aren't. We might should get her tested by a doctor."

"She's sure. Beginning to show. Thinks about four months."

Dennis thought for a moment.

"Of course, Flask, Carrie will have to drop out of school. Can't stay in school pregnant. Guess Casey could. She'll probably want to leave town. Imagine the Simses will want to leave town too. In my experience, preachers don't stand up to shame well, especially stuff involving sex. I can check on homes for unwed mothers for you, if you'd like me to. Then, I guess, there's always abortion."

Peter felt a chill.

"Hear it's available in New Orleans. Some woman down on Cartels Street is supposed to be good with a coat hanger, long as she's good and sober . . . did one for somebody here in the county couple of years ago. Far as I know went okay . . . but I can't imagine anybody risking that. Wouldn't chance it with my daughter."

"Casey is definitely gonna marry her, Money Clip."

Dennis gave Peter a warm, affectionate smile. After all, Casey Montgomery was Casey Montgomery.

"I've lined up my sister Evie in Jackson for them to live with. Actually, she seems excited about them coming, living alone so long like she has and all."

"That sounds perfect. Casey might even keep on in school and grad-uate. 'Course a pregnant girl can't continue in school anywhere I know of . . . considered too bad an influence."

"I've promised to help them with a car and any money they need. Don't need any help with the money. What I need your advice and help with is a car."

"What kind of car are you thinking about?"

"Certainly not a new one. Just something to get around . . . get to the hospital, if they need to. Wondering if you have any bank repo that might do?"

Dennis got up and stuck his head out the door.

"Mildred, call Tom and see if we have any car repos."

They sat quietly and waited.

"Won't take long," Dennis said, to break the silence. "We usually don't have but a few, often none."

Mildred put down the phone and came to the door.

"Tom says we have one . . . neat little green Ford. Two hundred dol-lars. Says it's got some miles, but it seems in good shape."

"I'll take it," Peter said, looking at Dennis, then at Mildred.

Item number two checked off.

"How much money do you think I should give them?" Peter asked.

"Oh, start them off with a hundred dollars. You've been making good money and that shouldn't be much for a well-heeled guy like my Flask." Dennis went to the door again. "Mildred. Look up Peter's ac-counts and let us know what's the best of his accounts to draw about three hundred from."

Sitting back down, he said, "Flask, I know you're upset. Can happen to anybody. It'll work out."

Peter sat, expressionless.

"Can't understand what's taking Mildred so long. This is not that big a bank," Dennis said.

Finally, Mildred came to the door. "I see two accounts. A savings account in the name of Mrs. Emma Bateman Montgomery with a balance of $16,125.12. A joint checking account in the name of Peter Montgomery and Emma Montgomery with a balance of $28.70. I don't see any account from which Mr. Montgomery could draw more than $28.70."

"You positive?" Dennis said. "Go look again."

"I've already looked again . . . and again. That's what took me so long. I'm positive this bank has no account from which Mr. Montgomery could withdraw more than $28.70."

Dennis saw on Peter's face a look he had never seen before: a mixture of shock, embarrassment and anger. Peter sat for a minute saying nothing, then he said, very sternly, "I'll be back." With that he walked out.

"I'll hold the car for you," Dennis shouted after him but Peter did not look back.

Speeding on the streets of Glasper on a Monday morning was bound to elicit comments, and Peter gained some attention this particular morning. He arrived shortly in front of his house, shaking with anger.

When he went in, Emma was sitting in the kitchen in a cotton print housedress, unkempt, barefoot, sewing and drinking coffee. She was shocked to see him at this time on a Monday morning. It was immediately obvious that something was wrong. She had never before seen her husband looking like this, red-faced and trembling with rage.

"What do you mean putting all my money only in your name?" he shouted.

She made no immediate response, struggling for an acceptable answer.

"Damn you, woman! What do you mean putting all my money in your name?"

"It's not all your money. How much do you need?" she finally said. Then she shouted back at him, "And you'd better not cuss me again like that if you know what's good for you!"

He stood for a moment, continuing to shake, his face getting redder.

"Five hundred dollars!"

"What do you need that much money for?" Only another woman or gambling debts could be involved at that level.

"You'll find out soon enough!"

"Then you're not getting it!"

They glared at each other.

"I want half of it . . . and I want it today!"

"You're not getting it!" There was no way some other woman would take her money and leave her and her son in want like her father had done.

Peter went to their bedroom and pulled a drawer with some of his clothes completely out of the chest. He turned and walked past Emma and outside, drawer and all.

"What are you doing?" she said when he came back in for the second drawer.

"I'm leaving you, woman . . . and I'm not coming back. I've worked hard for that money, but you keep it . . . and that's the last damn dime of mine you'll ever get."

With that he continued making trips to the Ford.

Sensing that this might be a developing crisis she didn't want, Emma said on one of his return trips, rather reluctantly, "All right, I'll give you your five hundred dollars." He ignored her, continuing to take his things out to his car.

Peter drove back to the bank and parked in front. For ten minutes he sat in his car, trying to calm himself, not wanting to make a public scene. Then he walked across the street, into the bank lobby and straight into Dennis's office, uninvited and unannounced. Dennis's secretary, Mildred Avery, looked up in alarm as he stormed by, but she could do little. Peter was already seated in front of Dennis, who looked up at his friend.

"Got your money business worked out?"

"You could say that. Told Emma to keep the damn money. I'm leaving her."

"Don't you think that's overreacting a bit, Flask? A judge would give you at least half." Dennis was not about to preach reconciliation; he had never cared much for Emma, knowing she had trapped Peter into marrying her.

Peter sidestepped the issue. "Guess I need a loan."

"How much?"

"Maybe five hundred: two hundred for the car; a hundred for the kids; two hundred for me . . . to find a place to live and start over."

Dennis called Mildred. "Fix a note for Mr. Montgomery . . . five hundred dollars, due in a year, two percent."

This was not exactly the way Peter had envisioned it taking place, but items two and three on his initial list could now be checked off. At this point it was up to Casey and Carrie . . . well, Carrie, he thought. Casey would do whatever she wanted.

CHAPTER 22

A FOUR-SENTENCE PRAYER

Later that afternoon, a calmer Peter was sitting in his office at the pulp mill, smoking his pipe, fidgeting with fifteen twenty-dollar bills and a bill of sale for the car, contemplating not only his son's future, but his own. School let out for the day and out the window he saw Casey coming down the dirt road that led into the pulp mill. His son came in and sat down in one of the office chairs.

"See the green Ford Coupe out front?" Peter asked.

"Yes, sir."

Peter handed him the keys. "It's yours."

Casey tried to act excited and he was, but the overall weight of the occasion, the wedding talk that was coming, tempered his reaction.

"That will sure help us . . . thanks."

"Let's go check it out," Peter said.

They went out and got into the Ford Coupe, Casey behind the wheel.

"Crank her up," Peter said, and Casey did. They smiled at each other, pleased at the powerful steady purr of the motor.

"Want to take her for a spin?"

"I think we need to talk about the wedding, Papa. Carrie's made some decisions."

They got out and went back into Peter's office. Peter preempted him again.

"I talked to Evie and she says you and Carrie can live with her for a while in Jackson, and here's some money for you." On impulse, he handed Casey ten twenty-dollar bills, keeping the rest for himself, not exactly what he had represented to Dennis when he had borrowed the money.

"We can go live with Evie? That would be great . . . Gosh! We don't need this much money." Casey stared at the money in his hand, by far the most cash his hands had ever held.

"Then don't spend it unless you need to." Peter thought it was about time to get to the point.

"What did you and Carrie decide?"

"She'll let the parents come to the wedding if you can get them to agree that it will be just her way, and no changes . . . and we mean *no* changes. She wants parents only, no brother or sister. She wants it outside on the bank of the Duncan County Lake in the afternoon right before sundown. She wants it done by some judge or somebody . . . no preacher. And she wants the shortest ceremony possible."

"Is that all?" Peter said.

"All I can think of . . . but Papa she really means this. If anyone else shows up, if any changes appear to be coming, we're gonna leave . . . gonna walk away and try to get married somehow, somewhere else. Carrie wants to be married by Sunday."

Peter lit his pipe with a series of short, hard puffs, then slowly exhaled a long stream of gray smoke, which formed a misty cloud above them in the small office. "Sounds like she's only giving me a few days to work this out," he said.

"Yes sir." With no more news to report, Casey asked, "Can I take the car and go see Carrie now?"

"Sure."

Outside as Casey approached the car, he heard Peter calling from the office door. "Come back. I forgot something."

When Casey walked back, Peter handed him a small object. "You may want this," he said.

Casey opened his hand, saw a small gold wedding ring. Somehow a fourth item had crept onto Peter's list. Tears formed in Casey's eyes and he hugged his father.

Casey said nothing more. He walked back to the car, started it, and drove away, still teary-eyed and with a lump in his throat . . . feeling so blessed to have his papa.

$\sim$

The day was ending and Peter was still sitting in his office. He would usually be going home at this time, but he didn't know where to go. He could sleep in his office for at least this night. While he was considering the possibilities, Dennis showed up in his office doorway. "Damn, Flask. How do you stand all this smoke?"

Peter got up, opened the only window, and cracked the door.

"How you doing, buddy? I'm a bit worried about you."

"I'm fine. Just got to figure out some plan."

"Come drive somewhere with me. Got something to show you."

They got into Dennis's Buick and headed west out of town, toward the setting sun. After about five miles, Dennis pulled into a gravel drive with large spreading oaks on each side, heading up toward a modest white farmhouse.

"Let's go check this out."

At the house, they walked up five wooden steps onto a porch running its full length. The place needed painting but showed little rot. Dennis got out a large ring of keys and tried several until he came upon the right one. Inside, it needed obvious repairs, but nothing that appeared major. Dennis worked the key off his key ring and handed it to Peter.

"Move in here for a while. My sister and I bought this place not long ago as an investment, came with a hundred and twenty acres. We have no immediate plans and someone staying here will keep the vandals out. If you and Emma don't get your problems worked out, you may want to buy it."

$\sim$

"Something's wrong with this picture!" Peter thought to himself that night as he lay on the bare floor in this abandoned house, some clothes under his head for a pillow, his overcoat and boots still on to keep him warm. "I'm not the one who got her pregnant, not the one who is pregnant. But I'm the one who has to tell her parents and get them to agree on this wedding like she has dictated it must be. How did this happen?"

Peter had no idea what to say, how to say it, when and where to say it.

He was beginning to wish he had never come out with his Golden Rule statement. But at this point there seemed no turning back; he had made a commitment to help the kids out.

He decided to show up just after seven, time for the preacher and his missus to have completed their evening meal, but before they would be in bed. At the parsonage door, Peter was still struggling with what he should say. He had never felt as inadequate to any task in his life, nor dreaded any more. Carrie's parents had faithfully attended school and athletic events since they had come to town. Both families knew their children were dating, and they had exchanged pleasantries from time to time, but little else.

Carrie's father came to the door. He was a small, lean man, even smaller than Peter, clean-shaven, fastidious by any measure, dressed in formal black shoes, pants to a blue suit, and a white collared shirt. Maybe he had been to a funeral or some such occasion and taken off only his coat and tie.

"Could I talk with you?" Peter asked.

"Certainly. Come in."

After years in the ministry, Reverend Robert B. Sims was accustomed to impromptu visits by those feeling a need for counsel or advice about the issues of their lives, and not only by folks from his own flock. He showed Peter to the parlor and invited him to sit down. "Good to see you, Mr. Montgomery. What can I help you with?" he said in his trained voice of concern and sympathy.

"I'd like to talk to you and Mrs. Sims together."

Robert Sims's countenance changed abruptly. "Something wrong with Carrie? Has she been hurt?"

"She's fine, but I need to talk to both you about her."

"Irene, come here!" he shouted back into the bedroom. "Something has happened to Carrie!"

Dressed in a simple housedress and slippers, certainly not dressed for company, Irene Sims came quickly out to join them. "What's happened?"

"She's not hurt," Peter said, in the most reassuring voice he could muster, "but she does have a problem. Please sit down."

They did, but on the edge of their seats. Peter could see no other way to get to the point. "Carrie's pregnant. She and my son Casey want to get married."

"Oh, no! Oh nooooo," Irene wailed.

Robert Sims's face reddened and he began to shake.

"I knew he was a bad boy," said Irene, sobbing almost hysterically, "a boy who would take advantage of my Carrie and mess her up . . . if he could. Robert, we should have never let her fool around with that boy!"

Robert Sims remained silent.

Irene kept wailing, "We taught her right . . . We tried to make her into a good Christian girl." Irene Sims looked at Peter with hatred in her eyes. "Your boy's such a bad boy to ruin Carrie's life like this."

"Carrie had her part in it," Robert Sims said in a loud voice. "She's the one who ignored what we tried to teach her. That boy didn't do anything she wasn't willing for him to do!" Peter wanted to verbally agree with that comment, but he tactfully refrained.

Robert Sims lowered his voice, but it had a sinister tone. "That boy of yours better be intending to do the right thing and marry her."

Peter had opened with that, but it appeared to need repeating. "Of course, he is."

Peter proceeded to explain that they had intended to run away somewhere and get married, but that he had prevailed upon them to let the parents attend the ceremony. Carrie had agreed, provided it was all exactly as she decreed.

Irene Sims had stopped wailing, but tears were still flowing down her face.

"Surely she will let us have a private service at the church or here at home with a preacher and not some justice of the peace or somebody like that marrying them."

"Right now, I'm not thinking Carrie deserves much of a formal wedding," Robert Sims interjected, in a tone of contempt for his daughter.

"It needs to have some dignity," Irene said, again beginning to wail. "She's made a mistake, but she's not trash."

"She's been acting like it," her husband said.

Irene wailed louder.

Robert Sims then fixed his gaze on the floor in front of him, in a strange glassy-eyed trance. He began to tremble and Peter sensed a mounting intensity in his being, and fully expected him at any moment to turn upon him with a verbal assault, even worse than that of Irene. But it didn't happen.

"All I know is what Carrie told me about running away and getting married," Peter said, ready to consider his mission accomplished, and ready to leave this strained scene. "And your daughter seems to be one who means what she says . . . and is going to go through with what she says she is going to do." The Simses would not argue with that. Peter added, "I try to be a man who honors his word. If they want a car and some money to run off and get married I *will* see that they have it. I do wish you would consider going along with this and letting me try and handle it for all of us."

"We'll have to think about it some," Robert Sims said. "This has caught us off guard and we are most upset."

"I know you are, and you need to have you some time to think about it," Peter said, getting up to leave.

~

The wedding was to be the following Sunday afternoon at five, on the south edge of Duncan County Lake, in the parking area of a boat launch. Making the arrangements, Peter knew all the details. Others had been notified of the date and time but had only been told they would be given the location an hour or two in advance. As Carrie said, "No uninvited guests, no changes, no fanfare . . . *if so, we're gone.*"

That day the temperature had dropped into the high forties and a chilly north wind rolled small whitecaps toward the scene. Peter prevailed upon Elmer Johnson, a local justice of the peace, to perform the ceremony. Elmer was a functioning alcoholic. His Sunday routine was to be sober for morning church, try and not drink until five on Sunday afternoon, but he was most ready for a drink by five. Elmer wanted to move the wedding up to three, but Carrie didn't approve. Peter solved yet another problem by promising him a bonus. Thankfully Elmer was not a Methodist and a member of Robert Sims's congregation.

On the lakeside, three old, flat-bottomed johnboats had been pulled up on the bank and turned upside down. Carrie and Casey were the first to arrive, and they got out of their car, walked over and sat on the middle johnboat. Ten minutes later Peter and Elmer Johnson arrived in Peter's Ford. They had one additional passenger who had been cleared in advance with Carrie: Evie.

These five assembled in front of the johnboats, the best apparent backdrop for this planned outdoor wedding. Elmer handed Casey a small notebook containing his standard wedding ceremony. Casey handed it to Carrie, and she looked at it carefully. Indeed, it was as minimal a ceremony as Elmer could use and feel right accepting his fee. Next to arrive were the Simses, in a well-used Chevrolet, appropriate for a country preacher. Last to arrive was Emma, in a Ford truck she had borrowed from her youngest sister's husband, Donnie Ray Dudley.

The dress for the occasion was truly eclectic. Most wore their best Sunday church clothes, except for Elmer Johnson and Peter. Elmer Johnson—whose slight slur indicated he was operating on Eastern and not Central Standard Time—had on denim bib overalls, his work boots, and his horse-feeding brown jacket. Peter had on a new blue suit he and Evie had picked out when he was in Jackson helping her get ready for the newlyweds. In front of Elmer Johnson stood Casey and Carrie, behind them in a straight row stood the others. Emma made a point of positioning herself next to Peter and attempted to hold his hand. He refused.

"You need to act right . . . act like we are a family. Act like we love Casey and are with him in this," Emma muttered in a tone of scorn, loud enough to make Peter uncomfortable, loud enough for most of the others to glance inquiringly in her direction. Emma had never learned the fine art of whispering. Fearing a scene, Peter reached out and took her hand. She squeezed his hand; he did not squeeze back. Emma looked like she was about to lose her temper. Feeling a mounting anxiety, Peter weakly squeezed her hand. Mercifully the ceremony began. When it did, Peter relaxed his hand and pulled it away.

"Dearly beloved," the justice said, reading from his notebook, balanced on his prominent belly. And so began what was to be as short and to the point a wedding ceremony as Carrie could have ever asked for.

"Who gives this woman to be married to this man?" Elmer Johnson said, rather dramatically.

Robert Sims was caught unprepared—there being no wedding rehearsal—but he was quick to respond. "Her mother and I do," he said in a firm, strong voice.

When the time came for the exchange of rings, Casey was ready with the ring he had been given. Carrie was ready as well. Knowing Casey had his ring for her, Peter had purchased a small man's wedding ring in a pawn shop when he was in Jackson with Evie, and he had slipped it to Carrie.

"I now pronounce you man and wife!" proclaimed Elmer. "You may kiss the bride." A weak, lips-to-lips embarrassed peck followed. At that point something occurred that surprised everyone except Elmer Johnson, Robert Sims, and Carrie.

The day before, Robert Sims had approached his daughter in the kitchen and made a private request. "When you are pronounced man and wife, could I please bless your marriage with a short prayer?" he had asked.

"I'll think about it," she answered, somewhat surprised, since he had been treating her with such disdain.

The next day she privately gave him her answer. "You can pray, but it can be no longer than three or four sentences."

Elmer Johnson remembered his cue, one of his most outstanding wedding moments. "And now the bride's father, the Reverend Robert Sims, will bless this occasion with a word of prayer," he announced in a loud, pompous voice.

Carrie's father stepped up beside Elmer Johnson, faced the group, and prayed. "Dear Lord, we thank you for Carrie and Casey. Bless their marriage and bless this child that Carrie nurtures within her. May they always love each other, love others and love You. In Christ's name, we pray. Amen." Robert Sims had honored his commitment to brevity.

"AMEN!" Emma said in a loud voice, echoing Reverend Sims, in the tradition of her fundamentalist faith. Not being of quite that vocal a tradition, somewhat surprised, the rest of the group glanced at her, with the exception of Peter, who stared ahead with clenched hands, anxious for the ceremony to be over with no unpleasant incident. He had done what he set out to do; he had seen that his son and Carrie Marie Sims were married with grace and dignity, in the presence of their loving parents, without an iota of hypocrisy.

CHAPTER 23

EGO NEEDS

F ollowing their wedding, Carrie and Casey packed their belongings in
the Ford and headed to Jackson. Evie was excited about them coming
and spared no effort or expense to ready her place for them.

The first of Lila and P.W.'s two children, Evie had always been gangly
and rawboned, long-faced and buck-toothed, but very smart in school.
In adolescence she had been several inches taller than the boys her age.

In 1917, she became restless while her younger brother was going to
Europe to fight. She was stuck in a dull, unexciting life of working long
hours at Montgomery Mercantile. Moving to Baton Rouge in early 1918,
she began training as a nurse, hoping to join the war effort, but the war
ended first.

Upon finishing her training, Evie took a job at a local Baton Rouge
hospital, where in 1927, soon after her thirtieth birthday, she met a Cajun
by the name of Auguste "Gus" LeBlanc. At forty-four, Gus was a bald,
big-bellied, ruddy-faced fellow who had come under Evie's care after suffering serious injuries in an oil refinery accident.

One day when Evie was changing the dressing on his badly-injured
leg, he had said, with a distinct Cajun accent, "I really do like the way
you touch me, you pretty little sweetie. You sure are a beautiful little
lady. I know all them men around here are after you . . . for sure." As
he talked, he looked her up and down admiringly, rolling his eyes as

seductively as he could from his bed, like she was a beauty beyond belief.

She had ego needs; he had his needs; and within six months, Evelyn Montgomery became the third wife of Auguste "Gus" LeBlanc. LeBlanc was from Plaquemine, a town a short distance south of Baton Rouge. He was from a big, boisterous Cajun family, and soon Evie was in a completely new world: a world of Cajun food and traditions, Cajun parties and festivals, and a Roman Catholic world at that.

Evie loved this family and this life. A thirty-year-old lifelong wall-flower, heir to a Scots-Irish Protestant tradition of church revivals and old-time gospel music, she learned to overeat, drink heavily, laugh loudly, to dance with men she had just met. As the third wife of Gus LeBlanc, a new woman was born: Evelyn LeBlanc, a happy, fulfilled woman by any measure.

In her second year of marriage she became pregnant, and in 1929 she and Gus had a son they named Auguste Claude LeBlanc. A big baby, with a birth weight of over eight pounds. Gus nicknamed him "Gator," thinking this would be imposing and macho. Evie didn't care. She loved her baby; and she loved her man.

Then in the spring of 1932, disaster struck. One weekend she was assigned duty at the hospital and Gus was to care for little Gator. Ever the restless type, Gus put the child in the car and headed out for Plaquemine, where he wound up at a festival in a park on the banks of a local bayou, perfect for drinking and flirting.

Suddenly, Gator was missing! In time, the child was found and pulled from shallow, murky waters at the edge of the bayou. Efforts were made to revive him, but they were unsuccessful. Hours later, a drunk Gus LeBlanc badgered his mother into going to the hospital in Baton Rouge and breaking the tragic news to Evie, telling her that Gus was so distraught he had to be sedated. Evie never cried aloud, never said anything at all for hours, simply sat in a chair with clenched fists, weeping softly. Then Evie was the one who did have to be sedated. Gus began to find more and more jobs that kept him away from home for weeks at a time, and when he was at home in Baton Rouge he would come in at all hours, drunk and smelling of his lifelong penchant for bars and the women found in them. Gus LeBlanc would be the main man Evie would

ever love, but her love would never be the same and she had begun to realize that having some men could be worse than having no man at all.

Their marriage, in any meaningful sense, was over. Evie was neither
cold nor warm toward him, just stoic and dutiful. As she would for the
rest of her life, she turned to her work for happiness and took refuge in
the response of her patients to her care.

Then, on a rainy Wednesday afternoon in the fall of 1934, Evie came
out of a patient's room to find Gus's mother, along with his sister Rosalie
and their parish priest, standing in the hall. The women had been crying and the priest had a sad look. They brought Evie to a patient waiting
room and broke the news to her that her Gus was dead, shot to death in
a dance hall incident outside the northeast Louisiana town of Homer
where he had been working on a pipeline.

In the summer of 1936, Evie moved back to Mississippi, and she
found a job worthy of her training and experience in Jackson, at the
hospital near the center of town.

Gus had a life insurance policy, offered through his employment—
premiums deducted from his pay—that paid Evie $20,000. With the
money, she bought a spacious three-bedroom Victorian cottage in a quiet neighborhood not far from her hospital and the local Baptist church
she was attending.

She had planned to rent a room or two, but never did, enjoying the
extra space for Peter when he came to visit, and even some of Gus's relatives on occasion. Always painted a sparkling white, long before it needed repainting, Evie's house had intricate Victorian woodwork on the
eaves, a gray slate roof, and a large porch in back with spindled banis-
ters. Inside was the essence of bright and happy Victorian country casual. Outside was the suggestion of English country garden. In time the
Montgomerys came to call it the Gingerbread Inn.

～

After marrying Carrie and moving in with Evie, Casey felt he should get
a job to help support his new family, and Peter found him one in Jackson
with a friend at a local lumberyard. Carrie worked to help Evie get the
house ready for the baby, while she also studied and tutored Casey. Irene
Sims had worked out an arrangement with the superintendent of Glasper

High School that Carrie and Casey could privately take the final exams given the other students and, if they passed, they would be awarded their high school diplomas at the same time as others in their class, but not participate in the graduation ceremonies. Carrie had almost perfect scores, the highest in the class, and Casey was not far behind.

~

On the morning of April 5, 1940, Carrie and her newborn baby boy came home to the Gingerbread Inn. It was a beautiful spring morning with watermelon-red azalea blossoms standing out against the white picket fence in the corner of the front yard. All four grandparents had visited Carrie and the baby in the hospital, with Peter and Emma still being estranged, and Peter being careful not to confront her. Irene Sims came to visit and stayed a full week. The baby boy weighed only five pounds, eight ounces at birth, but was healthy, perceived likely to be a wiry redhead like his mother, looking not much like his father. But that did nothing to deter them from naming him Casey Bateman Montgomery, Jr.

As young as they were, and as abruptly as their lives had changed, Carrie and Casey adjusted to parenthood well. Carrie thought she should find a job, but Evie would not hear of it. She was to "stay home and take care of that baby." And Evie did so love Casey Junior. Maybe he was little Gator, reincarnated in a much smaller, much ruddier version.

PART THREE

World War II

CHAPTER 24

THE NURSE IN THE PICTURE

P eter had joined the fight in World War I, without being drafted. Early one evening, in mid-July of 1940, Casey let Carrie and Evie almost finish their evening meal, then announced in a matter-of-fact voice, "I joined the Army Air Corps today."

Stunned, the two women said nothing at first. Then Carrie asked, in a low, shaky voice, "Why did you do that?"

"Because that's what I decided I should do," Casey responded, in his characteristic unembellished manner.

Casey had initially wanted to be a pilot, having been fascinated at sixteen with some barnstormers he saw at an air show Peter took him to in Biloxi. When he was informed that he'd failed the vision part of the physical and couldn't be a pilot, he was astounded. How could that be, when he could see the baseball and the basketball goal better than almost anybody! The problem: he was colorblind, not acceptable for pilots.

He wound up a turret gunner in a B-17 Flying Fortress, and by the end of World War II he had flown thirty-four combat missions against German targets.

Numerous times his big, lumbering B-17 limped back to base badly damaged, and several times they returned with wounded crewmen, twice with one who was dead on arrival. But Casey survived without wounds, when the life expectancy of a B-17 crewman was but twenty-one missions.

Carrie wrote to Casey almost every day. She got only occasional letters in return, but she was undeterred, sensing that he realized what he might write back would only enhance her apprehension. She sent him pictures often, but he sent back only two: a formal pose in his dress uniform and a picture of him in a pub with several buddies. Carrie framed the first picture and kept it at her bedside; the second one she put in a drawer, where it stayed.

Hitler committed suicide in his bunker on April 30, 1945. The following week, German forces all over Europe were surrendering to the Allies.

About this time Peter did something he had wanted to do for several years, since learning that Casey was based at Thorpe Abbotts Airfield, located some hundred miles north of London in English farm country, near Norfolk. He wrote Casey a letter with a unique plea.

With the war over, there was little for Casey do but wait to be sent home. He understood that he might have to wait for months, as there were millions of American military personnel in Europe, and much of the available shipping was committed to the continuing war in the Pacific.

Casey lay on his bunk dreaming of home.

"Mail call!" came the announcement. Casey wandered up to take his place in line. With gratifying frequency, he had mail but this day he had three pieces: a letter from Carrie, another from Evie, both telling him how much they wanted to know when he would be coming home, and a surprising envelope from his father. Inside was a letter, along with a four-by-six faded picture. Casey studied the picture first, a picture of a Montgomery in an English pub.

The soldier was a young Peter, and the woman with him was a pretty, slightly-built young woman with dark hair. Peter had on his basic military uniform. The woman had on a white blouse and a pendant around her neck. They both had beer steins in front of them; they had obviously been drinking; and both were smiling happily at the camera. Young Peter had apparently already started smoking a pipe and was holding a small brown one, not his meerschaum. Casey then turned to the undated letter and Peter's scrawled, difficult-to-read handwriting, by far the longest letter he had ever gotten from his father.

Son,

I need a favor. I want you to go an see if you can find a woman for me. I married your ma and we lived together for a long time. But this is the only woman I ever really wanted. Now this won't come to anything. She is probably married now to somebody else. And besides, even after six years apart Emma says no chance in hell she'll give me a divorce. But I've thought about this woman all these years and I'd just like to know what ever happened to her. And you there in England and the war over an all.

Her in this picture—English nurse. Took care of me all those months in the hospital after I got shot and brought back to England. I got out of the hospital an they put me in a barrack. We started seeing each other an I guess you could say for a few months we was lovers.

They sent me home. Tried to write and keep up. All that was hard then—and I'm not much of a writer. Then I got involved with your ma and we got married and all. But I never stopped thinking about this woman an thinking about her has always made me have a funny feeling inside. Like nothing else ever has.

All I got for you to go on was her name was Elizabeth Baker an she was a nurse at Edmeter Hospital in London. And you have this old picture of her. Hurry home.
Papa

Also, if you find her—buy her some flowers an catch her alone if you can and show her the picture and tell her the flowers are from me. I'll pay you for them when you get home.

Suddenly a veteran of thirty-four dangerous bombing missions had a new mission; a mission that left him bewildered and concerned. He would never want to let his father down but had little idea where to start this search. In addition, he was feeling concern about what he might learn if he did find her. What if his father was one of many lovers and she had no recollection of the young man in the picture, almost three decades in the past? In that event, Casey determined, he would lie and tell his father that he did not manage to find her.

~

Early the next morning, Casey went to see his commanding officer, Major Cliff Hadley, a stocky, balding, thirty-six-year-old Iowan who in peacetime had been a lawyer with a solo general practice in Cedar Rapids, Iowa. Casey had served under Major Hadley for almost two years, and knew him to be a kind, knowledgeable person from whom he could seek advice. Hadley's office, at the back of a round-domed Quonset hut near the center of the base, was sparsely furnished, with only a gray metal desk, three matching chairs, and a matching metal bookcase, filled with a mixture of books, manuals and periodicals.

Holding the letter from his father and the picture, Casey took a seat in front of Hadley, who was sitting behind his desk.

"What can I help you with, Sergeant Montgomery," Hadley said, in a warm voice.

"Sir, I don't know if this is appropriate. It's a private matter, not a military matter. But I have served under you for a long time now and know those under your command can talk to you about most anything."

"That's part of my role as a good commanding officer. What's this about, Sergeant?"

Major Hadley leaned back in this chair, propped his feet up on the corner of his desk, pulled a government-issue pack of Camels from his pocket, lit up.

"You care for one?"

"Yes sir, if you think it's all right."

Hadley flipped the cigarette pack across his desk to Casey, followed by the book of matches, and Casey followed suit.

"It involves my father who was here in World War I—wounded in France in 1918—shot in the leg. Yesterday I got this letter from him."

Casey handed the letter across to Hadley.

"He's the best father ever, and I want to do whatever I can for him, but I have no idea where to start."

The major read the letter, studied the picture, inhaled from his Camel, blew out a stream of smoke, and then looked up directly into Casey's eyes with a sympathetic countenance.

"This touches me. I can't imagine loving a woman like this for this long, not being able to have her, and not ever being able to get over her."

"Any advice?"

"If it was me, I'd go to London, try and find this hospital, and maybe somebody who was there back then and recognizes this woman in the picture . . . then go from there."

Casey looked at the floor, trying to envision how he would go about doing so. London was about a hundred miles away, but in his three years in England he had not been there.

"Let me see what I can line up," Major Hadley said. "You can have any leave you want, and I'll try to find you a way to London. We have military facilities there, and I can look for you a place to stay. Come back by this afternoon about three."

~

"I've got good news and bad," Hadley said when Casey returned. Casey looked at him with anticipation.

"The bad news is that the closest place I can find you a bunk is at Eighth Bomber Headquarters at High Wycombe, which is about thirty miles northwest of London."

He paused, dramatically, then smiled and said warmly, "The good news is that I told them Sergeant Montgomery is on official business for me and will need a jeep and driver."

CHAPTER 25

RED ROSES SAY LOVE

T he next morning, shortly after eight, a jeep rolled up in front of the unit mess hall. Casey was outside smoking, standing with his green duffel. Picking up his duffel, he approached the jeep on the passenger side.

It was a tired old jeep, with a dented left front fender, a small crack in the headlight beneath it, and a rusted spot on the hood the size of a slice of bread. It was open but had a canvas top that could be pulled across it and snapped to the high square windshield. The heavy, lugged tires were complemented by a similar spare mounted on the rear. Welded to the back was a small shelf, on which sat two five-gallon gasoline cans.

"I'm Private Rhodes, here to pick up Sergeant Montgomery. Are you Sergeant Montgomery?"

"Yes," Casey answered, with a broad smile, in a chipper tone. He was most happy that what had been promised had been delivered.

Casey pitched his duffel in the rear, and Rhodes helped Casey close the door, which required slamming it hard twice. Then he got in on the driver's side. He appeared younger than Casey, slightly built, with a youthful face, medium dark hair, augmented by a greasy hair cream, well overdue for a haircut.

Both Casey and Private Rhodes wore light olive drab trousers over ankle-high mahogany boots, topped by a standard-issue field jacket, required by regulations for going off post. Casey's clothes were impeccably clean and pressed, Private Rhodes's far from it. On Casey's left chest were two rows of service ribbons, Private Rhodes had none. They both wore standard-issue garrison caps, Casey's with blue air force piping, Private Rhodes's plain and unadorned.

"Sergeant, I understand I'm to take you to London, and was told to pack like we might be gone for several days. What are we going for?"

Caught off guard, Casey had to ponder an answer. "I'm not at liberty to say. It's a secret mission."

"Really? I've never been part of a secret mission. Top secret?"

"Not top secret . . . medium level."

Rhodes had a distinct syrupy drawl that let Casey know he was definitely Southern, but probably not from his part of the South.

"Where you from, Private?"

"West Virginia . . . well not the state West Virginia, you know, but the western part of just plain Virginia. Four miles out from Honaker, that's the closest town . . . and it ain't very big."

"How long you been over here?"

"Only about four months."

"What made you decide to join?"

"Oh, Lord, Sergeant, I didn't join. One day I come back to the house from slopping the hogs, and Mama was standing in the door, looking like something was wrong. 'Dusty,' she says, 'something come from the Draft Board today.' Dusty's what they always call me—what I'd rather be called—Delbert is my real name, you know, named after Mama's Uncle Delbert Lampkin. But I don't care much for Delbert . . . then Mama handed me this piece of paper and we figured out I had been drafted, you know."

"At least you got drafted so late that it was about over. You didn't have much risk of getting killed, not getting to go back to your hogs."

Private Rhodes made no immediate response, then said, rather dryly, "I understand, Sergeant Montgomery, I'm to drive you to London. Where in London are we going?"

"Edmeter Hospital."

"Where's that?"

"Don't know, and nobody here at headquarters seems to know. Know your way around London, Private Rhodes?"

"Lord no. In my four months, been there only once, driving Colonel Ratliff, but he knew where we were going and I followed his directions."

"Then head in like you did driving Colonel Ratliff . . . if you remember."

Casey lit another Camel and they started out. The bright sun reflected off high cumulus clouds billowing up across the flat landscape of East Anglia, its fertile fields stretching out for miles, some green with new growth and others plowed for the planting, occasional rows of trees breaking up the agricultural patterns.

They passed quaint villages, with stone cottages topped in thatch, surrounded by gardens of vegetables and flowers. The apple trees were in blossom, and Casey spotted familiar flowers: sweet William, delphinium, and phlox. The engine and transmission of the old jeep whined, and the lugged tires hummed loudly.

It took them almost three hours to reach the outskirts of London, where they began to see scenes of destruction from the Nazi bombing: homes destroyed; buildings gutted, with random walls still standing; massive holes along the road; obvious patches in the roads to fill bomb craters. Parcels of vacant land in parks and along sidewalks had been planted with vegetables.

Traffic was sparse, no doubt influenced by the acute shortage of fuel, and Casey began to suspect this old vehicle had been chosen because it was equipped to carry cans of extra fuel.

They came to what appeared to be a police station on the left.

"Stop here and wait," Casey directed.

Once inside he approached a stocky young woman with short dark hair, dressed in a blue uniform, seated at a desk. She looked up at him and smiled. "Can I help you?"

"I'm looking for Edmeter Military Hospital. Could you give me directions?"

The young woman looked off into space, as if deep in thought, then she looked directly at Casey. "Never heard of it." Two males, also in uniform, were behind her, one seated at a desk, the other standing at a counter.

"Either of you ever heard of Edmeter Hospital?" she shouted back to them. Both walked up. One was tall and gaunt, appearing to be in his mid-thirties. "What hospital, you say?"

"Edmeter Hospital," she repeated.

"Never heard of it," he said, and went back to where he had been standing.

The other man was of medium build, younger. "Nor have I," he said, returning to his desk.

Casey got back in the jeep and they headed deeper into the heart of the city. "Maybe we should look for an older person," Casey said in time.

"How about that guy?" Private Rhodes said, pointing to an elderly gentleman walking along. He was gray and stooped, wearing a black Edwardian derby, baggy brown pants, topped by a darker brown thigh-length jacket. They stopped.

"Sir!" Casey barked out to him, in a voice strong enough to be certain to get the man's attention. He stopped, turned, rested his cane on the sidewalk, and looked at them.

"Can you tell me how to get to Edmeter Hospital?"

He mulled the question. "Never heard of such a hospital." Casey felt a deep sense of despair. But, after a short pause, the man then added, "Back in the first war, my cousin was at Edmonton Military Hospital for a time. Edmonton Military was what North Middlesex Hospital was called for a time, there in the first war . . . North Middlesex it is now. But don't know about any Edmeter Hospital. You did say Edmeter Hospital, didn't you, laddie?"

Casey felt a surge of hope. Maybe it was Edmonton, not Edmeter. He said, "Where's this North Middlesex Hospital?"

Armed with directions and renewed hope, Casey set off for North Middlesex Hospital. When they found it, some of the hospital complex had sustained bomb damage and there was a large bomb crater across the street. Casey left Private Rhodes with the parked jeep and walked into the main entrance, approaching the first person he saw, a petite young woman seated behind a simple metal desk.

"Can I help you?" she said in a pleasant voice.

"Was this once Edmonton Military Hospital?" Casey asked.

"Think maybe it was . . . long time ago," she answered. "I've only been here a year. Why?"

Casey realized he should have prepared for this moment. Clearing his throat, he finally said, in a low, humble voice, "I'm trying to find a woman."

"What's her name?"

"Elizabeth Baker."

The woman thought for a few seconds. "Don't know her."

"Anybody you know been here a long time?"

"Maybe Gertrude. She's probably been here longer than anybody."

"Where can I find Gertrude?'

"Second floor." She pointed to her right. "Stairs are down that way. At the top, turn back left."

Casey followed her instructions. Going down a second-floor hall, he came to a nurses' station, beyond which was a ward with patients. A woman was leaning against an open counter, writing on what appeared a patient chart; a tall, broad-shouldered woman, with white hair and a horse face.

"I'm looking for Gertrude."

"I'm at least one Gertrude. What can I help you with?"

"I'm looking for a woman who was a nurse at Edmeter Hospital, or maybe Edmonton Military Hospital in 1918," Casey said in the most polite, humble voice he could muster. "Her name was Elizabeth Baker. Did you ever know an Elizabeth Baker?"

"Sure, I know her. We worked together for fifteen years. . . at least me and some Elizabeth Baker."

Casey showed her the picture.

"Lord, that's an old picture, but that's her. Why are you looking for her?"

"That's my father and he wants me to find her."

Gertrude raised her eyebrows, gave Casey a canny smile. "Last I knows she's nursing at Netley."

"Where's that?"

"Royal Victory Hospital at Netley, down by Southampton, about two to three hours southwest if you're driving. Got a ride?"

"Got a jeep," Casey responded, proud of his status as an American airman, commissioned by his commanding officer for a special mission. "Thank you," he said, walking away, happier than he had been in a long time.

"Where to now, Sergeant?" Dusty said when Casey got back in the jeep.

"Southampton."

"Where's that?"

"About three hours southwest of here."

Casey thought for a moment. "I don't know how to get there and this day is almost gone. Major Hadley says we have a bunk reserved at High Wycombe, which is about an hour. Dusty, let's go there and spend the night."

⁓

Early afternoon the next day, Casey arrived at Royal Victory Military Hospital in Netley on the outskirts of Southampton. The enormity of the facility was intimidating: a quarter mile-long multi-storied complex, surrounded by acres of lawns and landscaping. As before, leaving Private Rhodes with the jeep, he summoned his courage, walked in, and began asking questions, usually showing the picture of his father and this Elizabeth Baker, hoping for some response of familiarity.

After numerous fruitless inquiries, he walked down a long hall on the third floor of the west wing. A man approached him hurriedly from the other direction, middle-aged, lean and thin, appearing from his dress to be a doctor.

Casey stopped him. By now, his approach had become straight-forward, polished and direct.

"Sir? Maybe you can help me. I'm trying to find a woman my father knew in London in 1918. Here is a picture of her back then."

The man looked annoyed at the interruption, but he glanced at the picture, casually. "Don't know her, mate," he said, walking away. Then he stopped and turned back. "Wait! She's a lot older now, but that looks like Elizabeth. Elizabeth something . . . can't remember her last name. She's a nurse who usually works over in Ward 366 on the East Side."

Casey found Ward 366, one of the more-than-a-hundred large wards of black iron beds. The minute he saw her, midway down the ward attending a patient, Casey felt positive he had found his father's Elizabeth. Retreating to a bench at the entrance to the ward, he sat and watched her, trying not to be noticed. This definitely appeared to be the woman in the picture. She had aged, but she was still very attractive.

Suddenly Casey felt an anxiety bordering on terror. Now that he had found her, he was unsure what to do next. He left, going back to the jeep.

Private Rhodes sat in the shade on the ground next to the vehicle, legs stretched out in front of him, smoking. Spotting Casey, he got up and took his seat behind the wheel. Casey stood for a moment, his fingers mindlessly stroking the rusted spot on the hood, pondering what to do. Then he took his place in the passenger seat.

"Making progress with our mission, Sergeant?" Dusty asked, when Casey got in.

"Definite progress."

"Where we headed now?"

"Looking for flowers."

"Flowers! What kind of flowers?"

"Red roses, twelve red roses . . . with long stems."

When Casey's son was born, Evie had bought twelve long-stemmed red roses at a florist near the hospital. Giving them to Casey, she instructed him, "Go in there and give these to Carrie. Red roses tell her you love her—and you sure better—after all she's gone through to give you a beautiful son." These were the flowers Casey needed now. Something told him that with a suffering population, committed to growing vegetables wherever they could, this would not be easy.

As they got closer to the city center, evidence of bomb damage was everywhere. Casey couldn't help but notice several large bombed-out churches, which gave him a strange feeling as he thought about the churches of his heritage being destroyed by bombs. There was no way for him to ignore that his bombs would kill German people, even children, destroy their homes and factories. He now realized that these bombs were also destroying places of worship, sacred places that had endured for generations.

"Roses! We're growing cabbages, turnips and carrots these days, young man," said the haggard-looking woman behind the counter at the first place they stopped, in a tone that evidenced contempt. Casey left and pressed on, inquiring where he could, continuing to get a similar answer. Three more times he got a negative response, but this time, as he was about to get back in the jeep, an old woman called out to him, in a high, raspy voice, "Come back, young Yank!"

She was old and stocky, with a pronounced dowager hump, close-cut snow-white hair, her straight, print dress of mixed blues wrinkled and hanging to her ankles. She looked at him with intensity, and said in a much softer voice: "Why do you want these roses?"

Casey thought a moment. "I guess it's about love," he said with honesty, about as specific as he could be. The woman gave him a stern, suspicious look. She turned her back to him, stared out toward the ocean for a moment, then said in a low, clear voice, still looking away, "I think I may can help you. The first war got my man; this one got my baby girl; but I still got my roses, and maybe I still need to believe in love."

She led him to a small, tile-roofed stone cottage not far away, and they walked around the left side, along a path through a garden replete with colorfully blooming flowers. In the back were several large, rambling rose bushes, one with bright red blossoms. Looking beyond them, Casey saw the ragged remains of several bombed-out buildings.

"Take what you want," she said, and she walked away.

Some blooms were impressive, but a long stem was not to be found. Casey worked to put together the best bouquet he could. They would have to do, regardless of their crooked, twisted stems. This much was certain: these were very special roses; to an old woman, to a young American airman, and, potentially, to two other people.

Leaving, Casey tried to pay her, but she wouldn't accept his money. He leaned over, took the woman's hand, and kissed it. "Thank you. You're a beautiful lady."

The old woman responded with a warm, lingering smile.

When Casey got back in the jeep, Rhodes looked for a moment at this newly-found bouquet. "Back to the hospital?" he asked, with a hint of sarcasm. Even for a naive young guy from "west Virginia" this "classified mission" was beginning to look a bit suspect. Something about it had been suspect almost from the beginning.

"Back to the hospital," Casey replied, in a tone and with a look that made it clear he did not appreciate sarcasm and Rhodes had best respect his rank. "But it will have to be tomorrow." He guessed Nurse Baker's shift for the day would have ended by this time.

~

The next morning, Casey sat on the same bench outside the ward, roses in hand, carefully wrapped in soft green paper. He discreetly watched Elizabeth Baker among the patients in their beds, her white nurse's veil occasionally catching bright sunlight coming in the high windows. She was smiling at patients, talking to them as she went along. Casey didn't know exactly how he should handle this, but he knew it would not be in the ward with all the patients. After a while, she walked past him toward a nursing station, looking down at him and smiling warmly. Casey determined that when she headed back he would ambush her, and he did.

"Ma'am," he said, standing up, blocking her in the hall. "I have flowers for you." Elizabeth looked at him, a bit bewildered.

"And who are you, young man?" she said.

"Casey Montgomery."

"They're pretty, but why are you giving me flowers?'

"They're from my father."

"And who is your father?"

"Peter Montgomery," Casey said, showing her the picture.

The recognition was instant.

"Peter," she said, in a soft voice. With the flowers in one hand and the picture in the other she went over and sat down on the bench, staring down at the picture. She moved to the side of the bench, which Casey took as an invitation to sit beside her. She never looked up from the picture and never looked at him.

She began to cry. "What is this about?"

Casey knew no response he could make, and so he said nothing. She stopped crying and pulled off her glasses, wiping the tears from her face on the shoulders of her dress. Then she looked directly at Casey, a tone of anger in her voice, "Why is he doing this to me?" Casey noticed her hands were clenched and that she was trembling.

Knowing no answer he could verbalize, Casey reached into his shirt pocket and retrieved the letter from Peter that had accompanied the picture. Saying nothing, he handed it to her, still folded. Slowly and carefully, Elizabeth unfolded the letter and began to read it.

She began to cry again.

"I don't understand this. I loved him so much, and he left me without even saying goodbye. In all these years, I've never heard a word from him. I imagined that maybe he had died, like so many were at that time, and no one knew about me to let me know. At times, I felt that he had lied to me when he said he didn't have anyone at home waiting for him, and he went back to her and didn't care about me . . . that he was just using me while he was here in England. If he loved me, how could he do me like he did?"

"I don't know much ma'am . . . but I know my papa ain't no liar. If there ever was a man who weren't no liar, that's him. And I know after he left England he nearly died. He caught that flu and was in the hospital in New York, they thought he was gonna die. For months he was there in the hospital in New York before coming home. My grandma told me he was still sick for a long time after he came home."

Elizabeth had quit crying. She put the letter in her lap and moved the picture on top of it and sat looking at the picture.

"And I always heard this and I'm sure it's true. My papa didn't meet my mama until he came home, came back to Glasper after all those months he was in the hospital in New York. And he met my mama on account of she was working at our store in Glasper when he got home from the war."

Elizabeth said nothing for a time, continuing to look at the picture, as if in a trance. Casey could think of nothing else he could say.

"That still doesn't explain why he never wrote or contacted me, when he finally could, why he went on and married someone else," she said, in a low sad voice. "And it doesn't explain why, after he's gone on with his life, married and had a son, he wants to come back into my life like this." Looking up at Casey, Elizabeth tried to hand the letter and the picture back him.

"I think he would want you to keep them," Casey said. "He ain't lived with my mama—ain't had nothing to do with her—for about six years, and I think he may be wishing he could come back into your life."

Neither of them was ready for the conversation to end, nor did they know what else to say. Casey realized that he was left with a big unanswered question. He tried to think of some adroit, indirect way to get the answer, but could think of none.

"I don't know how to ask you this, but just ask it. I think my father is going to want to know about you . . . especially he's gonna want to know if you've got a husband and family now and all."

"No . . . I raised your brother, well, your half-brother—by myself—as best I could . . . with quite a lot of help from Dr. and Mrs. Prince." She paused. "When he left, I was pregnant with your father's child."

Casey found himself stunned and speechless. Questions flooded his mind, but he was unable to articulate any of them. Finally, he did the best he could. "As you can imagine, ma'am, I'm shocked about all this, now finding out I have a half-brother here in England that I knew nothing about. I want to meet him, find out all about him. What's his name?"

"Peter Prince Baker was his name . . . he's dead." Elizabeth began to cry again.

Casey got out his handkerchief and handed it to her. She took it and wiped her eyes.

"Mr. Montgomery," she said, when she calmed, "we apparently have much that we could talk about, but this is not the time and place. People are wondering what is going on, and I need to get back to work. I live alone. I have nothing else to do. If you would like, you can come by my flat or we can meet somewhere and we can visit at length about all this. There is quite a lot that has caught us both by surprise. Perhaps I could find answers to questions that have haunted me for most of my life. You could learn a trifle about your brother, if you have interest, and maybe see some pictures of him, that's all I've got left. You would no doubt be proud of him; and—were he alive—no doubt he of you."

"I'm stationed up out from Norfolk, Thorpe Abbotts Airfield . . . waiting to go home . . . with nothing to do. I'm not that much to be proud of, but I'm proud to still be here, alive and all. I've been in England for almost four years . . . managed to survive thirty-four bombing missions."

"Your brother didn't make that many. He was killed when his Lancaster was lost in a night raid over Berlin in November of 1943. I think it was his ninth mission."

~

A letter went out to Peter, first-class priority, letting him know that his Elizabeth Baker had been found, her address, and that she was unmarried and living alone. Casey didn't know whether to tell his father about his other son, finally deciding that should be left up to Elizabeth.

CHAPTER 26

DOUSED WITH ALE

F rom the time he found her in the last days of May 1945, until he left
to return to the United States in late August, Casey visited Elizabeth
three more times. For his next trips, he took a regularly-scheduled
bus from his airbase into Norfolk, then connected with public transportation to London, and on to Southampton, where he found an old but
adequate hotel near the train station.

Elizabeth lived alone in a tiny bottom-floor flat on the outskirts
of Southampton, commuting each day by rail or bus to the hospital in
nearby Netley. Her building was stone, aged and stained, one of identical
dozens, sidewall to sidewall, stretching down a long narrow street, separated from the street by a stone walk.

Casey's first visit was a week after he located her. He knocked on
the heavy wooden door and announced who he was. Elizabeth opened
the door with a pleasant expression and cheerfully invited him in, seating him on a couch, taking her seat in an armchair to his right. She had
on a dark gray knee-length skirt, topped by a long-sleeved white blouse
with a loose embroidered collar, interlaced with a red ribbon. Her shoul-
der-length graying hair was tied back over her ears with a broad black
band.

Her flat was three main rooms: a parlor upon entry, with accompa-
nying kitchen and eating area to the left beyond, then a bedroom and

bath through a door to the right. Unlike the dreary exterior, the interi-
or was bright and cheerful, a sea of color. In contrast to the dark wood
floor, the parlor furnishing was centered on a warm cream rug, with a
couch of blue-and-green plaid, accompanied by two matching blue arm-
chairs, topped by numerous colorful throws and pillows. Some lamps
were brass, others glass; all had light cream shades. On a side wall of the
parlor was a brown bookcase, with more framed pictures than books,
almost all of them of Peter Prince at various stages of his life, many
with the two of them together, several including an older couple. A small
dining table of blond wood was against the wall, with three matching
chairs, on top of which was a clear vase filled with the roses.

"I'm so glad to see you. Did you have any trouble finding me?

"No ma'am," he lied. Finding her particular flat among so many, so
identical, and with the unfamiliar numbering system had not been easy.

Casey expected her to immediately start telling him about his
half-brother, but she didn't. She inquired about his mother and any siblings, his grandparents; but it was obvious her main interest was Peter
and his present situation.

She offered him tea. Casey was a coffee man but could drink tea
when that was the offering. She got them both tea, talking as she prepared it, and sat back down. "You say your father separated from your
mother about six years ago? Hasn't lived with her since?"

"Yessum."

"Can you tell me anything about why?"

"No ma'am. Not much. My papa don't talk much about it. He ain't
one to run her down, at least not around me. But I'll have to say my
mama ain't that way about him. I did hear a rumor had gone around
town that it was about some money he said she stole from him."

"And in these six years, as far as you know, Sergeant Montgomery,
your father has shown no interest in any other woman?"

"No ma'am. Not that I know anything about . . . small as Glasper is,
not much like that misses attention."

"Where has your father lived these six years?"

"He bought a farmhouse and a hundred-twenty acres about five
miles out. I hear he's fixed it up real neat. Lives there with Pepper, that's

my horse I had when I was a boy . . . and I hear a little stray hound has taken up with him since I left."

Elizabeth sat, pondering, trying to take it all in. They both sipped the last of their tea.

Then she got up and walked to the bookcase, picking up one of the pictures and walking back. She handed it across to him. "This is Peter Prince . . . your brother. You and he do favor one another. He had your father's beautiful wide-set blue eyes and broad forehead, like you do. But he was not as tall as you are, more your father's size."

Casey handed the picture back to her and walked over to the bookcase, slowly examining the pictures, one at a time.

"These elderly people, they your parents?"

"No. I grew up in an orphanage and never knew my parents. That's Dr. and Mrs. John Prince. They took me in when I was twelve and were the closest thing to parents I ever had. I would not want to think about what my life would have been if not for them. When I was sure I was pregnant I went to them, struggling with what to do. I was young and scared. They insisted I move in with them. Their daughter had married and moved to Lancaster about 1910. She had no children. They had a son, who never married, and was killed at Verdun. Peter Prince was the grandchild they never had, and they loved him so."

Casey returned to the couch, picked up his empty teacup in a fidget; put it gently back down on the saucer.

"I shall fix us a trifle to eat . . . will have to look a bit. I don't keep much around that would tempt a big young man like you, with a bit of a hunger. I do have some fresh shepherd's pie."

"I don't expect you to feed me, ma'am. You don't need to do that."

"I want to, if you can eat shepherd's pie."

"Don't know if I've had any of that, but I'd like to try it."

"Then I shall certainly get it prepared."

They ate their shepherd's pie and talked on, mostly about her life and raising Peter Prince with the help of the Princes. She offered him a second serving of shepherd's pie and he took it.

"This is mighty good, ma'am. What's in it?"

"It's minced lamb and vegetables, topped with mashed potatoes, cooked until brown on top."

"It's great. We never ate lamb back home, not my family."

When he had finished his second serving, they moved back to their original positions on the couch and side chair. Elizabeth insisted she fix them another cup of tea.

"When I first met your father, he was suffering from a severe leg wound. Did it finally heal well, leave him with no disability?"

"I guess you could say it healed, but he's always had a limp . . . and I think it always hurt him, but he was never one to complain. I think the limping made his back hurt some too."

"He so loved baseball. Was he ever able to play baseball again?"

"No, ma'am. But he sure did like to watch me when I got to playing. He never missed a game."

Casey began to worry that he was staying too long and would wear out his welcome. "I must go now. I know you will need some rest if you are going to work tomorrow." Then, he said, with a teasing chuckle and a broad smile, "I shan't ever have had a better time."

"I shore did enjoy it myself, I shore did," she said, with a smile and chuckle of her own, taking her best shot at imitating his Southern drawl.

~

In the last week of July, Casey visited Elizabeth again in Southampton. She had been given a specific date for his visit and decided to have a traditional English dinner. It was pricey, but she was able to find roast beef, which she would serve with traditional English mustard, Yorkshire pudding, roasted potatoes, carrots, and peas, topped off with a custard tart. Thinking he might like a beer, she bought a half dozen bottles of Bass. It had been a long time since Elizabeth had been this excited preparing a meal for a man, a long time since Casey had enjoyed a meal specially prepared for just him.

"Go sit on the couch and let me pick up the dishes and put away the leftovers," she instructed him, when they had finished. Casey did as instructed. "Maybe you can enjoy this while you wait." With that she came over and handed him an opened Bass.

She cleaned off the table, put the dirty dishes in the sink, and covered the leftovers. Then she sat in her usual side chair with an open Bass of her own. Elizabeth put the Bass down on the table and walked over to the bookcase, coming back with a newly-framed picture, the picture Casey's father had sent him. She sat with it in her lap, looking at it wistfully.

"I guess you can see from this picture, I'll drink a beer with a handsome young man."

"You were beautiful . . . still are."

"Well, I was a skinny young thing then. Guess I'm a skinny old thing now." She paused, then added, in a low matter-of-fact voice, "But your father never seemed to hold it against me."

She took the picture back to the bookcase and returned with several letters in her hand. "I have gotten three letters from your father in the last several days. One of them was eight pages long." Casey imagined that taking his father almost a full day, since he was not much of a writer.

"I'm sure there's a lot he wants you to know," Casey said.

"He told me when he got back to your Glasper he started writing me every day at Edmeter Hospital in London, that's all he knew. Of course, there was no Edmeter Military Hospital, and Edmonton Military Hospital was in North Middlesex, not London. Casey, there was little hope of those letters getting to me, but I do wonder why they were not eventually sent back to him—at least some of them—so he would know they weren't getting to me."

Elizabeth stopped talking, sitting with the letters in her lap.

"And he keeps saying, over and over, in every letter, how much he loves me, that I'm the only woman he ever loved."

"One would have to wonder why he ever married my mother. They never seemed very happy together."

This put Elizabeth on the spot. After all, Emma was Casey's mother. "Sometimes things just happen that make people get married when they are not ready to, when that's not what they want," she finally said.

Casey had finished his beer. Elizabeth shuffled through the letters, pulling out one page from the third one and handing it to him.

"Every person deserves to respect their mother," she said. "But respect for your father is as important. You know that your father left me here, an unmarried woman, pregnant with his child, subject to ridicule and scorn. That said, your father is indeed a good man, as good as they get. You deserve to know that."

Casey looked at this page she had handed him, his father's familiar scrawled handwriting, and then he read the first paragraph:

"No man ever had it no worse than to be tricked into marrying a sorry lying woman he didn't love—Emma telling me she was pregnant when she weren't—and not getting to marry a good woman I did love, her who was the one who really was pregnant. I loved you so much. I just thought I had to do the right thing—from what I knew then."

Casey looked up at Elizabeth. She was looking down, at the letters in her lap. He didn't know what to say, so he said nothing.

"He says he wants to divorce your mother, come to England and marry me, take me back home with him to Glasper," said Elizabeth. "He says he has a very good position with a lumber company and can support us both well without me working."

Casey thought for a moment, trying to phrase a response.

"What do you think about that?' he finally said.

"I don't know . . . it's been such a long time. No doubt we have both changed so, and he might not like what he found when he saw me today. I probably still have some bitterness that I would have to get over. And certainly, I would not want to be the cause of your father divorcing your mother."

She looked down again at the letters in her lap. "But I do think he is the only man I shall ever love."

Casey found himself facing a cold, hard reality; he wanted his parents divorced, and as soon as possible.

⁓

On August 16, 1945, Casey made his final visit to see Elizabeth in Southampton. The next day, he was departing the docks at Southampton for New York on the *Queen Mary*, now stripped of luxury, windows covered, painted gray, and stuffed with triple-decker bunks.

They went out to celebrate, winding up in a neighborhood pub that Elizabeth suggested. Instead of her usual white blouse over a dark skirt, she wore a light beige skirt, topped with a colorful print blouse of red and green, with a tailored collar and puffy sleeves, tucked into her skirt. Her hair was tied back by a bright red ribbon, and around her neck was a red pendant on a gold chain. His uniform was pressed to perfection, his shoes shined impressively, and on the left side of his chest was a whole new row of campaign ribbons.

"Look at you! All those new ribbons," she said, when she first saw him.

"I guess they wanted to get it all to me before I went home and try to make me arrive looking impressive."

They were able to find an intimate back booth, which was good since the pub soon became crowded and noisy.

"The Toad in the Hole is their specialty, and it's quite good," Elizabeth said, after they were seated. "It is basically sausages covered with batter, much like Yorkshire pudding, then roasted."

"Sounds great. I may have had that once at a pub in Norfolk. If that's what you recommend, that's what I'll get."

"Well, I think I'm going to go with fish and chips, for sentimental reasons; that's what your father and I had, the first time we went out."

"Then that's what I want . . . for sentimental reasons."

The waiter approached, chubby, middle-aged, poor slouched posture, dark hair thinning at the temples, thin black mustache that matched his thin bow tie. Casey informed him that they would both like fish and chips.

"Shall we both get a glass of beer?" she asked.

"What about a pitcher? The picture with my father says you don't shy from a pitcher."

"Oh, we shan't want that much."

Casey ignored her. "Pitcher of Bass," he said to the waiter.

"He has a distinct West Country accent," Elizabeth commented, as the waiter walked away. "That's what I hear most here in Southampton."

"How did you get to Southampton?"

"It's a long story, but here is the short version. When Peter Prince was killed, my friend Janet had become head of nursing here and she insisted I come and join her. She knew my great pleasure in living with the Princes and raising my son there. But Dr. Prince had died, and Mrs. Prince was being moved to a home for the aged. Janet thought getting away from London would be good for me, and I had no real reason not to."

"Have you been happy here?"

"Took some getting used to, but as happy as anywhere. I believe you find your happiness mainly from within yourself. Inside I need to be needed, and if I'm nursing patients who need me, I can be happy."

They sat for over two hours, drinking Bass, eating fish and chips, and then drinking more Bass. Before, they had mostly talked about Elizabeth and her life, Peter and his. This night was a night for Casey to talk, and for some strange reason he felt compelled to tell Elizabeth about getting Carrie pregnant, and all Peter had done to help them at that time.

"That's the kind of man I knew he would be," she said. "He was the kindest, gentlest, most lovable man I ever met." Her upper lip became taut as she struggled not to cry, all to no avail. "And I loved him so," she said, suddenly overcome with emotion. Casey, even drunker, tried to hand her something to wipe away her tears, and in the process knocked a half-full stein of ale straight into her lap.

"I'm so sorry," he said, quite embarrassed, as he rushed around to her side of the booth to help.

"It's my fault . . . for being so emotional," she said, as she leaned over and hugged him. "I've survived more than one dousing of ale in my time." Then Casey hugged her back, pulling her into his muscular chest. They laughed together, her face still wet with tears.

"You're so great!" he said, looking down at her.

"And you're a wonderful man . . . Like your daddy."

That night Casey Montgomery and Elizabeth Baker found a special bond, a bond grounded in a deep love for the same man. Leaving Elizabeth, Casey found himself wishing that she could somehow be a part of his life forever.

CHAPTER 27

CROW CALL

It took Casey almost two weeks to get home from Southampton. Five days at sea to get to New York; four days getting processed for discharge at the military facilities on Governors Island; a day by train to Washington; another day to Atlanta, a final day on the leg to Jackson.

Earlier, he had informed Carrie and Evie that he was assigned to leave Southampton in August but could offer no further specifics. In great anticipation, they bought new curtains for the kitchen, and a new bedspread and sheets for Carrie's bedroom. They shopped for the latest, most stylish makeup for Carrie, each bought a new dress, and they had their hair professionally styled. Casey, Jr. got a haircut, a new sailor suit, and new white shoes. They did not know exactly when, but Casey was finally coming home and their excitement knew no bounds.

Shortly after midnight on Wednesday, August 29th, Casey arrived in Jackson by train. Three cabs were at the station hustling fares, and he got the third. Once out of the cab, he stood on the sidewalk, looking at the Gingerbread Inn. If anything had changed in his absence, he couldn't see it. He went up the walk, up the steps, and stopped on the porch. Would Aunt Evie still be keeping it there after all this time? He walked softly down the porch to his left and felt inside the lip of the flowerpot, where his fingers touched the key, right where it had always been kept.

He unlocked the front door, and went in. The parlor was illuminated by a single table light to his left near the kitchen door.

Dropping his duffel, he surveyed the scene. He remembered the two closed doors at the end of the parlor leading to two bedrooms, and that Carrie's room would be the door to the right. Where would his son be sleeping? He was reluctant to go right in, fearing they might be terrified to suddenly find a man in their bedroom in the dark of night. Should he just announce himself?

He didn't need to. The door on the left flew open and there stood Aunt Evie, in a long print nightgown, her pale face highlighted by light-gray hair.

"HE'S HOME! HE'S HOME! CARRIE, HE'S HOME!" she shouted.

Evie lunged for him and embraced her beloved nephew.

"Get out of my way, Evie," came another female voice.

And suddenly Carrie was kissing him passionately, like she couldn't get enough.

Casey finally pulled away from her, his smile wide. "My! This is some homecoming."

"I want more." Carrie started kissing him again.

"You folks have an audience," Evie announced.

Casey, Jr. was standing in the doorway, frightened, tearful.

"This is your daddy!" Carrie shouted. "Your daddy's come home!"

Casey knelt down and stretched out his arms. "Come here, little man. Come to your daddy."

Casey Jr. stopped crying, got a stiff upper lip and said in a firm, indignant voice, "I'm not a little man. I'm a medium man."

Casey went over to his son, picked him up and held him in his arms. He met his son's eyes. "What a big man you are."

"No, Daddy, I'm still just a medium man."

"Well, your daddy's so glad to be home with his medium man. How could I have ever made such a mistake?" Everyone laughed and the celebration resumed.

In time, Evie managed to get a protesting, reluctant Casey, Jr. to finish the night in her bed, with Casey and Carrie going to Carrie's room, where they made love until dawn, with all the passion and stamina befitting four years of separation.

~

Five days later, Casey set off on a trip south to visit his father in Glasper. Carrie and Evie had carefully maintained the wedding present Ford and it had held up well, necessary in wartime if they wanted an automobile. Carrie had started teaching English at a local high school and could not accompany him.

For the three-hour trip south, the road was a paved two-lane. Some of the Glasper streets were paved, but as he headed west, not far out of town, the road turned to gravel. It had not rained in almost two weeks and a cloud of beige dust rose behind him, drifting across the roadsides.

He rounded a curve and a crow was feasting on the carrion of a squirrel that had been killed in the road. Contemptuously, the bird waited until the last possible moment, then flew up and out of the way, leaving Casey to straddle the squirrel carcass.

In two more miles he turned off the public road and wound his way up beneath Peter's canopy of big oaks, and then Casey parked in front of the house's chest-high steps. The late afternoon sun, low in the sky, raked across the landscape. On the porch were four identical rockers, two on each side of the door.

Dressed in khaki pants and a bluish-green plaid shirt, Peter sat in the first rocker to the left of the door, smoking his pipe. Beside him was a medium-sized hound, alert to the approaching guest.

Peter wanted to dash down the steps and jerk open the driver's door, but he refrained from acting on that urge. His dog showed no such restraint, wagging his tail and sniffing Casey's pant-legs the minute he stepped out of the car. Casey bounded up the steps, the dog in hot pursuit. Peter got up from his chair and the two men hugged warmly, Peter holding his smoldering pipe out behind Casey's back.

"I'm so glad you are safe and home, son. I've missed you so. Stand back and let me look at you. My! . . . You left here my boy . . . you done come back a man, and quite a man. I hope I ain't changed as much as you have."

He had, even more, but Casey wasn't about to say so.

"You sure got yourself a friendly pup. Heard about him in one of

Evie's letters. What's his name?"

"Enos. Named him for Enos Slaughter . . . you know, the Cardinals slugger. Hit a home run the day this fella showed up."

"He ain't much watchdog. About as friendly as they come."

"Never met a stranger. Only thing he watches for is the squirrels, and I think he just harasses them. Don't think he would catch one if they sat still and let him."

Casey petted Enos on the head. Enos wagged his tail harder.

"There's a good breeze blowing out here across this porch. Right hot inside. You sit down here on this chair beside me and I'll be right back out."

Casey took the rocker beyond his father's, the one most out of the hot setting sun. Taking his pipe with him, Peter went inside.

The profound improvement in the property in four years became obvious to Casey. The steps and porch had new boards and were well painted. The shrubs were trimmed back, and the drive even showed new gravel. But where the trees allowed grass to grow on the lawn, Casey noticed it was high in seed heads. The lawn could definitely use some attention.

Peter returned, holding two bottles of beer in his right hand, bottle necks between his fingers; in the other hand he still held his pipe, gone out long ago.

"When you called and said you were coming, I got us some beer, even got a good block of ice to get it cold. If you been in England for four years, bet you been drinking a lot of beer."

"That's for sure. But this Pabst Blue Ribbon will beat that government Club Lager I've had so much of."

Casey pulled a pack of Lucky Strikes out of his left shirt pocket, together with a matchbook, lit the Lucky, rocked back slightly, and exhaled a stream of smoke out in front of him.

"Guess most everybody goes to smoking when they get in the military," Peter said matter-of-factly. "That's when I started." He walked over to the edge of the porch, carefully scraped out his pipe, sat back down, pulled out his tobacco pouch and packer, repacked the pipe, and lit it. His stream of smoke joined his son's in the fading light.

A tension built. Both men knew they had decisions to make, issues they so wanted to discuss. Each had directions they wanted this night's conversation to go, but neither knew quite how to get there. The small talk prevailed.

"Old Ford seems to be holding up," Peter said. "Good buy we made in that one."

"Yeah. Carrie and Evie have taken mighty good care of it."

"While you were away, I been driving up to visit them every now and then. Evie's got that fine house now I can stay in."

"It's a mighty nice house. In their letters, Carrie and Evie told me about your visits."

"I do love that Carrie of yours. Nobody's got no better daughter-in-law."

"Well, you know I love her too. And we have us a fine Little Casey now. Don't think he likes his mother kissin' on another man, though."

Peter chuckled. The conversation languished.

Then Casey moved to a subject that had been eating on him, something he felt Peter might understand. "I'm home and with my family I love, them that love me, but I feel so empty and lonely."

Peter relit his pipe yet again, and he took a long, deliberate draw. As the smoke drifted, Casey remembered tobacco smoke in a backyard under a big oak tree on a prior occasion years before.

"You ain't gone over there and gotten involved with another woman, have you, son?" Peter asked. He was all too aware that war, with death ever-present, tended to blur one's vision regarding the boundaries of morality and commitment.

"Oh, no. Nothing like that, but I sorta had a special family over there too: Billy Frank, and Tommy, and Willie Earl, Ralph and Danny . . . and them others. We was family too. We bunked in the same barracks . . . ate together, flew missions together, knowing we might die together. We tried to look out for one another, and when we could and we partied together. We was a kind of family. Now I don't have 'em, and it makes me so lonely all a sudden. You ever feel that way when you came home and left all those fellas you were fighting with?"

"I had some of that," Peter said. "It's like the only family you know, and you care about them other fellas, and all a sudden they is gone. I'll tell you this, when one of 'em gets killed, it's like you lost a brother. I never had nobody die hurt me worse than my friend Arthur, when he got killed. But I wasn't over there near as long as you was. Wasn't even a year before I got shot and shipped to England."

"But you felt that way?"

"Sure I did."

Casey knew the rest of the story: Peter had not just lost his band of brothers; he had left behind his one true love. Casey started to move to the subject of Elizabeth Baker, knowing his father would be so wanting to hear about her; but he decided not to. The sun was setting, and this subject was likely to be extensive.

"Let's go inside and light some lamps before it gets too dark to see the wicks," Peter said. And lamps it would have to be, for it was much too hot for the fireplace, and electric power had not reached this rural area.

After they opened the door and entered into the dim light of the main room, Peter took the globe from a large brass lantern, lit the wick, replaced the globe, and adjusted the flame. A hospitable yellow light flowed across the room, furnished with a worn but serviceable brown plaid couch, two brown side chairs, a coffee table, several side tables, decorative lamps, even a dark green rug, a sturdy desk, and an ornate bookshelf.

Evie's influence seemed to be everywhere, since Peter had never evidenced the slightest interest in or knowledge of home décor and had left Emma whatever furnishings they had during their years together.

"Have a seat, son, while I light one in the kitchen."

Casey took a chair in the corner with the best view of the adjoining kitchen. Noticing numerous magazines scattered about, he got up and gathered a small batch and sat back down with them in his lap. He flipped through them in curiosity: *Field & Stream*; *Pine and Pulpwood Market Journal*; *Progressive Farmer*; *Sears & Roebuck* sales fliers. There were even three copies of *National Geographic*, and atop one stack of magazines was a familiar Bible, well-worn from backyard worship services under the large spreading oak, an object indelibly imprinted in Casey's memory. His father had never been much of a reader, but that seemed to have changed. The magazines may have been his, but all the books would likely have been a part of Evie's décor.

Casey went over to the bookcase. Eclectic randomness here as well: more issues of some of the same magazines, stacked loosely on some of the shelves; and dozens of books, many that even showed evidence of pages having been turned down to mark a spot.

The first one that caught his eye was a rather large bound volume. Casey picked it up and looked at the title. *Moby Dick,* by Herman Melville. Then he moved his eyes down the shelves. *The Sound and the Fury; A Farewell to Arms; Walden; The Grapes of Wrath; Tom Sawyer; Huckleberry Finn;* another big thick book with the title of *Ulysses.* He couldn't imagine his father reading any of these big thick books. Peter came out of the kitchen and sat on the couch, and Casey returned to his chair.

"Looks to me like Evie's really tried to fix up this place for you . . . make you look like a country gentleman," Casey said. "It sure is nice now."

"She's made it mighty pretty and all for me, hasn't she?"

"Even got you a bunch of fancy books to make you look scholarly."

"That wasn't Evie's doing . . . that was your Carrie. After she got to going to that college, she'd pass along literary books after she got through with them."

As Casey knew, when their baby was a year old, with Evie's encouragement, Carrie had gone to Belhaven College, a short distance from the Gingerbread Inn. By going twelve months of the year, and taking some courses at nearby Millsaps College, she had graduated with honors in three years, majoring in English literature. By the time Casey returned, she had gotten a job teaching English at a local high school, the baby being placed, when necessary, in a daycare facility adjacent to Evie's hospital.

"I'm so proud of that Carrie," Peter continued. "She's the smartest, most book-learned person we've ever had in our family."

"You read any those books?" Casey asked.

"Tried to read 'em all. Some I could, some I couldn't stay with," Peter responded. "Liked that *Farewell to Arms* . . . lived a bunch of that myself, first war and all. That big *Moby Dick*, read about a quarter of it and quit.

Too much malarkey, not enough whaling. The Faulkner one . . . some of them people is like them that's peopled my world, and some of them places was like around here, but them long sentences was hard for me to keep up with. That big *Ulysses* one . . . didn't get far in that one."

At the bookcase, Peter scanned the titles of the books Carrie had brought him, refreshing his memory. "'Of course, I loved the ones about that Tom Sawyer and that Huck Finn. Saw a lot of me growing up—and you too—in them fellas."

The two Mark Twain novels were among only three that Casey had read. "Don't think I was quite the character those two were," he said.

Peter was deep in his own thoughts. "And those Twain books weren't only about those boys having fun," Peter continued, musing. "That fella, Twain, he was trying to tell us some stuff . . . like ain't nothing right about no one man owning no other man . . . and them that don't know it ain't got no religion and ain't got no right God."

"I read *Walden* in high school and liked it," Casey injected, not wanting to appear completely illiterate, Clemens' moral truths not being the high points of his recollections of Huck and Tom.

"Think I may have read *Walden* in school, too," Peter said. "But I read this copy Carrie brought. Lot of good stuff about living in that one. That Thoreau fella would probably think this place was a whole lot more house than I need." He made a sweeping gesture with his hand, intending to make Casey gaze around his modest, Evie-decorated farmhouse. "Maybe, son, if you'd read it again, you'd get more out of that second time, like I did."

Peter pulled the Steinbeck off the shelf and thumbed the pages. "Liked this *Grapes of Wrath*," he said. "Could relate to them folks. We had a lot of that around here during that Depression, and we didn't have no dust bowl . . . just a *nothing in the bowl*, bowl." He grinned broadly, pleased at thinking he might have succeeded at being humorous. "Let's go in the kitchen and look for some supper."

They went through a doorway into the country kitchen. Casey was impressed by the white-painted walls, floor painted gray enamel, open cabinets painted white, a sparse bright white set of dishes, and the L-shaped gray counter with a variety of items for daily use. Conspicuously, in the corner of the L-shaped counter, sat three unopened bottles of Old Crow.

On the counter was a colorful red canister set, in the shape of huge apples, with green stem handles, and by the window was a small square table with two chairs. On the table was a slick, red-checkered tablecloth, and in the center was a small green vase with artificial yellow flowers. Like everywhere Peter sat for long, the table had a simple glass ashtray. An iron wood stove was on one wall, pipe stuck through the wall above.

"Have a seat," Peter said, gesturing to a chair at the table. Casey sat down and gazed out into the gloaming through the large adjacent window. In the dim light he saw the barn and what looked like a horse and some cows beyond.

"What's that tank and little building?" Casey asked, pointing out the window to nearby structures.

"Kinda proud of that," Peter responded. "Go open that door and look in there." He pointed to a door to the right. Opening the door, Casey found a basic bathroom: toilet, wash basin, and shower.

"That was once a big pantry," Peter said. "But with Evie having that big fancy house in Jackson, I couldn't let them have to go to an outhouse when they're of a mind to come here. That little house is my generator and batteries, and that tank is for the water . . . and I put in a septic. Not as fancy as Evie's, but a lot better than that ole one-hole outhouse that was here before. Made another one upstairs, about like this one. That's why the tank is so tall."

"What'd you do upstairs?"

"Two little rooms, and that little bathroom. Evie and Carrie put beds and things in there too. One to the right at the top of the stairs is where you'll sleep." Obviously, Evie and Carrie had taken a serious interest in fixing up Peter's house, and it was apparent that he was proud of it. He was definitely excited about this homecoming celebration.

"Went in to McBee's grocery and got us some good T-bones to grill, and some big ole potatoes . . . and some budder beans. Even found an apple pie. Let's go out back and light up the grill." To the back porch they went. Peter lit a lantern and carried it out with them to light up the scene. Right beyond the back steps, Peter proceeded to light a charcoal fire in a grill made from an oil drum cut in half.

"Dennis gave me this," he announced, looking back over his shoulder, referring to the grill. "Dennis comes out some, mainly when his wife goes to see her people in Atlanta."

He came back to the porch and sat alongside Casey, in one of two rustic chairs with a table made from a tree stump between them. Peter lit his pipe, and Casey pulled cigarettes from his pocket and lit up, blowing a big puff out into the glow of the lamp Peter had brought out and placed on the porch floor.

"Now that you've taken up smoking, your Luckies and my P.A. ought to keep them skeeters off us. You drinkin' any whiskey these days?"

"Not above it."

"I'll get us a drink of whiskey. This may be a night for us to share more than a little beer." Coming back, he put a just-opened bottle of Old Crow, two glasses filled with ice, and some water in a fruit jar on the tree-stump table.

"Old Crow." Peter held up the whiskey bottle to the light of the lantern. "I drink what Dennis buys. He gets it in New Orleans . . . usually buys that good Black Jack. Said, with the war and all, this was the best he could get. Said Old Crow ought to be cheap, but high as hell right now. Ever had any Old Crow, son?"

"You bet. Bunch in basic. Elmer Wright would buy it. Said it was right cheap, but good stuff. Tasted good to me. He claimed General Grant favored it, and Lincoln wanted to get him a barrel, when he got to whipping us. Elmer even claimed that ole Mark Twain drank it."

"Well, then, let's let the crow caw," Peter said, trying again, rather weakly, to be comedic. "Even got two more bottles Dennis brought. Want any water in it?"

"I'll take it with only ice . . . let the ice melt, and sip."

"Why not?" Peter agreed, following suit.

They allowed the fire to burn down. Sipping their first drink, they prepared their meal. While they ate, they indulged in safe conversational topics: Carrie's job; the medium man; Evie's life; Casey's schoolmates, those who had gone to war, and those who had not; those who had returned alive; and those who had not. Neither mentioned his own combat experiences . . . and neither got to the subjects they so wanted to discuss.

CHAPTER 28

A NOTE OF CONCERN

T hey put the dishes in the worn farmhouse sink, picked up their glasses and the whiskey, then retired to the parlor, where the lantern was still brightly flickering. Both lit up and blew out long, slow puffs. Peter took the lead.

"Got any idea what you gonna do, now that you're home, son?"

"No . . . kinda feel lost. All I know is fighting the war and shooting my turret gun. Now it's over and I'm separated from all my friends . . . don't know how to do much else."

"You were only eighteen when you joined. Hadn't had much time to learn about anything to make a living at."

Casey thought for a minute, then turned and looked directly at Peter. "And so were you."

"Well, most of us don't have no good plan all the time," Peter said. "Sometimes you have to take what's there . . . until something better comes up. I love being a wood buyer, but I didn't know anything about that when I was your age. It just happened. We're both empty. Let me get us some more ice." He picked up their glasses and went to the kitchen, visiting his new indoor facilities in the process.

Peter refilled their glasses while Casey took his turn in the new bathroom. Then they both sat again, thinking, Peter swirling his ice in his whiskey.

"Know Wyatt Young'll take you back at the lumberyard . . . says you was one of the best he ever worked."

Casey took a big sip of his whiskey, which was virtually straight, little ice having melted at this point. "Maybe that would be a start. But I don't want to pull lumber orders all my life . . . Carrie's gone to college, don't want her to have all the education . . . me not know enough for her to talk to me about her kind of stuff . . . Don't think she'll want to come back to Glasper."

"I've read some of her books, and we can talk about them, and I don't have no college."

"Yeah. But maybe if you had some college you could have gotten through some of those others."

The minute this came out Casey was sorry he'd said it. Peter looked hurt.

"Don't take that wrong, Papa. They might have been just as boring."

"No. You're right. You oughta go to college, like Carrie. Think you're gonna be in for some good government help, and you know I'll give you money if you're needing it. Maybe you could study to be one of those engineers that designs fancy things."

Casey filled their glasses. Not enough time had elapsed since the last refill for there to be much need for more ice. They were getting drunk. Casey sat staring into his glass; Peter sat looking at him, trying not to be too obvious, awaiting a response. He had thought he would like to have been an engineer, been the one who designed the machines they used in the paper mill.

They sat, pondering and sipping their whiskey. Peter put his glass down and lit his pipe. Casey finally looked up from his glass. "I think I may want to be a lawyer," he said in a slow, distinct voice.

"Why a lawyer?" Peter asked.

"Two years in England . . . my commander was Major Hadley. He and I got close and we talked some. Both of us had a baby boy we didn't know except in pictures. He already had a little girl, too. We'd show each other pictures when they came. Major Hadley was a lawyer before the war."

Casey reached for the Old Crow, which by then had only an inch left in the bottle. "You're out of luck, Papa, I'm killing the Crow," he said, draining the bottle.

"Not so . . . got more." Peter got up and retrieved another bottle, pulling off the top and stumbling as he came back through the cased opening. He topped them both off and smiled, nearly missing his own glass with the first pour.

"Don't know why, but Major Hadley was always trying to encourage me to be a lawyer, mainly after I made Sergeant and got to be over other people. Claimed he liked the way I handled my men who had problems, guided them to do the right thing . . . said that was a lot of what a good lawyer had to do. He said lots of lawyering—at least his kind—was about things that didn't have no clear answer, just about judgment. Major Hadley thought I'd be a good lawyer, thought I'd have judgment and do good at getting people to do what would be best for them. He said lots of folks wouldn't follow the best advice, 'less it was what they wanted to hear."

"Being a lawyer would take a whole lot of schooling," Peter said.

"I know, and I'd hate to move Carrie and Little Casey out on Evie— all a sudden—about the minute I got home, so I could go off to law school. Can tell Evie's mighty happy having them there, gotten mighty used to not being by herself, and Carrie's made a commitment to her teaching. I think she likes her school. Doesn't seem right to mess them up on everything so I can go off to law school. And I don't want to leave Carrie again and go off to school by myself."

"I don't know anything about law school," Peter said. "We'll have to study about it some."

They sat quietly, continuing to sip their whiskey, until Peter got up abruptly, and left the room. He returned with a picture of the older Elizabeth Baker, standing on her doorstep in a dark dress, a photograph Casey had taken and sent soon after he found her.

"She's still mighty pretty, ain't she?" Peter said, wistfully.

Casey looked at the picture, handed it back, and went out the front door. Peter heard the door to the Ford slamming, and Casey came back in, handing his father two pictures, taken of him and Elizabeth in the pub the night before he left on the *Queen Mary*. Casey had her hugged against him and they were smiling at the camera, both appearing quite intoxicated.

Peter studied them intently, switching from one to the other several times. He was obviously enthralled.

"Don't think I was ever able to get her quite that drunk."

Peter got up again and left the room, returning with yet another picture, handing it to Casey.

"Here's a picture of your brother she sent me."

Casey studied it and handed it back.

"She says he looks just like you, and he really does, wish we coulda known him."

Peter sat intently studying the picture of Peter Prince in his lap.

"Guess she's right. Couldn't deny him, as they say."

They sat for a full minute, Peter continuing to study the picture.

"Got to pee," Peter announced, stumbling back toward the bathroom. Casey opted for a pee off the porch in the front yard. They both got back and topped off their glasses, unconcerned about any ice. The second bottle was nearly half gone. They had been drinking together for almost four hours. Casey had consumed more, but Peter was the drunker. Casey had been drinking almost daily in England; Peter was older, had been eating and sleeping little, and was considerably smaller.

"I loved her so," Peter said, his speech slurred. "Still do . . . think about her all the time. You think she'd marry me . . . if I went to her and was divorced?"

"Yes, Papa, I do."

"You really think so?"

"Yes, Papa, I do."

Peter downed the rest of his whiskey in two big gulps, shuddered, wiping his mouth on his right sleeve.

He sat staring at his empty glass, cupped in both hands in front of him. Then his countenance changed. Peter became flushed and began to shake. "Mean, conniving woman!" he said in a low voice, before stumbling to his feet and suddenly hurling the half full bottle of Old Crow through the parlor window. Fortunately, in the heat of the night, the windows had been raised, leaving only the screen in its path, little match for the half-full bottle of whiskey. Pieces of the ripped screen were left dangling against the dark of the night. With the throw, he stumbled to his knees. Reaching to pull himself up on the table, his hand contacted his beloved meerschaum resting in the ashtray. He gripped it by the barrel and stood up, wobbly and still shaking.

"Mean, conniving woman!" he shouted again, throwing his most precious material possession, his beloved meerschaum, on a path to follow the bottle. It glanced off the windowsill and sailed out into the darkness.

He sat down. "The woman is gonna have to give me a divorce. One way or another I've got to make her understand that." Peter leaned forward, putting his elbows on his knees, where he remained, sobbing softly.

"Papa, something will get worked out . . . it will have to."

Peter's shaking began to subside, and he said in a rather soft monotone, "The sorry woman is a lying, conniving woman."

He stood up for a moment, an unsteady, wobbling drunk, and threw his glass at the window. This time his aim failed him, resulting in a direct hit on the windowsill, the glass breaking with a crash, only a small part of it clearing the window.

He turned and looked at Casey through glassy eyes.

"I'm going to bed. You're upstairs. There's a flashlight by the stairs."

Peter stumbled out, crashing into the face of the doorway, bouncing off, and disappearing from Casey's view.

Casey sat for a time, trying to come to grips with what he had witnessed, trying to make drunken sense of it all. He had never before seen his father drunk, nor seen him in a fit of anger. Two large moths had already found the missing screen and hovered around the lantern. A mosquito bit him on the hand. He got up, pulled the window down, pulled the curtains together, and went back to Peter's room, where he found his father, passed out on the bed, still fully clothed.

Finding the flashlight by the stairs, he went out into the darkness and around to the side of the house, looking for the bottle and the pipe. The bottle he located easily, over an inch of whiskey still left in it. The pipe was not so easy, but eventually Casey located that, much closer to the house. He came back in, sat back in his chair, pouring what was left of the second bottle of Old Crow into his glass, then placing Peter's meerschaum gently back in the ashtray. He sipped the rest of his whiskey and smoked another Lucky, after which he went up the stairs to his assigned bedroom, stripping down to his underwear and getting in bed, a disturbed young man. He didn't know what his father might do, never having seen him like this.

Casey did not sleep well; he kept waking up and staring up at the dark ceiling. The first rays of light that came through the window were merciful. He dressed and went downstairs, found Peter where he had left him, in his bed fully clothed, snoring loudly, the room having the distinct smell of a human body trying to detoxify itself from too much alcohol.

Realizing it would be hard for either of them to talk about the events of the night before, without it being most awkward, he wanted to gracefully leave before his father awoke. Finding a pencil and piece of paper in the parlor, he sat at the kitchen table, drinking his coffee, and scrawled his father a note.

Papa
You were sleeping too good for me to want to wake you
Needed to get back
Glad to be back from over there
Enjoyed last night. See you soon.
Casey

He sat for a few moments, staring at the note he had written, pressing his hand hard into the table, still gripping the pencil and he wrote beneath his signature:

Papa, please. Please don't do anything until you talk to some lawyer. Until you at least talk to me.

Driving back to Jackson, Casey passed where the crow had been the day before, reluctant to leave his carrion. Off to the side of the road he saw what had been a squirrel, now reduced to a bushy tail, a few small bones, some tufts of dusty fur. All the way back Casey had a queasy, empty feeling. He felt he should do something. But what? Maybe his father would see a lawyer; maybe a lawyer could help.

CHAPTER 29

A VISIT TO A LAWYER

Peter awoke dizzy and thirsty, with a deep, throbbing headache. He stumbled to his new bathroom, found two aspirins, then headed to the kitchen, getting a glass of water and sitting down at the kitchen table. Taking the aspirins and drinking the water, he found himself becoming queasy, so he went back to bed.

An hour later, he opened his eyes and stared weakly at the ceiling. His head was still hurting, but he was no longer queasy. This was his worst hangover ever.

At eleven in the morning, he arrived at his office at the pulp mill, still afflicted with a throbbing headache, and in the grip of an all-consuming anger. Documents for several prospective wood purchases were on his desk and needed attention, but concentrating on his work was impossible. He smoked, pondered, brooded . . . His hands shaking, he repeatedly clenched his fist.

"Sorry woman," he muttered to himself every few minutes. "Woman is going to have to let me go." Finally, he did control himself enough to decide to see a lawyer, and the lawyer he wanted to talk to was Benjamin Levine.

~

As Peter's timber-buying acumen became obvious, Dennis Langley saw further opportunity to use Peter's talents. Dennis and Peter formed a partnership: D & P Investments. When they saw a bargain, D & P Investments bought not only the timber, but the land as well. Peter found the deal; Dennis had financing and contacts; lawyer Benjamin Levine closed the deal. In time, they would sell the land for substantial profit.

Levine and Peter were as different as two people could be, but Levine was the lawyer Peter knew well, and trusted. He had a corner office on the ground floor of a traditional two-story red brick building in the middle of Glasper, right up the street from Dennis Langley's bank. Clarence Townsend's drugstore shared the building's first floor. Upstairs were two other law offices and an insurance agency.

Peter had paid little attention to the time, and he got there at ten past noon. He walked up to the door, entered, and looked around, finding no one there. A one-lawyer office in a sleepy country town, with one secretary, could be expected to be out for lunch at noon. The rhythm and routine of the town was familiar to him, as to most people. He knew Thelma Bradley, Levine's longtime secretary, had gone home to lunch. Almost inevitably, if he went to Maude Powell's café down the street, he would find Levine, sitting alone at his traditional table enjoying the daily special, and reading his latest available copy of the *Wall Street Journal*. He also knew from prior experience that Levine did not intend for this read or his lunch to be interrupted by legal business.

Peter went back and got into his car. He filled his pipe; lit it; and waited. Fifteen minutes later, Thelma appeared at the door, opened it, went in. Peter opened the car door, scraped out his pipe on the street, put it down on the metal dash, and followed her. She was middle-aged, gray, plain, and pleasant, with a broad, square face, and an equally square hairdo.

"Got us another deal today?" she said in a friendly tone, when she looked up from her desk and recognized Peter.

"Not today. Need to talk to Mr. Ben about something personal."

"He should be back any time."

"I'll just wait here." Peter took a seat in the reception area across from her desk. The office was elegant and formal: walls of dark varnished mahogany, with wide crown molding and thick matching door facings, replete with framed memorabilia, diplomas, certificates, and awards. Behind

Thelma's spacious mahogany desk was a large gold-framed landscape with billowing white clouds. Two broad street-front windows with white curtains further tempered the otherwise dark scene. Peter Montgomery sat in a red leather chair, waiting the return of Benjamin Levine.

At seventy-two, Levine had maintained a solo practice in this small storefront office on Main Street for more than forty years. He was the only Harvard Law graduate to ever practice in the county. Widely respected, he was smart, hard-working, fair, compassionate, frequently giving of his time to a wide variety of legal and civic efforts.

A small, thin man, Levine was always impeccably dressed in custom-tailored suits, and never without his trademark, a stylish bow tie. He had never smoked, and the only alcohol he drank was expensive Scotch that he sipped straight, after his evening meal, beneath the high ceilings of his elegant study. To find competition for his passions, bridge and chess, he traveled extensively. Levine's grammar was perfect; his enunciation precise.

Benjamin and his wife Edith were the only Jewish residents of this rural county with a population of only nine thousand. The son of a moderately successful Brooklyn jeweler, Benjamin had met Edith Warren, a petite blond, at a party on Long Island in the summer of 1893. He was in his second year at Harvard Law School, she a liberal arts senior at Vassar. They married upon his graduation in 1895.

Edith was the daughter of Jonathan P. Warren, who had amassed a fortune in early oil wells in Pennsylvania and West Virginia. Not long before Edith and Benjamin married, Jonathan had invested a substantial portion of his fortune in over thirty thousand acres of virgin timber in South Mississippi. The purchase included five thousand acres of fertile river bottom land, interest in two banks and a railroad.

On the five thousand acres was a large, white-columned antebellum mansion, set back amid spreading live oaks, seven miles out from Glasper. Right out of law school, Benjamin agreed to come to Mississippi to help manage these investments. This he did until Edith's brother Johnny graduated from Wharton in 1899 and came to take over these family interests. Edith had come to love her stately home, where she had developed extensive gardens, and she did not want to leave. So, in 1902, Benjamin Levine went off to Glasper to hang out a shingle, to become the lawyer Peter wanted to talk to this fall afternoon of 1945 about a divorce.

Levine immediately noticed Peter sitting in his office when he arrived fifteen minutes later. "Good afternoon, Mr. Montgomery," he addressed him, ever deferential and respectfully formal. "You and Mr. Langley about to make another good land deal, I take it."

"He needs to talk to you about something personal," Thelma interjected, before Peter could respond.

"Well, go in my office, Mr. Montgomery, and have a seat." Benjamin Levine took off his dark gray fedora and slapped it sharply, as if to knock off dust, then hung it on the hat rack. The hat was not the least bit dusty. There were those in town who claimed he bought a new one every month. "Hate this dust," he said. "Hate driving a dirty car, but no point in washing it right now." He was not known to drive one of those long either.

It was well known that Levine was extremely wealthy and practiced law for a simple reason; he loved the law and he loved the feeling it gave him to help people, the more common the better. He had helped so many for so long, so often without remuneration, that Benjamin was known as impossible to beat in Duncan County.

Levine's inner office was a repeat of the dark mahogany, but brightened by floor-to-ceiling bookcases, filled with books, almost all with wheat-colored binding. It was considered the most extensive private law library within several counties, and Levine was known to be generous in allowing other lawyers to use his books, so long as they were faithfully returned to Thelma within a day.

Levine came in and took a seat behind his large, ornately-carved desk. Behind him, in a break in the bookcases, was a six-foot-wide counter, stacked with files. Over the counter was another landscape painting, a colorful impressionistic street scene, this one vertically-oriented and also framed in gold.

"What can I help you with, Mr. Montgomery?" Levine asked, looking over his thin wire glasses.

"I want a divorce."

"Well, perhaps I can help you with that. Why do you want a divorce?"

"Don't love the woman. Haven't lived with her in over six years . . .

not going back."

"Well, it's pretty well known around the county that you and Mrs. Montgomery have been separated for a long time. What's her attitude about a divorce?"

"Every time I talk to her about it, she says no way in hell am I going to get one . . . that I'll get a divorce over her dead body."

"That's rather morbid histrionics," Levine said. Peter gave him a blank look. "Unnecessarily dramatic," the lawyer added, realizing his poor choice of words. Having years of experience in these matters, Levine was tempted to ask Peter if he had found someone else, but he decided against it.

"Well, if she decides to fight it, you will need some recognized statutory grounds for divorce, and some evidence to support it. Does she have a lover?"

"Be hard to believe."

"Has she ever struck you?"

"No."

"Ever cursed you?"

"Emma believes most cussing is a sin . . . against the third commandment and all. She did tell me to get out of the goddamned house once . . . then went to praying for forgiveness, right out loud, with me a-standing there."

"That the only time?"

"Think so."

"Does she berate you?" Again, Levine got a blank look. "Scold you? Criticize you? Run you down? Constantly nag you?"

"Well, she criticizes me and scolds me some."

"About what?"

"Mostly—before I left her—if I try to smoke in the house, which I haven't done in years . . . and she accuses me of being out drinking sometimes, though I don't let her catch me at it, and I don't admit it."

"You have any witnesses who would say she constantly nags and criticizes you?"

Peter thought for a moment. "Not that I can think of."

"Does she refuse to have sex with you?"

"Of course, I haven't had anything to do with her in six years, but before I left her, if I give her three days' notice of when I think I might want to do it . . . sometimes she was willing . . . maybe half the time."

Levine was getting desperate. "What's the worst thing you can think of she has ever done to you?"

"Well, she took over fifteen thousand dollars of my money and put it all in her name."

"Did you ever demand that she give it back?"

"Well, kind of. I started asking for half, but I changed and asked for five hundred dollars of it, to give our son, who needed it."

"How many times?"

Peter had to ponder this one as well. "Well, we had a big fight about it . . . finally told her to keep the damn money, but I was leaving."

"And you never asked her for it again."

"No."

Levine struggled with what he should say. Then he looked over his glasses at Peter, a look of compassion and concern, and he said in a softer voice. "Mr. Montgomery, some states may have no-fault divorce statutes, but one has never passed here. In Mississippi, to get a divorce, you have to prove one of the statutory grounds, and I don't think you can."

"You don't think I can get a divorce?"

"Maybe if your wife softens and doesn't contest it, but not if she decides to contest it."

Peter sat and looked at the floor.

Levine added, "Mr. Montgomery, why don't I write her a letter and tell her you have contacted me about a divorce and you would make her a generous settlement, if she is interested, and to contact me or have her lawyer do so, if she is?"

"How long would we give her?"

"No specific time is necessary. Are you in a hurry, Mr. Montgomery? You have been separated for over six years."

"Yes."

Benjamin Levine pondered whether to ask the question he had previously shelved, and then decided, given this response, it would be appropriate. "Have you found someone else, Mr. Montgomery?"

"Well, kind of," Peter answered, looking up at him. "Name's Elizabeth. But I ain't seen her since I left England in 1918."

Benjamin Levine thought this might be a truly interesting story, but one that would involve more of his day than he had available. The letter described to Peter would go out the following day, and they would wait and see if it brought any meaningful response.

After leaving, Peter cranked his car and put it in gear to back out and leave. Then he stopped and shut it off. He sat for a minute thinking; then he got out and walked across the street and into the bank lobby. Mildred Amos, Dennis's secretary, looked up and greeted him.

"Mr. Langley has gone to the barber shop, Mr. Montgomery. He should be back soon."

"Only need something to write a letter on."

Mildred got several sheets of paper and an envelope out of her desk. "I have some plain paper, but my envelopes all have bank letterheads. Wait! Here's a blank envelope."

"Thanks."

"Need a stamp?"

"No. I'll need special stamps at the post office."

Peter went over to an island counter in the lobby and picked up a pen, secured to the counter with a small chain, and started writing.

> *Dear Elizabeth,*
> *Talked to lawyer about help to get divorce today.*
> *He is going to try and help me. Want to be with you*
> *real bad. Hope you are well—*
> *I love you*
> *Peter*

At the post office, he sat frozen in his car as anger began to well up within him. Then, inexplicably, the anger subsided and an empty, helpless feeling came in its place. Peter tore the letter from the sealed envelope and sat staring at it for a few moments, then he crumpled the letter and the envelope together, threw them on the passenger seat and cranked the car. "What's the point of it?" he thought, dejectedly, as he drove off. Things needed his attention at his office, but he was not up to dealing with any of them.

Leaving town, he ran into a hard rain. By the time the short stretch of pavement ran out, rivulets of muddy brown water were streaming off the road and down roadside ditches. When he pulled up to his house, the downpour was still unabated, with big, windswept torrents rolling across the landscape. Turning off the car stopped the clapping of the wipers, a blessed relief for his still-aching head and fragile psyche.

Clutching the crumpled letter and envelope, he got out of the car and strode into the house, at a pace no different from what it would have been on a sunny afternoon. Drenched, he sat down at his kitchen table, putting the crumpled paper in front of him. The water running into his eyes began to annoy him, so he got up and retrieved a dish towel beside the sink, wiped the water from his face, sat back down. He opened the now-wet letter and folded it out on the table in front of him, where he stared at it blankly.

The last of the three bottles of Old Crow that Dennis Langley had brought him was in the corner of the kitchen counter. He got up, picked up the bottle, looking briefly at the label; then, with the help of a kitchen knife, he removed the top. Pulling a water glass from a shelf, he sat down at the table with the Old Crow and filled the glass to within an inch of the top, which took half the bottle.

Peter sat at the table drinking straight bourbon, staring at the wet letter, his mind far away in time and space. He was in Europe in 1918, on a battlefield in France, amid the dead and dying; he was in the south of England, in a hospital, severely wounded and in great pain; he was in a one-room flat in the north of London, with a beautiful little woman named Elizabeth, both of them naked in her bed.

Outside the window a bright flash of lightning streaked across the sky, with a clap of thunder, then another. The glass of whiskey was less than half full as he took another gulp, now almost tasteless. His mood turned morose. He saw himself in another room, with another woman, both fully clothed. He was trying to reason with her, plead with her, beg her, and all she would say was, "No way in hell . . . you'll get a divorce over my dead body."

Suddenly there was a huge, blinding explosion and a cannon-like boom, as lightning struck a large oak not a hundred feet away. Startled, Peter knocked over the glass of Old Crow, and the whiskey ran across the table, soaking the letter. Through drunken, lifeless eyes he watched the glass roll slowly around on the table and stop, just inches away from the edge. Quite drunk, Peter put his head down on the table, wet with bourbon whiskey, and he fell into a stupor.

CHAPTER 30

TWO TURDS

Emma's response to Benjamin Levine's letter came the day after it was mailed. Thelma had been at the office a mere thirty minutes. Benjamin had just come in, taken off his hat, sat down at his desk, and begun to look at his morning mail.

The front door burst open with a forcefulness that caused it to shudder upon its hinges. There, standing in front of Thelma, was Emma Montgomery, all two hundred pounds of her, not so much fat as stout, a chunky, thick-bodied woman. She had on no makeup, her hair was short and straight, and she had on a baggy cotton dress, hemmed just below her knees. Her round face was red and she had fire in her small, closely-set eyes.

"Where's Levine?" she barked. Then, not waiting for an answer, she burst into Benjamin Levine's office. The stately lawyer tried to rise respectfully, but Emma did not give him time, so he sat back down.

"Here's your answer!" she said, in a loud, angry voice, throwing the wadded letter across the desk. "And tell that damn little turd he'll get a divorce over my dead body." With that she started out, as abruptly as she came in. But, right at the door, she turned and addressed Levine again, pointing her finger at him. "And you're a damn little turd, too." She exited the office, again punishing the vintage door and its antique hinges.

Levine got up and went to stand before Thelma at her desk.

"My. Glad I'm not married to that," he said.

"Do you want me to call the law?"

"Of course not. She didn't hurt anybody nor break anything."

"You going to let her call you a little turd, Mr. Ben, and not do anything about it?"

Not answering, Levine turned toward his office, only to come back. "Do you think calling someone a damned little turd violates the Third Commandment?" he asked her, with a rather perplexed look. Thelma showed no comprehension. "I guess it depends on what force in the universe is in on the damning," he said, answering his own question. "Call Mr. Montgomery at the pulp mill and tell him Mrs. Montgomery has given us her answer, and I'd like him to come by my office to discuss it, when he can and I'm free. And don't tell him anything about what Mrs. Montgomery said when she was here."

"Surely, you're going to tell him Mrs. Montgomery called both of you damned little turds, aren't you, Mr. Ben?"

"No."

"Why not? He ought to know what she said about him."

Benjamin looked at Thelma, giving her a slight frown.

"Because that would not represent good judgment, Thelma."

~

Peter had managed to devote his day to making contacts with landowners about timber purchases, and it was late afternoon when Thelma was finally able to locate Peter in his office at the pulp mill. He came immediately, and was soon sitting across Levine's desk from him, two relatively small men, not an ounce of fat on either of them, both recently dubbed little turds. "She's given us her response," Benjamin said.

Peter said nothing, but raised his eyebrows, inquiringly.

"She says she is not interested in a divorce."

"How'd you hear?"

"She came by my office, first thing this morning."

"That's all she said?"

"Yes."

"None of that . . . *no way in hell . . . over my dead body* stuff?"

"She is not interested in a divorce," Levine said, rather firmly, with a tone of finality.

Peter started to shake, and he calmed the shake by forcefully gripping his knees. The back of his arms felt strangely cold. Both said nothing, as Levine let Peter try and collect his composure.

"Then there is nothing I can do about getting a divorce?"

"Well, you could file a divorce suit against her, claiming *habitual cruel and inhuman treatment*, that's the language of the statute, knowing you probably don't have sufficient proof to support it in a trial, but hoping the suit will cause her to soften, want to get it over with. Sometimes it does that. But it might also make Emma mad and even more unreasonable."

"It might make her madder, but she couldn't be more unreasonable."

"You could wait a while and hope maybe she finds someone else and then she wants a divorce. That happens quite often. Many women, when they finally accept that their husband is definitely not coming back, tend to start wanting to find another one."

"Fat chance of that."

"Do you want me to prepare and file a divorce complaint, like I mentioned?" Levine said, wanting to tactfully wind things up.

"Let me think about it some."

Giving Levine a disgusted frown, Peter got up and walked out, not even speaking to Thelma as he went out the door.

"What's he going to do?" Thelma came to Levine's door and asked.

"He wants to think about it."

"Mr. Ben, I can't see thinking long about staying married to that."

"Who knows?" Levine reflected. "She might suddenly decide she's as ready for a divorce as he is. Women can be fickle and unpredictable, you know."

"And men can't?"

"Thelma, my dear, there are substantial gender differences between the minds of men and women."

"Probably so, and you men are impossible to understand!"

~

After leaving Benjamin Levine's office, Peter went out to his country house and sat on the back porch for a time, staring into space toward his barn and pasture. The time came for him to eat his evening meal, but he had no appetite; actually, he felt nauseated. A cottontail rabbit munched the few remaining weeds along the fence line. The rabbit had grown accustomed to Peter, felt no threat from him, paid him no attention. From his position, lying at Peter's feet, Enos could not see him.

As it grew dark, Peter went in and lit two lamps, one in the kitchen, another in his bedroom. Finally deciding to try and eat, he found some cornbread, salted ham, and sweet tea. After a few bites, he pushed it aside.

Sitting at the table, Enos at his feet, Peter attempted to evaluate his options. Maybe he could go to England, make Elizabeth love him enough to come home with him, live with him in sin, as he had always heard it called. Certainly, it would matter little that he gave Emma grounds to divorce him for adultery. But he couldn't imagine Elizabeth being willing to do that, nor him wanting her to.

Maybe he could go to England, lie to Elizabeth, tell her he was divorced, marry her in England, never come back, hope no one ever discovered his crime. He was not much concerned with going to jail if his lie was detected, but he could not see doing that to Elizabeth. Her whole life would be based on a lie.

Why? Why wouldn't the woman give him a divorce? She knew he wasn't going back. Why did she have to be so mean and heartless? He kept seeing her in front of him, always shouting, "Peter Montgomery, there ain't never going to be no divorce! Not now! Not ever! Peter Montgomery, you'll get a divorce over my dead body!"

Peter visited the bathroom, returned to the kitchen, turned out the lamp, retired to his bedroom. He took off his outer clothing, turned off the bedroom lamp, got into his bed. He lay on his back, looking up at the dark ceiling.

Eventually, he fell into a restless sleep. Peter had always been prone to dreams: sometimes pleasant ones of playing baseball in his youth, fishing with his father; his times with Casey, Dennis, Hannah; so often of Elizabeth. Then there had been the nightmares: his time in the trenches; on the battlefield; in pain in the hospital; wretched times on the verge of dying with the flu; unpleasant events with Emma. Often, he awoke realizing he had been dreaming, but with little recall of what they were about.

Other times, when he awakened, his dreams were still vivid in his mind.

Toward morning, Peter was dreaming that he was marrying Elizabeth. The ceremony was taking place in the Glasper Baptist Church, the church of his heritage. It was mid-afternoon on a sunny autumn Saturday. Although Methodist, Reverend Robert Sims was conducting the ceremony. Elizabeth wore a beautiful white wedding gown, with much satin and lace. She carried a bouquet of red flowers. Janet was her maid of honor; Evie and Carrie were bridesmaids. His father was his best man; Dennis and Arthur were groomsmen. The bridesmaids wore red satin dresses. All the men were dressed in matching dark suits.

"Dearly beloved," Reverend Sims was saying. "We have gathered here together today to unite this man, Peter Montgomery, and this woman, Elizabeth Baker, in the bonds of holy matrimony."

Suddenly there was a shout from the back of the church. "Stop! You stop! There ain't gonna be no marriage! Not now and not ever!"

It was Emma. Red-faced and angry, in her usual dowdy cotton dress. She had a long-barreled pistol in her hand.

Emma walked through the wedding party, right between Peter and Elizabeth, pushing them aside, and up to Reverend Sims. "You get! You get outta here! You put that Bible down and you get!" With that, she pointed the pistol toward the face of Reverend Sims. Robert Sims went around her and started down the aisle toward the rear of the church.

Emma approached Elizabeth, who was holding the bouquet in front of her, and pointed the pistol at Elizabeth. "And you get! You get back to wherever you come from . . . and don't ya ever come back. He's mine and ain't nobody else ever gonna have him. Not now and not ever. You get!"

Emma turned toward the stained-glass window behind the altar, aimed the pistol from the hip, and pulled the trigger. Multicolored glass shattered and fell.

"All of you get!" she shouted. "Anyone goin' slow may get some of these other bullets in this here gun." The wedding party scattered, most going toward the rear of the church. Peter grabbed Elizabeth's arm and pulled her toward a side door.

Peter awakened from the dream, sweating; his heart was pounding. For over two hours, he lay in bed, overcome by depression, his mind alternating between despair and anger.

Finally, he got up, put paper, kindling, and wood in his cast-iron stove, and lit it. Pumping the bellows a dozen times to enhance the flame, Peter closed the stove door. He washed out his coffee pot, put water and coffee in it; sat it on the stove to await enough heat to boil the water.

He returned to his bedroom, putting on the same clothes he had worn the day before, went to the kitchen table, and put on his work boots, methodically tightening and tying the laces.

The water began to boil in the coffee pot and it began to perk. Peter kept a large cast-iron skillet at the back of the stove, always greased and ready for use. It was hot enough now for his usual bacon and eggs. He put two slices of bacon into the skillet, poured a cup of coffee, sat down at the table, giving the bacon time to cook. When he sensed the bacon should be ready, he got up, took out the bacon, cracked two eggs into the skillet. Standing over the stove, he watched until the eggs fried hard.

Back at the table, Peter sat in front of his bacon and eggs and a cold biscuit. He knew he should try to eat, or he would likely be hungry later in the day. He ate one piece of bacon and part of one egg, then pushed the plate away to the middle of the table, drinking his coffee.

Peter couldn't get his mind off Emma. How had he let her come into his life and ruin it like she did? He could try to blame Dennis, but he knew he didn't have to go with Dennis to Joe Don's Place, didn't have to get drunk, knew that the minute he became conscious of what Emma was doing he could have pushed her away. No. He couldn't blame any-one but himself. He had never tried to before, and he wouldn't now. His life was what he had made it. But now he had a chance to make it what he wished it had always been.

Peter got up from the table, put the now-empty coffee cup on the counter by the sink, and walked out the back door of the farmhouse, down the six broad wooden steps. As he cleared the bottom step, Enos followed in his wake.

Well out in the pasture, Pepper heard the door slam, whinnied, gal-loped to meet him. Pepper was a quarter-horse gelding Peter had bought for nine-year-old Casey in 1931. They had named him after Pepper Martin, the Cardinals outfielder and hero of the 1931 World Series. Peter had wound up with Pepper when Casey married and left home.

At the barn, Pepper was waiting for him at the gate. Peter went into the tack room, filled a bucket with oats, sprinkled a handful of sweet feed on top, put the bucket outside the gate, and shut it. Pepper proceeded to munch away.

Back at the farmhouse, Peter retrieved his cup; refilled it; sat back down at the table. Enos came up and put his muzzle in Peter's lap, wagging his tail. Peter patted him on the head, then took both his hands and rubbed Enos's floppy hound ears simultaneously. Enos closed his eyes to savor the moment, and his tail loudly thumped on the gray wood floor.

The day before, Peter had obtained two wood buys for his company. He had other prospects he could approach today, but he was in no mood to do so. He was in no mood to do anything, unless maybe die.

Leaving his coffee cup on the table, Peter returned to his bedroom and lay down on the bed, not even bothering to take off his boots. He lay thinking about Elizabeth; thinking about Emma; reliving his dream of the night before. He lay on the bed for another hour, in the grip of a mind-numbing depression.

When he decided to get up, Peter sat on the edge of the bed for a few minutes, leaning forward, staring at his work boots. Walking to the pantry he retrieved his shotgun, propped in a corner. The only time he had touched it in years was to move it when necessary.

Peter's shotgun was a double-barrel Parker, twelve-gauge, double trigger, circa 1915. His father gave it to him new when he returned from the war in 1918, thinking it would be the perfect gift, a source of envy in their hunting culture. But when he left Europe in 1918, Peter never wanted to touch another gun. In twenty-seven years he had not shot it, something he had carefully kept from his father.

He sat at the kitchen table, shotgun in front of him, his right hand resting on the stock, thinking about Elizabeth, thinking about Emma, reliving his vivid dream of the night before. Emma was the mother of his only child. He could never hurt her, but maybe he could threaten her and make her think he could; make her be reasonable. Make her let him have Elizabeth.

Peter thought about shotgun shells. It was deer season when his father had given him the shotgun, and his father had given him a box of buckshot with the gun. The box had never been opened. He retrieved the shotgun shells from the pantry, sat back at the table, fumbled with the tab at the top of the box to open it. He took two shells out, staring at them. There was no stained-glass window where Emma lived, but there were windows with many panes. He doubted he would do anything like that, but if it would let him have Elizabeth . . . he might.

Picking up the shotgun, Peter walked through the dining room and living room to the front door. At the front door he realized Enos was not behind him. "Come on Enos! You gotsta go out!" Peter called back to Enos, who followed him down the steps.

Standing by the old Ford, he put two shells in the Parker, leaving the breach open, and he got in, placing the gun on the passenger seat. Backing up and turning around in the yard, he drove out and took a right onto the country road, a mixture of dirt and gravel, wide enough for two cars to pass, always dusty or muddy, never long in between. Today it was dusty, very dusty. As he headed east toward Glasper, the morning sun hit the accumulated dust on his windshield, making it hard to see. He flicked on the wipers, which flapped loudly on the dry windshield, clearing away most of the dust.

When he pulled up outside the house, much had changed about the place since he moved out six years earlier. The old azaleas, hollies, and nandinas he had so painstakingly pruned and restored were straggly and overgrown. The white paint was peeling in places, showing brown wood, particularly in areas most exposed to the west sun. The lower left pane in a dormer window was cracked and a third of it had fallen out; several spindles were missing on the front step rails.

It was now almost ten o'clock, bright and clear, temperature approaching eighty. For ten minutes, Peter sat in his car, staring at the house, his Parker double-barrel draped across the passenger seat, breach open, two buckshot firmly seated in the chambers.

He could picture her in there, probably seated at the table where she sewed, obese, hair unkempt, barefoot, in a dowdy cotton dress. When she saw him come into this room for the first time in six years, her look would likely be what it almost always was, in their last years together: a look of contempt and scorn.

He tried to picture her reaction when she unexpectedly saw the shotgun, wondered if she would fear death. Probably not. She'd likely just laugh and sneer at him, realize he was probably bluffing, wouldn't make good on any threat he made; that she could stare him down, put him in his place, once again take advantage of his disdain for friction and conflict.

Peter stepped out of the car into the sunlight, snapped shut the breach of the shotgun, and started across the lawn.

CHAPTER 31

HIS PEACE BOND

"E MMA!" he shouted, as he mounted the steps and threw open the front door. There sat Emma's sewing group, sewing in their laps, all neighbors, all women Peter knew well: Gina Townsend, the local druggist's wife; Myrtle Peters, an older widow who sometimes helped Emma with her sewing; and Tina Elliott, whose husband was a traveling shoe salesman. All four women's faces registered shock.

Peter was taken aback at the unexpected presence of the others, but he was completely out of control and not to be deterred. He shouted as loud as he possibly could. "WOMAN! YOU'RE GOING TO GIVE ME A DIVORCE! YOU UNDERSTAND! YOU LISTEN TO ME, WOMAN! YOU'RE GOING TO GIVE ME A DIVORCE!"

He paused a moment, staring at Emma, then continued, hyperventilating and shaking, "I'VE GIVEN YOU A HOUSE. I'VE GIVEN YOU MORE MONEY THAN MOST ANY WOMAN IN THIS TOWN. I'VE SUPPORTED YOU AND OUR SON! ALL I WANT FROM YOU IS A DIVORCE! YOU ARE GOING TO GIVE ME A DIVORCE! YOU UNDERSTAND ME, WOMAN? YOU UNDERSTAND ME?"

He pointed the shotgun at the front door and pulled both triggers. It blew a hole at the top the size of a pie plate.

Gina Townsend flew out the back door screaming, "HELP! HELP! HE'S GOING TO KILL HER . . . HELP! . . . HELP!"

Tina Elliott fled to the bedroom and cowered in the corner behind the bed. Myrtle Peter fainted dead away. Emma wanted to get up and flee, but Peter stood over her, gun in hand. He had gone crazy. She dared not move.

Peter lowered the gun, looked at Emma, and said in a soft, clear voice, "Woman, if you don't give me a divorce, I don't know what's gonna happen to either one of us." With that he walked out the front door, now mutilated by buckshot, got into his car, and drove off.

Leaving, he was not in any mood to go to the pulp mill. He did make two stops on the way home. He went by the bank and withdrew a thousand dollars cash, having a sense he might need it, and then he stopped by Herbert Manning's carpentry shop.

"Need to replace the front door on the house Emma and I own out on East Main, it's damaged beyond repair," he said to Herbert. "How much will it be?"

"What kind of door you want?"

"Best house door you got."

"About forty dollars."

"Can you do it now?"

"Probably be next week."

Peter handed Herbert four twenty-dollar bills.

"Would that get it done today?"

"Before dark," Herbert said, smiling as he put the money in his front shirt pocket.

~

Later that afternoon, Peter sat in wait on his front porch. He had calmed, and he was smoking his pipe. He held out his hands, across his lap in front of him, trying to imagine how handcuffs would look and feel on his wrists. Twice he filled his pipe and smoked it down. He walked out to his barn and fed Pepper a bucket of oats; he stopped at his car and checked the oil; ultimately darkness came, with no visitors.

He went inside and lit lamps in both the parlor and the kitchen. Having had no lunch, he found some salted ham and cornbread, and he tried to eat it, but after two bites he lost interest in food. Coffee appealed to him more, and he perked a pot. He definitely expected a visit from the constable or a deputy sheriff, and he would offer them a cup; he knew them all.

At almost eight he heard the car driving up. Going out on the porch with a lantern, Peter saw two unrecognizable figures getting out of a vehicle and starting up to his house. "Come on in," he shouted out into the darkness. "I've been expecting you." When they came up into the light of the lantern, the two figures were not at all among those he had been expecting, but they were quite familiar.

One of his visitors was Wiley Watson, the sheriff himself, not a deputy. Peter and Watson were lifelong friends. They'd started to school together and graduated together, one of a class of seventeen, only eight being boys. Peter was center fielder on their high school baseball team, Watson the catcher. The sheriff and his brother Vernon had quail-hunted on Peter's property twice during the last quail season. The other was Joe Earl King, one of the three justices of the peace in the county. King and his family were long-time patrons of Montgomery Mercantile, and Peter had waited upon King while working there; he had even bought his company pulpwood from King in 1941. The sheriff was a big, blond man in his early fifties, with large, widely-spaced eyes, dressed in uniform. King was a man of average size in his early sixties with thick gray hair and a small, yet noticeable, potbelly.

"Come on in. Was expecting a visit from the law but weren't expecting it to be you fellows. Like some coffee? Perked a fresh pot."

They both declined.

"Okay if we sit here, Peter?" the sheriff asked, taking a seat on the couch. King sat down next to him. Not wanting to be looming over them, Peter dropped into his reading chair. He was expecting to be arrested but didn't know an arrest went like this.

"I have a warrant for your arrest," the sheriff informed Peter, firmly but politely.

"Was expecting it. What am I charged with?"

"What's he charged with?" the sheriff asked the judge, who had prepared and issued the arrest warrant the sheriff was to serve.

"Well, sheriff, that's been quite an issue. Emma first wanted to charge him with attempted murder, but she came in with this Elliott woman, who was there all the time and knew it all. When I got to questioning them, they agreed he could of shot her, as easy as he shot that door, if he'd a wanted to kill her. Then she wanted some kind of trespass or assault, or something about destruction of the house, but he owns the house much as she does. They agreed that he never touched anybody. He shouted and threatened a lot, but he didn't even curse or call anybody any names. Finally, we settled on disturbing the peace. He sure as hell disturbed their peace."

"You're under arrest, for disturbing the peace," the sheriff said to Peter, handing him the arrest warrant. "Here's the return," he said to the judge, handing him the document. "We going to let him go on his own recognizance, I take it? We know he's not going anywhere."

"Well, we would," Judge King responded, "but she claimed she's scared of him and wants him kept in jail. I told her we couldn't do that on a disturbing the peace charge, when he hasn't been convicted, but she could ask for a peace bond. She swore out a complaint for a peace bond."

"What's that?" Peter asked.

"A bond you post, that can be forfeited if you disturb her peace again," the sheriff answered. "I think you've disturbed her peace all you're likely to, but she's got a right to ask for that. You got the forms for a peace bond?" he asked King.

"Wasn't coming out here without 'em."

King looked at Peter. "How much peace bond can you post?"

"What do you need?"

"How about two hundred fifty, can you get that? We can give you until tomorrow when the bank's open."

Peter pulled out his money and peeled off two hundred sixty dollars in twenties and handed them to Judge King. "Don't have any change, so let's set it at two-sixty."

The peace bond documents were signed and all the official documents for this judicial proceeding were held by the judge, folded in his lap.

"Don't you go telling I came out here and did this," King said to Peter. "Ain't in no habit of going to people's houses to hold court. But the sheriff asked me to and I did it for him. Ain't no getting elected a judge in this county if Sheriff Watson ain't for you." King looked at Watson, who couldn't suppress a weak smile at the compliment.

"I sure won't," Peter said. "And next time we need wood, you folks are going to be the first I ask."

When they got to the door to exit, the sheriff turned around and addressed Peter. "That Emma's got a reputation around town for being a loud, tough woman folks don't dare cross. Most people always wondered why you married that woman . . . stayed with her long as you did. Lotta folks'll be happy you finally stood up to her a bit." Watson turned and went down the steps. Peter heard them drive off in the gravel.

He went back to his favorite chair with a cup of coffee, his pipe, and his Prince Albert.

Thirty minutes later he was in his bed, under arrest and under the influence of caffeine. But Peter slept better than he had in a long time.

～

Midmorning the next day, Sheriff Watson was in his office at the courthouse, feet propped up on his desk, reading the county newspaper that had come out the day before. Emma Montgomery stormed in.

"PETER IS OUT OF JAIL!" she shouted. "OUT OF JAIL!" She had to stop to catch her breath. "Gina Townsend looked out the window of the drugstore a while ago and saw him coming out of the bank!"

The sheriff never took his boots off the corner of his desk. If she could burst in, showing him no respect, she deserved none. "What's wrong with him having banking business?" Sheriff Watson asked.

"He's supposed to be in jail. You're supposed to have arrested him and put him in jail."

"I arrested your husband last night. He is to appear in court to answer your charges and he also posted a peace bond that will be forfeited if he disturbs you again." The sheriff leaned back a bit more, but kept his boots hanging off the side of his desk.

"But I think he may kill me. You've got to do something, Sheriff. Somebody's got to do something."

"Nothing else I can do."

"Can't somebody do something?"

"Maybe you," the sheriff said. He paused for a full ten seconds, wanting to add drama to his words. Then he looked at her, as sternly as he could, adding in a soft, sincere voice, "Maybe you ought to give the man a divorce."

Emma started to say, "No way in hell . . . over my dead body." She had mastered those lines to perfection. The words wouldn't come out.

"You think he'll kill me, Sheriff?" she said, in an uncommonly low, humble tone.

"It's not likely, but he could. Men do get mad enough at women, from time to time, to kill them. Happens every year or two 'round here, somewhere."

Emma looked at the sheriff and said nothing.

"And then some men, depressed as he is, just kill themselves. How would you feel about that?"

Emma stared at the floor for a few moments.

"You think he's gone crazy?"

"All I know is when a man goes to shootin' holes in doors with buck-shot, he's acting mighty crazy."

Emma's face lost color and her lower lip stiffened. She got up and slowly walked out, with no further comment. She did leave the sheriff's office a changed woman. For all of her life she had coped with insecurity by stonewalling reality. It was a talent she had lost forever.

In Glasper, nothing was more than a few blocks from the town center. Emma's house was little more than two blocks from the sheriff's office. A hard tightness gripped Emma's throat as she walked home in a deliberate pace; tears came and subsided as she walked. Only three cars passed her, and each time she tucked her head and looked down, lest someone notice her distress.

She had never bothered to lock her doors; virtually no one in town did. She walked through her impressive new door and locked it, then went to the back door and bolted it as well.

From early afternoon until well past midnight, she cried off and on, pondering recent events, her situation, her future, grappling with the main issue confronting her. Was staying married to a man who had not lived with her in over six years, and was obviously not coming back, worth *any* risk to her life, or his?

⌇

Mid-morning of the next day, Thelma Bradley looked up from her desk and saw Emma Montgomery entering the Levine law office. From the inception, things were vastly different from her last visit. Rather than a red-faced, loud, angry woman, Thelma faced a woman with a drained, weak, and weary look, humble and speaking in a soft, defeated tone. "I'd like to please see Mr. Ben, if I could," she said.

"He's gone across to the bank, but he should be back soon."

"Could I sit here and wait for him?"

"That would be fine. He should not be long."

Ten minutes later Benjamin Levine returned and immediately noticed Emma Montgomery.

"Good morning, Mrs. Montgomery," he said pleasantly.

"Could I please talk to you, Mr. Ben?"

Levine noticed the transformation in appearance and tone. When anything out of the ordinary happened in Glasper, news spread fast, and both Thelma and Benjamin had heard of the recent dramatic events at Emma's house, an episode now being called "the buckshot sewing party." But they had no reason to expect this visit.

"I want to give Peter his divorce," she said, in a humble and resigned tone, without even getting out of her chair.

"Well come into my office, Mrs. Montgomery, and let's talk about it."

In Levine's office, she took a seat across his large, ornate desk. Levine gave Emma a questioning look.

"You sure about this, Mrs. Montgomery?"

"I want to give him his divorce. How do I do it?"

"I would like for you to have your own lawyer, Mrs. Montgomery. There are two good lawyers upstairs who would do you a good job. There are others around. I am confident Mr. Montgomery will be fair and generous. We would want to talk about you dropping your criminal charges."

Leaving Emma seated, he went out to Thelma. "Thelma, call around and see if you can find a lawyer to talk to Mrs. Montgomery about a divorce. If you get someone, tell them I will be representing Mr. Montgomery and I will guarantee their fee."

Turning back to Emma, he reemphasized it, "You can certainly pick any lawyer you want and I will see that Mr. Montgomery pays their fee. If they want a retainer, tell them to call me."

"Thank you, Mr. Ben," Emma said as she got up to leave. At the door she turned back, looked directly at Levine. "I'm sorry I called you a little turd, Mr. Ben. Please forgive me for that."

"You were upset, Mrs. Montgomery. Your apology is accepted. Please close the door for me as you go out."

When there had been sufficient time for her to leave, and Levine was positive she was out of the office, Benjamin went out to Thelma's desk. "Call Mr. Montgomery at the pulp mill and tell him he's getting his divorce and I'll be getting back with him on the details."

"I heard her apologize for calling you a little turd."

Benjamin smiled. "Don't guess she could apologize to Mr. Montgomery since we never told him she called him that."

"Matter of fact she called him that again, right before she left," Thelma said.

"She did?"

Thelma looked at Benjamin with a sad face, and he thought he saw a little moisture in her eyes.

"After I got her an appointment with a lawyer, she stood here sobbing and she said to me, 'You know I did so love that little turd. I loved him so much. I guess I didn't know how to go and show it . . . and I guess he didn't know how to go and know it.'"

They pondered those comments a few moments, then Benjamin said, "Thelma, sometimes the relationships between men and women bring grief and sadness to both parties. At times, two people can't make it work." He went back into his office. Watching him leave, Thelma concluded that he hadn't stated anything that profound; he had simply stated the obvious.

In this small county, Thelma knew the history of Emma and her family. What was saddest to Thelma, after Emma had left, was the feeling that Emma's marriage to any man was probably doomed to failure when she was but a little girl; doomed to failure in 1904, when her father ran off to Texas with another woman, abandoned her, her mother, her three siblings. This marriage was doomed to failure when Emma's father taught her the basic nature of men; that they were congenitally, irrevocably, and unpredictably sorry; that she could never really trust any man, even with his own money.

CHAPTER 32

COMING FOR YOU

At Peter's kitchen table, spread out in front of him, were four completed pages of a letter to Elizabeth. He was starting on a fifth, by any standard being written on stationery ridiculous for a man his age: Valentine's Day stationery Townsend's Drugs had not sold in three years. Each page was in the shape of a heart, with a one-inch red border circling a white center. His tacky choice of stationery was just part of his hurricane of emotion.

Peter knew he wasn't much of a writer, but he was trying to tell Elizabeth about the divorce, tell her how much he loved her, how much he wanted her, all the hopes and dreams he had for them together.

Yet there was insecurity, fear, and confusion. How could he get to England? What would happen to his business while he was gone? Would she actually want him? Would she want to come to Glasper with him?

Midway into the fifth page, he wadded it up and put it out in front of him, then did the same with the other pages, one at a time. He sat in front of the wads of paper, trying to come to grips with it all. Finally, he took a new sheet of paper and he wrote:

Dear Elizabeth,
Emma's going to give me a divorce.
I hope you want me because

I'm coming for you—soon as I can.
I love you—always have—always will.
Peter

The envelope was square; but, true to its purpose, a large red heart was printed on the front, coming out nearly to the edges. Peter addressed it to Miss Elizabeth Baker, 3140A SE High Street, Southampton, England, carefully writing his return address on the back.

⌣

Bonnie Patrick, the postmistress, looked at the letter, and then looked at Peter, with a sly smirk. She was most familiar with the appropriate postage, without having to look it up.

"Let's double it. I want to be sure it's enough," Peter said.

"Seems foolish to me. I've sent many a letter to England and I know what it takes."

"Double it. I want to be positive it gets there," Peter said, flatly.

Bonnie added double postage.

⌣

Fog creeping in from the Atlantic felt unusually chilly, and it seemed to Elizabeth that fall was coming early this year. Standing outside her front door, she tore open the envelope with the bright red heart and read Peter's short letter on the unusual heart-shaped page. She went in, took off her jacket, and sat down at the kitchen table, where she spread it out on the table, flattening it with her fingertips. His message was terse and straightforward. He was getting a divorce and coming for her, as soon as he could.

Reality came sweeping in upon her. For these months, their correspondence had been a romantic diversion, adding excitement to her life, but she never actually expected to see him again. Now she realized that Peter was serious enough to get a divorce, serious enough to be coming to England to get her; that he expected her to marry him; return to America with him.

What did she know about this man after so long? What would he now be like? Would he want her when he saw her with all her wrinkles and graying hair, and sagging—and old? Would she still love this man?

Whatever else she had in her life, she had found stability and a secure routine, lonely at times though it might be.

Elizabeth opened a dresser drawer and took out a box of stationery and found a writing pen; then sat back down at the table, once again looking at Peter's letter on the strange heart-shaped paper.

I hope you want me because
I'm coming for you—soon as I can.
I love you—always have—always will.

If Peter was making plans to come to England, thinking he was coming for her, he deserved an immediate response. She had to admit the truth. If he was serious about coming, she wanted him to. But she was terrified about it just the same. Like him, she started pouring out her heart, writing about how many wonderful memories she had of their time together, so long ago, writing about how lonely and empty and sad she had been when he suddenly, inexplicably, walked out of her life. She stopped short of writing it, but she wondered if she would want to leave her home, her friends, her country, and go to America with him, if that's what he expected.

Then, across a broad ocean, she did exactly what he had done. She wadded up the letter she had written, one page at a time. And she wrote on a single page, well down from the top.

If you want to come to England to see me,
I would love to see you.
She thought about his words:
I love you—always have—always will.

Should she, could she, say something like that to him? She sat for several minutes, staring at what she had already written. Then she simply closed with:

Love,
Elizabeth

That was all she could bring herself to say. Her response was carefully folded and placed in an envelope, licked and sealed, then addressed to Mr. Peter Montgomery, Post Office Box 134, Glasper, Mississippi, U.S.A. She would mail it tomorrow. She knew it was time for her to eat, but she wasn't hungry. She fixed a bowl of porridge and sat down to eat it. With less than half of it eaten, she put it aside and walked away to a sleepless night, her mind alternating between excitement, anxiety, fear, and doubt.

In the morning, Elizabeth went back to the table and found the porridge stiff and cold. She picked up her letter and stared at the address. Whatever her doubts, fears and insecurities, she must admit the truth; she wanted him to come back to her, and she would be devastated at this point if he didn't.

Elizabeth walked to a chest next to her bed and opened a little box there containing her jewelry, found what she was looking for, and took it out; a small pearl, mounted on a gold chain. She put it around her neck, and looked in the mirror, not closing the clasp, just holding it behind her neck with both hands. Then she sat down on her bed, held it in her hand, looked at it again, this piece of jewelry that was her most precious. She had not worn it for years, perhaps for fear of losing it; perhaps because it was associated with pain and loss. Elizabeth put the pearl necklace back around her neck, closing the clasp to keep it there.

CHAPTER 33

SOMETHING LEFT OUT

Wednesday, November 21, 1945, was the day before Thanksgiving, sunny and mild, with a midmorning temperature in the high fifties. Fall foliage had reached its peak, and the Glasper landscape was most vibrant and colorful. Everything about this morning gave Benjamin Levine a warm, positive feeling as he walked back from the judge's chambers at the courthouse.

He entered his law office and gave Thelma Bradley a broad smile. "Call Peter Montgomery and tell him I have his final divorce decree in hand . . . that he is no longer a married man. Tell him he can come pick it up any time he wants to." Levine took off his fedora, hung it on the hat rack in the corner, went into his private office and shut the door.

~

Twenty minutes later, Dennis Langley's long-time secretary, Mildred Avery, saw Peter coming through the main door of the bank. For years, he had visited her boss at least once a week, an extremely polite, soft-spoken, mild-mannered man. But on a couple of occasions, he had come in and breezed into the bank president's office without a word, as if she did not exist. From the minute she saw him, she knew this was to be such an occasion. Dennis had finished talking to a local contractor about a commercial loan, ushered him out with a handshake, and returned to his desk.

"Money Clip, look at this. Just got it from Mr. Ben . . . finally got my divorce."

"Great! Flask, I'm so happy for you," Dennis said, his voice not so much one of joy as one of affirmation. "What do you intend to do now that you have it?"

"I want to go to England, quick as I can."

"That's what I'd be expecting."

"Don't have any idea what I've got to do to get there. Never been any farther away than Jackson to see Evie . . . without the government taking care of it."

"Maybe I can help. You go get to work on how you're going to leave the wood yard and working out things with the paper company and I'll start thinking about how we can get you to England."

"It's a good time of year for me to take off, right this close to winter and bad weather and all . . . and I've got them pretty stocked up," Peter said, pondering his new situation.

"I'll call you this afternoon, after I have had time to work on it a little for you . . . give it some thought . . . maybe make a few calls."

Peter left, and Dennis picked up the telephone, dialing a familiar number.

"Benjamin Levine's office," Thelma Bradley answered.

"I need to speak to Mr. Ben."

"Good morning, Dennis," Levine said when he got on the line.

"As soon as it's convenient, I need to talk to my lawyer about a very important issue for the bank. When could you see me, Mr. Ben?"

"You can walk on over now."

Dennis Langley was ushered into Benjamin Levine's office by Thelma Bradley.

"I appreciate you seeing me so quick, Mr. Ben."

"I've been representing your bank since your father owned it. I don't have a more important client. When the Bank of Glasper has what you call a very important legal issue, I will do my best to make time for you. What kind of legal issue do you have?"

"Well, it's *kind of* a legal issue. But it's more than *just* a legal issue. I've decided that there will be substantial investment banking opportunities in England, now that the war is over, and I want to send a representative of our bank to England to explore such opportunities on our behalf."

Benjamin Levine's little pince-nez glasses had ridden down his nose, and he looked up over them at Dennis with a puzzled frown.

"International investment banking in England? Don't you think that's a bit out of our league with our small-town bank?"

"Well, I'm determined to investigate it . . . it's important to me."

"And does the bank have anyone you could count on to send on our behalf . . . who could remotely know a good investment opportunity over there? Are you thinking of anyone in particular?"

"Yes sir, Mr. Ben. I think I want to send Peter. He has a nose for a good investment of any kind."

A faint smile came across the face of Benjamin Levine. "I think you're right. Peter Montgomery is definitely a man who appreciates a good investment opportunity, and I think that would probably even be true in England."

Dennis returned the smile. They had made the connection.

"I don't have much idea how to get him to England. But if I know anybody who can help, it would be you, Mr. Ben, as much as you travel, with all your chess and bridge tournaments, and all the trips to Washington you make."

Dennis knew that Benjamin Levine had been heavily involved in the election campaign of Senator John Easterman, in 1940. He knew that Easterman respected Levine's legal scholarship, as well as his family wealth, and had a penchant for calling Levine for advice on issues involving legislation of importance, having confidence that Levine could give him a quick neutral assessment of how proposed legislation would impact his constituency. Levine would have the knowledge and the contacts he and Peter needed, if anyone would.

Levine summoned Thelma Bradley. "Thelma, see if you can get Gordon Holworth in Senator Easterman's office on the phone for me, please."

Several minutes passed. Then Thelma stuck her head in the door. "Mr. Holworth is on the phone, Mr. Ben."

"Hello, Gordon," Levine said. "How're you and the Senator getting on, there in Washington? . . . no . . . no . . . Don't need to talk to the senator . . . no . . . no . . . he'll hand me off to you, anyway." Dennis sat patiently, listening only to Levine's side of the conversation.

"I have something here I need your help and advice on. The bank I represent here, the Bank of Glasper, needs to send a representative to England. We need your advice on the best way to get him over there, want to fly him if possible . . . and maybe a little help with any necessary papers, that's primarily why I'm calling." Moments passed. Dennis continued to sit patiently.

"Yes . . . yes, I heard that TWA was getting some new competition . . . AOA, isn't that the new airline . . . we'll go with them, if that's your advice . . . we knew you would be a good place to start for advice, and especially on the necessary papers . . . not sure about that, let me ask Dennis Langley, our bank president, he's right here with me."

"When does he want to go?"

"As soon as he can."

"Soon as he can . . . His name is Peter Montgomery . . . oh, yes, I guess you would recognize the name . . . worked hard for the senator in the campaign . . . buys wood for the paper company, contacted lots of landowners for us."

Dennis uncrossed his legs and crossed them in the opposite direction.

"Oh, we wouldn't want to put you to all that trouble. Well, that would be nice . . . yes . . . yes . . . we'll be around the rest of the day."

"He will work on it and call us back," Levine said to Dennis, as he hung up. "I'll let you know as soon as I hear from him."

Dennis Langley left, returning to the bank where he would await being contacted.

"'The course of true love never did run smooth,'" Benjamin muttered out loud as Dennis cleared the door, talking to himself.

"What?" Thelma said.

"Just something that popped in my head . . . Shakespeare . . . *A Midsummer Night's Dream* . . . Lysander to Hermia, I think it was."

I do work for a strange little man, this Mr. Ben, Thelma thought to herself, on the way back to her desk, *talking to himself and using funny words like he does.*

∽

A quarter past two, the call came. "Mr. Ben is on the phone for you," Mildred Avery notified her boss. Dennis picked up.

"We have it all worked out. Gordon Holworth and I have taken care of everything, provided you and the bank are willing to go to this much expense."

"It's very important to us here at the bank. I don't think expense will matter much, but how much are we talking about?"

"About as much as your new car cost, about a thousand dollars."

"We'll have to pay it. I knew exploring international investment opportunities in England would be expensive for our bank."

"We're talking about one way."

Dennis swallowed. "We'll pay it. This is important, Mr. Ben. I'll call Peter and tell him to come in to see Thelma . . . that she will have all the details for him."

Ten minutes later Levine called back. "I've thought of one small detail that the senator's office left out."

"What could it be, Mr. Ben? Seemed like Gordon thought of everything."

"He left out something I think is important."

"We sure don't want that . . ."

"I don't think we should send our representative to England, seeking international investment opportunities, without someone there expecting him."

∽

When Elizabeth got home from work two days later, a telegram was posted on the door of her flat.

Elizabeth. Divorce final. Coming to England. Soon.
Flying. I love you. Peter

She was gripped by a fluttering sensation in her stomach, a strange mixture of apprehension and excitement. Excitement did seem to predominate.

CHAPTER 34

A HAPPY MAN

Ten days later, Elizabeth got off the tram and started her two-block walk to her flat. All day she had thought of Peter and their times together twenty-seven years before. Could he actually be coming back into her life?

It was a gray day, damp and cold; throughout the early morning it had rained intermittently, followed by an afternoon of damp, chilly fog, much like that day so long ago when she thought a young American soldier had gone out of her life forever, only to find him leaning against a wall at a hospital exit, waiting for her. As Elizabeth approached her flat, she saw a figure seated on the doorstep, slumped over his raised knees, face buried in his arms. Peter Montgomery was asleep.

For a few moments she stood over him, caught up in memories of so long ago when she stood over him sleeping in the hospital. She reached out her hand and touched him gently on the shoulder. He raised his face and they were looking at each other for the first time since 1918.

Neither said anything, both savoring the recognition, struggling with the emotion of the moment. In his face Elizabeth saw deep fatigue. Beside him was an oilcloth bag, damp on the top.

"Peter!" she exclaimed, "I'm so excited to see you. Get up and come in."

"I'm so happy to see you," he said, following her through the door.

Elizabeth took off her coat, laid it across a chair, turning to place her hands on both of his shoulders. "Let me look at you," she said, looking up into his face. The years had taken their toll. His hair was graying and receding at the temples, his skin weathered and beginning to spot and wrinkle. But he was still lean and muscular and still had those beautiful crystal-blue eyes, tired and weary though they appeared.

"Peter, the years have been kind to you." She moved forward and hugged him, placing her face against his chest.

"Elizabeth, you're so beautiful."

He placed his hand behind her head and gently held her against him. The years had taken their toll on her as well, primarily in the graying of her hair, now a pronounced salt-and-pepper look, wrinkles around her eyes, a thinning of her lips. But she still had what had captivated him in the beginning: a cheerful radiant smile; a voice that he could never hear enough of; a woman's smell and taste that stimulated him so. Just being in her presence had always given him a sense of euphoria. His passion for Elizabeth was like nothing he had ever experienced. Nothing had changed. He had a powerful urge to sweep her into his arms; carry her to her bed; make love to her again, like he had long thought about, dreamed about.

"You're a bit damp," she said in a pleasant, concerned tone, pulling away from him. "We shall need to get you in some dry clothes. I hope the clothes in your bag didn't get wet."

"Most should still be dry."

"Why don't you go in the bedroom and change? When you finish, I'd like to change, too . . . get out of my uniform."

He went through the door to the bedroom as instructed and she sat down on the blue-and-green plaid couch. He could be heard unzipping his bag, and she heard what sounded like him brushing his teeth.

Elizabeth was caught up again in that now familiar feeling of mixed excitement and apprehension. This time the apprehension was winning. What if he started telling her how much he loved her, and she was not certain of her feelings? She was confident she would still love him, but she wasn't positive. What if he wanted to immediately be intimate, go right into passionate sex like they were having when he suddenly disappeared from her life twenty-seven years ago?

He came out, wearing a broad smile, khaki pants, and a red-and-black plaid shirt. His previously rumpled hair had been combed. She could not deny that there was something about this man that so appealed to her, something about his innate gentleness, his quiet sincerity, something about an inherent goodness and honesty she'd once felt he had. And, now more than ever, she felt he was a man she could trust, a man who would strive to do the right thing, no matter what the consequences.

Her view of him when she was twenty had not changed; he was like no other man she had ever encountered, the only man she had ever loved. But that did not mean Elizabeth was not apprehensive; he had hurt her deeply, pain she did not want to feel again.

Peter immediately went to the bookcase and picked up one of the pictures of Peter Prince, the last one that had been taken of him before he was lost, a portrait in his uniform.

"This our son, the son I never knew?"

"He was so handsome, and such a fine person, and I loved him so, as did Dr. and Mrs. Prince. He was the grandson they never had."

"Makes me feel so strange . . . and so sad . . . that I had a son that I never knew I had, and he was gone before I ever got to know him."

"He looked so much like you. And some of his mannerisms, too. Something in the tone of his voice reminded me of you."

"Looks like he was a happy little guy as a child, smiling in all these pictures."

"He was a delight in every way. When I had him, it gave me a lot to live for, a lot to be happy about."

Peter sat on the couch beside her and put his arm around her, trying to pull her to him. "My turn," she said, getting up. "When I got your telegram, I bought you some pale ale . . . remembered that was your favorite." She went over to the kitchen area of her multipurpose room, retrieved a bottle of ale.

"Thanks," Peter said, in a soft voice, smiling up at her, adoration in his eyes. He tried to reach out, get his hand behind her waist, pull her to him, feeling a powerful impulse to put his face against her midriff, savor the scent of her, still indelibly imprinted in his memory.

She moved away. "I'll be back."

She went into the bedroom area, gently shutting the door behind her, where she took off all her clothes, folded them, put them away. Then she stood in front of a mirror that was over her dresser, studying her naked body, something she hadn't done in years. There was little sag in her breasts, not much there to sag. Even her pregnancy with Peter Prince as a young woman had not left Elizabeth with much permanent in that area. But her pregnancy had changed the shape of her once-tiny waist, and there were lingering hints of stretch marks on her stomach. It seemed that her arms and legs had lost size and firmness, and they never were much. She turned sideways, looking at herself from that profile. Her breasts may not have sagged, but her buttocks definitely had. Walking away from the mirror to pick out her clothes, she felt another wave of apprehension. She was definitely a middle-aged woman, and it wasn't only in matters of physical appearance. She couldn't help but wonder what it might be like to have sex again after so long. She felt the rush of apprehension mixed with excitement that had so colored her life of late.

Thinking about what to wear, she couldn't help but remember a time twenty-seven years before, when he found her coming out in a floor-length embroidered nightgown. This would not be a repeat of that. Remembering he had liked her in white, her hand went to a simple white cotton blouse with a button-up front and a wide shirt collar. She remembered a black skirt she had worn so often when they went out together. Elizabeth found a black skirt and put it on. She brushed her hair and freshened her makeup, then picked up a small bottle of cologne that Mrs. Prince had given her for her birthday many years back, something she had never used. She opened the bottle and touched some behind each ear; Mrs. Prince would be pleased. Elizabeth put her fingers under her small pearl pendant. Letting it drop back against her body, she went out to join the man who had given it to her so long ago.

"Now," she said, sitting down beside him on the couch. "We should be a bit more comfortable."

He shifted his bottle of ale to the other hand and put his arm around her. She looked up at him and smiled. He was caught up in the elation of being back with her after so long.

"I love you, Elizabeth. Always have and always will."

Her face had a strange look, almost like a look of pain. "Please don't say that to me, right now . . . I don't want you to say that to me . . . right now."

"You don't want me to love you? I thought everybody wanted to be loved, and hear they was . . . and you know I love you."

"Peter, this has come so quickly and unexpectedly. I need for you to give me some time to sort it all out . . ."

"I'll give you time, as much time as you need, and try and not say it anymore," he said in a somber voice. "If that's what you want . . . and all."

"Peter, I'm feeling scared I may be going too fast." She began to tear up.

Peter felt a disconcerting emptiness; his euphoria had proved to be most ephemeral. He had an impulse to pull her to him, to kiss her on her tearful face, but he just sat motionless and let her cry. He started to try and explain again, now face-to-face, what had happened, and why, but decided against it.

In time she stopped crying, wiped her tears with her hand.

"You must be starving. I know I am. Let's go out and find a place to eat. What kind of place would you like?"

"How about the place where you and my son Casey were when the pictures of you with him were taken? Some place where they will soak you in ale."

He smiled. He did not know the details, but he had some accurate suspicions. She smiled back. Both felt a sense of warmth. They had begun to reconnect.

Peter helped Elizabeth into her heavy coat, and he put on a leather bomber jacket Casey had brought him home from England.

"It's about four blocks and it's very chilly," she said.

"You've warmed me up with that good ale."

They went out and down the narrow street, not walking far before encountering bomb damage debris against the side of a building. They stepped around it and she reached out and took his hand. He squeezed her hand softly, and they continued on, hand in hand, like they had done so many times in 1918.

When they got to the pub, it was not crowded, but the table where she and Casey were in the pictures was occupied. "That's the one where the pictures of your Casey with me were taken," she said, trying to point it out unobtrusively. "Let's take that one over there. It's in a corner and shan't likely be noisy."

The waiter approached; he was the same one who had waited on her and Casey when they were there together, portly and grumpy, with his pronounced West Country accent.

"Why don't we get fish and chips?" she said, before the waiter could inquire, feeling a tinge of nostalgia. "That's what we had our first night together. I think that would be special for us."

"Elizabeth, it sure would be." Anything she wanted this night of her life he wanted her to have.

"It'll be fish and chips for the both of us," Peter said.

"Beer or ale?"

"And a pitcher of Bass." It was a night for optimism at every level.

The fish and chips were brought out, and they began to eat.

"Tell me about the hospital you work in now," Peter said.

"They say it's the biggest military hospital in the world. It takes up acres and acres."

"Sounds a lot bigger than Edmeter."

"Edmeter?" Elizabeth responded. "It was Edmonton! I wonder why that has been so hard for you!" She had a frustrated look.

"Wish I had gotten it right. Our whole lives could have been so different."

She chose not to go there. "Yes, Edmonton was small in comparison to Royal Victory."

This was a subject neither wanted to pursue further.

"You look so tired," Elizabeth said. "Like you haven't had any sleep in days."

"Not much. Haven't been in a bed in almost a week."

"Goodness! Tell me what it was like getting from Glasper to here with me tonight. Tell me what it was like . . . I've never been outside the south of England. Going across an ocean would be scary to me, and I've never been in an airplane."

"Well, my friend Dennis drove me to N'Olens and I got on a train in N'Olens and went to Washington . . . took two days. Then I went to New York on a train . . . took another day. Then I got on this big airplane with four big propellers. It flew to Boston and stopped awhile . . . then it flew to some place called a new found land, then we flew half a day across most of the ocean and landed at a place called Shannon . . . then we flew on to a place called Hurn, where there wasn't anything but the plane I was on and a whole lot of war planes. Then I got on a train for a short piece down to Southampton and walked to your place and I'm here with you . . . and so glad." He wanted so to say, "Because I love you and always have," but he had been forewarned.

"Tell me more about your Glasper, and the house you live in."

Peter described his house in the country, and the way Evie and Carrie had decorated and furnished it for him, and the drive lined with giant oaks, and his beloved acreage. He told her about sitting on his porch, smoking his pipe and watching little brown rabbits feed along the fence line, squirrels chasing each other through the trees, and the birds, some like the martins that came with the seasons, others like the mocking-birds that were his permanent friends. Elizabeth sat quietly, sipping her ale, acting enthralled, which gave Peter a positive feeling. Maybe she was seeing herself living there with him.

"How far is it to the next house?"

"Oh, I guess about half a mile, way farther than you can see . . . even in the winter when the leaves is off the trees."

It was a world as foreign to Elizabeth as another planet, but she liked the visions she was forming of it.

"Now me and Emma, we lived in town. Houses all around."

A stern, disapproving look came on Elizabeth's face. "Peter, you're here with me now, and I don't want to talk about you and Emma."

"Okay," Peter said, in a soft, flat tone. He liked this proposition. Thinking of Emma was definitely unpleasant and talking about it with Elizabeth would be even worse.

She smiled at him, putting down her ale and reaching out to squeeze his hand, feeling that an agreement to leave his marriage to Emma a thing of the past had been made. They both felt the road back to the love they once shared had taken an auspicious turn.

She wanted to know about his work, and he told her about the pulp mill and all the ways he went about getting wood for it. He even told her about his land deals with Dennis Langley and that he "sometimes made some good money." She continued to sit and listen, interjecting questions from time to time. Peter had never been much of a talker, but now he loved it, interest in his life seeming to spell interest in him.

"You look so tired," she ultimately said, sensing he was exhausted. "I've got to take you back and put you to bed and you get some rest."

Peter paid their bill and they left to go back to her flat. Again, she reached out and took his hand and they walked along together hand in hand. He might not be allowed to tell her he loved her *but he verily did*, and he was finally back with her again, holding her hand. Peter was a happy man.

CHAPTER 35

THE RIGHT WOMAN'S LOVE

A rriving back at her flat, Peter helped her out of her coat. She hung it on a peg behind the door, and he took off his jacket. "What do you want me to do with this?

"Let's hang it up here beside mine . . . here on the one closest to mine."

Peter felt she was teasing him, wanting more, wanting what they once had. Maybe he had gained a reprieve from the "don't tell me you love me." He started to do so but decided against it.

Elizabeth came to him and put her arms around him. She gazed into his eyes. "I've had so much fun tonight. I didn't know I could still feel this way."

He looked down at her; it seemed he could see desire there. Peter leaned down and kissed her on the mouth, not a deep, penetrating, passionate kiss, just a kiss of warm affection. He pulled away and looked at her again.

She smiled at him. "I always loved to kiss you," she said.

With that, he pulled her to him and kissed her passionately, letting his tongue stroke inside her lips, gently touching it to her tongue. She responded in kind, lingering there for two, three, four seconds, the kiss of lust and abandon they had shared so long ago. He reached down low and caught her, pulling her against him, trying to bring them together, reaching for as much intimate contact as possible.

She pulled away from him. "I'm still not ready for this. No, not yet . . ."

"Elizabeth, I'll never hurt you again. I never would have hurt you the first time if I coulda helped it." Then he paused, a long lingering pause. "Elizabeth it hurt me too . . . real bad . . . still does." He felt his eyes begin to tear and avoided her glance.

"Please be patient with me, Peter. I want to be alive and happy again, but I'm so scared."

"I'll be patient with you," he said, still looking away. "Whatever it takes. But you need to know I'll never leave you again . . . ever."

She put her face against his chest. "You know I think you are so wonderful." He made no response, and they stayed there, her face against his chest, for half a minute, feeling the mutual pounding of their hearts.

"Let's get you some rest," she said. "I'll sleep out here on the couch."

"I can't take your bed. I'll sleep out here on this couch."

"I'm much smaller than you, and this couch is big enough for me, but not for you . . . go put on your pajamas and I'll tuck you in."

"I don't have no pajamas. I always sleep in my underwear." She'd heard that before, so, so long ago.

"Then let's go get you out of everything but your underwear and get you tucked in." She got him by the arm and pulled him toward the bedroom. He sneakily tried to wipe away a lingering tear without her seeing him.

"Call me when you are in bed and I'll come tuck you in."

Elizabeth went out and pulled the door almost closed, leaving a four-inch gap. The flat was small and without much privacy. She could hear him relieving himself of some of the ale he had drunk earlier.

"I'm in bed," she heard him call, and she found him with the covers tucked up across his chest.

"I just wanted to give you one little goodnight kiss," she said, kissing his face gently, letting her hand stroke across his chest as she pulled away. Then she went out and pulled the door almost shut, leaving a small crack. Peter lay there in silence, fatigued but still keyed up, enjoying the comfort of his first bed in a week, with a growing awareness of how many aches and pains the past week had brought to his middle-aged body.

When he was almost asleep, Peter realized that she had quietly opened the door and come into the room. Had she finally relented to her desire? Then he realized that she was trying to quietly slip through to the bathroom, which could only be reached from the bedroom area. Both remained as quiet as they could. He wondered if she could hear him breathing. She went back out, again pulling the door almost closed, again leaving a crack. He wondered why she did that . . . maybe so the heat could circulate.

Having been now emotionally stimulated, he found himself again exhausted, his body wanting desperately to sleep, but his mind whirling, reliving events of the night, events of the last week, events of long ago.

Almost asleep, he felt a touch on his shoulder. Looking up, he saw her, dimly illuminated in the light of the city coming through the room's only window.

"I want to be in bed with you again," she said. "Let you hold me for a while . . . feel warm and secure again, like you always made me feel."

He moved over to the side of the bed and she got in with him, pulling the covers over them and putting her cheek on the pillow, close against him, her arm over his chest. Peter said nothing, reaching out and hugging her to him.

"I'd like to have you in bed with me every night for the rest of my life," he said. Again, he so wanted to tell her how much he loved her, but held back, heeding her admonition, not finding it easy.

Neither said anything for a full two minutes, as they cuddled, close and warm.

She said, "I so want to love you again . . . I so want to . . . but I'm so afraid I'll get hurt again. I loved you so much . . . and you left me, left me feeling so empty and so used like Janet had warned me against. Then I had your baby, our son, and I raised him and loved him so, and he got killed. Every time I've loved I've gotten so hurt by it." She made no audible sound to accompany it, but Peter sensed silent tears.

"I didn't want to leave you and hurt you any more than he wanted to get killed . . . it was just things that just happened."

She hugged him, perhaps a gesture signifying acceptance. He stroked her hair and held her close. They continued to lie there, him wondering if she was still crying.

"I'm going to let myself love you again," she said. "I don't have any choice . . . because I do . . . I love you."

"Why can you say that and I can't?"

"You can now, and you better . . . because I want you to, and I want to hear it."

"I love you, Elizabeth. I've never been able to love anybody else."

"Promise you'll never leave me again."

"I promise . . . I'll take care of you every day until the day one of us dies."

"I hope that will be a long time," she said, mustering a little chuckle.

"Then you'll marry me?"

"Yes. It sure took you a long time to ask me."

"I love you," he said again, struggling hard, but finding nothing else he thought he could add about why it took him twenty-seven years.

"I've got this strange happy feeling," she said. "I'm not supposed to feel this happy . . . but I do."

"I've never been so happy in my life," Peter said.

They continued to lie there together, neither saying anything more. Elizabeth broke the silence. "You can make love to me, if you want to. I think I want you to now."

"You know I do. You know I've been wanting to ever since I got here."

"Then take off your clothes," she said, getting out on her side of the bed, pulling her nightgown over her head and dropping it to the floor. Peter tried to get his off, being slower, having two garments to shed, and being taken by surprise. That's the way he remembered Elizabeth being, sensuously removing clothing a piece at a time never being her thing. When she was ready, she was ready, and clothes were the enemy, a foe to attack aggressively. When they were back in bed together, she again pulled the covers over them and kissed him, a kiss signifying all the passion she felt.

"You may have to help me to get ready. It's been a long time."

Peter quickly realized her concerns were ill-founded.

"I think you're ready," he asserted.

"Then let's take it and put it where it can make me feel so good, good like I haven't felt in so long."

Peter realized he had a problem: Elizabeth might be ready; he was most ready; but *It* was not ready at all.

There was a brief, awkward silence before he said, "I don't think I'm quite ready yet, ready as I need to be . . . big enough to do it and all."

"Then we need to see what we can do about getting you ready," she responded. And she did her best. Twice it seemed success might be at hand, but both times it was limited success and of limited duration.

Peter realized that he was no more ready for sex than he was walking away from the tram in the cold drizzle, fully dressed, fatigued to the core from a long trip across half the world. His age and his fatigue were now joined by a fear of impotence.

"I don't believe I'm gonna to be able to do it," he said, in a defeated tone. "I ain't done it in so long, I guess it's like an ole mule that ain't been worked in a long time . . . has forgotten how to plow, doesn't have no power left. Can't pull the plow no more . . . guess I'm not much of a lover no more."

Elizabeth put her face beside him, far enough away for them to have eye contact. "Look at me," she said. He turned, and she was staring directly into his eyes, a look reserved for the man she loved.

"There is nothing wrong with the mule and nothing wrong with the lover, other than no real sleep for a week and you being anxious and worried about it. Everything will be fine in the morning."

"You think so?"

"I'll guarantee it."

"How can you know? How can you guarantee it?"

"It's called faith. Faith helps make things happen. You will be fine in the morning."

"I love you," Peter said. "I love you so much."

"And I love you," she said. "I always have and always will."

"Thought those were my words."

"Maybe . . . but you will need to learn to share."

"I love you," he said again. He'd leave it at that, now that she had copped his line.

"Now," she said. "There is something I want you to do for me that is more important than sex."

"What?"

"Just lie here all night and hold me and let me be close. Sex can be good, but often what a woman wants most is to just be held and to feel warm and close and loved . . . feel protected and secure."

"I can do that," he said. And he did.

~

Peter woke the next morning with two simultaneous realizations: He was as physically ready for sex as he had ever been in his life, an impressive readiness indeed, and Elizabeth was acutely aware of his readiness, her eyes focused upon it.

"I told you all you needed was a little rest," she said, when realizing his eyes were open and he was looking at her.

"Look at this!" he said, in a dramatic display of his readiness. It was indeed one of his proudest moments.

Elizabeth, for her part, had a sense of pride all her own; she was proud of the demonstrated power of her faith. "I think the old mule can still plow . . . good as ever," she said. "Although I don't know how excited I am about the idea of getting plowed . . . believe I'd rather think about a lover still being quite a lover and being made love to."

"Can we make love, now?" he asked.

"Right now, Peter. I was lying here, waiting for you to wake up. I've never been as ready."

They made love, with all the passion they had for each other, and it was as good as it had ever been or ever could be. Elizabeth had given him a convincing lesson in an ageless and immutable truth: aphrodisiacs will ever be sought; aphrodisiacs will ever be touted; but there will never be an aphrodisiac with the innate power of the right woman's love.

Later, they got up and had a breakfast of porridge and tea, with a slice of toast and jam. Elizabeth sensed Peter was still hungry and offered him more toast and jam. Then they got back in bed, lying on their backs, close together, holding hands.

"Peter, I think you are the best lover there's ever been," she said, in a soft voice.

"I'm not that, but you make me more of a lover than I ever thought I could be. You sure do that."

"Maybe it's because I love you so," she said, squeezing his hand, worming her body even closer to his. They lay basking in a warm glow of happiness, confident they were meant to be together. Now, at long last, they finally were.

~

A week later Peter Montgomery and Elizabeth Baker stood at the altar in the Chapel of Royal Victory Military Hospital on the outskirts of Southampton, where they were married by the hospital chaplain. Their traditional vows ended with these words: "Until death do us part."

THE END

ALFRED NICOLS received undergraduate and law degrees from the University of Mississippi. Following military service, he had a career as a lawyer, a state trial judge, and a federal judge.

He and his wife Mary live on rural acreage in Mississippi, where their two sons have second homes. *Lost Love's Return* and its reader guide were written to leave his children and grandchildren, maybe others, insight into issues in life and the value of family ties, even to imperfect people.

ACKNOWLEDGMENTS

This novel would not have been written, nor would I ever have attempted to write fiction, were it not for the friendship and encouragement of Landman Teller, Jr. (1941-2016). Landy and I met on a freshman baseball team our first year of college and became lifelong friends. We went on to law school where we graduated in the same class, as a team winning the moot court competition our senior year. Over the years he would occasionally encourage me to write fiction. "It's something I want you to try," he'd say. Finally, in 2015, while hunting dove with me, he went on a hard sell. "Just do it. I'll help. Send me each chapter and I will edit and critique." Senior partner in his law firm, he was very busy. But I did, and he did. An English major, his critiques were usually a fourth the length of the chapter. Often, we would exchange three consecutive emails over just one potential comma. Then, in 2016, he suddenly and unexpectedly passed away. I plodded on.

At this point, after six-plus years, scores of rewrites and editions, I have so many to thank. I am fearful of leaving out someone who deserves thanks and recognition. I beg forgiveness.

I must first thank Josh Gray. Josh has a master's degree in creative writing and teaches creative writing for the University of Texas. An award-winning fiction writer, he has edited two different versions of the novel, several years apart. Josh quickly taught me that writing credible legal briefs and opinions gave me no ability to write creative fiction. He put me to work at studying the craft of writing creative fiction. I had much to learn!

The novel starts with battlefield scenes in World War I on the Western Front. I connected with Anne Webster, a renowned Mississippi historian. Among other books, Anne has published a book on letters home from Mississippi soldiers in World War I. Anne didn't just advise me on this feature of the writing, but she proofed and edited two different versions, one much longer than the final. Thank you, Anne.

My younger brother Randy Nicols, who passed away in 2019, worked tirelessly to help with historical research. He sent me a constant stream of period photos he had located, and suggested the quote from *A Midsummer Night's Dream*. Thank you, Randy.

Dana Isaacson did a complete professional edit of one version of the novel. He was of great help in refining the plot and in improving my writing, often by cutting unnecessary words, even scenes and characters. Thank you, Dana.

I am grateful to so many other kind and generous friends who have encouraged, beta-read, proofed, advised, edited, and critiqued, over the course of so many rewrites and revisions. Thank you: Linda Teller Parker, Elizabeth Guider, Beverly Craft, Sylvia Carraway, Mary Helen Bowen, Winnie Goodwin, Bertie Mae Young, Bennett Chotard, Anna Furr Dexter, Glynn Griffing, Bill Yates, Neil White, Sandy Feathers, Peggy Teller, Terryl Rushing, and Joyce Blaylock Wood.

Lost Love's Return would not have been published without the Books Fluent team's enthusiasm in acquiring my novel for publication. Thank you to my Books Fluent editor, Jana Good, who has patiently worked with me to polish it to its printed form. The book cover, designed by Stewart Williams, perfectly captures the evocative message we set out to create. My appreciation to my Books Forward team for promoting and marketing the book: Marissa DeCuir, Julie Schoerke, Jennifer Vance, and the entire team.

Lastly, I'm indebted to my sons, Lee and George, their wives Amanda and Jana, and to my five grandchildren, Mary Lee, Wallace, Gray, Reid and Owen, for the motivation to write this novel, and to Mary (without whom I would have none of them), for her almost six decades of patience, devotion and love.

READER'S GUIDE

1. When should we risk love? What happens to Peter when his relationship with Hannah doesn't work out? Why didn't it work out?

2. Peter heard his grandfather tell his father that he was afraid Peter was going to be a sissy, not a big man in the family tradition at all. What does it take to be a man? A real man? Did this experience later influence Peter to join the Army?

3. What did Peter do to make Sergeant Mulholland suddenly respect him? Isn't that often all it takes to command respect?

4. Arthur prays not to die. What is the value of prayer? How do we know if our prayers are answered? Is there meaning in unanswered prayers?

5. How does a man, raised in a hunting culture, who was so tender hearted he couldn't bear to shoot a squirrel and see it suffer, later come to kill numerous other men? Did these men deserve to die?

6. The most experienced sergeant on the Western Front couldn't kill Bruno the Rat with a rifle, after many tries. A young private his first week in the trenches killed him with a duckboard slat. What did Bruno do that cost him his life? How does that compare to texting when driving or going on open water without a life jacket? Can you give other examples?

7. Peter and Elizabeth were immediately attracted to each other. Why? What is romantic love? What makes love last? Is that the same thing as what makes marriage last?

8. Why did Elizabeth, a virgin until then, suddenly want to start a sexual relationship with Peter? Did her friend Agnes influence her? How much is our first voluntary sexual experience determined by the appeal of the other person vs. the pull of curiosity? Doesn't curiosity cause us to do much of what we do, often to our detriment?

9. Peter and Elizabeth's first sex was far from perfect. She is too tense to be physically ready, and he is all too ready. Did that have any impact on their ultimate relationship?

10. Elizabeth was thin and skinny, not voluptuous at all like Hannah, but she was warm, genuine, supportive, and fun, and she became the love of Peter's life. Isn't that all that really matters to most men?

11. Peter suddenly realizes how blessed he is to have family ties, even to imperfect people. Why did it take Elizabeth to make him appreciative? Why does it so often take being exposed to someone who doesn't have it, to appreciate what we do have?

12. When Sergeant Duck wanted sex with a prostitute he put in his order for the youngest one available. What is statutory rape? What is the legal age of consent? Does it matter if the victim is a prostitute? What if the victim's age is unknown?

13. Peter's discussion with his sister when he returns from the war goes to perhaps the greatest theological dilemma of all: Why does a loving God let bad things happen to good people and good things happen to bad people? Peter gives her the best answer he can. What would be your answer?

14. Getting drunk and losing control can have life-changing consequences. Drunk driving is the one that first comes to mind for most. What are others? Would regretted sex be a frequent one?

15. Peter's father pressures him to marry Emma. He says he does not intend to risk losing his first grandchild to an abortion. Would he feel the

same way today, if now available testing revealed the child would be born so severely handicapped that it would never be able to walk or talk, dress or feed itself, and by some twist of fate he would be responsible for providing the child with all those things for the duration of the child's life? What if Evie had been abducted, raped and impregnated at thirteen?

16. When Peter wants to talk Casey and Carrie out of eloping, he confronts them with *the Golden Rule:* "Do unto others as you would have them do unto you." Why is this principle considered the essence of universal morality? Carrie explains she may be a sinner but she doesn't want to be a hypocrite. What is a hypocrite? Peter wants to help Carrie deal with her guilt at being pregnant and her thoughts of the shame she has brought upon her pious family. How did Peter try to do that?

17. Peter joined the military without being drafted, as did Casey. Casey's driver on his mission to find Elizabeth was drafted. Should there always be a draft? What are the consequences of having no draft?

18. When Peter so desires to again have sex with Elizabeth, after twenty-seven years, he is humiliated by his impotence. Elizabeth gives him a short lecture about her belief in the power of faith. What is faith? Do you think there is power in faith? What part does faith play in our success and happiness, our ability to deal with our ultimate mortality?